CW01394309

BLADE OF DISHONOR

THOMAS PLUCK

Goombah Gumbo Press

This book is a work of fiction. Names, characters, places and incidents are either the product of the author's imagination or are used fictitiously. Any resemblance to actual persons, living or dead, or to actual events or locales is entirely coincidental.

BLADE OF DISHONOR

Copyright ©2013, Thomas Pluck. All rights reserved, including the right to reproduce this book, or portions thereof, in any form. No part of this publication may be reproduced, distributed or transmitted in any form or by any means, including photocopying, recording, or other electronic or mechanical methods, without the prior written permission of the publisher, except in the case of brief quotations embodied in critical reviews and certain other noncommercial uses permitted by copyright law.

ISBN-13: 978-1492253778
ISBN-10: 1492253774

Developmental Editor: David Cranmer
Cover art painted by Roxanne Patruznick, www.roxannepatruznick.com
Cover design and interior by Suzanne Dell'Orto, www.modomnoc.net

Goombah Gumbo Press
P.O. Box 1864
Montclair, NJ 07042
www.goombahgumbo.com

*For my great-uncles Frank, Phil, Butch and Jimmy Morrone,
whose service in World War II may have been less exciting
than the stories here, but are as heroic nonetheless.*

ACKNOWLEDGMENTS

THANKS TO David Cranmer for approaching me with the idea of a mixed-martial arts fighter getting caught up in a battle over a Japanese sword. We chewed the fat over it a while and this is what I came up with. I hope you enjoyed it.

Thanks again to my great-uncles, who inspired the World War II stories of the novel, and my mother and grandmother for hosting Sunday morning coffee where we all got together and chatted over *zeppole*. Uncles Frank and Phil served in the Pacific, and are no longer with us. Dominic, aka "Butch," and Vincent, aka "Jimmy," served in Europe. They don't like to talk much about the War. From how their faces changed when they thought about it, I knew how bad it must have been.

That covers inspiration. The perspiration was shared by Jaye Manus, Chad Eagleton, Josh Stallings, Holly West, and Neliza Drew, who all helped me edit the book.

I'd also like to thank my wife Sarah for always supporting my writing, and for enduring countless ninja, samurai, yakuza, and war movies like *The Devil's Brigade, Dead or Alive, Lone Wolf and Cub: Sword of Vengeance,* and *Revenge of the Ninja.*

I thank my trainer Phil Dunlap of Advanced Fighting Systems for teaching this clumsy hardhead how to fight halfway decent, and for helping choreograph the fights, and my friend Peter V. Dell'Orto for introducing me to Phil, hosting me in Japan and training with me at Kazeta Jin's Philoktetes shooto dojo in Kameda. Peter also answered many questions about Japanese language and customs. And thanks to my friend John Milkewicz for answering questions about serving in Iraq.

Jake Adelstein's excellent *Tokyo Vice: An American Reporter on the Police Beat in Japan* was a priceless resource on the yakuza's true role in Japan, without any Godfather-style glorification. Other books that informed my work were *Unbroken* by Laura Hillenbrand which tells the story of Olympic runner Louis Zamperini's life as a soldier and POW in the Pacific war; *With the Old Breed*, by E.B. Sledge; *Band of Brothers*, by Stephen Ambrose; *Black Rain*, by Masuji Ibuse; *When the Emperor was Divine,* by Julie Otsuka; *Sun and Steel,* by Yukio Mishima; *Guadalcanal Diary,* by Richard Tregaskis, *The Good War,* by Studs Terkel, *A Midnight Clear* by William Wharton, *Black Samurai* by Marc Olden, and *On Killing,* by Lt. Dan Grossman.

All the mistakes are my own. And don't recite Mikio's Japanese without looking it up in the included dictionary. That guy has a very dirty mouth.

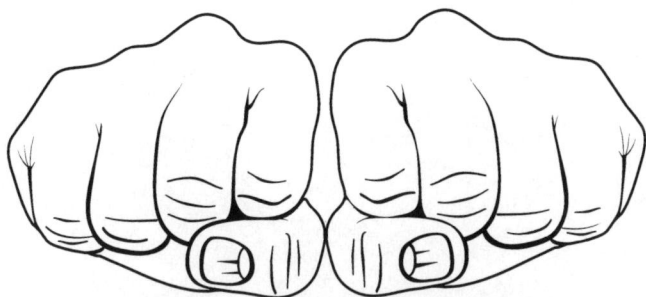

PART ONE

THE WAR COMES HOME

1.

WHEN THE MOTHER TRUCKER blew him a kiss, Reeves had already hit the ground walking. He gave her a half-smile and hefted his pack. The big rig honked and rumbled across the tracks. Past the rusty railroad crossing, dirty buildings huddled against the cold and a bullet-pocked sign read:

WELCOME TO BUTTZVILLE
A MINNESOTA STAR CITY

The star burnt out long before he left town, and had fallen from there. Reeves pulled his fatigue jacket snug around his broad shoulders and pointed his boots into town.

The trucker said Ironsides Surplus & Pawn was still open last time she'd come through. She pulled down her shirt to show the shiny nickel revolver she'd purchased there and kept tucked in her bra. There hadn't been much room in the bed in back of the cab, but it was warmer than the squats Reeves had holed up in on the way.

Big Chickie's still manned the corner, sooty brick and plate glass covered with taped newspapers. The old man made a good pizza pie, and his wife made good sausage and pepper sandwiches. The locals called the sandwiches a 'greasy dago,' but Reeves didn't. Mr. Ciccarone coached wrestling at Star City High, and took the team to the championships more than once.

Reeves had worked up an appetite paying for the ride. The memory of fried peppers and onions hung in the air.

He pulled the handle and the door rattled. He tried again.

3

Closed.

Reeves had changed in the seven years he'd been gone, and the town had, too. The shop's windows had been taped over with newspaper. Reeves leaned in to read a headline.

FORD PLANT ROLLS OUT FINAL MUSTANG

The photo showed smiling workers around a tricked-out GT convertible.

Reeves wondered what the hell the men in the picture were smiling about.

His stomach grumbled. All the trucker had was a Thermos of coffee, which sloshed in Reeves' bladder while he walked. He eyed the alley next to Chickie's and unzipped.

"Step away from the building," a voice said.

Reeves turned, snapping his fists into guard.

The sheriff popped the thumb break on his holster. Red-faced and cornfed, his big sandy moustache covered the harelip Reeves remembered from high school.

"Easy now, Reeves," the big man said. "Hate to splatter your brains all over the wall."

It didn't look like Tor Johansson would hate to do it. From the curl of his lip, it looked like he was doing it in his mind, over and over. Reeves had never poked fun at Johansson's lip scar, but a lot of kids had. When Tor beefed up into a linebacker, he took it out on every one of them, and anyone else who gave him an ounce of shit.

"You weren't gonna drain the snake, were you? That's indecent exposure," Johansson said. "Disorderly conduct. I'll toss your ass back in jail. We got a turd in the drunk tank who's either puking or crapping his pants all night. Sometimes both. I ought to stick you with him, down with the filth where you belong."

"This town looks pissed-on enough," Reeves said. He relaxed

and lowered his hands.

"Did I say to put your hands down? I could shoot you right here," Johansson said. "No one would give two shits."

Reeves figured that was correct. He judged the distance versus how fast Tor's reflexes had been back after graduation, when he'd busted a bottle of Hamm's beer over Reeves' head and left a shiny lightning-bolt scar down his sideburn.

"You robbed me of my one chance out of this town," Johansson said. He'd taken the Iron Cats to the finals, then gone to State. Came home to brag the same weekend Reeves celebrated his trainer getting him a tryout with the UFC. "Concussion syndrome. Bullshit," he spat. "I told 'em that's what helmets are for."

"Water under the bridge, Tor. You fouled up my exit, too." Reeves rubbed his hand, where the bones had knitted stronger than before. Lumps showed through the skin. The judge might've been Lutheran, but performed his most fervent worship at the college gridiron. He'd sentenced Johansson to time served, but tossed Reeves a dime to polish off at the penitentiary. Reeves chose the Marines instead.

"You're still a smart mouth," Johansson said. "So it's been ten years. All that gets you is no bullet in the back of the head."

"I'm gonna go before you say something you regret," Reeves said. "You wanna shoot me in the back, you go right ahead." Reeves shifted his pack and headed up the street.

"No one would miss you," Johansson said. "Not even your nasty old crippled grandfather."

"You can shoot me, if it means not having to listen to your sad sack bullshit," Reeves called.

Johansson followed him in a black Chevy Trailblazer ss and rolled down the window.

"I don't have to shoot you, Reeves. You'll trip on your own dick soon enough, and I'll be there to slap the cuffs on." The engine roared as he pulled away.

Reeves couldn't deny that was probably how things would play out.

2.

THE TOWN FELT BIGGER on foot. He'd always had a bike as a kid, held together with JB weld and duct tape, and later a dirt bike pawned by some teenager who knocked up his girlfriend. Reeves had felt spoiled, despite living on the wrong side of the tracks and growing up in the back of an Army-Navy store. When he and his friends played War in the woods, they used real World War II helmets and bounced deactivated grenades off their heads.

It didn't make up for losing his parents, but it wasn't a bad childhood. Grandpa Butch expected a lot, and there wasn't a day Reeves wasn't told he needed a kick in the ass. Butch had never delivered it. Had never laid a hand on him.

The closest was when Reeves took a Savage .22 off the shelf and used it in a battle of GIs vs. Nazis. He unloaded it and removed the firing pin, but Butch caught him sneaking back with it, and dragged him by the ear to the back of the shop.

"Didn't I teach you to treat every gun like it's loaded, you dumb shitbird? This ain't gonna hurt me more than it'll hurt you," Butch said from his wheelchair. "It ain't gonna hurt me one bit, unless I miss your skinny ass and hit my leg with the gun belt. I never laid a hand on you. Never kicked you in the ass, even when you deserved it—and just 'cause I only got the one leg don't mean I can't kick you in the ass—but you don't fool around with firearms, kid. I seen too many friends with their faces blown apart like a jack o'lantern thrown in the street to worry about you shooting your pecker off. Or shooting off one of your friends' peckers, for that matter."

He snapped the belt, and Reeves gripped the arm of the wheelchair.

"Boys are gonna play war. That's just how boys are. But it ain't no game. Looks like fun on the TV, but it's the worst hell mankind's ever come up with. It'll make you do terrible things, things people will tell you to be proud of. And that just makes it worse. You think on that. Think of your friend, that chubby I-talian kid, with his jaw blown off. Imagine it sitting in the dirt, like you were playing horseshoes. Him crying for his mama, except he ain't got no mouth."

The belt cracked. Reeves winced, but felt no pain. He looked over his shoulder and the belt came down again. Grandpa Butch cracked his own hand, and broke the skin. His eyes didn't even water.

Somehow that hurt Reeves worse than if he'd taken the whipping himself.

REEVES KNEW BUTCH would have choice words for him when they met. Maybe he'd plant his rock-strong hands on the arms of the wheelchair, and finally give him that kick in the ass.

Only one way to find out.

The Star Diner stood catty-corner to an abandoned Phillips gas station, its chrome liver-spotted with rust. The neon sign was out, and the waitress's smile flickered no more. A few banged-up pickups and a gold flake Oldsmobile coupe parked in the lot. Reeves dug in his pocket and found a few crumpled bills.

Inside it looked the same as he remembered, the Formica yellowed with an extra layer of grease. Augie, a bald walrus with a gray moustache, flipped burgers behind the counter. His apron was singed under his beer belly from where it skirted the grill. Men in trucker caps at the counter. Old women in the booths, life hanging heavy from their wrinkled necks and hefty arms. A few stared, then looked away as the bell dingled on the door.

Reeves set his pack down on an empty stool and squeezed past a waitress's round rump toward the restrooms.

"Bughouse is for customers only," Augie snapped.

Reeves held out his dollar. "Coffee and a buttered roll, then."

The cook scraped burger grease off the grill with his spatula. "With tax it's a buck oh five."

Reeves fished the pocket of his dungarees and found only a hole.

"Come on, Augie," Reeves said. "No veteran's discount?"

"You have my sincere thanks for your service," Augie said. "Which is worth exactly squat. Sorry, Reeves. We all got to make a living."

The waitress hustled back with her pot of coffee. Bright eyes and freckles on a young face creased early with well-practiced smirks. Fox red hair spiraled down her shoulders. She bumped past Reeves and slapped a nickel on top of the register.

"You can owe me," she said.

"Thanks."

The restroom was as cramped as the crapper on a submarine. Reeves straddled the toilet and sighed. He read the missives covering the walls.

A crudely drawn set of male genitals. Nobama. And scratched out, Tara is a dirty something or other. Someone had removed the paint with a car key to erase it. Reeves washed his big mitts. Considering the empty paper towel dispenser, he wiped his hands dry on the back of his pants.

The waitress flitted up and down the diner car with her coffee pot like a hummingbird in reverse, putting black nectar into patron's cups.

Reeves ate his roll and ignored the folks mumbling in their booths.

"Not too popular around here, are ya?" the waitress asked, as she stopped by for a refill.

Reeves shrugged. "I busted the champ linebacker's jaw, about ten years back. Grudges freeze up here and never go away."

"You're the one who popped Tor Johansson?"

"They call me Reeves."

"Tara." She picked his dollar out of her pocket and flattened it on the counter. "This one's on me, Reeves. That creep likes to use my back pocket for a mitten."

Reeves grinned as her shoes squeaked away on the linoleum floor. He rubbed his hands together. They didn't feel cold, but her pockets sure looked nice and cozy.

The bell rang and a skinny old man stepped in and lingered by the door. The folks eating turned to look, then stared down at their plates.

The old man took two quarters from his pocket and pinched them together. Reeves caught the scent then. Not unlike his fatigues after a long day in the sandbox playing babysitter to Army convoys. A customer wrinkled his nose. Another made a loud gagging sound.

Reeves spun slowly on his stool. He hadn't recognized the man shrouded in his shame. He'd been Big Chickie, once. Now he looked twisted and pale, like a gray dishrag life had wrung dry.

"Wait outside, you bum," said the biggest of four young men squeezed in a booth. Roughnecks for the taconite mine in Hibbing, from the embroidered caps they wore. "Stinks worse than a stopped toilet."

"Be right out with your coffee, Mr. Ciccarone," the waitress said.

The bell tinkled and the old man slipped away. The waitress filled a to-go cup. "Quit bothering the other customers, fellas."

"Or what, Tara? You gonna give us a tongue lashing?" Big Mouth said. His buddies snickered.

Tara bit her lip and packed the cup in a paper sack with a wad of napkins.

Reeves turned his head toward the table. He handed Tara back his dollar. "Bring him a bear claw, too."

Tara took the buck and filled the sack with sweet rolls.

Reeves walked over to the booth. "Have some respect," he said. "He's a good man who fell on hard times."

"I don't care if he takes the Vikes to the Superbowl," Big Mouth said. "That old dago stinks on ice." His pals laughed louder. Two boys, hiding behind men's scruffy moustaches. And a bald seatmate who tilted his bull neck, cracked a vertebra.

Reeves blocked Big Mouth in the booth with his hip and planted his boot on Baldy's chest. He ground his thumb into the nerves at the back of Big Mouth's jaw and prodded Baldy's Adam's apple with his steel-toe. Both men gagged and squirmed.

Tara grinned and took the sack outside.

"His name's Mister Chickie from now on," Reeves said. "Have some respect, or I'll beat it into you."

Augie rattled a rolling pin on the counter. "Settle down before I call the sheriff."

Reeves slapped them on the backs of their heads, then threw his pack over his shoulder. He stopped at the door.

"This town used to be good people," he said. "What happened?"

"We let in riffraff like you," an old woman sneered.

CHICKIE SAT ON THE GUARDRAIL, sipping the coffee. Reeves passed Tara on the steps. She gave him a smile and a pat on the behind. She slipped inside before he could respond.

"*Grazie* for the roll, Reeves," Chickie said.

"Funny how quick people turn on you," Reeves said, and sat beside his old coach, watching the failing sun paint the lake orange across the highway.

"Things go bad, people turn on each other," Chickie said. "Too afraid to risk banding together."

The bell rang and the four roughnecks piled out. Reeves set his camo ILBE pack by Chickie's feet.

"You can run," Chickie said.

"You know damn well I can't," Reeves replied.

The men rushed down the steps in a pack. Reeves raised his fists and smiled. He met their charge with a flying knee to Big Mouth's chest. The big bearded man reminded Reeves of Bluto from the Popeye cartoons, and he hit the ground hard. The two kids gaped, and Baldy clipped Reeves in the gut with a big elbow, sent him spinning.

"Legs, Reeves, legs!" Chickie hollered, rising to his feet.

Baldy had an easy fifty pounds on Reeves' middleweight frame but nothing on his speed. The two moustaches swarmed on him, grabbing for his arms. Reeves chopped one's thigh with his shin and sent him hopping. Baldy threw haymakers and clubbed Reeves on his arms. Reeves ducked and weaved. The other kid slashed with his wallet chain and caught Reeves on the ear. Baldy tackled him from behind. Reeves rolled with it. Baldy yelped as his scalp hit the pebbled asphalt.

"Good sweep, Reeves! Now finish him," Chickie hooted.

Reeves smiled and they hit the ground. He spidered to side mount position, throwing a knee to Baldy's ribs and an elbow to his skull. The wallet chain kid ran up with a kick and Reeves took it on the chest and hugged his boot. He fell back and twisted the kid's ankle. The kid cried out and tumbled. His cap rolled away, and Reeves torqued his work boot and levered the kid's outburst into a scream.

Baldy unclipped a razor knife from his belt and leaped on Reeves, his teeth gleaming red.

Reeves spun turtle on his back and pulled guard as the knife came down. He clamped both hands on the man's forearm. Grunting as the point needled his chest. Baldy groaned and put his weight into the stab.

Reeves shot breath through his clenched teeth and curled on his side. The knife ripped a jagged hole through his coat. The slice burned across his chest like a hot shell casing.

Reeves scissored his legs around Baldy's shoulders and hooked his leg over his head in an arm bar. He twisted the man's arm and leaned back until the elbow popped.

He left Baldy whimpering and tossed the razor knife to the asphalt.

"We done?"

The other kid rubbed his leg and helped Big Mouth to his feet. The big man's beard bubbled with vomit.

"Yeah, we're done," Reeves said, and checked his wound.

"Going to see Butch?" Chickie handed him a wad of napkins.

Reeves pressed them to his chest. "Yeah."

"Get ready for worse," Chickie said.

The diner crowd stared from the windows. Tara gaped from the doorway.

Reeves gave Chickie's hand a hard squeeze and headed up the road.

3.

REEVES PULLED HIS COAT CLOSED against the wind, thinking of the cold desert nights. That's the thing they didn't tell you about Iraq and Stan-land, how cold the nights got. The crazy heat during the day drove everyone mad, like the fear banded tight around your chest. Every car a bomb, every kid waving for bottles of water or candy bars a lookout, a runner, a triggerman for an artillery shell buried beneath the road, ready to shred your legs to *shawarma*.

Reeves couldn't help wanting to be a war hero like Butch, but the old man railed against it every chance he got. "It don't make you a man," he said, more times than Reeves could count. "It'll show you if you are one, but so will a lifetime of hard work." Reeves would sneak into the VFW bar to hear hard-eyed old men tell them the tales of blood and heroism that Butch never told.

So despite all the threats of a kick in the ass, when the judge told Reeves to sign up with the Marines or face ten years in Stillwater, he took the Corps. Reeves spent three months in County, on ten grand bail. Day he was booked, Butch rolled down the cell block with a bankroll in his lap that made the fat jailer whistle.

"This is for your lawyer, not you." He shook his head. "You stupid jerk-off. You're as hard-headed as your father was. You want to be dead like him?"

Reeves only remembered glimpses. A big man like a statue carved of sandstone, with a permanent grin. Reeves had been in the car when it had turned over. Racing a driver that had cut them off toward a one lane bridge, ignoring his mother's protests. Reeves flew out the window and his parents went through the ice.

"You can cool that hot temper of yours here until trial," Butch said. "I thought you training to fight would burn the fire out of you, but it's made you dangerous."

Reeves wanted to say that Tor and his two buddies had been hassling girls at the party. That he hadn't thrown the first punch. It didn't matter. He'd busted two jaws and cracked Tor's skull on the concrete floor.

The jailer reached to help turn the chair around, and Butch shoved him away. He spun one wheel, then pulled himself down the hallway with the sole of one worn brogan. Reeves bloodied his fists on the pale green cinder blocks.

He felt the ache in his fists now, and rubbed his knuckles when he didn't have his thumb out for a ride. The cars that didn't fly past slowed to show him a different finger.

An hour into his hump, a gold Toronado roared past like a rocket from planet '70s. It skidded to a stop in the gravel shoulder, brake lights aglow in the twilight. The car reversed toward him. Reeves skipped aside.

Tara leaned out the window. "Mr. Ciccarone said you might need a ride."

"Thanks." Reeves threw his pack on the floorboards.

Tara took off before he had the door closed. She'd changed into jeans, a Cheap Trick t-shirt with the neck cut out, and a hoodie with fake black fur around the neck like a shag carpet. The front seat was covered in a worn Winnie-the-Pooh quilt that she'd tucked under the head rests and cut holes in for the seat belts.

"You really tore those guys a new set of assholes," she said. "About time someone did. They hassle me, and they hassle everybody, but Augie won't toss out a paying customer even if the guy drops a steamer in the pie case, ya know?"

Reeves laughed. This gal was something.

"Chickie told me you'd be headed toward the pawn shop. Johansson came around looking for you."

"Yeah?"

"Yeah," she said. "You don't talk much, do you?"

"Nope."

"Typically it's cash, grass or ass for a ride in my Golden Oldie," Tara said. "Seeing that your ass is bruised and you're unlikely to be carrying either kind of green, a little friendly conversation would cover the bill. If that's not too much to ask."

Reeves arched an eyebrow. She drove with one hand on the wheel, the other slapping time on the seat to "Barracuda" by Heart fuzzing out the speakers. He admired the defiant set to her jaw and the way she filled out the seat.

"I been away ten years," he said. "Not much to talk about."

"Where were you?"

"Fallujah."

"That in Wisconsin?"

"Iraq," Reeves said. "Before that I was in Afghanistan for a stretch. Long enough to see we weren't doing any good."

"I don't follow politics," Tara said. "I support the troops, though."

"What about you," Reeves said. "I don't remember you from high school."

"I'm from Coon Rapids," she said. "Went to St. Cloud to get away, you know? Can't stand that town. Got my degree in design, that's why I'm waiting tables."

Reeves snorted, and noticed the cracked dash was sponge-painted in rainbow colors. He wondered what art lurked under the quilt.

"You're stuck here now," Reeves said. "This place is a black hole."

"You're a troop, right? I made decent tips today, if you want to crack a few Leinie's and dance around Ole's jukebox."

Reeves could use a hot shower and a soft bed, and Butch wasn't going anywhere.

Before he could answer, lights flooded the interior and a crash knocked them forward.

"What the hell?" Tara screamed, but took them out of the fishtail with ease.

A lifted Bronco with floodlights and a yellow snowplow filled the rear window, coming fast.

"Give it more pedal," Reeves said.

Tara obliged. The engine roared and the Toronado hunkered low.

A shotgun blast rattled their lungs. The driver either fired in the air or was a lousy shot, but Reeves felt the familiar weight in his gut, like swallowing cold metal.

Tara took a curve at speed, tires spraying gravel.

"Put the brights on," Reeves said, and slid up beside her and put an arm behind the head rest.

"I got this," Tara said, eyes darting as she scanned the road. "I can't choose men or careers worth a damn, but I can drive the shit out of my Olds."

"If there's buckshot flying, I'd rather it be in my arm than your brain pan."

The Bronco cut across a field and ate up their lead. Tara worked the gas and the brake as the spinning Ironsides Pawn sign peeked through the trees.

"Hang on, soldier," she hollered, and spun the wheel.

The tires squealed in protest as they executed a sharp drift. Tara toed the e-brake, then released it and gunned the pedal to launch them around the curve and into the strip mall's empty parking lot. The Bronco blew past and bounced through the weeds.

The pawn shop's lights were out. The Chinese place next door was open. "Go around back," Reeves said. The rear of the pawn shop was empty except for Butch's enormous maroon station wagon.

Reeves hopped out and tugged on the rear door. Locked solid.

The door to the Chinese kitchen was open and wafted the sweet smell of fry oil. Maybe Mr. Han would lend him a cleaver.

The Bronco bounced up the curb and blocked the exit. Four men limped out. Two brandished hockey sticks. Baldy swung an axe handle, and Big Mouth toted a Stevens twelve-gauge.

"Get in," Tara said. "I can lose them!"

Reeves ducked in the window to plant a kiss on her ear. "Thanks for the ride, but this ain't your fight."

"Screw you, Reeves," she said, and revved the engine. "I'll run your asses over!"

Big Mouth racked the shotgun. The shell casing clattered across the pavement. He leveled the twelve-gauge at the windshield.

Reeves put himself between the car and the barrel. Tara leaned on the horn. The men stepped closer. Their wounds fresh, their anger raw. Behind them, the pale walking corpse of PFC Jenkins, his throat spraying blood.

Reeves flushed cold head to toe. The bitter Fallujah nights. His arm around Jenkins' neck, clamping the wound shut with a compression hold. The young PFC's heart pounding, fading, fluttering away against Reeves' blood-slick biceps.

Jenkins mouthed silent accusations as the darkness took him whole.

Reeves stared dead-eyed toward the shooter. Could he break someone's neck after taking a chest full of buckshot? Time to find out.

He took a step forward.

The night exploded with small arms fire. The reports crackled off the trees and across the lake.

Reeves looked down at his chest. When he looked back up, Big

Mouth had his hands held over his head while hot piss spread over his jeans.

A worn sole scraped the pavement. Grandpa Butch dragged his squeaky wheelchair beside Reeves. A vintage M3 "grease gun" smoked in his lap. One big mitt on the trigger, the other gripping the 30-round magazine.

Butch had a head like a dum-dum bullet with a sneer gouged in the lead. "If you shitbirds don't wanna join the twenty Germans and eight Japs I got on my dance card, you'd better put your ugly faces in the dirt."

He sprayed another burst over their heads into the woods. The four men hit the ground before the brass casings finished tinkling across the asphalt.

Tara covered her ears and stared.

"Thanks, Grandpa," Reeves said.

Butch elbowed him in the jewels. "You're still a dumb little shit."

Reeves winced and rubbed himself.

"Quit playing with your nuts," Butch said, and jerked the grease gun toward the open door. "Go get that jerk-off sheriff on the Ameche."

4.

REEVES PUMPED JENKINS' CHEST and hollered into his drained face. The evac chopper tilted toward base. An RPG streaked past.

"Game over," Corpsman Milkewicz shouted. "You're just squeezing the blood out of him."

Reeves ignored him. It was his damn fault.

The chopper landed hard, and Reeves jolted awake.

"WAKEY WAKEY, HANDS OFF SNAKEY," Butch said. "We don't sleep in around here." He glared from his wheelchair. He kicked the cot again and raised a thick diner cup. "Coffee's on. Time to earn your keep. Make some eggs 'n' bakey." He scraped his heel on the floor and pulled his chair away.

Reeves sat up and rubbed the cauliflower lump on his ear. The stockroom contained boxes of junk Butch didn't have room to display, and a cot that smelled like mothballs and old man farts. Reeves stretched, banged out a hundred push-ups, and folded the sheets inspection-tight the way he knew Butch wanted it.

The fridge leaned in a corner like a polar bear playing hide 'n' seek. The top had an AM radio built into it. Inside he found butter, bacon, and eggs. But no hotplate. He headed out front.

Sun sliced through the dirty windows. Dust motes danced golden over racks of fatigues and wool coats stuffed airtight. Barrels of surplus bolt-action rifles, like planters sprouting iron bouquets. Mosin-Nagants. Mausers. Trapdoor Springfields. Anything you could stuff in your pockets that was worth a damn was behind the counter or in the glass cases.

Hunting knives and military antiques. A Nepalese kukri, a two-foot metal boomerang the could behead a water buffalo with a single chop. The usual used firearms—.22 plinkers, hunting guns. Stubby revolvers with the shine worn off from twenty years lying dormant in a policeman's holster.

The counter was neatly covered with the toys of Reeves' youth. Deactivated grenades, 20mm shells and rocket bombs, a bucket of bayonets and another of P-38 can openers. The leftover detritus of a century of war.

Butch had two MRE packets bubbling in its cardboard cooking sleeves. You added water and the chemicals burned hot. The phosphorus stink tanged the air.

"I was coming," Reeves said.

"So was Christmas," Butch said. "And put some pants on. This is a place of business."

Reeves pulled on a pair of camo pants from the rack and a black t-shirt with a pissed-off looking eagle on it from the bargain bin.

Butch opened the foil pack. "Jambalaya," he said. "All yours, kid."

Reeves emptied the tiny Tabasco bottle that came with every MRE into the caked glob of yellow rice, and choked down a spoonful.

"Don't tell me you like eating this crap."

"Beats the C-rations we had," Butch said. "I got ten cases without labels on 'em. Grab bag." He opened his packet. "Shit on a shingle," he said, and smeared the chipped beef onto stale, postcard-sized crackers. He crunched one down with perfect white dentures.

Reeves washed it down with bitter coffee from the tin percolator pot Butch had on the old Bakelite hot plate. Grandma Jean had liked making do with old things. When the cancer took her, the house became a barracks for a battalion of two. Butch the DI, and Reeves his single troop. They built a training gym in the basement.

Butch taught him to box, and Mr. Chickie coached his ground game. Backyard brawls in a makeshift cage, then all across the region to fight amateur, sleeping in the station wagon.

"What happened to the house?" Reeves asked.

"Didn't need it after you left," Butch said. "Got robbed while I was here at the store. Bunch of kids, they wrecked the place. Couldn't bear to go home to it after that." He looked up at a black-and-white photo of Grandma Jean, a platinum blonde beauty smiling down on him from a silver folding frame.

"Sorry," Reeves said.

"We're all sorry, kid." Butch crunched another cracker and brushed the crumbs off his thick flannel shirt. He wore a long-sleeve thermal shirt under it, and a wool blanket over his lap.

"I'm glad you're home," Butch said, and punched Reeves on the arm. He rolled his chair toward the front doors. "You can have my leftovers. Clean up when you're done. And take a bath, you smell like a bucket of assholes."

The old man had barely touched the food. Reeves choked it down. He knew it would pain the old man to see it go to waste. It came with surviving the Depression.

After he cleaned up, Reeves watched Butch go through the ritual of raising the security gates and hoisting the '76 Bicentennial flag out front. Old Butch still had a jaw like the prow of a battleship and a chest thick as a barrel, but the skin on his brick-like hands was thin as tissue paper and covered with age spots. They reminded Reeves of the sidewalk outside a bus station, speckled with a thousand pieces of chewing gum trampled into the concrete.

It made him feel glad he'd come home. The old man might have looked hewn from granite, but even stone wears down with age.

They sat behind the counter all day. Reeves watched Butch chew through two packs of Blackjack gum and chase out the few customers.

Two boys came in to play with the bayonets and ask the prices of everything while their mom used the laundromat on the other side of the Chinese place.

"Is that a machine gun?" the chubby boy asked.

"I told you last time, kid. It's a Browning Automatic Rifle," Butch said, flipping through the *Shotgun News*.

"How much is it?"

"More than you got."

"My Dad could afford it," said the other kid, a gawky boy with glasses. "Is that a real samurai sword?" He pointed behind the counter.

Reeves looked up at the black lacquered sheath on the top steel shelf. The sword handle was wrapped in milky stingray skin, like a molting snake's dead white eyes.

"The Japanese call it a *katana*," Butch said, and wheeled around the counter. With his shoe, he pushed out a milk crate stuffed with curvy-spined paperbacks and yellowed hardcovers of military history. "Stick your four-eyes in a book and read about it. Two bits each."

"What's a bit?" the chubby one said.

"It'll take too long to explain. A quarter, kid."

The two boys looked at the books, then each other. The skinny one fished two quarters from his pockets. "Wanna get one?"

"The laundromat's got Domo in the gumball machine," Chubby said. The kids nodded and hurried out the door.

The bell rang and the door swung shut.

REEVES REMEMBERED THE ONE TIME he'd touched the sword. Of all the deadly implements on display, it was the only one he'd been forbidden to touch. After the rifle incident, Butch made him field

23

strip every firearm in the shop. It felt like smoking a whole pack of cigarettes in the closet as punishment. The guns no longer held any allure, but the sword shone with twisted beauty, like the king cobra at the zoo.

The blade gleamed like a fang of oily polished silver. A zig zag of cloudy etchings ran from the iron guard to the chisel point. It was so sharp you couldn't see the edge, and when Reeves had tested it with his thumb, he thought he cut himself to the bone. He wrapped his shirt around it and carefully slid the blade back into the wooden sheath. It didn't make a sound. He thought swords sang when you drew them, like in the movies, but this one spoke only dead silence. He put it back, but Butch caught him over the blood-spattered sink, trying to tourniquet his thumb with a knotted wash rag.

"Stick your damn thumb in your mouth like a baby," Butch snapped and dug out a surplus medical kit. He gave Reeves his belt to bite while he stitched the wound.

"I told your dumb ass not to touch the sword," Butch said, squinting at his work while young Reeves fought back tears. "Of all the hell I went through, that sword's all I've got to show. That and an empty pant leg. So don't ever touch it again. Or you'll see a side of me you don't want to see."

Butch dabbed the cut with mercurochrome while Reeves put tooth marks in the belt leather. He wrapped it in gauze and tape and slapped Reeves on the behind. "Everyone gets a second chance, kid. But no one gets a third one. So quit being a shitbird."

Reeves ran outside and watched through the window as Butch balanced on one leg, took down the sword, and sat in his chair with the blade across his lap, studying it in the light. He sat there for hours, and Reeves knew what he was thinking about.

The war.

◆ ◆

OVER THE NEXT FEW DAYS, Reeves thought about his own war, while Butch paid too much for Walmart crap pawned by sad-faced men, then shooed them out when they stared too long at the cheapest pistols in the display case.

"This town's really gone to shit," Reeves said.

"Ford put the last nail in the coffin when they lit out for Mexico. Never trusted that Nazi symp."

The plant had built Mustangs and Ranger pickup trucks. Star City people had driven them out of pride, but not Butch. He drove a Buick Roadmaster wagon. When asked why his blood didn't run Ford blue, he said "Henry Ford would have pushed FDR down a flight of stairs and made Hitler President if he'd had half the chance."

Butch wasn't welcome at the VFW hall, and in his own words, couldn't give a shit less.

They had Chinese for dinner. Butch ate beef chow mein with chopsticks, doused with chili sauce. Reeves ate sweet and sour chicken with his fingers.

Butch only ate things on four legs. He'd grown up on a chicken farm, and hated the filthy things. Turkeys, too. Grandma Jean used to bake ham on Thanksgiving, spiked with cloves, pineapple and maraschino cherries, and called it Hawaiian turkey.

They watched the Packers slaughter the Vikings on a pawned big screen TV, and Butch nodded off in his chair. Reeves watched the old man hunched over in dreams, his big hands clenched as if in prayer.

Butch still had the dreams. Reeves had his own. He hoped they'd be gone by the time he was Butch's age, but knew they'd follow him like a second shadow, one with pieces missing.

Butch murmured to himself and stomped his foot. He opened his eyes, blinked, and untangled his fingers. "Time to hit the sack," he said, and rolled toward his room.

"I'm going out, Pop."

"Keys are on the nail," Butch said. "Curfew's at . . . hell. You're a grown man. Just don't wake me up, and don't get in trouble. And put gas in the Buick if you run it low."

"Thanks, Pop."

Butch rolled into his room, holding up an open hand.

5.

REEVES LEANED ON THE LIGHT POLE outside Augie's diner and waited for Tara to finish her shift. A sleek black Lexus SUV the size of a small bus sat in the diner parking lot. Probably some real estate guy, looking to buy up half the town for a song.

Tara looked tired, and shivered when the night air hit her face.

"Hey," he said. "Danica Patrick."

"Hey yourself, " she said, and smiled, laughed. "I don't know the names of any UFC fighters."

"Rich Franklin," he said. Reeves liked Franklin. He had brains *and* heart. He'd fought through a broken arm and took out "Iceman" Chuck Liddell.

She unlocked the car. "Thanks for the fun last night. Scared the hell out of me, but that's the most excitement I've had since I got stuck in this burg."

Reeves shrugged. "Glad someone appreciated it."

"If you wanna jaw-jack, get in. It's cold. And you owe me a drink."

Reeves got in.

She turned the heater up and hit the highway.

"So who was the high roller?"

"Japanese businessmen," Tara said. "They don't tip for shit."

"Maybe they want to buy the old Ford plant," Reeves said. "Make Toyotas or something."

"They could turn this place into one big sushi bar for all I care."

"You ever have sushi?" Reeves had tried sushi on R&R during training at 29 Palms. He liked it as long as there was plenty of the spicy green stuff, wasabi, to go along.

"I like the cooked stuff," she said. "You?"

"Love it," Reeves said. "My Pop hated fish after the war. I only ate fried walleye on a stick at the State Fair."

Tara made a face. "Funnel cake for me, thanks."

Ole's was a double-wide with deer heads on the walls, a Centaur pinball machine and a permanent tilt to the right. The pinball machine had two legs under halves of an old phone book to keep it level.

They clinked bottles of Leinie's and navigated the flannel shirt crowd to the jukebox. Tara fed it quarters, then beckoned Reeves with a finger. On the tinny speakers, Cheap Trick told him to "Surrender," and he did.

A half dozen Leinie's later, they steamed up the windows of the Oldsmobile until Reeves eased a thumb beneath her bra strap, and she tapped his nose like a naughty puppy's.

"Easy, tiger."

He held his hands up with a sheepish grin.

"You first," she said, tugging his shirt hem.

Reeves peeled his shirt off. In the dashboard light, he looked like a statue of wind-scoured sandstone.

Tara whistled, then weaved fingers with him, like they were play-ing a game of mercy, and held him down to mete out punishment. Her hair smelled sweet and warm. Not smoky like the trucker gal's, or greasy like the dog tag chasers who'd swarmed him in the bars outside 29 Palms. Her hot breath on his chest melted the ache deep inside.

Something slapped the roof, and harsh light glared through the fogged windows.

"Wake up in there," a voice boomed. "Take it home."

"Oh shit." Tara fixed her shirt and rolled down the window to

Sheriff Johansson's reddened face.

He shone the flashlight on Reeves' bare chest. The shrapnel scars gleamed silver.

"Tor—"

"Tell him to put a shirt on," Johansson said, looking away.

"I'm sorry."

"Yeah." Johansson sucked his upper lip and tapped the door with his flashlight, then walked back to his cruiser.

Tara drove Reeves back to his car. "Heaven Tonight" by Cheap Trick on the tape deck, while Reeves pulled on his coat.

"If he gives you static—"

"What, you gonna break his arms and go to jail?"

"No," Reeves said. "Just saying. I'll take the heat from that prick."

"He means well," Tara said. "He can be a hardass, but it's got to suck having everyone look at you, and only see what you should have been."

"Tell me about it," Reeves said. "Anyway, Tor and me've been screwing each other's lives up since high school. No reason to stop now."

Tara kept her eyes on the road until she dropped him off, and let him out with a weak little wave.

6.

THE NEXT MORNING REEVES WOKE to his internal alarm and Butch's snores. He found some eggs and a pack of cheese curds in the ancient fridge and fried them up in a blackened skillet on the hotplate. Butch rolled in with the blanket over his lap and his teeth in a cup.

"Smells like you had a good time," the old man said, rinsing his dentures in the shop sink. "Who was she?"

Reeves smelled his shirt. Tara's powdery perfume lingered. "Some waitress."

"That cute little chippie works over at Augie's? You're my grandson, all right. She reminds me of your grandmother. Got fire in her." He slipped in his teeth. "How many scoops you put in the coffee pot?"

"Six, and one for the pot."

"Good man."

They ate cheesy scrambled eggs and watched the sun burn the fog off the lake across the highway. When they were done, Reeves rinsed the plates and Butch picked through curls of lined yellow scrap paper tucked under the avocado-green rotary phone. He handed Reeves a torn-off corner marked with chicken scratch.

"Your old trainer called a lot," Butch said. "He's out in Vegas. Seen him on the TV. He still calls, about once a month. That's his number. You should call him, get back in the cage."

Reeves looked at the paper, then the arm he'd put around Jenkins' throat.

"I dunno, Pop. Thirty's kind of old, ain't it?"

"Tell it to Randy Couture, you little pussy," Butch said. "He was champ at 46."

Reeves stared at the numbers.

"It's what you do, kid. You take things apart. If I left you alone in here you'd disassemble every damn thing to see how it worked. You couldn't put Humpty Dumpty back together in a million years, but you were always a damn good fighter. Technical, honorable, smart as a whip in there. You're dumb as shit most of the time, but put you in a cage, and you shine like a new dime."

Reeves nodded, absorbing the closest Butch had ever come to encouragement. He thought of how pathetic Sheriff Johansson looked. He'd been a prick kid and now he was a prick cop, but if Reeves hadn't busted Tor's skull and his own hand in the process, maybe he'd be coaching on TV by now. Chumming with Rich Franklin and the boys, instead of back where he started.

"Maybe I need to do something else, then."

"Like what, coach?" Butch sneered. "Those who can, do. And you can. So quit bellyaching and give him a call."

Butch ended the argument by rolling out front to flip the sign to OPEN. The black Lexus idled in the parking lot. He squinted at its tinted windows.

"Some fancy car out there." Butch rolled behind the counter and warmed his hands on his coffee cup.

The bell rang. A strongly built Japanese man in a black suit held the door, and a slim man, also Japanese, stepped inside. He looked over the store's contents with disinterest, through gold-framed lenses. The two men exchanged whispers, and the spectacled man gave a curt nod. His stocky counterpart stepped to the counter and made a slight bow.

His cheekbones thickened, his knuckles sharp. Reeves nodded

back to him, in recognition of another fighter.

His boss stepped forward with a curt nod. "Mister Sloane. My name is Takehiko Yoshiro," he said in perfectly unaccented, anchorman English. He tugged off a doeskin glove and offered Butch his hand.

Butch shook it. "Butch Sloane. But you know that already. Who's Silent Sam, behind you?"

"He is my driver, Mikio."

"*Ohayo*," Mikio said.

"This ain't Ohio, pal," Butch said. "It's Minnesota."

The bodyguard's face did not register insult or disrespect.

Takehiko smiled. "I would like to invite you to dinner for a business proposition."

"So, you collect war memorabilia?" Butch said.

"No, sir, I am a real estate investor."

"You're in the wrong place, then. This town's slated for the garbage heap."

Takehiko chuckled. "Yes, Star City has seen its heyday long ago. But unlike other shortsighted businessmen, I see its strong and proud history, and imagine its potential."

"You gonna build Toyotas here?"

"No, sir, I am no industrialist. I groom forgotten towns like this one, which have fallen a little behind, to make them attractive to factory owners, who can breathe new life into them."

"I get it. You're gonna bring in condos full of cake-eaters and their Range Rovers."

Takehiko chuckled. Reeves watched Mikio, part with his natural fighter's curiosity, part out of boredom at the conversation. The man stood stock still, like a guard dog. His eyes settled on everything and nothing at the same time. He breathed maybe twice a minute.

Reeves shifted on his feet and rolled a kink out of his shoulders.

"I know what you're thinking," Takehiko said, "But converting Star City to an affluent suburb would make no sense considering its location. Revitalizing it as a town where people can come to work and raise a family is the ultimate and most profitable goal." He gave a brief smile. "I assure you, I'm no philanthropist. Think of me as a promoter, and Star City as a contender fallen on hard times. Some shortsighted men would abandon it, let it become a cream puff that other fighters use on their way to the top. I'm not that man, Mister . . . Butch. I think this town has plenty of fight left in it."

Butch grumbled to himself. "So what's your play, Yoshiro-san?"

Takehiko leaned over a glass case festooned with Wehrmacht helmets and Nambu pistols. "My accountants have done their research, and I would like to purchase this lot, and everything in it, for the value appraised on your taxes, approximately three times the going market price. Four hundred and seventy thousand dollars."

Butch grated his calloused thumb against his chin stubble.

"Pop, that's a lot of money," Reeves said. He hadn't had anything close since his hazard pay in the Marines, and that all went into stripper's thongs and bartender's tills.

"Ixnay, kid," Butch said. "I got tenants. Mister Han and Sally the laundry lady. I can't toss 'em out in the street."

"While our planning has no place for a pawn shop or a military surplus store, we can put it in writing that when we raze this property, we will fully compensate them for any moving costs incurred in relocating their businesses in the new town center. Would that ease your mind?"

Butch nodded. "I'll have to think on it."

Takehiko nodded. "Of course, Mister Sloane. But opportunity only knocks but once. We will return this evening to hear your decision. And remember, the offer is for everything. Not just the land and the businesses, but everything in them as well."

"I thought you didn't care about antiques."

Takehiko grinned. "I have done my due diligence, sir. We already have a buyer for the lot. We pay in cash, and you would have the weekend to vacate the premises."

"What's the big hurry?"

Takehiko turned and surveyed his future possessions. "This will be our planning headquarters. If you accept, we move in on Monday, to pump new blood into Star City. If you do not, we have other worthy candidates, and when we come to buy your lot, our budget will require us to offer a sum more in line with its market value."

"Uh huh," Butch said.

Takehiko turned and bowed. "We look forward to your decision. *Sayonara.*"

"Don't you mean *mata, atode?*" Butch smirked.

"Hai," Takehiko said with a tight smile. *"Dewa, mata chikai uchini. Mou osoi node watashi wa kaeri masu."*

Butch and Reeves watched him leave. The bodyguard grunted and followed his boss out the door.

7.

"YOU CAN'T SELL THE PLACE," Reeves said.

"Why not, kid? I sold the house. All I got here's three graves—your grandma, my poor daughter and your dumb shit father—saving a place for me."

Reeves had grown up here. The place still smelled stale, of mothballs and cosmoline, but it was the air he knew. He never wanted to inherit it, but he thought it would always be there, just like he thought Butch would never look drawn around the jawline, and have skin like sagging tissue paper.

"I just . . . ." Reeves said, looking away. "Where you gonna go?"

"Hell if I know," Butch said. "Vegas? Someone's got to watch over your dumb ass. They might start another bullshit war, and you'll sign up before your title fight."

"I didn't sign up, Pop."

"No, you did something stupider. See what I mean? You'll pick a fight with some mobbed-up kid, or get drunk and try to impregnate a slot machine."

"There's nothing out there for me, Pop."

"Call your damn trainer before you say that," Butch snapped. "Didn't you hear what that Japanese fella said? You're not some cream puff, and you know it."

Butch rolled behind the counter. "Go and call him. I'll man the register. The customers are coming in waves."

Reeves uncurled the scrap of paper and dialed the rotary phone. He thought of what to say while it spun through the numbers.

"AJ Perry speaking."

"Hey, uh, Arnie. This is . . . this is Reeves."

"Rage Cage Reeves? Well butter my ass and call me a biscuit," Arnie said. "How you doing, Rage?"

Arnie had coined Reeves' fighting name. His mouth was a mint of such phrases.

Reeves told him how he was, and how Butch was, when he asked.

"What's on your mind?"

"I want back in."

Shouts and the slap of flesh on the mats filled the background while Arnie thought on it. "How far you out from fighting weight?"

"I'm more of a cruiserweight now," Reeves said. "All we did was lift weights and eat in the Corps. I dunno, maybe two, three weeks, tops. And you know me, I cut hard."

"Yeah, you can hit the scales with barely a teacup of water left in your whole body." Arnie laughed. "You animal. Weigh-in's in two weeks. You ready to train that hard?"

"More than ever, Coach. I need this."

"UFC will love it, you got a story, you're a war hero. Get your ass out here. I can't fly you out, Rage. I'm sorry, but I got all my green tied up with my boys. I want you back, and there's an undercard on the next UFC show that I can pull strings on. No guarantee it'll be shown on cable, but the audience will see you tear things up before Franklin defends his title."

The phone's Bakelite receiver crackled under Reeves' grip. "Next week, Arnie. Swear it. Me and Butch are driving in. You got room for a couple cots?"

Arnie laughed. "I got a guest room with a double bed, long as you don't mind Holly Hobby on the canopy."

Reeves laughed like a boy, and hung up to tell Butch the news.

"I told you so," Butch said. "Been telling you thirty years. About time you listened."

Reeves shook his head, then looked over the small arsenal behind the counter. "They like guns out in Nevada," he said. "You could open a new shop."

"We'll open a gym, knucklehead. Think of the future. I know I raised you in the past, but I thought kids all wanted to fly to the moon, learn computers and crap."

"Not me," Reeves said. "I like it right here."

"Well pack your fart-sack. We're going to Vegas."

8.

REEVES DIDN'T HAVE ANYTHING TO PACK. He helped Butch—when Butch would let him—unroll a few duffels and fill them with clothes and personal effects. A photo album. His grandma's jewelry box. The GI .45 Butch kept under his pillow. Reeves shouldered one, and Butch rolled out with the other.

Reeves packed the bags in the station wagon and filled up with MREs, bottled water, and a pair of widemouth canteens to minimize the rest stops. The bench seat had seen better days, so he took a clue from Tara and lined it with a wool blanket, and threw in two spares in case Butch got cold.

He stopped at Mr. Han's and picked up a pint of house special chow mein for Butch and a quart of steamed chicken and vegetables for himself, back in training mode. He stuck a pair of chopsticks in Butch's container.

Butch sat with the sword in his lap. He stared at the wavy pattern on the blade, like mountaintops in morning fog. Reeves stopped at the door, not making a sound. He'd seen Butch like this before. The old man didn't drink, and never talked about the war. He sat with the sword, paying silent penance. Eyes rheumy and stone jaw atremble. The first time Reeves saw it, Grandma Jean told him Butch was not to be disturbed.

The door creaked and betrayed his entrance.

"I thought your grandmother would be the one I lived my life with," Butch said. "But this damn sword's been with me longer."

Reeves bit his tongue.

"You got a buck?"

"Yeah, why?"

"Because I'm handing this down to you," Butch said. "And it's bad luck to give someone a knife. I figure that counts for a sword, too."

"But, Pop—"

"Just gimme a dollar."

Reeves took a damp bill from his pocket.

Butch sheathed the sword and handed it to him. "It's yours now, kid. I know, I know. I'll tell you all about it on our trip. You promise to take care of it?"

"I promise." Reeves slid an inch of blade from the scabbard, then snapped it shut. "I got chow, Pop."

"Thanks, kid. Now put that away."

Reeves set the sword on the shelf. They ate in silence.

"You should go tell that chippie goodbye," Butch said.

9.

REEVES DROVE THE WAGON past the diner, but her Olds wasn't there among the lunch crowd. He found it parked outside Ole's gin-mill. Another shiny black SUV took two parking spots. He squeezed beside it and climbed out the passenger side.

Ole had the heat on full blast, but the room felt colder than a well digger's ass. The regulars huddled at the bar muttering to themselves. The bandaged and bruised diner douchebags, surrounded by more friends, all sneered at a Japanese man drinking alone by the jukebox.

Takehiko's bodyguard Mikio had three dead soldiers at his table, and nursed a fourth.

Tara leaned against the bar, arms folded, a Leinie dangling from her hand.

Bigmouth and friends parted for Reeves, and Ole offered him a longneck. Ole was bald on top and heavily bearded, like his head was on upside down.

"Club soda and lime, Ole. I'm training."

"Good to hear it, ya?" Ole said. "Always liked going to your fights. I was never late getting home."

Reeves took his drink and squeezed up to Tara. "Hey."

"Hey yourself," Tara said, and drained her bottle. "I guess Johann Law don't scare you."

"Nope."

"Maybe you should kiss me, so he arrives to break things up," Tara said. "Trouble's brewing."

The crowd grumbled to itself, low and muddy. Angry words

bubbled to the surface. Words like "Japs," "rice burners," and "job stealers."

Mikio drank and ignored them. There was an unspoken distaste for the foreign in an auto plant town. The only Japanese cars were junkers that car dealers let you hit with a sledgehammer for five bucks a pop, and the last mayor caused a minor scandal when his wife bought a Volvo. She traded it in for a Lincoln, but he was still unseated in the next election.

A squat man in a down coat broke from the pack and dropped a coin in the juke. Guitar notes tinkled the opening to "Turning Japanese."

The crowd roared with laughter. "Good one, Craig!"

Mikio's face remained stone.

Craig looked miffed that his insult was either misunderstood or ignored. He crouched in front of Mikio's table and squinted his eyes, pulling the lids in a slant with his fingers. He bucked out his chipped yellow teeth and babbled nonsense in mock sing-song. The crowd cheered him on as he stomped like a sumo wrestler to the beat.

"Dance with me, Honda boy!" Craig hollered.

Mikio drained his beer and set the bottle down with a dismissive grunt.

Craig grabbed for it.

Mikio's hand snapped like a bear trap, clutching the man's hand around the beer bottle. Craig swore, tried to jerk his hand away, then threw a clumsy punch at Mikio's face. The crowd rooted him on.

Mikio leaned away and the fat fist swept his bangs. "He throw first punch," Mikio announced, then clenched his fist.

The beer bottle shattered in Craig's hand, and he fell to his knees with a girlish cry.

The bar patrons gasped and two drinkers stepped forward. Reeves blocked them with his arm. "You don't want any of this," he said.

Three then rushed from the crowd. Two tree-like Finns and one short, hard-edged iron miner.

Mikio smiled and shouted "*Kocha koi!*"

He kicked his chair at the first tall comer, who stumbled over the table and sent the beer bottles clattering to the linoleum.

The other two split up and circled. Mikio kept his grip on the screaming man's hand, throwing a quick sweep to the miner's ankle. The big Finn threw a rangy hook and Mikio yanked his captive into its path to block. The short miner threw quick chain punches, sinking at the knees like he'd boxed, or at least hit a punching bag before.

Mikio weaved so gracefully that his dodges seemed accidental. He snapped what first looked to Reeves like an uppercut, but turned out to be an elbow. The miner's boots gained liftoff, and his back landed flat on floor. The remaining slugger went for a tackle, and Mikio back-stepped like a bullfighter, tripping the man up with the 'cape' of his whimpering hostage. The Finn skidded to one knee and Mikio smiled, falling to sumo stance and bringing the anvil of his forehead down on the man's temple.

The big Finn crashed to the floor before the first fighter had gotten back on his feet.

Tara whistled. "You showed 'em!"

"Settle down, now," Ole shouted.

"*Yowayowashii,*" Mikio chuckled.

The last man skittered back to the crowd. Knives clicked open and men hefted stools.

Reeves set down his glass and stepped forward. "Let him go," he said. "He's learned his lesson."

Mikio rolled his knuckles and ground the man's fingers into the broken glass. Craig slumped, face white from the pain.

"That's enough," Reeves said, and snapped his hands into guard.

Mikio chuckled and let the man drop. Triangles of brown glass poked from his palm. He offered up the shards to Reeves. "Shake," he sneered.

Reeves gripped his hand and squeezed. Mikio's expression did not change as their arms flexed. Neither did Reeves'.

The only sound was the crunch of glass and tearing flesh.

"Stop it!" Tara said, and pulled their hands apart. "What are you, psychos?"

Blue lights flashed from the parking lot.

Reeves released, and Tara brushed the glass from his hand, blotting it with a napkin.

Mikio held out his bloody palm. A shark's fin of glass jutted from the flesh. He pinched it between calloused fingers and let it *tink* on the floor.

"I DON'T HAVE TIME for this crap," the sheriff said to the crowd. "Loomis had an armored car go missing. The State Police want us to assist in the search. Anybody sees a Brink's truck, call 911."

Mr. Takehiko arrived shortly after in a Russian fur hat and camel hair coat. "Despite the fact that my bodyguard was clearly assaulted, I will gladly pay for the damages, officer."

"Can I go?" Reeves said.

"Yes, get out of my face, Reeves."

10.

TARA INSPECTED HIS BLOODY PALM in the parking lot. "You can't drive with this," she said.

"I don't have insurance," Reeves said. "And the closest VA clinic's down in Hibbing."

"I got a first aid kit at my place."

Her place was a tiny attic apartment in a big house with flaking, peach-colored shingles. The walls tilted inward with the pitch of the roof, and were covered with acrylic paintings of what seemed to be geometric shapes getting frisky with balloon animals. And a creased Foghat poster.

"This all your stuff?"

"Yep," she said. "You don't have to say anything. It would be like me saying you're a good fighter, when you know I don't know a damn thing about it."

Reeves nodded. "Good point."

"Take your shirt off," she said. She turned on a little boombox, and Foghat ground out blues guitar.

She washed his hand in the sink and they sat cross-legged on her futon while she bandaged him.

"I'm guessing you like Foghat," Reeves said.

"Ya. Something wrong with that?"

"I'm not gonna mock the musical taste of a woman with a big needle in her hand," Reeves said. "Just always thought it was a funny name. What is it, a hat you wear in the fog? Does it have a light on it?"

"I always thought it was a drum," Tara said. "Like high hat? You know, fog . . . like funk? A funky drum?"

Reeves shrugged. "Or maybe you're supposed to say it *Foh-got*. They Foghat to wear their fog hat."

Tara laughed, and jabbed him with the needle. "Ooh! Sorry."

Reeves hadn't flinched. "You're making a big deal out of nothing," he said. "But you're pretty good at it. Maybe you could be my cut man."

"I've had practice," she said. "I'm an EMT. Well, I used to be. Got tired of digging dead drunks out of their flipped-over Broncos."

Reeves stared at one of her paintings while she finished. Images of Hummers gone turtle on desert roads.

"What's on your mind, big guy?"

"Something I saw in a movie." Reeves made a fist around the bandages, released. "That fighter, he's missing the tip of his pinky finger. In Japan, that means you're in the mob. If you screw up, you cut off part of your finger to show you learned from your mistake."

"That's pretty harsh," Tara said. "Maybe he just likes playing with broken bottles."

Reeves snorted.

"What about you?" She traced the scars from shrapnel, barbed wire, and playing war with dulled bayonets as a kid. "Got any parts missing?"

"Nope," Reeves said.

"I'd like to see for myself," she said, and leaned in for a kiss.

He showed her.

THEY STARED AT THE BEIGE CEILING. She felt warm and soft under the quilt. Her hair was down, spilled over his chest. Her lip fluttered with a quiet snore, knocked out by afternoon delight. Reeves gave her milk-white bottom a hungry squeeze.

Tara cracked an eye. "Mmm."

"Said you wanted to be up by nine."

"I got the graveyard shift," she said, stretched.

Reeves reached for her, and she patted his hand away. "No thirds. I'll never get to work."

She pulled on a t-shirt. "I wanted to ask. Why do you fight?"

Reeves stretched. "Makes me feel alive."

She winked and pulled the quilt off of his waist. "What about me, did I make you feel like that?"

Reeves grinned. "Like a god," he said. "Fighting's different. It's who I am."

"Hurting people?"

"Nah," Reeves said, and pulled the quilt over himself. "Fighting's mental, too. For me, it's about taking apart the other guy's game."

Tara thought on it. "It's cool to watch, but maybe you should try chess," she said, and tickled his earlobe. "No one ends up with cauliflower ears."

"Yeah." *Chess players don't get an arena full of people going wild, either.*

"You wanna pick me up for breakfast?"

"Sure," Reeves said. "We'll meet you on our way down to the Interstate."

"Where ya going?"

"Vegas," Reeves said. "I'm gonna fight again. Those Japanese dudes are buying Butch's shop. It's gonna be great, we gotta tell Chickie! He'll wanna go!"

Tara stared. "And you just forgot to mention it?"

"I . . . Foghat?" Reeves grinned.

Her lower lip shriveled into a wedge of blood orange.

"You didn't really give me a chance—"

"What's that supposed to mean?" Tara pushed him out of the bed with cold feet, and threw his boxers at him. "You got what you wanted, now split town."

"Hey. I'm sorry, it's not like that."

"Just go," she said, and pushed him toward the door.

"Wait a minute," Reeves said, as she threw his jacket and jeans. He ducked and grabbed his boots.

"Send me a postcard, asshole."

11.

REEVES WALKED BACK TO HIS CAR IN THE COLD.

You made me feel so good I forgot about going to Vegas, he should have said. *Come with us. If you don't like it, I'll buy you a ticket home with my first purse.*

The Lexus was gone from Ole's parking lot. Reeves looked at his hand and the cut on the palm, then drove back to the shop.

Butch snickered at Reeves' mussed hair. "Kid, didn't your trainer say that women give you weak legs?"

Reeves took a shower, and tried to wash off the feeling that he'd done a good woman wrong.

The sun winked out behind thunderheads, and distant rumbles echoed through the darkness. Chickie came in with a bag of sweet rolls from the diner. They ate them at the counter with a fresh pot of coffee.

"Your Tara's been giving me all the day-old," Chickie said. "She's a good girl, that one. Said you bumped heads with that Japanese *cafone.*"

Reeves sipped his black coffee, and kept his hand in his pocket.

Butch took a cruller and softened it in his cup. "You still haven't learned, have you?"

"I didn't start it, Pop."

"I had to blow through half a box of GI hardball to save your ass last time you didn't start nothing."

"Some fights you got to fight, Butch," Chickie said.

"And some you don't."

"They were calling Mr. Chickie a bum, Pop," Reeves said.

"He's weathered worse," Butch said. "Everyone knows you're a tough guy now, kid. Especially that waitress. That's all that was about, and you know it. And now you're messing with your only ticket to a second chance. I know you're a Marine, but you abuse the privilege."

"Butch, the boy just came home," Chickie said. "Can't you go easy on him?"

"I went easy on him all his life," Butch said. "That's why he's such a hot head. You want Jerk-off Johansson to lock you up again? I know you're smarter than that. You just never act like it."

"I'm going for a walk," Reeves said, and pulled on his coat.

"Go ahead. Run away. You're good at it. Make a habit of it."

The bell tinkled, and Takehiko and his bodyguard opened the door. Mikio carried a steel suitcase, the kind with a handcuff. The cuff was locked around the handle, as if to say his grip was the more ironclad of the two.

"Good evening," Takehiko said. He smiled at Reeves. "Ready to go, I see."

Mikio set the case on the counter and stepped aside.

Takehiko opened the case, half full with banded stacks of cash in varying denominations.

Chickie whistled.

"Four hundred seventy-five thousand, two hundred and twenty-two dollars," Takehiko said, and spun the case so it faced them.

Butch ate the last of his cruller and washed it down. He rolled up to the case and peered inside. He took out a stack of fifties and flipped them like playing cards. "Nothing smells like money, does it."

"We eagerly await your decision, Mr. Sloane."

Reeves cracked the first knuckles of both hands.

"Looks like we have a deal," Butch said, and slapped a manila folder on the counter. "Here's the deed."

Reeves exhaled.

Chickie smiled and took a bite from his apple fritter.

Mikio leaned in to whisper to his boss.

"The deal is for everything on the premises," he said.

"Except our things," Butch said. "I've packed our personal belongings in the Buick."

"Does that include items that were displayed for sale when we arrived this morning? Because one is absent."

Butch grinned, and tossed the fifties back into the case. "I made a sale today." He reached under his blanket and took out Reeves' crumpled dollar bill. "Anything that's not here has been sold."

"Pop, what are you doing?"

"Quiet, Reeves," Butch said. "Adults are talking."

Mikio grunted with a sly grin.

His boss's face showed no such amusement. "You are making a grave mistake, Mr. Sloane," Takehiko said, removing his glasses. He slipped them in his pocket. "Altering a business deal. I thought you were a man of your word."

"I am," Butch said. "So what makes you think I'd let your family have the *Honjo Masamune* after all these years?"

Takehiko smiled. "My *oyabun* says I favor my grandfather. I wouldn't know," he said. "You stole him from me."

"Like he stole the sword," Butch said.

"It belongs to those capable enough to possess it," Takehiko said. "My grandfather will not rest until I avenge this dishonor. You should take the money I have been generous enough to offer for what is rightfully mine."

"It's always the brats who stayed home who make war about honor," Butch said. "Your grandfather was a beast on two legs. He didn't get half what was coming to him."

"I see his cut took your leg, Mr. Sloane," Takehiko said, showing teeth. "Don't make me take the rest."

Reeves jumped over the counter. Mikio snapped into guard, and so did Reeves.

"Reeves," Butch snapped.

Reeves and Mikio pressed forearms together, and shifted balance from foot to foot.

Takehiko chuckled. "Perhaps they can fight for the sword? But that would be foolishness. Its destiny lies with the Gantetsu clan, Mr. Sloane."

Reeves flicked his eyes from Butch and back.

"It belongs to Japan," Butch said. "Your grandfather stole it, and murdered the priests who held it in his care. He told me, young man. He told me everything, because he thought I was going to die. He was talky like you, he kept babbling right until I cut his shitbird head off."

"Enough," Takehiko said through gritted teeth. "The money for the sword, Mr. Sloane. Or we take it. And your lives."

"Go for it," Butch said, and slammed the case of money shut. "My kid'll kick both your asses."

"But Pop, what about—"

"Some fights you have to fight," Butch said.

"You Americans," Takehiko said. "This is no playground dispute. The sword is a stolen Japanese treasure. Your grandfather will die penniless and disgraced, like trash upon the waves."

"You made a promise, kid! Fight for the sword."

"You just cursed me out for fighting a dumb fight and shit-canning my future."

"Butch—"

"Stay out of this, Chickie," Butch said.

"Omae no manko wa kusai," Mikio sneered.

Reeves sighed, and stomped into the back room. He unwrapped the sword from its protective cloth, and shoved it into Butch's hands. "I don't want it anymore. I can't tell what the hell you want!"

Reeves turned around, and Butch heaved himself up on his hands in the chair and planted a swift kick to Reeves' backside.

Reeves snarled and instinctively snapped his hands into guard.

Takehiko barked a command, and Mikio flipped over the counter in a kick.

Reeves took it on the shoulder and fired a speed combo on pure instinct. Mikio weaved and countered, and Reeves slipped the blows, driving him back.

Takehiko reached for the sword and got the barrel of Butch's grease gun in the nose. "This'll be a fair fight. Your family's never been good at those."

"Bukkoroshite yaru zo!" Mikio charged, eating a jab to get inside. He snapped the uppercut elbow, and Reeves stepped back and heaved a roundhouse kick to the hip that sent Mikio tumbling into a barrel full of rifles.

He leapt into a flying knee to Reeves' chest and ripped the back of his suit open. Reeves fell over a box of books and through a coat rack. While he got to his feet, Mikio tore the rest of his jacket off and loosened his tie.

The two fighters circled, kicking debris and obstacles to make a ring. They moved in inches, heads bobbing side to side, knees sinking, the planes of their bodies shifting with each step.

"Fight, dammit!" Butch hollered.

Reeves snapped a jab and Mikio cut his cheek with the counter punch. Reeves gave him a hook to the ribs for the privilege. They slugged and dodged and traded knees to the body. Reeves dodged a head butt and shook Mikio with an elbow to the ear.

"Come on, Rage Cage!" Chickie shouted and clapped hands. Butch kept the grease gun trained on Takehiko.

Reeves leapt on Mikio's back and snaked his arm around his neck. Mikio slammed him into the counter and shattered the glass, then pushed his thumb into Reeves' palm and jammed it into the wound.

Reeves grunted and dropped, and jacked back the thumb.

Mikio grunted and pulled away, but Reeves gripped the arm and threw his leg into a flying armbar. Mikio's eyes flared as he saw his mistake, and slammed Reeves into the hardwood floor again and again.

"Don't quit!" Takehiko snarled.

Reeves leaned back and felt Mikio's tendons torque to their limit, tight as guitar strings.

"*Kono yaru!* Coward!" Takehiko snarled.

Reeves felt Mikio's arm begin to go. He knew guys like Royce Gracie who were triple jointed, or immune to the pain, who'd sucker you the moment you let go. Not this time.

Mikio snapped quick kicks at Reeves' head, then crushed down to try to break through the armbar. When he got close, Reeves whipped a left hook to his jaw.

He held the armbar as Mikio's eyes fluttered, and they both crashed to the floor.

Takehiko's face burned red. His hand drifted toward his pocket as if to retrieve his glasses.

"Hands down, *kuso tori.*" Butch laughed, and sighted the grease gun on Takehiko's chest. "Your gramps was a sore loser, too. Get your fighter and piss off out of town."

Reeves untangled himself from the unconscious Mikio and eased him to the floor. His head lolled from side to side.

Takehiko huffed and backhanded Mikio across the face.

The knocked-out fighter's eyes snapped open and he jumped to his feet, hands in guard. Then winced and clutched his jacked shoulder.

"Ow," he groaned, and frowned at Reeves. "You are fucker."

Reeves slapped his hand. "Good fight."

Mikio grunted.

Takehiko took his glasses between fingertips and slowly placed them on. He pushed the briefcase across the counter. "Take your money, and spend it quickly. The Japanese authorities will come for the sword, Sloane. And they will give it to me."

"Not while I breathe," Butch said.

Takehiko smiled. "So be it."

He slammed the glass door open as he left. Mikio bowed and ran after him.

12.

"COME WITH US, CHICKIE," Butch said, as they shared a steel cup of Early Times. "What've you got here except free donuts?"

Reeves moved an icepack back and forth from his knuckles to his face. "I need you, Chick. My ground game's gone to hell."

"I dunno," Chickie said. "This town was good to me. Seems a shame to leave her 'cause she's not pretty no more."

"I'm the old one here," Butch said. "You're talking like it'll kill ya. What'll kill ya is staying here moping over what was. You can still coach. Man who don't work's half dead already."

A black police truck roared into the lot and rocked to a stop at the door. A police cruiser joined it, lights strobing.

"What the hell's this," Butch said.

Johansson pushed the door open. Two uniforms followed him. "You screwed the pooch this time, Reeves."

"The hell are you talking about, Tor?"

"Put your hands on the counter," Johansson said, hand on his holster.

"It's not against the law to sleep with your girlfriend."

Johansson's face reddened. "This involves another matter, Reeves. Now put your hands on the counter before I have the boys tase you."

Reeves smirked and placed his hands on the counter.

"Got in a fight, looks like," a blond officer said. "Just like the driver told us."

"He just got in a brawl with that Japanese fella's bodyguard,"

Chickie said.

Butch sneered, lower lip aquiver. His eyes settled on the steel briefcase.

"This looks like the case, sir," another officer said. He tugged on blue nitrile gloves and unsnapped the locks and opened it.

Johansson whistled. "Those bands say Loomis armored."

"Whoa," Reeves said. "We just got this from the Japanese guys, the businessmen. Ask them where it came from."

"The armored car driver says a guy six two, sandy hair, Army fatigues. That don't sound like no Jap to me," Johansson said. "Cuff him."

"But—"

"Zip it, kid," Butch said. "Save it for the shyster."

Reeves held his hands back for the cuffs. He let out a long sigh. "When did they hit the truck? I was with Butch, or Tara."

"Tell it to Judge Storsved," Johansson said. "I wish we'd have you longer, but the State cops are coming for you in the morning, to take you to Arrowhead. Real jail."

THE CELL HADN'T CHANGED. The graffiti had. The smell seemed to have intensified. Sour drunk vomit and old piss. A dispatcher watched old *Seinfeld* episodes on a fuzzy portable TV, and answered calls with an audible roll of the eyes. Tor had taken a picture of Reeves in the cell with his phone before strutting out.

At least he was alone. Reeves lay down on the hard bench and stared at the ceiling, thinking of Vegas and the second chance he never got. He punched the wall and rubbed his sore knuckles.

"YOU'VE GOT TO TAKE CARE OF EACH OTHER," Grandma Jean said, and gripped his hand like the reins of a jumpy colt. The cancer had turned her skin waxy, her face angular and alien, but had taken little of her wiry strength. "Promise?"

He had promised. And he'd let her down. Forced off to war. And now back in a cell. Her skeleton watched from above, through the ceiling, shaking her head. Shedding her fine locks in sheaves, ashes coming down.

Reeves woke to a clang, panting.

Takehiko wouldn't take no for an answer. He'd set him up. Got him jailed so he could take the sword. The sword he'd promised to protect.

Another promise broken.

Two shadows at the door.

"He has to watch," Johansson said, leading Tara by the wrist.

"You're a sick fuck, Tor." Her waitress apron still on.

"You're Catholic, you should know how to do penance."

Reeves sat up. Smelled ethery vodka in the air.

"What are you doing, Tor?"

"Sheriff Johansson, Reeves," he said. "Have some respect. Neither of you got any respect."

Reeves held his head in his hands. "Let her go, *sir*," he said, with the disrespect only a front-line grunt could muster. "It's me you hate. Cuff me to the damn cell and take it out on me."

"I oughtta," Johansson said. "You know what, Reeves? You're not worth the paperwork. I already wrote you up, and I'd have to type it all over again, saying you resisted, and we had to give you a little wood shampoo to clean your head. But you know what? You're good as gone. It's Fireball here who needs the lesson."

Tara tugged her trapped wrist.

"I used to think you were all right, Tor." Reeves smirked. "You took a lot of crap. I liked when you gave the bullies a beating. But you turned into one of them."

"Ooh," Johansson said. "Real deep. Well, I didn't need your pity then, and I don't want it now. Some rat from the shit side of town, with your horseshit-smelling grandma acting like Dale Rogers."

Reeves gripped the bars. "Shut your rabbit mouth."

Johansson flexed and strained against an invisible leash.

"Ow!" Tara said, and gripped his hand.

Johansson pushed her away, and unsnapped the stun gun from its holster. The electrodes crackled blue. "This won't leave a mark, Reeves. Don't tempt me."

"Come on, Tor. Open the cell. I know you want to."

Johansson laughed and holstered the stun gun. "So you can kick my ass? See, Reeves, that's what the badge is about. You can kick my ass. You're the tough guy. But you'll always lose, because I'm a cop and you're shit."

Reeves kneaded his temples, fighting back the fury. "The Japanese set you up, Tor," he said. "They robbed the truck. They're gonna rob Butch's store. His sword is some sort of treasure."

Johansson shook his head. "You can't talk your way out of this one."

"Go check the store," Reeves said, leaning on the bars. "Please. He's an old man."

"Old men die all the time, Reeves," Johansson said. "And you know what? Maybe that'll make us even. That and you watching Fireball here do what she does best."

Johansson bent backward, shuddered. He fell and gripped the bars. Reeves jumped back from the shock.

Tara held the stun gun to Johansson's butt cheek until he wet his pants and slumped to the floor twitching.

"Oh shit," Tara said, and dropped the Taser. "Oh shit oh shit oh shit, we're screwed."

"Get the keys," Reeves said. "Might as well get blued and tat-tooed."

13.

THE DISPATCHER, a large woman whose bust had settled below elbow level despite the valiant efforts of her brassiere, watched Kramer wig out on her Sony portable TV. And she watched the prisoner and the sheriff's fuck-buddy run into the parking lot and peel away in a gold Oldsmobile.

"Listen, I didn't tell you I was leaving because you made me forget," Reeves said.

"Just can it," Tara sighed, pushing the pedal to the floor. "Nothing you say is gonna make me stop being angry. I just assaulted a cop because of you."

"Whoa. I appreciate you getting me out of there, but I didn't ask. I know Tor. I'd have gotten him pissed off enough to get in arm's reach."

"Oh ya, you were doing real great all by yourself. Just shut up."

The Toronado got air as they hit the pawn shop parking lot, bottomed out and slid to a halt with the tang of hot rubber.

They knocked on the back door until Butch opened it in his longjohns. Grease gun across his lap.

"You stupid jerk-off," Butch said, smacking toothless lips.

"What? I'm here to protect you!" Reeves said.

"I don't need protecting. Get inside, numb nuts. You too, young lady," Butch said, and spun his chair back inside.

Chickie rubbed his eyes. "What are you two doing?"

"They broke out of the damn jail, that's what," Butch said. "Help us pack up, Chick. We gotta blow town."

"You wanna go to Vegas?" Reeves grinned at Tara.

Tara put her palm to her nose like an oxygen mask. "I think I'd better patch things up with him."

"Honey, that big *stronzo* is never gonna take his hooks out of you," Chickie said. "He won't chase you. Reeves, he will. You, he'll be ashamed."

"I need to go get my stuff," Tara said. "Meet me at my place? I bet Tor's coming straight here as soon as he changes pants, so don't dilly-dally."

She kissed Chickie on the cheek on the way out.

"I didn't get a kiss," Reeves said, stuffing his ILBE pack.

"You're not a gentleman," Butch said, fitting his dentures. "Enough grab-ass. Take the BAR and the FG42, we can hock them in Vegas for seed money." He spun his chair toward Reeves, offering the handle of the Masamune.

"It's yours now, Reeves," Butch said. "Take it."

Reeves reached for the sword and the lights went out.

"The hell?" Chickie said.

Butch chambered a round in the grease gun. "Get down!"

The glass front window exploded inward with the *whump* of det-cord. Ceiling tiles tumbled in showers of dust and black shadows flickered in the dark of the shop.

Razors flickered in the air. Reeves brought his hands up, and groaned as the blades struck.

Butch fired three quick bursts. The grease-gun's muzzle flash and deafening roar filled the room. A masked body clothed in black skidded to the floor at their feet.

Reeves yanked the star-shaped blade from his forearm and threw it at the first thing that moved.

Men in black leapt from aisles. Two fell on Reeves and he twisted and blocked, grunting as he took the blows. He countered and they simply weren't there. They moved no faster than some he'd fought, but in ways he'd never faced before.

"This is *pazzo*," Chickie said and ducked behind the register.

Butch's gun roared as he rolled behind the counter. "Chickie! Get the Luger from the register, you little bastard!"

Reeves ate a punch to the nose and ducked to let the man's fist crunch on his skull. The man grunted in pain and Reeves kneed him in the gut, clinched, and spun with the man's body to slam his other opponent with it. The ninja in Reeves' grapple shrieked. Three red-feathered darts had pierced his back.

Chickie popped shots from behind the counter with the Luger as Butch reloaded. A red-feathered dart hit Butch in the chest.

"Son of a bitch!"

Chickie grabbed his shoulder and pulled the dart out. It had skewered the silver framed photo of Grandma Jean.

"Show me it," Butch snarled. Chickie obeyed. The dart hadn't marred Jean's face. "Haul ass, you crazy I-talian, I got men to kill!"

Two more ninjas flipped over the coat racks with spinning swords and Butch fired a long burst.

Another swordsman swung for Reeves. He yanked a Mauser from a barrel and blocked. The ninja drove him back to the counter with slashes. Reeves dodged his thrust and clocked him across the jaw with the stock. The ninja's chest jumped as Butch riddled him with bullets.

"Get behind the counter, shitbird!"

Reeves tumbled over it and panted.

"Load the Browning and make yourself useful!"

Reeves shouldered the shelf and caught the heavy automatic rifle as it fell. Butch rolled behind the cash register for cover and throwing stars spanged off the pale green metal. He hooked an ILBE pack strap with his foot and kicked, spilling the magazines out to the

61

floor. "They're reconnoitering for a second wave, we don't have much time. Load up and get me a Garand, soldier!"

Chickie dialed the rotary phone, spitting Italian curses at it. "You couldn't get a modern phone?"

"It costs five extra bucks a month!" Butch snapped. "I'm on a fixed income!"

"Can you argue that later?" Reeves handed Butch the Garand and slapped a mag into the Browning Automatic Rifle. Footsteps pattered across the roof, and tires popped and hissed in the parking lot.

"Laundry's closed," Butch said, and yanked back the bolt of the Garand. He held back the charging handle and fed it an 8-round spring clip while scanning the smoky ruins of the shop. "Hope Mr. Han's all right."

"Why can't we give them the sword, Pop?"

The handle of the sword stuck out from the wheelchair where Butch had tucked it.

"Because I gave my word! And so did you. Doesn't that mean anything? Quit being a dry-balls and let's blast our way through these bastards."

Chickie talked into the phone. "Hello, Sheriff's office? We've got—"

A black arrow sank in his chest to the fletching, and the roof of the store exploded and caved in with smoke. Silver blades flashed in the murk.

Butch and Reeves screamed and fired at the shadow shapes hurtling through the dust. The BAR slugged Reeves' shoulder like a heavyweight and punched fist-sized holes through a ninja's chest. Butch swept the room and fired with precision.

Reeves dropped his weapon when Chickie folded in half. The old man gulped air like a dying carp. Reeves snapped the head off the arrow. "Stay with us, Chickie!"

"You're no medic! Pick up your weapon!" Butch hollered, and the Garand's empty spring clip hit the floor with a *ting*.

A black-clad Takehiko swung through the gaping hole in the roof on a rope, sword in hand. Butch blocked his cut with the Garand's barrel. He butted Takehiko in the shoulder and kicked the floor hard, rolling his chair back to the wall as the ninja's sword flashed.

"Pop!"

Reeves leapt for the Browning and two ninjas dropped from the ceiling, stomping him flat with split-toed boots.

Butch fed the Garand a stray round of 30-aught six and fired. Takehiko's blade shattered.

Takehiko tossed the broken weapon aside and skated to Butch's chair on one knee, striking him in the gut.

"That all you got?" Butch snarled, and yanked a commando dagger from under his blanket.

Takehiko sprung back and drew the Honjo Masamune from Butch's chair. Butch threw the knife and Takehiko struck it from the air, and pinned Butch's shoulder to the chair with a deep thrust of the blade.

Butch screamed.

Reeves lashed and kicked, leaping to his feet. A ninja whipped a chain around his throat and yanked him flat on his back. The floorboards cracked with the impact. The ninja held the blade of a sickle to Reeves throat while his comrade hog-tied him with a silken rope in seconds.

Reeves struggled and spat. "I'll kill you!"

The ninja wrapped the silk over Reeves' mouth and left him trussed.

Takehiko chuckled and slid the blade from Butch's wound. It exited silently, without a drop of blood. Butch stuck his fist in the cut, and gritted his teeth.

"My grandfather misses you, Mr. Sloane," Takehiko said. "I pray for him at the Yasukuni shrine, and he screams out for vengeance."

"The shrieks of a coward facing justice," Butch gasped.

"You took his head," Takehiko said. "And I will take yours."

Reeves tugged at his bonds and groaned a muffled scream.

Butch planted both hands on his chair. He set his jaw in a sneer and pushed himself up on one wobbly leg.

"He died cowering," Butch said. "I'll take mine standing."

Takehiko laughed. "Do you know how ridiculous you look?"

Butch glared, fists at his sides. "Your family never knows when to shut up. May that sword curse you and all your blood until it's returned. Do it, you evil sonofabitch!"

Takehiko swung the Masamune in a whispery flash.

Butch hit the floor. His leg toppled after him.

Reeves screamed.

"The sword belongs to the Gantetsu," Takehiko said. "You don't have a leg to stand on." He burst into hysterics.

Butch dragged his legless body toward him, leaving a slug's trail of blood.

Takehiko kicked Butch onto his back. "Grandfather, may your *kami* find rest."

Tires screeched outside. The ninjas looked to their leader.

Reeves chomped on the gag and spun turtle, jerking his captors off balance. He head-butted the nearest in the face and sent the man sprawling with a shattered cheekbone. The ninja's chained sickle clattered to the floor. The second rose to strike and Reeves lashed out a kick to the back of his knee, toppling him.

"Reeves!" Johansson shouted from the parking lot. "Get your ass out here!"

"Leave him," Takehiko swore. "Take care of the cop!"

The two battered ninja ran outside.

Reeves thrashed out of his bonds and clutched his grandfather. "Pop!"

Butch stared at the half moon through the smoldering holes in the ceiling, then reached up and patted Reeves on the cheek. "I'm done, kid," he wheezed. "Protect the sword. Pay my debt for me." His hand fell and his eyes went flat.

"Pop! No!"

"You will crave justice," Takehiko said, and sheathed the Masamune. "This *is* justice. Let it end here, or your life will be one of pain."

Gunshots rang outside, then a ragged cry.

Reeves charged.

Takehiko flipped back and away with a plume of smoke that stung Reeves' eyes and choked his lungs. Two incendiary grenades exploded at the door. A wave of flames crashed over the ceiling, and Reeves dived into a rack of wool coats for cover.

He pushed the rack of coats toward the window to smother the flames, and leapt out into the parking lot.

Johansson leaned on a police cruiser, clutching his gun arm. A ninja lay crumpled a few steps away. Takehiko bolted toward a pair of black SUVs.

"Put your hands on the hood," Johansson growled.

"Give me your gun," Reeves said.

Takehiko opened the truck's door and lobbed a fly ball. As the grenade's spoon pinged Reeves dropped and tackled Johansson away from the police car.

The cruiser's hood exploded open and the windows spider-webbed and collapsed. Reeves covered his face from the falling debris. Johansson winced as the hot shards rained down.

"What the hell," Johansson said.

"War just hit home," Reeves said. He wrenched Johansson's side-arm from the thumb-break holster and fired at the fleeing black truck.

The slide locked back. Reeves dropped the pistol to the asphalt.

Johansson stared wide-eyed at the blazing shop and his smoking cruiser.

Reeves checked the sheriff's shuriken wound. "Keep pressure on it," he said. "Move away from the vehicle, it might go up. And call for backup."

Johansson nodded, face glazed in cold sweat.

Reeves ran for the second SUV. The gas tank blew with a spray of glass and flame. Reeves hit the dirt and covered his head.

A shape struggled inside the front of the truck. The fire closed in. Reeves climbed to his feet and yanked the door open.

A bound and gagged Mikio sprang into his arms. Reeves dragged him from the wreck and tore off his duct tape gag.

"*Domo, domo,*" Mikio coughed.

Reeves dumped him by Johansson. "You're the cop. Interrogate him." Reeves ran around back and ducked into the burning building.

THE AIR INSIDE THE STOCKROOM felt hotter than the desert at noon. Reeves crawled beneath the waist-high ceiling of smoke. Rounds popped as boxes of ammo cooked off.

Reeves belly crawled to Butch and closed his eyes gently.

He knelt for a long moment at the side of his fallen grandsire, coughing into his sleeve as sparks and embers fell, snowflakes from hell.

Reeves tucked the photo of Grandma Jean into Butch's pocket.

"I'm sorry, Pop. I fucked up, I know." A beam cracked and Reeves swatted a red coal from his shoulder. "I'll get your sword back. I don't know what it means to you, but I'll get the damn thing back, I swear."

He crushed Butch's limp form to his chest and set him down. He pulled the blanket from the wheelchair and covered him with it, and pulled a coat over Chickie's corpse as a box of MRE heaters went up and showered him with sparks.

Reeves pulled his coat over his mouth and scrambled out the back. The Buick wagon had four flat tires and the paint had already blistered off the hood from the heat. He busted the window with an elbow and tugged out his pack. Popped the glove box, and Butch's .45 and a battered metal can rattled out.

Reeves racked the Springfield .45, engaged the safety, and tucked it under his coat. He picked up the small metal brick. A rusty can of Tetley tea bags. Orange pekoe. He opened it and a crammed stack of yellowed letters busted out. He crimped the box shut and stuffed it into his cargo pocket.

Out front, Johansson paced with his cell phone. The sirens of the volunteer squad echoed across the lake. Smoke plumed from the building's funeral pyre, staining the rosy winter dawn.

A pair of headlights twinkled through the trees, coming fast. Reeves heaved Mikio to his feet and headed for the road, dragging him by his zip-tied hands.

"Where you think you're going?" Johansson sputtered.

"I've got a ride to catch," Reeves said and kept walking.

"What the hell is going on here?" Johansson gripped Reeves' shoulder. Reeves wrenched away, and drew the .45.

Johansson showed his hands.

A weary war cry came from behind. A wounded ninja ran for them, sword held high. Mikio wheezed and kicked the ninja in the gut. The .45 boomed twice, and Johansson ducked the ejected shells.

The ninja stumbled and raised his blade once more.

The Toronado screeched past on smoking tires to plow through the swordsman. The car jounced over the body.

Johansson stared open-mouthed.

"Holy shit," Tara said, and leaned out the window. "Where'd he come from?"

"Japan?" Reeves shrugged. "Pop the trunk."

"Oh my God," Tara said, gawping at the ruins of the shop. "What about—"

"They're gone." Reeves lifted Mikio in a fireman's carry and dropped him on top of the spare. He mashed the trunk closed on his protests, then climbed in the passenger side.

"What's going on?"

Reeves squeezed Tara's hand over the shifter. "I'll tell you on the road. Just head north."

"This ain't over," Johansson shouted, stumbling after them. He slapped a mag into his service Glock.

Tara cut the wheel and broke the tires loose. The sheriff fell flat on his ass as the Toronado roared out of town.

PART TWO

DEVILS AND DRAGONS

14.

THE FEAR OF DEATH WAS NOTHING compared to the fear of being seen as a coward.

Ernest "Butch" Sloane, Jr. stared out the jump doors and swallowed a mouthful of bile. Two weeks ago he'd been a park ranger in Superior National Forest, and his knees turned to water when he had to climb the ladder to the fire tower.

Compared to flat Minnesota, the Montana mountains had seemed enormous. From his perch in the shaky twin-prop, they looked like lumps in a plate of mashed potatoes. What if he busted his legs, and spent the war pushing pencils in a wheelchair? What if he pissed his pants?

The paratroop instructor hollered "Jump, you shitbird!" over the roar, and Butch leapt into the emptiness.

Fear struck him like a fall through the ice in Lake Superior. Parachutes blossomed open below, pale flowers against the rich green fields. Butch closed his eyes and tugged the cord.

He felt a yank and heard the flap of fabric, but when he looked up there was nothing.

Panic fluttered through his loins. His balls crawled up inside, using the rest of his body as a shield against the earth fast approaching. The instructor made them pack their own chutes. Butch had been riveted, but what if he'd mucked it up? It would be his own damn fault if he wound up a splat of bird shit on a mountain.

His heart punched at his throat. Every inch of his skin told him to scream and flail as the wind slapped his cheeks.

Butch set his jaw and remembered what the big-nosed jump instructor had said to do. He reached back and caught the strip of fabric, keeping his legs out to slow his descent. He tugged and felt the chute spill out his back like the guts of a strung-up deer. His hand got tangled as the chute deployed and yanked him up, spinning him in dizzying circles. He lost his glove getting free and watched it flutter away like a blackbird.

The rush tingled him from toes to scalp. He was going to live. He was a paratrooper.

Butch Sloane laughed like a tickled child as he floated down to the airfield with his comrades.

HE WOULD HAVE PREFERRED to spend the war chasing poachers and watching gophers fornicate, but he was a crack shot with a trapdoor Springfield, and his father—a chicken rancher and a die-hard Farmer-Labor man—had taken him aside and explained that the worst thing in the world wasn't a Republican, but wasted talent. So Butch enlisted at Camp Ripley, standing in line with the mopes holding draft cards, watching the 4-F rejects pretend to be disappointed when they got the heave-ho.

When the recruiter saw "Park Ranger" on Butch's application, he pulled him aside. The beak-nosed pencil pusher asked him if he'd done any tracking, and Butch told him about the time a bank robber from Roger Touhy's gang escaped from Arrowhead. Butch came down from his fire tower to join the posse. Three days later he caught the man sipping water from a creek. The sparkle-eyed sonofabitch raised the revolver from the guard he'd killed, and Butch blew a hole through his chest with his 30-aught six. He didn't tell the recruiter how he threw up after. Or that the guy's face haunted his dreams.

The recruiter picked up a phone and parked Butch on a bench, where he twiddled his thumbs until two hard looking men with blue garrison caps and no answers to his friendly attempts at chatter came in and marched him onto a train with blacked-out windows.

None of the soldiers on the train talked either.

The train stopped three hours later to fill up with Canuck soldiers dressed every which way, in kilts and tam o'shanters, fatigues and shorts cut off at the knees.

The men were to a one taciturn. Several stretched out to fill both seats as a short Indian looked for a spot. Butch had run-ins with Indians as a ranger. They all seemed to have a chip on their shoulder. He looked straight ahead as the Indian took the seat beside him.

"What do you do if you swallow a bullet?" the Indian asked.

Butch frowned and said nothing.

"Praise the Lord and pass the ammunition."

Butch laughed, and the kilted men frowned, and by sundown Butch and Jimmy Prince were lying like old friends, about who shot a sixteen-point buck and who caught a muskie as long as your leg.

The train stopped in Montana at Fort William Henry Harrison, where a lieutenant with piercing eyes and a nose as thin as an axe blade told them they were now part of a special joint American-Canadian force chosen for their wilderness survival skills.

"I am Lieutenant Frederick, and those of you who don't quit will fight in the 1st Special Service Force. You will climb mountains. You will parachute from airplanes, and you will be instructed by Norwegian commandos to ski in formation. You will fight as an elite sabotage unit, and strike at the heart of the enemy," the officer said, sweeping them with his glare. "Every operation is a suicide mission. Extraction will not always be possible. You will take no prisoners. Your skills as woodsmen will ensure your survival and escape. And if you speak of any of it to anyone outside this unit, you will hang as traitors."

The men nodded. And they trained hard.

Barrel-chested Butch was given the "Johnny gun", the M1941 Johnson light machine gun, with a 25-round magazine of 30-aught six that jutted out sideways and made it tough to balance. A slow-talking Southerner showed him how to brace it and fire on the move. It was a lot different than leading a whitetail from a blind, but the gun had a flat trajectory and didn't rise much, and soon it felt as natural as his old Springfield. They trained in German weapons—the "burp gun" machine pistol and the Mauser rifle—until they knew them like their own.

A skinny, big-nosed Irishman named O'Neill taught them to fight like the Japanese. An old China hand, he told them tales of fighting Japanese spies alongside the Shanghai Municipal Police. He threw even the biggest bohunks around like rag dolls, taught them to jab and gouge and make every blow count, not to trade punches and dance like a boxer. Each man was issued a combat dagger with a skull crusher pommel and taught to hook an arm around a sentry's throat and knife them in the kidney to ensure swift silent death.

Jimmy Prince could throw his knife twenty-five paces into a sil-ver dollar sized target, and he taught Butch to do it as well. Butch had a knack for body blows that stole the wind out of his sparring partner, and he showed Jimmy how to get a knuckle through the ribs and hit the lungs, and get under to hit the liver.

Fierce-eyed Lieutenant Frederick trained alongside them, and O'Neill led from the front. They jumped from planes with full packs and landed ready to fire, and an old blue-eyed Italian taught them to rock climb like the mountain goat he resembled.

They fought and scaled and ran and marched until the huskiest was cut to muscle and bone, and on weekends they hit the town's only dance hall. There they traded nods and shots of whiskey with old cow-punchers, and danced politely with the town's women under the watchful eyes of seasoned lawmen.

BUTCH FELT LIKE HE COULD SPRING OVER THE ATLANTIC and punch Hitler in the mouth. Jimmy Prince couldn't get a drink despite his uniform, so Butch ordered two, and brought them back to the table.

A big red-faced man with a handlebar moustache sauntered over, his dull gray Colt loose in the well-worn holster. "I appreciate you boys going to fight, but no Indians drink in my city limits. You'll have to leave, son."

"These are for me, sheriff," Butch said, and hammered back both shots.

The lawman narrowed his eyes and lumbered away.

Jimmy shrugged, determined to have a good time. There were more soldiers than women, so they danced together to make the ladies laugh, showing off their freshly minted fighting physiques.

Butch never drank much—just slugs of aquavit when ice fishing—and the local redeye stoked the fire in his belly. One of the girls had a smile that shone like a new dime. Platinum blond with a sharp smile, strong legs and a fire inside that her friends huddled around for laughter and warmth. Butch crossed the room and asked her to dance.

His cheeks were red, but the liquor hadn't made him any less gentlemanly. The girl's friends egged her on, and she reluctantly took his hand. Her name was Jean Marie Dundee, and she kept looking over Butch's shoulder when he wished she would put her head on it.

Butch gave her a twirl to show her he wasn't as tipsy as he looked. There hadn't been much to do back home except dance with big blond girls and keep them warm in the winter, and Butch was good at both.

"You dance like a bull in a china shop," Jean said, and tugged his arm like the reins on a draft horse. "You stomp my toes and I'll make a steer out of you."

She kept him at bay with a firm hand on his shoulder. Her full lip had a permanent smirk, and Butch tasked himself with making her smile.

"What do you do if you swallow a bullet?" he asked over the country fiddle coming from the speakers.

"Shoot yourself with the other five for being a jackass," was Jean's reply.

At the first slow song, his hand drifted from her waist to her hip and she gave him a slap.

The boys laughed at him, and for the next weeks of training they ribbed him about it. But it only strengthened his resolve.

MONTANA WINTER HAD NOTHING ON MINNESOTA, but the mountains shaped the wind into icy fists that battered Butch's cheeks on the slopes. Norwegian commandos harried the troops until even the clumsiest bastard could shush and slalom in formation. Motor pool pencil-necks instructed them in the use of the M29 Weasel snow-ready tread vehicle. It became clear that their mission would be in the ice and snow.

As the days got colder, Butch began to think of how warm Miss Jean Dundee would be in his arms. She spotted him coming across the dance floor and tilted her head with that same wry grin.

"You come back to tell me something?"

"I was hoping you'd give me a chance to turn the other cheek."

Butch fell in love with the smile she gave.

He did his best to see more of her smiles in the few weeks they had left together. But smiles were all he got. Jean was the only child of a cattle rancher who treated her almost like a son, and was used to getting her way. And her way was chaste.

Butch heard from the other soldiers that plenty of cowgirls had gone for hay rides, but Miss Jean would have none of it. He would walk her to her horse, a big paint, and she'd lean over to kiss him on the cheek before she trotted home. Any time Butch felt tempted by one of the frisky chippies, he thought of Jean's platinum blond hair framing her sharp smile. He imagined her out of her clothes, too, but it always came back to that smile and the half a sly wink she brought with it. Rumor had it the Army put saltpeter in the rations to dampen the soldiers' libidos, and Butch wished for a double dose.

He was dreaming of her riding down the mountain naked as Lady Godiva on the morning the bugle call roused them early to hear the Lieutenant's speech.

As they marched to formation, each man was handed a new insignia. A red arrowhead with USA at the point and CANADA printed down the center.

"You men are the tip of the spear the Allies will stick up Hitler's keister," Lt. Frederick said. "But first you have an appointment with the Empire of Japan, in the Aleutians. You have trained harder than any brigades under Allied command. The Japanese are a warrior culture. You will not be fighting the squinting midgets on the war bonds posters, but hardened men who have trained since birth to die for their Emperor. They will not surrender. They will not die easy. Do not underestimate them.

"Pack your chutes and clean your weapons. You have R&R until curfew this evening. Any soldier missing curfew will be court-martialed. Any soldier who comes back too drunk to stand will be horsewhipped."

Frederick scanned his men with glossy black eyes. "Tomorrow you will show the enemy your mettle, and *you will not fail*."

◆ ◆

BUTCH PACKED HIS CHUTE THREE TIMES until he was satisfied, then hopped in a Jeep with Jimmy Prince and a couple of Cajuns who cursed the cold. Miss Jean wasn't with her friends. A short brunette hanging on a kilted Canuck's arm told him she'd gone home.

Butch took the Jeep back to base. The MP guarding the motor pool frowned. "You're back early."

"Yeah, there was a big fight, I wanted no part of it," Butch said as he passed. He quickly turned and put the man in one of O'Neill's sleeper holds. "Sorry, buddy." Butch set him down gently behind the guard shack.

He roared through the gates behind the wheel of an M29 Weasel trainer. By the time the MP loaded his rifle, Butch was already off zig-zagging through the trees.

The mountain road was dark, muddy and rutted. He passed a wagon sunk to its axles, abandoned in the dirty slush. The Weasel's one headlight cut through the gloom, illuminating a lone rider trudging up the hill.

The horse shied and kicked as Butch pulled alongside in the halftrack. Jean tugged the reins and stroked the paint's neck until her steed calmed.

Butch killed the engine and stood to face her. "I don't even rate a goodbye?"

Jean looked away and chewed her lip. She eased her horse closer. Silver trails traced her cheekbones in the moonlight.

"Don't you go die now, you sonofabitch," she said, and leapt into his arms. Her hat fell into the mud. Butch cradled her in back of the halftrack.

"I'll be coming back with Tojo's head on a bayonet," Butch said. "And if you marry some cowpunch, I'll kick him right in the ass."

She planted a fierce kiss on his mouth and kneaded his shoulders. Butch opened his winter fatigues to keep her warm, but she was plenty warm already. Her boots crossed behind Butch's back as he clutched her tight.

The horse nickered and pranced away, nibbling the weeds that peeked through the snow.

15.

REEVES FLIPPED THROUGH THE METAL TETLEY TEA BOX he found in Butch's pack. Medals in their cases. Letters to Grandma Jean. He left them unread, out of respect for the dead.

Tara had the wheel, a scowl on her face. Broke up over Butch and Chickie's deaths.

Reeves was, too. He'd gone cold inside.

They had lost Takehiko's truck even with the speedometer pinned. He had too much of a lead.

"We're driving blind," Reeves said.

"We'll catch up," she said.

"Pull over. I gotta take a leak."

She sighed and coasted down to double digits, then skidded to a stop on the shoulder. Reeves leaned over her thighs.

"Hey."

He took the keys from the ignition and walked around to the trunk. He opened it with his fist cocked.

Mikio blinked at the hazy sunlight. Crusted blood flaked off his face and moustache.

"Where's Takehiko, shitbird?"

"Kutabare," Mikio spat.

Reeves raised his bandaged fist.

Tara stepped out and lit a smoke, her fur-topped boots crunching the gravel. She sat on the edge of the trunk and offered Mikio a drag. "If you want to warm up in front, tell us where your boss is headed."

Mikio grunted and took a puff from her Marlboro.

"Let me deal with him," Reeves said. "I left three of his limbs working. Where's your tire iron?"

"Manko," Mikio said.

"I don't know what that means, but I'm pretty sure I don't like it," Reeves said. "You can freeze back there."

Tara came around with a Thermos of coffee. "Sit him up, Reeves."

"Tara, he—"

"He's a human being, and this is my ride," she said. "So my rules. Got it?"

Reeves nodded, and helped stand Mikio up. Tara snipped the zip ties on Mikio's hands with a multitool, and Reeves stuffed him in the back seat. They piled in and slapped their hands to drive out the chill.

Mikio wormed his good arm out of the quilt and sipped the coffee Tara handed him from the passenger seat. "*Domo,*" he said.

Reeves took the wheel, and watched trucks roar past.

"Your boss left you holding the bag," Tara said. "I know you guys got honor and stuff, but . . . who'm I kidding, I only know what I know from the movies, right?"

"Get to point," Mikio said.

Tara smirked. "Okay. What do you owe this asshole?"

Mikio looked into his cup, then drained it. He handed it back to her. "Go north," he said.

"See, was that so hard?" Tara said.

Reeves hit the pedal and the Toronado spat gravel. Mikio rubbed his shoulder and winced.

"Let me look at it," Tara said. She leaned over the seat and prodded Mikio's arm from shoulder to elbow. "Eyes up here, buddy."

Mikio chuckled. "No."

Tara cuffed him on the side of the head, and sat back on her seat, buttoning her coat closed. "Your arm's not busted. You guys get in the ring and pound each other's faces in, then you whine about the tiniest little thing."

"You ever been hit before?" Reeves said.

"I busted my collarbone once," Tara said. "When me and my bestie Lynn drove down to Apple Valley for the Black Sabbath reunion show. This suburban brat in his mom's Volvo rear-ended her Scout, and I slammed right into the dash. No seat belts." Tara pulled her shirt down to finger the knot in the bone. "Snapped my clavicle like that." She clicked her tongue against her cheek.

The men nodded.

"And I still went to the show," Tara said. "Handful of Advils and my hip flask of JD. We weren't missing Ozzy for anything. Lynn chipped a tooth and swallowed it. Her boyfriend stayed home with the sniffles. The sniffles! Little whiner was cheating on her. Sniffles, my ass."

"I hit harder than the sniffles," Reeves said. "Give him a break."

"Not that hard," Mikio said.

"Knocked you out," Reeves said.

"Luck," Mikio said.

"Stop fighting, girls, you're both pretty." Tara laughed. "Sounds like you're both coming down with the sniffles."

16.

ALASKA WAS A BUST.

They chuted in and trained their guns on abandoned camps and machine gun nests. Jimmy Prince and a tracker from Texas poked through the leavings and estimated that the Japanese troops had evacuated months before.

The lieutenant booted an empty fuel can and pointed to his aide de camp. "Note that we have struck the Japanese," Frederick said, and turned to the men. "Now let's go get Jerry."

THE 1ST SPECIAL SERVICE FORCE hopped so many planes that Butch felt like a baby being delivered by a drunken stork. They hit the shore in Casablanca to attach to the American 5th Army, and shipped to Italy to break the Gustav line. The Italians had surrendered, but the Germans held the mountains. A handsome general with a bad case of Long Island Lockjaw briefed them.

"The Jerries have a weapon we call screaming mimis," the general honked. "They call them the uh, *Nebelwerfer*. That's Kraut for smoke mortar, except they aren't blowing smoke. They're chemical warfare cannons. We've hit these ss head-on, and each time they gas us and rain hell with their 105s."

Lt. Frederick spoke next. "Men, we're going to climb up Jerry's back door and kick those gas rockets right up Heinrich's heinie."

Jimmy was part of the recon force. When he returned from debriefing the brass, the men huddled around him for the skinny. "I hope you liked climbing with full haversacks," he said. "Bring all the ammo you can carry. The peaks are lousy with Krauts."

The mountains blossomed with fire. They climbed under the cover of an artillery barrage unlike anything Butch had ever seen.

"Fire on the mountain, run boys run," the rangy, weak-chinned man they called Kentucky twanged, and hammered a piton into the rock.

The climb was virtually sheer. The constant flicker of explosives lit the shadowy crags and goat trails, and the blasts peppered them with rock fragments from above.

Butch dug his boots in and followed Kentucky up the rope. The thin air choked out their fear. The rumble of artillery buffeted them, angry drumbeats coming from all sides. And halfway through the ascent, the skies opened up with their own battle song of thunder, lightning and the sizzle of freezing rain.

"Tie yourselves together," Butch hollered, and knotted his reserve rope around him. He tossed it to Jimmy down the line.

"Put a pro on your Johnson," O'Neill called back.

Butch bit the corner off a condom package and spat. He unrolled the rubber over the muzzle of the Johnson light MG, and planted his feet for the slippery ascent.

They climbed slow. Butch swore he saw a mountain goat fall ass-first off the mountainside, and hoped it wasn't a comrade. The Kentucky boy bellied over the edge of the precipice and waved them over. Butch skittered and Jimmy grabbed him by his web belt, giving him a brief view of the rocky abyss below before dragging him to safety.

Guttural shouts echoed across the peak. Flares arced overhead. O'Neill threw a leg over and punched Butch in the shoulder. "Attack!"

They charged.

Stars flickered on the mountaintop and the gravel at their feet flew like popcorn. The German machine gunners were everywhere, raking the mountaintop. Men tumbled over the cliff and Butch knew he couldn't hear them scream over the shelling, but heard it anyway, as their shocked faces plummeted from view.

O'Neill slapped Butch on the shoulder. "Big man, give us fire from that angle, now!"

Butch ran serpentine to the far flank and planted behind a scrub pine. He lined up the big sight of his Johnny gun and feathered the trigger, pocking the nests with three-round bursts. The strafe of the German guns snaked through the rock shards toward his position.

Bullets snapped past his ears. His cheeks tightened in a rictus as he screamed and returned fire.

Shoot-through grenades whistled overhead and their report echoed down the peaks. One machine gun nest's star-flicker winked out. Then another.

O'Neill waved men through the cleared field of fire and Butch followed. Platoon leaders took over the nests and turned the guns back on the enemy. Butch and Jimmy followed O'Neill and his men toward the smoke mortars.

Jimmy crept down to perform a quick recon with binoculars. "Don't look like they know they've been breached, sir. If we follow their supply lines, we can get right on top of them, one by one."

O'Neill and Jimmy led the ambush. O'Neill with a suppressed Sten gun, and Jimmy with a pair of commando daggers. Butch pulled the rear and covered them with his support weapon.

The *Nebelwerfer* resembled a honeycomb of rocket tubes, and each was manned by five soldiers. Two got a knife in the back and the third caught a machine pistol burst full in the face. Butch caught a flash of the man's obliterated features before the corpse toppled over the edge. Stomach acid flooded his mouth and he choked it down.

Two riflemen dived for their weapons and Butch put a burst

of 30-aught through their backs. Jimmy retrieved his blades and they rearmed with German weapons so the unique report of enemy weapons would not alert their prey.

O'Neill waved them ahead and knelt to plant a demo charge under the rocket mortar. They had almost reached the second target when the blast went off and alerted the crew. The Germans turned just in time to get hosed down with the Devils' captured burp guns. It felt unsportsmanlike, as they traversed the ridge and left howitzer crews face-down and riddled in their wake.

"Like slaughtering hogs come Easter," Kentucky said.

The distinctive patter of the machine guns etched the shocked expressions of the dead into Butch's mind forever.

"Feels wrong shooting them in the back," Butch said.

"I like it just fine," Kentucky replied. "Better'n lookin' 'em in the face."

O'Neill handed Butch his burp gun and plucked an olive metal lollipop from a dead soldier's pack. "*Panzerfaust,*" he said. "Like a bazooka."

The final *Nebelwerfer* crew pitched potato masher grenades down onto the trail and blew Kentucky clear off the mountain. His flailing looked like jumping jacks on the way down.

Butch didn't feel so bad about shooting Germans in the back anymore. He, O'Neill and Jimmy took cover behind a rock crest.

"Ditch the bullet sprayers," O'Neill said. "Put your rifles over the top and pin them down."

O'Neill cocked his .45 and broke into a run with the *panzerfaust* in his other hand. Butch strafed the ridge in short controlled bursts. Jimmy held the Garand to his cheek and picked off Jerry helmets as they gophered up to return fire.

Butch heard the panicked hammering of .45 caliber rounds and his legs sent him after O'Neill against his will. The Irishman had squeezed himself against the mountain while three riflemen took turns shooting creases into the rock face. Butch roared around the corner with the Johnny gun and swept them with the trigger pinned, cutting two in half. The last German ran and Butch followed.

They rounded a corner and the German tumbled like a bloody sack. A half dozen Germans huddled around a *Nebelwerfer* spraying the path with fire. Hot pain seared Butch's thigh, ribs and cheek as he screamed and swept the barrel from one target to the next until the machine gun clicked dry.

Smoke enveloped Butch as the *panzerfaust* rocket struck the base of the cannon and shrouded the enemy in white-hot flames. One ran past them shrieking. Butch pulled the trigger on an empty magazine.

O'Neill swept the burning man's boot, then stomped the back of his skull as he hit the ground. The *Nebelwerfer* teetered over the cliff, taking its scorched and dying crew with it.

"You did good, lads," O'Neill said, and slapped Butch on the back. "Let's move. There's plenty other mountains just like this one."

The constant gunfire echoed off the mountains like sheets of lead rain. The machine guns dueled long into the night.

17.

SNOW CAME DOWN LIKE PLAYING CARDS tossed across the highway at the windshield. "Keep my baby under a hundred," Tara said.

Reeves sighed and eased off the pedal. "You want to drive?"

"Actually, yes." She dragged her behind across his lap and they switched spots. The tires nicked the rumble strip and sputtered complaint.

Reeves eased the Springfield 1911 in his belt and rubbed where it had dug in. He set it on the seat, and turned to study Mikio's hangdog face. The old fighter might have been counting snowflakes.

"You fight Shooto?" Reeves asked. "Pride, maybe. You look familiar."

Mikio nodded. "Not champ." He searched for the word. "Contender."

"I liked Pride. Better rules than UFC. Wish I could've fought over there."

Mikio grunted.

"Here, it's all promoter shit," Reeves said. "I mean, it's the only game in town, and I wish I hadn't messed up and lost my chance at a title fight. But we might as well be pit bulls in some scumbag NFL player's fight farm, for all they care. Fight us until we're used up, and kick us to the curb."

"Same in Japan," Mikio said.

"Yeah?"

"After my fight, three ribs broken. My . . . promoter, bring in *manko*," Mikio said, and chuckled. "Pussy man?"

"A cream puff?"

"No," Mikio said, and put on a fake smile. He pantomimed putting on makeup.

Reeves laughed. "A baby face? Pretty boy. Yeah, we get them, too. Sometimes they got talent, but funny how they get the easy fights to pad their record so they make it big. While the technical guys, the good fighters, they gotta take shit until the fans demand they get a fair shake."

Mikio nodded. "Pretty boy puncture liver," he said, slapping his side with the good arm.

"Sorry I kneed you there," Reeves said.

Mikio smirked and waved a hand. "Pretty face got title fight. He lose, but take my place. Contender."

Reeves nodded. He'd seen it with fighters he admired, getting shot down before they had their shot. Sometimes it made him glad he'd been in the Marines instead. There, brass sprinkled you around like roach killer, but they let you rest. If you could rest while mortars thumped around the perimeter and choppers landed in the middle of the night hauling in more of your blown-up friends. Even now, Reeves woke at the slightest noise, wondering which soldier was going home a few limbs short.

Didn't matter whether it was the battlefield or the ring. Someone higher up was gonna throw you into the meat grinder.

18.

AS HE CRADLED THE HEAD of the sleeping SS soldier whose throat he'd severed, Butch thought of the letter he'd received in Anzio. Jean said they'd had a rough winter, lost some cattle, and she couldn't listen to Ernest Tubb without crying. Butch had wanted to tell her he wished he had her warming his tent in the mountains, but the SSF—now dubbed The Devil's Brigade, after the name *Schwarzer teufel*, black devils, that the Germans had given them—were not allowed to write home.

He jammed his forearm over the dying soldier's mouth and tilted the chin down over the gaping neck wound. When the body stopped twitching in his sleeping bag, Butch stuck the Devil's Brigade's death sticker over the SS skull insignia on his helmet.

The sticker read *Das dicke Ende kommt noch*.

The worst is yet to come.

Jimmy blinked three times to signal he was done with his side. Their faces blacked with boot polish, every jangly bit of metal muffled or removed. Two men stood guard with suppressed Sten guns while they slit every throat but one, then crept out of camp in the chill night air.

The poor bastard would wake up in a slaughterhouse.

They were the terror of the Winter Line. The Herman Goering Division and *Panzergrenadiers* whispered of them, the Black Devils who struck only at night. Whetting their daggers on the throats of sentries. Their bullets riddling every convoy foolish enough to not travel in force. The Germans surrendered in droves when they saw the red arrows on their shoulders, then kicked the ground and cursed when they saw their true numbers.

Jimmy wiped his blades on a captured Nazi flag, and let it drift into the mud as they exfiltrated into the woods. For a while, Butch had used their flags for TP, but now the consensus was that seeing the swastika soiled with the blood of the fallen was more demoralizing to the enemy.

That, and they were itchy.

Back in camp, Butch traded his chicken C-ration for Jimmy's hash. The taste of red meat was too close to blood for Jimmy, and Butch had eaten chicken so much as a child that he'd smelled like one, and thought he was turning into a damn plucked rooster every time he got goose pimples. But it beat chalky K-rations, and anything was better than the bully beef and hardtack the British got.

"Remember what food used to taste like?" Jimmy asked over the fire.

"Just chicken, and I'm trying to forget." Butch had his boots over the flames. His feet had gotten frostbite on a previous raid, and they'd ached in the cold since.

A replacement, a tall Canadian named Turritin, shared smokes and joined their fire. "What are you gonna do when the lights go on again?"

"I was a butcher," Jimmy said, looking in his can of chicken. He jabbed a spoon around in it, then tossed the can into the fire. "Not doing that anymore."

"They're dropping bombs on women and children all over London," Turritin snapped. "Think of them, not the bloody Jerries."

Butch wiped the black from his face. "Wait until you're on night patrol, kid. Until then, keep your mouth shut."

"Keep the smokes," Turritin said. "I know where I'm not wanted." He shuffled away.

Butch thought about chasing deer poachers. Finding piles of spilled guts in the woods, tracking blood trails. "I just want to look my girl in the eyes and not scare the shit out of her."

"Didn't she crap the first time you met?"

"Like a Clydesdale."

IN THE MORNING, Lt. Frederick said the night patrols were over. "Slaughtering Nazi supermen may be a heroic cause," he said, "But tomorrow we cross the Rubicon and follow in Caesar's footsteps. We will take the Eternal City back from the Hun. The battle will be fierce. We have the German on the run, at his most desperate since he decided to throw his weight all over Europe. They will not take our advance easily.

"They have tanks, they have snipers. They have their misguided, fierce Teutonic pride. A German Shepherd has lifted his leg on the great city of Rome, boys. It's time to smack his nose with the newspaper."

If only it had been so easy. Their spearpoint gouged against the anvil of Monte Cassino.

"Keep up, you big bastards!" O'Neill hollered. Jimmy, Turritin, Butch and Andre the Cajun hauled ass through crumbling ancient stone toward a squad of German engineers holding the bridge to an island in the middle of the Tiber river. The Germans had a disabled tank for a pillbox, and swung its massive turret their way.

The Devils split and took cover as the shell punched a hole through the flipped personnel carrier they had been using for a shield. Butch leveled the Johnny gun and clanged a burst off the tank's armor. O'Neill and Turritin pincered around the pillbox while Jimmy and Andre sniped with captured FG42 paratrooper rifles. Mustangs zipped and buzzed overhead, punching out tanks a block away.

Butch laid covering fire until the tank gun swiveled his way. He belly crawled behind the demolished facades of a Roman temple and took shelter behind the marble bosom of a beheaded goddess. The spot he'd inhabited moments before erupted with debris and the tank shell cratered the cobblestones. Butch's head rang like Bugs Bunny had crowned him with a frying pan.

The world spun, and Butch thought of one of Jimmy's stupid jokes about the Hunchback of Notre Dame falling off the steeple of the church. Something about a dead ringer. He spat a mouthful of dust and saw his crew firing into the tank hatch. They'd taken the position.

Butch stumbled to his feet. He couldn't hear anything, but saw a donkey bray silently across the plaza with a soldier bayoneting its flank, forcing it to pull an impossibly heavy load. A 20mm cannon with four Germans in tow.

Fear goosed Butch like a hot poker. He let the MG hang from its strap, the way he'd been taught to shoot and ski, and broke into a full run. He came at the Germans circling a fountain fouled with corpses and blood, hollering nonsense he couldn't hear himself.

The Germans opened up with the 20mm and two Devils came apart in chunks. Turritin hurled grenades, his mouth frothing while anti-aircraft rounds sparked off the tank around him. Butch howled around behind them and hammered the gunners with his 30-aught six. The big rounds punched through the wagon and tore the Germans' legs out from under them, burst their guts out their bellies like streamers from battered piñatas.

The donkey fell to its side kicking. A German sank behind it and fired his sidearm, his lips peeled back with terror. Butch riddled the donkey's corpse until the German fell on his back and panted at the bright blue sky. Butch took the Luger from the dying man's hand and aimed at his forehead.

Butch looked away, fingered the trigger, then sank to his ass in the rubble. He uncapped his canteen, took a slug, and wet the German's lips with his finger.

"*Veilen dank,*" the man wheezed, and panted until he seized up and went silent.

Turritin sat gasping, covered in blood. Butch slapped him on the shoulder and helped him to his feet. The rest of the platoon marched past to man the bridge.

O'Neill picked through the splattered remains with his fighting knife until he came up with dog tags. He pushed them into a pocket, and wiped his face on his sleeve. A tall Quebecker jogged over to relay him a message.

"The lieutenant has asked for us personally," O'Neill said, lighting a smoke. He snapped a command toward a sad-eyed kid named Irving Hoddeson who they called 'Berlin.' He'd quit Juilliard to join up.

"Berlin! You're with us now."

O'Neill drank from Butch's canteen and pointed up the mountain, where a monastery perched in the rookeries of Monte Cassino.

"That there's full of Kraut commandos, keeping us from Rome. Let's show 'em who's king of the mountain, boys."

Berlin collected burp gun magazines from the dead. "ss?"

O'Neill nodded, and flicked his smoke into the raging river below.

88S WHISTLED DOWN and shook the road as the Devils ran through terraced farms up the hillside. Allied guns returned fire, but the angle of the peak sent most shells over the target. The monastery loomed, and the fuzzy cotton ball of the sun peeked through the haze of artillery fire.

Butch hopped a stone wall and huddled with his squad. Rounds snapped overhead and the men shuddered at the friendly artillery landing short, cratering their path to the castle. The grass rolled in waves and the shock rippled downhill, tossing the men as if God whipped the earth like a bed sheet.

Butch felt his jaw moving but couldn't hear himself scream.

He swore to himself that if he made it home, he'd convince Jean to leave the mountains for the Minnesota prairie. Where you could see what was coming for miles around.

When the thunder ended, the silence was the loudest sound Butch had ever heard. O'Neill slapped each of his men on the shoulder and directed them with jabs of his fingers. They ran through shell-holes and shreds of tangled barbed wire over crumbled walls, trading fire with equally panicked Germans, who slid down the terracotta roofs screaming.

Snipers pinned them in the vineyards until O'Neill ran halfway down the mountain and hauled up a bazooka. Jimmy stared wide-eyed, and Butch nodded to him. Their squad leader's disregard for his own life shone bright in a company of men renowned for it. He blasted the top off the bell tower and they charged, stomping the grapes in their wake. The church bell clattered down the mountain, ringing out a chaotic toll.

The vineyard erupted with dirt clods and severed legs. Turritin howled and the platoon jolted to a stop.

Minefield.

Butch ran in the shattered men's footsteps while snipers picked off his frozen comrades. He fired a burst that shattered a row of roof tiles, then ducked to grab Turritin by the belt and drag him from open ground. A Devil two rows over somersaulted, the ground exploding beneath him. His boots went a different direction.

Butch hit the ground behind a wine press and tied Turritin's leg off with his belt. Jimmy followed his path and snagged the man who'd lost his feet and dropped him alongside. Jimmy traded shots with snipers while Butch dumped sulfa on the wounds and stuck the wounded with morphine syrettes.

"Best we can do for now," Butch said, and passed Turritin his sidearm.

The big Canadian shivered and checked the chamber.

O'Neill and Berlin waved from the other side of the courtyard. Jimmy returned the signal, and they charged behind an empty stable, meeting with the rest of the squad.

"Andre the Cajun's men are hammering the front door. We're going through the wine cellar," O'Neill said. "Butch, hit the windows. Rest of you, grenades ready. In twos."

Butch crawled around the corner and put a burst into the clay window grates on either side of the cellar steps, then kicked and rolled when his cover splintered to pieces under MG42 fire. The German squad machine gun stippled the stable walls and mowed down the first wave of men. Butch found a horse stall with a loose slat and surveyed the castle. The MG42's distinctive trumpet muzzle nosed out a corner tower window.

Butch whistled, then sent burst after burst up into the window, ricocheting big rounds in the round room while Jimmy led the grenade charge. The MG42 rounds sparked off the bricks, firing blind at the grenadiers who crushed themselves up against the castle wall. The pineapples thundered below and the cellar entrance billowed smoke.

Berlin disappeared down the dusty cellar. Butch took a captured Luger from his boot and pumped his legs across the courtyard. A scatter of lead fragments peppered his back as he jumped down the stairs. They burned like cigarette ashes spilt down his shirt. Above, he caught a glimpse of the machine gunner hanging out the window, another man holding him by the boots.

In the cellar, O'Neill and Jimmy traded rounds with three Germans curled up in a pile of shredded barrel staves. Berlin strafed them with his burp gun, then stomped the throat of the last man moaning. He picked a twisted magazine from the wreckage and tossed it. Jimmy and O'Neill shouldered their rifles and switched to Sten guns in the close quarters. Butch collected Luger magazines from the fallen.

Berlin led them up the spiraling stairs, his gray eyes cool as thunderheads. He had piano player's fingers and they tickled the triggers as smoothly as they once had the ivories, coaxing single rounds, doubles, and triples at will. He'd had plenty of practice with the BB guns in Coney Island, before his father dragged the family to hole up in the Catskills after Lindbergh had praised Hitler. Papa had smelled a pogrom coming. In a cold whisper, he told young Irving of the terror the Cossacks had brought to their *shtetl*, which now only existed in memory.

His son never shied away from a fight.

Two tall soldiers sporting the ss lightning bolts rounded the hallway. Berlin put two rounds in the chest of the first and one in the face of his brother. Shouts echoed down the hall. Berlin crossed the threshold and waved up his comrades.

They soft-shoed to the corner tower and bounced a potato masher into the room. Berlin stitched the MG42 gunner up the back, then folded against the wall. An officer shot him through the biceps with his sidearm. Jimmy and O'Neill perforated the shooter with their Sten guns.

Berlin stuck his dead arm into his shirt Napoleon style, and looped the strap of his burp gun over his neck. "I can cut the mustard," he said.

Butch picked through the guns stacked by the window and slapped a fresh belt into a light MG34 machine gun. He folded the bipod and heaved the sling over his shoulder. "I'll take point."

At the top they found monks huddled in their cells and the double doors to the great hall barricaded. They heard the roar of *panzerfaust* from beyond the doors, as the last of the ss held off Andre's head-on attack.

Berlin dragged an old monk out by his hood. The friar jabbered in Italian while O'Neill dug deep for Latin phrases the priests had drilled into him. "Tuck here says we can drop in on those krauts through the chimney, if we take the roof."

The monk led them to a stairwell that opened to the pocked and shattered rooftop. Butch peeked over the top and saw a row of legs where snipers leaned against the balustrade, shooting down from the roof. He quietly extended the bipod and pulled the trigger.

Nothing.

Butch hadn't racked the bolt.

One of the snipers reached for the ammo box behind him, locked eyes with Butch, and froze.

Butch yanked the bolt. All five riflemen's heads jerked around at the clang. The MG34 roared, and Butch swept back and forth across their waists and mowed the snipers over the railing.

The Devils clambered onto the roof and huddled over the chimney, arguing over dropping their last grenade.

"Surprise is all we got," O'Neill said.

"Sarge, we have no idea of the numbers," Jimmy said. "You can't—"

O'Neill's answer was to throw his legs over the chimney and shinny down like a big-nosed Irish Santa Claus. Jimmy gritted his teeth and followed, small and nimble. He stopped when O'Neill reached up and squeezed his knee. Two men stuffed in the chimney ready to drop.

Butch watched over the edge as Berlin stalked through the

ruins of the rooftop for hidden snipers. O'Neill rolled the grenade into the room and made the sign of the cross. It whumped and he dropped, firing and running. Jimmy dropped next and immediately fell back against the sooty bricks and clutched his side. More rounds hit the stone around him, and he shriveled into a ball.

Butch did not think. Later, he wished he had. He jumped over the rim and landed hard. It felt like his leg shot up through his knee. He fell flat on his stomach with a scream and saw O'Neill curled under a shattered desk, firing blindly with his Sten at half a dozen Germans crammed behind a toppled dinner table.

One of the Germans hosed the fireplace with a burp gun. It felt close enough for the muzzle flash to singe Butch's eyebrows. The German was no more than a boy, his lips curled with a desperation Butch knew by heart.

Butch lay into the MG34 as rounds ricocheted all around him. He shredded the boy and his comrades until the last of the ammo belt snaked through the bolt and the barrel glowed red.

The shock of the busted leg saved Butch from feeling the burning wounds that cut across his back, but he felt them plenty on the rocky ride to the field hospital with the rest of his squad.

The Devils had led the Allies to Rome. Their reward was the guilt and lonesome heartache of survivors who question why they had lived while so many brothers died in the needless, brutal slaughter.

19.

TARA PULLED AROUND A SALT TRUCK, skirting the stormy gray chop of Lake Superior. Reeves and the Japanese fella had talked for nearly an hour, and Mikio nodded to her dismissively each time she told him they were coming to a junction.

Each time, it ticked her off further. This wasn't a damn limo service.

Besides, hadn't this guy's boss killed Reeves' grandfather? And they talked like two old friends, throwing mock punches, reliving old fights. Maybe he was buttering the guy up, but she'd had enough. The road forked ahead between the north shore and the Iron Range.

"We going right or left?" Tara asked.

"And then he sinks his hooks in, I swear he's gonna pop the guy's head off." Reeves laughed.

"Hai, hai," Mikio responded.

The Toronado shuddered and both men gripped the rear seat. Tara pumped the brake and they skidded to a stop, the car's nose plowing into the virgin snow.

"Whoa," Reeves said. He caught the Springfield as it slid off the seat.

"Enough bullshitting," Tara said. "Where we going?"

Mikio grunted. "Airport," he said, and pointed out the window at the sign. "Eerie."

"Ely airport?"

Mikio nodded.

"Thank you," she said, and pulled away in second gear, tapping the brake and the gas to keep the tail straight until they got up to speed.

"What the hell was that about?" Reeves said.

"I'm glad you two are getting along, but I'm tired of playing chauffeur to the Fight Club twins. An hour ago you wanted to shoot him."

Reeves shrugged. "You wouldn't understand."

"Try me," Tara said. "If you think I'm stupid, you can get out and walk."

Reeves sighed. "I didn't say that. You saved my ass three times already. If you're stupid, I'm a damn moron. I just mean you're not a fighter."

"Honey, I'm—"

"I mean in the ring," Reeves said. "It's like we're both military. It stays with you, if you do it long enough. Are EMTs like that? Kinda like medics?"

"Yeah," Tara said. "I was an ambulance driver. But that's a boy's club. They shoved us around, didn't think we belonged there. I was the only girl in my bus, and when I crossed paths with another gal wearing the uniform, we were like sisters. It was a tough gig."

"There," Reeves said. "That's it. You give each other respect, unless they're a damn shitbird." He looked out at the snow, catching himself using Butch's words. "You speak the same language. There's a little something there, brotherhood. Maybe more."

"Yeah," she said. "I should've stuck with it."

"Why didn't you?"

Tara kneaded the wheel. "I didn't want to be stuck on the volunteer squad forever, and I couldn't cut pre-med."

Reeves nodded. "So why art?"

"I dunno," Tara said. "Because I liked it. What about you guys.

What did you like in school?"

Reeves shrugged. "Girls?"

Mikio laughed and slapped him on the shoulder.

Tara shook her head and flipped on the fog lights, then cut north to the Iron Range.

20.

WHEN THE MEDAL BEARERS CAME TO the repo depot to award him for the minefield rescue, Butch rapped on his cast and told them to give his medals to Turritin, who'd lost his leg.

"We sent them to his family," they said. "He didn't make it."

Butch watched the rest of the Devils go back to the front. The survivor's guilt hurt more than his wounds. What stung most was hearing that Lt. Frederick had taken command of the 1st Airborne after the fall of Rome.

Butch bit back tears. Others shed them openly.

Butch saved his for when his closest buddies left to chase the Germans through French villages. Jimmy Prince was the last to visit the hospital and squeeze his hand.

"See you when the lights go on again, you crazy Indian."

Butch's cast felt like an iron shackle when bulldog Jimmy marched out the door.

Each morning Butch woke to the memory of a young German soldier's face ripping apart while he lay in bed, waiting for his leg to knit. He tossed his wheelchair for crutches, and hobbled around Rome with the convalescents, visiting the ruins of empire and tossing candy bars to gangs of children who followed them crying, *"Americano, dove é mia cocciolata, per favore?"*

Anyone who could walk on two legs was a malingerer in his book. Pinching nurses's asses with two good hands while their comrades fought on the front? What kind of man could do that? Not Butch.

He walked alone, heaving himself with two crutches, then one, then he begged the docs to cut the damn cast off. Better to give it time, they said. Wasn't sunny Rome a treat?

It was torture. Smoking in a hospital bed, worrying that some green replacement was lugging the Johnny gun for your buddies instead of you. Some fresh-faced kid who might get them all killed.

Butch lost himself in history, visiting fountains and temples older than Christ, and by writing letters to Jean Marie. He hobbled back from a tour one afternoon to find three envelopes in his hospital bed. Jean wrote of the brutal winter and the lonely spring.

I was riding Copper along the ridge just before sunset when I came upon a mountain cat stalking one of our calves. I gut-shot her, and tracked her back to an old dead oak tree that I used to climb as a child.
After I put her out of her misery, I imagined a little girl swinging from the branch like I had done. The craziest thing is, she had your eyes.
I wish I could see those eyes again.

WHEN THE BONE DOC CAME BY, a short man with a pencil moustache and a head as bald as an egg, Butch showed him the Swiss cheese holes he'd gouged in the plaster of his cast so he could scratch the itches with an untwisted coat hanger.

"You don't take this damn thing off soon, I'll smash it to pieces myself."

The doctor scrunched up his charcoal moustache. "We can take it down to the knee, Corporal Sloane. I can't spare the resources to cut that off and then plaster a new one on just because you have ants in your pants."

Butch slid the knife from his boot. "Ants? I ain't got ants, I got the creeping crud, and I'm sick of it!"

Butch slammed the pommel of his dagger into the yellowed plaster of his cast. Crumbs and shards fell to the floor.

The doc stumbled back. "Orderly! Get an MP!"

"That won't be necessary," boomed a familiar voice.

The wounded sat up straight in their beds as a long-faced officer with a heap of fruit salad decorating his uniform strode in flanked by two stony men in jaunty garrison caps. Butch dropped the dagger on his bed and struggled to his feet to salute.

"Sir," he said.

"At ease, Sloane," Major General Frederick said, returning the salute. "Doctor, I need this man on his feet, *tout suite.*"

"General, I understand, but we can't waste supplies," the doctor said.

Frederick nodded. "We have plenty of supplies headed to Bastogne," he said. "I could arrange for you to join them."

The doc blanched.

Frederick handed Butch a crutch. "Doctor, we'll be needing your office for a briefing. When we return, I want this man X-rayed. If you can spare a little gauze and plaster, and find a cane, I will have the quartermaster fully replenish your stores after a thorough audit."

Butch followed Frederick to the doctor's office. The aides closed the door.

"Sergeant O'Neill recommended you for a mission I put together as a final hurrah for the Devils," Frederick said, relaxing against the desk. "You boys are scattered all over Europe, and I can't take the best men in the whole damn Army away from the front. But I can nab a few of you before you're sent as replacements for who knows what unit. The brass doesn't know what to do with you.

"But I'm the brass now. Youngest fool with a division command. You know damn well I'd rather be leading you fine men in the charge straight down the Fuhrer's throat, but Brad and Ike have other plans. They want you boys using your snow training to occupy Norway, which is a waste of our seasoned fighting men.

That's pogue detail."

Butch nodded, and looked down at his cast.

"I know it must be killing you to be stuck here, Sloane. So I'm promoting you to sergeant. You will lead a squad I've collected, of Devils like you, who are raising hell in field hospitals, chomping at the bit to get back in the fight. And I think you will be pleased. You were present for our first campaign in the Aleutians, if I recall, were you not?"

"Yessir. The Japs dodged us."

"Well they won't be dodging you this time. A Ranger battalion under General Frank Merrill was recently disbanded, similar to ourselves. They call them the Marauders, and they gave the Japs hell in Burma. The jungle was unkind to them. Trench foot, dysentery, and diseases you never heard of. They have intelligence that may shorten the island-hopping in the Pacific, but they need survivalists. It'll be hot as hell, and you'll miss the party when we stick it to Hitler, but the Emperor and his fanatics need to feel the pain only the Devil's Brigade can inflict. Are you ready to kick Tojo in the ass?"

"With both feet, sir!"

TWO MONTHS LATER, a six-foot Japanese held Butch's life in his hands over the Leyte Gulf.

Johnny Nagaki piloted the glider while Butch and five Devils huddled in the cargo bay around a Jeep fitted with an anti-tank gun. They prayed as flak explosions rattled the fuselage and warship cannons thundered miles below.

Butch hadn't trusted the Japanese-American kid at first. None of them had.

The platoon of devils had met on recently captured Guam for mission-specific training. Andre the Cajun joined them, a new scar across his cheek.

"Long way to come, just for some killing," Andre said, chewing tobacco.

"The Marines can't have all the fun," Butch said.

"Now it our turn," Andre said. "I hear de Oriental woman, the cooch go sideways."

The men hooted and laughed, and Butch shook his head. He didn't like rude talk. The laughter went silent.

Three Japanese filled the rear door.

"I can assure you that rumor is untrue," the tallest said, a man with fine features and large, calloused hands. "But if I find one, you can go down on her and learn to play the harmonica."

Andre jumped to his feet, his face twice its usual red. Butch's leg throbbed as he tensed to spring.

"I'm Staff Sergeant Johnny Nagaki with the 442nd Nisei regiment," the tall soldier said. "We're all born American, we all speak Japanese, and between us we've killed enough Germans to fill a beer garden. We're here as your translators, but if you want to fight and get it over with, we'll be happy to kick your asses all over the barracks first."

Andre fished in a top pocket with two fingers and stepped closer. He cupped his hand to his face and locked eyes with the officer. The men behind Nagaki shot their cuffs and sank into combat stance.

Andre hummed out the first few bars of "The Caissons Go Rolling Along," then wagged a battered harmonica. "You lucky," he said. "I already know how to play!" He laughed and punched Nagaki on the shoulder. The tall Japanese-American returned the gesture.

The rest of the men relaxed, but remained guarded.

They talked battles. The three Nisei were part of an anti-tank battalion who had landed over the enemy line in gliders, covered the 7th Army's flank, and then joined in the rescue of the 141st Infantry, who were trapped in the Vosges mountains by the Germans. The casualties had been very heavy, with only five men unwounded. Major General Frederick recruited them from field hospitals with the 1st Airborne.

In return, Andre recounted their push through Italy and their regrets over not joining the invasion of France.

"They haven't told us the target, but don't you worry. We're headed for plenty of action," Johnny said.

Butch wanted to knock the smile off Nagaki's face.

"How do we know you won't shoot us in the back," Butch said. "Like you people did at Pearl."

"Easy, Sloane," a Canadian sergeant said.

Johnny shrugged it off. "My men always lead the charge. If you get ahead of us, try not to squint."

The men laughed, and Butch looked away.

It was a long week of training. They were given captured Japanese weapons. Ugly little Nambu pistols with the trigger guard stuck forward. The Type 100 side-feeding submachine gun, Arisaka rifles. And an enormous anti-tank rifle.

"They fire this from the shoulder?" Butch asked, hefting it. It must have weighed a hundred pounds.

"Too heavy for you, Sloane?" Nagaki smirked.

Butch heaved the monster to his shoulder. It made his hip ache. He was glad they had no ammo for the cannon.

The night before their mission, he thought of Jean. He had missed her as they hopped across the States, but not for lack of trying.

They were given no R&R. No fraternizing with other units. They began to realize the mission was not just secret, but something big. When they landed in Helena to resupply, Butch packed a new M1941 Johnson light machine gun and all the ammo he could carry.

That afternoon, he shaved a second time for Jean. The razor sang against the stubble. He slapped on some bay rum and frowned at the shadows beneath his eyes, like the empty sockets of the SS death's head insignia, the *totenkopf.*

When he smiled, it only looked worse.

After dark Andre and Butch hustled to the perimeter fence. The camp had actual security now, including a tower guard with a sweeping searchlight. The MPS were no challenge compared to the sharp senses of an SS sentry wired on months of endless combat. Andre tied a ribbon around the ladder for the guards to find on shift change, and they rolled under the fence while the searchlight scanned the motor pool.

"Tell the captain I'll meet you in San Fran for the flight out," Butch said, and followed the rutted tracks he'd left during his first escape. He found the road and hopped a cattle truck to town.

In the lot outside the general store, he patted the necks of two horses hitched to a wagon. Butch wondered where all the cars had gone. He waited for a copper-bearded fellow in a Stetson to exit the store with a sack of goods, and asked for a ride out toward the Dundee ranch.

As the horses clopped past a row of pickups sitting on bald tires in the weed, the old man told him that gas and tire rationing kept them on horseback most of the time. His sons had joined as mule skinners, packing cargo on horses and mules for the Army. The caissons kept rolling along, no matter what pulled them.

"You're going to see Miss Jean, I gather."

"Yessir."

"The Dundees have been hit pretty hard. Government isn't paying much per head. She's been looking for a foreman, now that Mr. Dundee fell ill."

Butch nodded. Couldn't go AWOL, but maybe he could help for a few days. He'd worked on the chicken farm, there had to be work he could do. But mostly he thought of making her smile, and getting his arms around her.

Over the rise, lights cut across the road. "Looks like someone might need a push," the old man said.

The light swiveled and blinded them. "Halt!"

Four MPs smiled from the back of an M29 Weasel blocking the road. One jumped into the mud. The MP Butch had put the choke on, all those months ago.

"Captain Bloomfield sent us to escort you back to base, Sloane," the MP said, holding his rifle at port arms. Butch hopped off the wagon, and held his hands up.

The driver of the personnel carrier revved the engine and dug the tracks in deeper. The horses neighed and shied away. The old man pulled the reins to veer them away, and the MP trained his rifle on him.

"There's no need for that," Butch said, stepping between them.

The MP shoved the butt of his rifle at Butch's jaw, and Butch dodged it. He twisted the weapon and looped the strap over the MP's neck, stepping aside to choke him with it. "You got me," he shouted. "Leave the old man alone."

The MP's rushed in and beat Butch into the mud with their rifles.

"Tell Jean I came for her," Butch called out to the old man, before a fist found his mouth and the MPs had their fun.

BUTCH LAY SLUMPED ON THE CONCRETE in the brig. Andre snored from the cot. The captain arrived with a bucket of water frosted with ice, and splashed them both awake. Andre shrieked and cursed in his patois. Butch groaned. The water felt kind of good.

"Your previous commander gave you quite a bit of leeway," the captain said. "But I imagine he would not take kindly to finding you drunk and singing in the town square, attempting to fornicate with the statue of Myrna Loy."

"She a pretty girl," Andre said, wiping his face.

"And four MPs in the infirmary." The captain sighed. "Sloane, save the fighting for the enemy. Any other mission and I'd put you in Leavenworth. Get to the barracks and clean up. We take off at oh four hundred."

They changed planes in San Francisco. On the tarmac, Nagaki looked out at the bay, hazy with fog. Butch lit a cigarette off a battered Zippo.

"You from here?" Butch asked

"Used to be," Johnny said.

"Don't hop the fence to see your girl," Butch said, and tapped the sutures on his cheekbone. "They ain't fooling around."

"I'd have to climb a lot of fences to get where she is."

"Yeah?"

"Arizona, I think," Johnny said. "Maybe New Mexico. Relocation camp."

Butch nodded.

"My folks are in Utah," Johnny said. "Camp Topaz."

Butch remembered when Roosevelt ordered that the Japanese be rounded up. He'd felt good, like they had finally hit back for Pearl Harbor. He imagined them huddled like rattlesnakes, waiting to strike. He never thought any of them would sign up to fight. He wondered if *he* would have, if the tables were turned.

Butch tapped out another Lucky and offered it up. They smoked, and the crimson spans of the Golden Gate emerged from the mist.

A CONVOY OF C-47 SKYTRAINS towed Butch and Johnny Nagaki's glider and nineteen like it. Five big enough to carry light tanks, five with Jeeps, and ten loaded with 28 men each, armed to the teeth. Small gliders could be picked up by tow cables. The instructor had told them about the rescue in Shangri-La, where a WAC Corporal had crashed in the mountains. They sent a six-man glider in, then came back and plucked them right out of the jungle.

This mission planned for no such extraction. They would land north of Tokyo and strike their target. If they survived, they had silk maps of the surrounding area. They were to live in the woods and use their issued survival kits with hooks, fishing line, and large leaf-bladed knives called smatchets. During the briefing, Butch felt like he'd swallowed a rock. Until General MacArthur told them the target.

While the Navy went head to head with the largest cotillion of Japanese ships left in the Pacific, at Leyte Gulf in the Philippines, the Devils would be towed in gliders at thirty thousand feet. B-29 bombers would hit Yokohama to feint and draw anti-aircraft fire, while the gliders landed in Ueno and Chiyoda parks, surrounding the Imperial Palace.

The target was Emperor Hirohito.

"While you boys were busy killing Nazis," General Mac said, "We took Saipan. And ten thousand civilians jumped off cliffs rather than surrender. The Emperor told them they'd be warriors in heaven, or some such malarkey. The loss of life in taking Japan will be unfathomable. Your mission will save countless American and civilian lives.

"The Japanese have proven a brutal adversary in Bataan. But I get no joy from our victories when it sends conquered women leaping to their deaths with their children. Perhaps the capture of their Emperor will end this madness, or perhaps it will increase it a hundredfold. That is not for you men to contemplate. Think of the million American lives our bean counters have decided it will cost us to take Japan."

WITH A BOOM, the glider shuddered and torqued, slamming Butch into the Jeep. The Devils rocked and bounced off the wooden frame of the glider. Butch fought to get to the cockpit, but the gravity felt

BLADE OF DISHONOR

like quicksand.

They were going down.

His stomach churned. The world spun and the glider tore itself apart. It landed hard, and the Jeep tumbled through the rice field and crushed the men who gripped it for dear life.

Butch opened his eyes to the sky on fire. He struggled to his feet in the muck and cut away the straps of his parachute with the smatchet. Tracer fire lit up the clouds with streaks of orange, hyphenating into the heavens like lightning in reverse. Butch ran toward the severed cockpit of the glider. He pulled at the hand of a soldier who lay facedown in the mud, and came away with just an arm.

He dropped it and hacked his way into the wreckage. The copilot had a crushed mess where his chest had been. Butch slapped Johnny awake and pulled him out. At the edge of the fields, silhouetted figures began to shout. Johnny grabbed his survival kit, and the two of them loped into the foothills, taking cover in the scrub of stout little evergreens as bombs whistled down.

They ran all night. Scattered bombs hit the village, and smoke trailed in wisps to the sky. Search parties and rescue vehicles echoed from the valley below. They took turns sleeping on a bed of pine needles while the other held Johnny's sidearm and kept guard, belly down in the brush, watching the sun rise pink over the sea.

They shared a K-ration bar and Johnny spread his silk map over the browned pine needles. "My guess is we're somewhere south of Yokohama, in the hills around this bay."

Butch nodded. A necklace of little islands dotted the map. "Think we could make it to one of these? I'm not gonna last real long if we get spotted, but I can fish like nobody's business. At night, or through ice. That's all there is to do in Minnesota. Fish, drink and screw."

"Until we find some *sake*, you can fish."

They moved at night, keeping low of the ridgeline and following the crude map, skirting the village on the water aglow with lamplight. Snowflakes as big as silver dollars began to waft to the ground. They crouched in the woods above a small temple with red gates.

"We'll freeze out here," Butch said. "The temple may be empty."

After the lamps went out, they crept down the hill. The blanket of snow hushed their descent. Johnny held up a hand and scouted the building. Butch crouched by a statue of a raccoon with a bottle of *sake*. It sported a straw hat and had a pair of testicles to beat the band.

Outside a church, even. What kind of country, Butch thought.

Johnny waved him in. Butch flinched at the bald man in the red robe who greeted him solemnly.

"It's okay, he's a priest. He said we can stay the night, but have to run in the morning. He won't snitch, but he won't lie, either."

Butch nodded, and when Johnny bowed to the man, Butch aped him.

The priest shook Butch's hand. His grip was like stone.

The temple was also home to a plump white cat with a black nose that made it look like Hitler. It licked itself while the men shared a meal. Butch thought its nuts could give the raccoon statue a run for its money.

The priest brought two rice balls and hot tea, and they split a K-ration with him.

The priest and Johnny spoke softly while Butch scratched the cat's ears.

"His name is Kazeta. He was a soldier, once," Johnny whispered. "He fought in China, and went AWOL after Nanking."

Butch nodded. He remembered being a teenager in the '30s, when his pals thought it was dumb that girl couldn't buy silk stockings anymore, just 'cause the Japanese had killed a bunch of Chinamen. When they heard what the invaders had done, the boys shut up about it.

They slept on the hard *tatami* mats while the cat purred and picked its teeth with its back claws.

THEY WOKE TO THE SHUSH OF QUICK FEET IN SNOW. Butch drew his blade and rolled to the wall. The priest was already awake, putting on his slippers. A smaller robed man panted by the door, whispering in short, desperate bursts. The priest filled the doorway and muttered to the man. Johnny crept beside Butch and cupped his ear.

"Pack your gear," Johnny whispered. "This don't sound good."

The priest barked a command, and turned with a sigh. His eyes scraped the floor and he waddled to a corner to pull up a floorboard. He took a wrapped package from below.

Johnny bent behind the priest and whispered.

The priest uttered a string of firm grunts, and drew a gracefully curved blade over his head. Butch scooted back.

"He says soldiers are coming," Johnny said, translating for the priest.

Butch moved to bolt, but Johnny stayed him with a hand. "He wants us to take the sword. He says it is a treasure, stolen by . . . zealots, when the war began. It was supposed to make them invincible. He stole it from them when he went AWOL."

The priest sheathed the sword silently and pushed it into Johnny's hands. When Johnny took it, the priest popped the snap on his holster and took Johnny's sidearm. He barked commands, his face trembling with import.

Johnny nodded and bowed. He and Butch ran into the snow and up the hills. Behind them, a troop carrier crashed up the wooded trail to the temple. Soldiers surrounded the building, and a slender, spectacled officer stepped out of a little scout truck driven by his aide. A sword jangled at his side.

Butch and Johnny watched, huddled behind a squat pine.

Reports echoed up through the trees. The soldiers dragged out the priests and pushed them to their knees. A bloody patch spread on the shoulder of the priest who'd given them shelter.

The officer smiled and circled his prisoners. The shorter priest screwed his eyes shut and forced his head low in supplication. In one swift movement the officer drew his blade and severed the praying man's head at the neck. The bald head rolled away in the snow.

Butch clutched a handful of pine needles.

The head's mouth gaped like a fish. A thin spray of blood flowed from the severed neck like a red veil in the wind.

Kazeta, the big priest, raised his chin in defiance. He pressed his fist into his wound. The officer shouted a taunt and his blade sang once more. The priest's left hand flopped on its back in the snow like a dying spider.

Kazeta grimaced and tied off his wrist with a section of robe.

Johnny stared at the butchery until Butch tugged his collar, and they crept through the trees. Johnny used the sword as a cane, unsure on his feet in the snow, while Butch hopped like a hare.

The officer shouted something and laughed, and his men laughed with him. He wiped his blade on Kazeta's robe, then barked a command and pointed at the temple with his sword. The soldiers swarmed to search it.

Johnny slipped and skidded downhill on his behind. Two soldiers clambered up after them with a shout. Butch ducked behind a tree and threw the smatchet into the first rifleman's back. The second pinned Johnny's hand to the ground with his bayonet. Butch picked up the dropped Arisaka rifle and clocked the bayonetter across the head.

Johnny gritted his teeth and Butch tugged the bayonet out. Butch gave him the rifle and shoved the sword in his belt. He turned to run when a truck hit him in the ass. He tumbled into Johnny and they both spilled down the hill into the shouts and sharp boots of the Japanese soldiers.

An infantryman reached for Butch's sword, and two pistol shots puffed the snow by his hand. The soldier froze. The officer strode to him purposefully. He handed the man his pistol, then knelt to retrieve the gleaming black scabbard.

Butch lay panting, applying pressure to the exit wound on his leg.

The officer drew the sword and its silver blade glowed among the tumbling snowflakes. The soldiers gasped and whispered. The officer beamed.

Johnny clamped his pierced hand under his armpit. The officer touched the sword edge to his neck. Johnny winced and pulled away. His skin parted like the petals of a blooming flower, and blood trickled down his shirt.

"I am Gantetsu Mutsuhiro," the officer said. "Only my blood-line may touch this holy blade. You have betrayed your true people, Nisei. I should behead you, but that would be too honorable a death, one which you do not deserve."

"Butchering the priests was honor?" Johnny said.

"Urusai, benjo mushi!" Mutsuhiro backhanded him across the face. "He dared steal the *Honjo Masamune,*" he said. "This blade is the very . . . soul of Japan. It belongs to the Gantetsu clan."

"You steal sword," the priest growled. *"Shinobi hiretsukan!"*

Gantetsu laughed, then spat commands to his troops. The soldiers dragged their prisoners to the troop carrier. Butch passed out when they dumped him to the floor.

21.

THE SNOW BATTERED THE WINDSHIELD and whited out the road like television static. Tara pulled off the road toward a spinning gasoline sign. Short Stop, it read.

"What are you doing?" Reeves reached for the wheel.

"I'm starving and I gotta pee."

"We can't lose any more ground," Reeves said. "Stick your ass out the window."

Mikio chuckled.

Tara pumped the brake and cut the wheel, sliding them into the driveway by the frosted coin-op air pumps and vacuums. Reeves gripped the dash.

"I can't see a damn thing, Reeves. Quit being an asshole." Tara fixed her hair in the mirror, adjusting the bobby pins that held her locks in check. "You know what that means? No plane's taking off, either. So let's get some pancakes and think up some kind of plan."

Reeves chewed his lip, then nodded.

Mikio tucked his bum hand into his pocket, and Reeves draped Tara's spare down jacket over his shoulders for him. They shuffled into the diner area, and people stared at them from the booths.

A chunky-armed waitress brought three laminated menus and hustled them to a booth. Tara asked her to bring three coffees and a pitcher of cream.

Mikio sneered at his pink jacket. "I look asshole," he said.

"We catch Takehiko Yoshiro, I promise we'll get you a whole new wardrobe," Reeves said.

"Not real name," Mikio said, and drank his coffee black. "Real name, Gantetsu Takehiko. He *wakagashira* . . . underboss? Of Gantetsu yakuza clan. Wants Japan go back to . . . military." He waved his cup, searching for the word. "Old ways. Fool."

"Then why are you working for him?" Tara asked.

Mikio shrugged. Reeves ordered a steak and vegetables, Mikio got a cheeseburger and fries, and Tara chocolate chip pancakes with whipped cream.

When the food came they attacked it like wild dogs.

Mikio grunted after downing half his cheeseburger. "After I lose contender fight," he said. "No more money. Children need to eat. Takehiko tell trainer, make Mikio throw fight. Big money. Throw one fight . . . ." He looked outside at the blizzard, and shook his head. "You throw all fight. Then no more fight. Need money, work yakuza."

Reeves nodded and sawed into his steak. He knew fighters who fought four, five hundred fights to put food on the table without ever throwing one. He couldn't respect a man who threw a fight, but he could understand why they did it.

"Sorry about the arm," Reeves said. "You should've tapped."

Mikio chuckled. "No cage, no tap."

"So you came here in a private jet," Tara said. "But you had to rob a bank for the sword money. I don't get it. If he's a crime boss, he's acting strange. What do I know? All I know is movies."

Mikio picked at his fries. "He no tell me plan. Something with erection."

Reeves laughed, and Tara elbowed him.

"Election," Mikio said, concentrating. *"Mukou ike."* He gave Reeves the finger.

"That's all right, Mickey," Tara said. "I bet we sound funny talking Japanese."

"Mickey, like mouse?" Mikio chuckled.

"How do you say my name?" Reeves said.

Mikio thought, his moustache crinkling. *"Paizuri Tatsujin."*

Tara grinned. "What about me?"

"Oppai ii desu akane," he said. "Mean very pretty, red."

"What's mine mean?" Reeves said, smirking.

"Fearsome warrior," Mikio said, and finished his coffee.

The snow had not let up, so they ordered another round of coffee and sweetened it with the flask in Tara's purse.

"So Takehiko, whatever he calls himself. He said his grandfather knew . . . ." Reeves flexed his fist. "That his grandfather knew my grandfather. Butch never talked about the war. Except maybe to Mister Chickie, and they killed him, too."

Reeves set the tea box on the table, and pushed it away.

Tara picked through the photographs in the tea box. "Who's this beauty?"

"Grandma Jean. Died when I was ten. Cancer."

Tara read the letters while the two men talked fights. Mikio had done a lot of work for the Gantetsu, but had been a pawn in their game. He told Reeves they began working with Japanese nationalists a few years after he joined, to make up for gambling revenue lost with the economy tanking. The nationalists had deep pockets.

Mikio called them *issunbosi,* and made a small measurement with his thumb and index finger that showed what he thought of their manhood.

"Mickey, did your grandfather fight in the war?" Reeves asked.

Mikio shrugged. "Every man fight."

"Did he ever talk about it?"

Mikio shook his head. "Die when father little."

"What did he do?"

Mikio furrowed his brow. "Black . . . smith."

"He made swords?" Reeves perked up.

Mikio shook his head. "Kitchen knife. For sushi." He reached into his shirt and produced a small, wedge shaped blade forged rough from unpolished steel. He handed it to Reeves handle first. The handle was hammered round like a short length of pipe, making the knife resemble a spearhead.

Reeves smirked. "Thanks for not pulling this in the fight."

"Boss say fight, not kill." Mikio smiled and sipped his Irish coffee.

22.

THE MEDICS PATCHED Butch, Johnny and Kazeta expertly before they were handed to the camp guards to be beaten and tortured.

It felt like a fever dream. The camp prisoners were emaciated Westerners, hunched short and hollow-eyed so they resembled the Japanese caricatures on the propaganda posters. The guards were fit and strong and often tall, completely unlike the sniveling weasels he had been told to expect. Gantetsu forced the prisoners to file out and watch the punishment of their new cellmates.

The three new fish ran the gauntlet of the guards back and forth while the starved men watched at bayonet point. Fists, boots and bamboo sticks rained down until Butch staggered and crawled, his stitches torn. If they stopped and curled into a defensive ball, Gantetsu pricked them with his officer's sword.

The POWs turned their backs. They squeezed their eyes shut and endured the shouts, the jabs of bayonets and rifle butts demanding that they watch. Gantetsu ordered the cooks to pour bowls of hot miso and set them in the dirt.

Men who had subsisted on starvation rations for years, alive only because of what rotten food they could steal or beg through the fence from villagers, began to weep as the heady scent of the broth tickled their noses.

One man turned and his comrade slapped his hand. The guards laughed and brought them spoonfuls. A sunken-eyed Italian-American with a crooked smile swatted the spoon away. The guard punched him in his anvil of a chin. Another prisoner turned and scrambled for the bowls, and two of his scrawny compatriots tackled his boots.

"Ganbarre!" the officer shouted and cackled. "Fight! Keep going!"

The prisoners pinned their comrade and smothered his whimpers in the dirt.

Johnny Nagaki rolled onto his back, eyes swollen near shut. "You can't beat them," he shouted. "And you won't beat us."

The prisoners cheered. Butch waved a fist. The priest collapsed when a guard kicked his stump.

Gantetsu marched to Johnny's side, kicking over the soup bowls as he went. He drew back his boot and planted it in Johnny's ribs.

"This man is a traitor to his race," Gantetsu snarled to the prisoners, then repeated it in Japanese for the guards. He yanked Johnny to all fours by his hair.

"Go ahead," Johnny said through shredded lips. "Cut my head off."

Gantetsu drew his pistol and shot Johnny through the spine.

Butch shouted curses until a guard kicked him in the temple. The world blurred, and the voices bubbled like he was underwater.

Butch rolled to his belly to see two guards drag Johnny's moaning body to the latrine pit. They lowered him in boots first, exchanging glances as Gantetsu shouted orders in a froth. Johnny clutched the guards' sleeves. Gantetsu bent back his fingers until they cracked like green twigs.

Butch and Kazeta crawled toward the latrine's edge. Gantetsu tugged off his soiled gloves and flung them into the muck, where they fluttered to either side of Johnny's face.

Butch and the priest swung their hands over the edge to reach him, to swim the distance. Guards yanked them back by their belts as they teetered over the crumbling dirt.

Johnny struggled to remain upright, shuddering with the effort.

He gave one last scream and submerged to the nostrils, eyes darting as the filth bubbled around his face.

In Butch future nightmares it took hours. He told himself Johnny's death could not have lasted more than a minute.

Johnny rolled his eyes, and with a spasm his head disappeared beneath the oily effluvium.

Moaning in the prison hut, Butch prayed for Johnny's sake that it had taken only seconds.

23.

"**DAMMIT, REEVES,**" Tara said, rubbing her eyes. Between two fingers, she held a yellowed letter covered in careful script.

"What did I do?" Reeves said. He stared out the window at the driving snow. The waitress glared from the coffee station, arms folded across her chest.

"Not you, your grandfather. He really loved her," she said, and slid the letter across the table. "You have to read these. He's such a sweetheart."

"Was," Reeves said. "He was a real hard-ass by the time I came along."

"Only after your grandma passed on. I bet that broke his heart."

"It broke everybody's heart," Reeves said.

Grandma Jean was something else. A real cowgirl angel. She would ride her horse along the lake into town, packing a six-gun loaded with snakeshot. She never learned to drive. She told her grandson Little Butch Reeves that the town might have gone all modern, but she never would. There was no use changing just for change's sake.

"You learn anything useful?" Reeves said.

"Don't get snippy, tough guy." Tara spied for onlookers before sweetening her coffee from the flask of Wild Turkey. "I would've loved to meet her. Her letters are like poetry. But there's nothing in here about swords. Not yet." She unfolded another page and spread it flat on the gold-speckled Formica tabletop.

"Mickey," Reeves said. "What kind of plane is it? Maybe I can call my old commander and get DHS out there."

Mikio wrinkled his sparse moustache. "Look like plane."

Reeves smirked. "Come on."

"Red nose," Mikio said. "Four . . . ." He twirled his index fingers close to his chest.

"Pasties?" Reeves said.

"Propellers, dummy," Tara said. "It's a prop plane. How many of those can there be? Call your Army guy."

"Okay, gimme your phone."

"I don't have a phone," Tara said. "I drive a '69 Toronado. It has a tape deck."

Reeves scanned the diner for a pay phone, then threw a smile to reel in the waitress. She hustled over and slapped the bill on the table. "Getting near closing time."

Reeves eyed her name tag. "Diane . . . is there a pay phone?"

Diane arched her sharply painted eyebrows and pointed an amber fingernail at the snow-spattered glass doors.

"Honey, can you bring us a fresh pot and maybe a few bear claws?" Tara asked. She leaned close. "I wait tables myself. We'll take care of you."

"I don't care if you lift your skirt for the Indians at the casino," Diane said. "We're closing on account of the weather, so you can settle then get the hell out, *honey.*"

The waitress shuffled away.

Mikio grunted out a chuckle.

Tara narrowed her eyes and stalked across the seat. Reeves put a hand on her shoulder. "It's not worth it. Can you get the bill, and give me some quarters for the phone?"

Tara flared her nostrils three times before handing over the keys. "There's change in the ashtray."

Reeves Frankenstein-walked through the deep powder in the

parking lot. The Olds was frosted thick. He swept the snow off the driver's window with his elbow and climbed in to pilfer the ashtray.

He had dug three quarters and a guitar pick from the hobo jackpot when the whited-out windows glowed blue and red. Reeves carefully peered out the quickly fogging glass.

Two state cops with hunting caps stomped into the diner.

Reeves keyed the engine. The wipers struggled against the snow coating. The 455 Rocket V8 burbled hungrily as he circled back and aimed the front end toward the highway. The Toronado's front wheel drive made it the king muscle car of the snow belt. He shifted into low gear and it pulled itself through the tire-slashed blanket of snow.

Inside, the cops hovered in front of the booth, hands on their weapons.

Reeves took the .45 from the glove box and tucked it in his belt.

Tara argued, waving her arms. The cop caught her by the wrist and spun her, bending her over the table, reaching for his cuffs.

Reeves stepped out of the car and walked to the police cruiser. The Staties had left the engine running, the heat on full blast. Reeves tugged the handle. Locked.

The headlights of a snowplow sliced through the flakes hitting the highway. Reeves smashed the cruiser's window with his elbow and tugged the shifter into reverse. He ran around to the front and pushed on the hood, combat boots skidding in the snow.

The snow chains caught and Reeves fell face first into gray slush. The cruiser rolled across the highway until its rear bumper crunched against the guardrail.

The snowplow blared its horn in protest and locked its snow-chained tires. The cow-cutter nose impacted the cruiser with an echoing boom and crumpled in half, blowing out the windows and grinding chunks of it off the median. The plow scraped to a halt, and the driver stood looking out the door.

"Oh boy," he said, gaping at what he'd done.

Reeves took cover behind the Toronado. The cops rushed outside to stare at the wreckage. The cruiser's light bar blinked weakly from beneath the truck.

"Holy moly," said one Statie to the other.

"Ya," his partner replied.

Mikio leapt from behind and shouldered one cop into the snow. Reeves hip-checked the remaining officer on top of his partner and held them down with a knee on the spine.

Tara ran to the Olds with a handcuff dangling from her wrist. "Get in the car, shit heads!"

She hit the pedal before they had the doors closed, rocketing the gold missile through a snowbank onto the highway. Mikio hooted and watched out the back window as the cops scrambled for their radios.

"You some drag racer," Mikio laughed, patting Tara on the shoulder. "You real drag queen."

Reeves laughed. "I assure you, she's not a drag queen."

Tara swatted Reeves with her cuffed hand, then joined them in laughing off the adrenaline rush.

24.

BUTCH AND KAZETA carried Nickel's body across the frozen ground of the camp. It was stiff as a board and weighed less than a child. Butch had lugged heavier packs in the field. The bitter cold and meager rations culled the weakest, and the man they called Nickel, for resembling the Indian on the coin, was the latest to succumb.

The guards had stripped Kazeta of his robes and given him an ill-fitting uniform. Butch thought Kazeta looked kind of like Paul Muni in *The Good Earth,* before his hair started growing in. Now, he looked kind of dapper with the moustache. Clark Gable's dour Japanese cousin. They had shared a cell for two months while they healed. Now, Kazeta just looked like Kazeta.

They set the body down at the edge of the pit and turned their backs. The two stone-faced guards kicked the body into the hole. Kazeta took the pick and Butch took the shovel. Kazeta heaved the pick one-handed over his shoulder and broke up the frozen dirt pile, which Butch shoveled into the grave to give poor Nickel a blanket for the winter.

The two guards neither smoked nor made a sound. There were two distinct groups: the stony men who obeyed Gantetsu without question, and the men whose fear and distrust of their leader betrayed itself in trembling chins and darting eyes. These two were the former.

Kazeta called the stone men *shinobi*. Butch called them Ball Busters. The rank and file he called Ass Kissers. Butch would snap every one of their necks if it meant freeing the camp, but he felt a wisp of sympathy. They were enlisted men, under the command of a psychotic whose retinue of fanatics had definitely received elite combat training. Standing up to them would be suicide. But serving and obeying an evil man killed your soul, one icepick jab at a time.

They set down their tools when the Ball Busters whistled to signal that the job was done. The guards followed them to the prison hut, Butch limping and Kazeta with the stump of his wrist jammed in his pants pocket against the cold.

On their first night in the communal POW barracks, a raw-boned shitbird named Fowler attempted to rouse the prisoners into killing Kazeta.

"He's not just a yellow swine, he's another mouth to feed," Fowler said. "Hold him down, I'll do the strangling. But I want his ration for myself."

Butch pushed himself up and hobbled to the corner, dragging his bad leg. "This man protected me," he said. "You want him, you kill me first."

"Maybe we will, gimpy," Fowler said. He had a pushed-in nose, and enough muscle left on him to make trouble. "You know how many brothers we lost? What's one Jap?"

The skinny sunken-eyed Italian called Zee walked over. "They want us to kill him. Why else would they put him here? You want to make Gantetsu happy?"

"Why not, maybe we'll get a damn full meal for once."

Zee shook his head. "They'll punish us anyway. They want to break us down, make us inhuman. Men who would tear a cripple apart with their bare hands. We're not those men, are we?" He addressed the room. "Are we?"

Slowly, the prisoners shook their heads. All except Fowler. He walked over to Butch and poked him in the chest. "You gotta sleep sometime, crip."

"I sleep real light," Butch said.

ZEE HAD BEEN RIGHT. The next morning their Ass Kisser guards looked puzzled when Kazeta showed his face. They muttered to themselves and hurried out.

A short while later Gantetsu appeared with a pair of Ball Busters. He paced with a rolled-up magazine, his polished boots clicking on the floor of the hut. "I gave you a gift last night," he said. "But you refused it. How uncivilized you are. You do not even know to take revenge." He swatted Kazeta on the back of the head with the magazine.

"Perhaps you were merely cowards? Even wounded, this misguided fool is still a fierce warrior," Gantetsu said. "But no. I know your true nature. You will murder him in his sleep, once he is weak."

Butch hadn't had a beating in a few days and it emboldened him. "What makes you say that?"

"Because you are savage," Gantetsu said, and waved the magazine. "Let me show you what kind of man your dead cripple president was."

Butch pushed himself up with a snarl, and one of the Ball Busters kicked his bad leg out from under him. Butch hit the floor ass first. He rubbed his leg.

Gantetsu read from the copy of *Life*. "President Roosevelt was given a letter opener, made from the carved arm bone of a slain Japanese soldier." He then stepped around the room, showing each man the photo.

"Animals," he spat. "Carving up the dead like cattle, allowing yourselves to be captured when you can still fight. Cowards! You have no honor even in death."

"This is who you protected," he shouted in Kazeta's face. He flipped the magazine open to a photo of a pretty young secretary admiring a trophy on her desk: a bleached human skull, minus the jawbone. He shoved the page into Kazeta's face and barked at him in Japanese. Kazeta looked away, revolted.

"This is why we treat you as beasts," Gantetsu shouted. "Because you are below animals!" He threw the magazine on the floor and stomped out.

The prisoners took turns reading it. Most of the pages had been torn out. All that remained were images of severed Japanese heads staring from atop Sherman tanks. Skulls hanging from signs that read "Tarawa recruitment center," and a cartoon with a proud mother asking her son to bring her home a necklace of trophy ears.

"They beheaded us, too," the hangdog American pilot called Pappy said, his lip twisted into a sneer. "I don't know who started it, but the islands were pure hell."

ZEE HAD FLOWN B-24 LIBERATORS out of the Samoan islands, and his plane went down on a search and rescue mission. He survived thirty-three days on a raft in the open sea, only to be captured soon as he hit land. Pappy's bomber had been shot down over Truk. The two of them were born survivors, the unspoken leaders of the POWs. They taught Butch how to stick it out. Don't smart off, and work until you drop, because to quit was an insult to the man who had issued the command.

Zee and Pappy said the Japanese must be getting desperate, because the rations for both the soldiers and the prisoners had dwindled away. They had made friends with a Japanese cook who sneaked them scraps. Meager and often rotten, but enough to keep the weakest of them alive.

Until recently.

The winter was a harsh one. Butch and Kazeta dug often.

At night the guards demanded quiet, but during the day the prisoners could play cards, or checkers they'd made from scrap paper. There was no contact with the Red Cross or the outside world. When Butch told them that Saipan had fallen, the POWs cheered. Some had been imprisoned for nearly three years, and were relieved to hear that the Marines had finally taken Guadalcanal.

As the red sun hovered low in the sky, mocking him like the face of the Japanese flag, Butch listened for the approaching bootsteps that meant guards were coming to drag him and Kazeta to Gantetsu's hut for a random beating.

Zee patted Butch on the shoulder. "I was his redheaded stepchild before you two came along," he said.

"Glad we could be of service," Butch said.

"It's worse not knowing," Zee said. "Every day, expecting the crazy bastard to beat the hell out of you. At first it felt good when he didn't, now it feels worse. You know it's coming. Just not when." The other men nodded. Their eyes sank to dull pits, as if pushed in by calloused thumbs.

"YOU WILL DIE BEFORE THE EMPEROR," Gantetsu told Butch and Kazeta one evening, after using them as living punching bags in his private dojo. The pair slumped against each other, hands bound. The *Honjo Masamune* gleamed from a lacquered display rack. Gantetsu took the sword and turned it over in his hands. He addressed Kazeta in Japanese, then reached out gingerly with the blade to brush Butch's neck.

Butch tensed and the bare edge razored half a day's stubble from his skin.

Kazeta nodded somberly.

"If you two are bargaining over my head, I'd like a say in it," Butch said.

"Kazeta just saved the lives of five prisoners," Gantetsu replied. "He will restore this sword to its former magnificence. You have nothing to fear, Sloane. Not even fear itself, as your fallen leader said. You will be saved for the *Kempeitai*," he said and smiled. "The Secret Police. They will learn all about your plan to kill the Emperor."

"I'll tell 'em what I told you," Butch said. "To go screw."

"You will tell them," Gantetsu said, stepping around them, testing the sword's perfect balance. "Without a drop of your blood being spilled. They questioned me, once. Tested my loyalty. Something you *gaijin* would not understand."

Gantetsu twisted the blade in the lamplight. Motes danced along the edge. "They say this sword cuts light itself," he said, staring at the starry display. Butch and Kazeta found themselves entranced as well. It resembled a string of diamonds, water droplets in the icy dawn. "That it can make a man invisible, if he is a pure-hearted warrior. Foolishness. But if it were so, I could not demonstrate it.

"The *Kempeitai* won't hurt a hard man. They know better. When they came for me, they brought my wife. They dipped her feet in boiling water," Gantetsu said. "But I kept my secrets. She walks with a cane now, but bore me a healthy son. Is that what the spirits want? For us to remain strong, even as our heart is torn from our chest?"

Kazeta grunted.

"You will never never shine for me," Gantetsu said, holding up the blade. "For my son, perhaps. *Shatei!* Take them away." As Butch and Kazeta were dragged back to the prison hut, Gantetsu's silhouette drank from a bottle of *sake* and stared at the Masamune's blade.

KAZETA SPOKE NO ENGLISH and the Allied POWs knew only a smattering of Japanese. They slowly taught each other their respective languages. The rest of the prisoners shunned Kazeta, so he and Butch had plenty of time to practice.

Some of the prisoners were disgusted at the photos in *Life* magazine, but most justified it as revenge for Pearl Harbor. Fowler bragged that he'd collected a necklace of gold teeth before he was captured.

"They called me the Jap Hunter," Fowler said. "They sent me into the jungle after slant-eyed snipers. I hammered out their teeth while they were still wriggling," he said to Kazeta. "You hear me, Lefty?"

Kazeta ignored him and folded a piece of scrap paper into tight little creases in a corner of the floor.

"Yeah, stare," Fowler said. "Stare like you all do." He walked around a card game, sneering at the player's hands.

Butch stretched his leg. The stitches had healed over a hard knot with a squishy center. It hurt when he pushed on it. He tried not to think about it as he limped over to Kazeta. "What you got there?"

Kazeta held up the paper. He had folded it into the shape of a slender water bird. "Origami," he said, and placed it in Butch's palm.

Butch smiled. "Thank me? Thank you. I should be saying thank you."

"No *arigato*," Kazeta said, *"Origami."* He pantomimed folding the paper. "Make bird."

"This is how Americans make a bird, Jap," Fowler said, and stuck out his middle finger.

"Arigato," Butch said, and set the tiny crane on his bunk.

"Itashimashite," Kazeta responded, with a deep nod.

"Gesundheit," Fowler said to scattered laughter.

Let crazy Fowler laugh. When the snow cleared, Butch was getting out. With Kazeta and the sword if he could. Alone if he couldn't. No one else had the stamina. If he could get a rifle and a knife, he could survive. Mount his own guerrilla campaign.

At night the buzz of bombers droned to the south. B-29s hitting industrial zones. Distant echoes of explosions across the water. Closer and closer. Pappy told them how they'd welcomed the sound of incoming planes on Truk until they realized the Allies had no way to tell prison camps apart from soldier barracks. Pappy had survived by pure luck when half his hut was obliterated.

Butch wasn't going to get killed by his own side. He would go down fighting. He stashed his share of the dry rice Zee begged from the cooks in a discarded burlap sack. When he scrubbed the kitchen, he palmed matches. He stored his contraband beneath a rotting floor joist.

Kazeta found a bent nail and sharpened it on a piece of flint to make a tiny sword. He decorated it with scraps from his work on the Masamune. Butch was damned if it didn't look like a miniature version of it.

Butch found him another nail and pantomimed unlocking a door with it. Kazeta took the nail and nodded. He patted his chest, pointed at Butch, and then to the mountains.

Butch nodded back. "Yeah, buddy. I'm thinking the exact same thing."

25.

REEVES PICKED AT THE HANDCUFF with a bobby pin while Tara cruised with one left hand on the wheel, and shook her head. "Ma was right, this damn car is gonna wind me up in jail!"

Her father had loved driving in the snow and the rain, and took Tara along to get away from Ma's drunken arguments. He taught her to drive from his lap until she could reach the pedals, and they'd stop at an A&W drive-in for a milkshake. He had a heart attack during a screaming match with Ma when Tara was thirteen. Ma pacing and yelling into the phone while Tara beat on his chest, trying to remember what they'd taught of CPR in health class.

"It's cool," Reeves said, and squinted at the lock. "I packed snow over your license plates."

"How many gold '69 Toronados are on the road, ya think?"

"They won't remember anything," Reeves said. The pin popped out of the keyhole. He went back at it. A buddy who'd served in the Security Guard battalion showed him how to pick handcuffs once, but they'd been buzzed on hooch smuggled on base from Qatar in mouthwash bottles.

Tara sighed and eased up on the pedal. Mikio snored from the back seat. The snowflakes had shrunk to powder, peppering the windshield like rice thrown at a wedding.

"Trust me," Reeves said. "I bet you don't remember what the cops even look like. They won't remember you either. They're not trained for it, they're backwoods Barneys."

"And you're what? Just 'cause you don't wear boxers doesn't

137

make you a commando."

Mikio blinked himself awake. "So loud," he said.

"Sorry to disturb your beauty rest," Reeves said. The bobby pin snapped it half. He tossed it on the floor mat. He dug in the ashtray for another and came up dry. "You got something back there I can use for a lockpick? A needle or something?"

"Use dick," Mikio said, and settled back down to sleep.

Tara snorted.

Reeves flipped through the letters. Reading them felt wrong, like he was rifling through Butch's things, looking for cash. He found a bulging air mail envelope, silky and thin. Inside, oddly shaped scraps of paper. One crumbled to fish food flakes in his fingers. He carefully picked out another, a fist around his heart as he squinted at Butch's chicken scratch.

I don't know if you'll ever read this. I tried to see you when we were state-side, but the MPs caught me. I know I said your town smelled like cow crap but there's nothing I want more than to shovel a mountain of it, long as it means I can be with you.

He saw Butch grinning in his chair from the back porch, while Grandma Jean showed Reeves how to clean Rocky's stable. When she didn't know Reeves was looking, she came up behind Butch and kissed the thick lines on the side of his neck. They smiled at each other, something unspoken, now laid bare.

Reeves looked out the window at the expanse of dead white.

"What's wrong?" Tara said.

"Nothing."

"I'm sorry you lost him," she said. "I wish I got to know him."

"Me too," Reeves whispered.

"Not long until we hit Ely," Tara said. "You got a plan?'

Reeves shrugged. "Find the plane, get the sword. Break it off in

Takehiko's ass."

"They're not gonna let us in the airport, dummy. You're gonna have to think of a way in."

"I'll figure it out when we get there," Reeves said, and went back to the letters. The last was on good paper, barely aged. When he unfolded it, a flattened *origami* dove fell into his lap.

Tara gave it a glance. "Your gramps was money," she said. "Folding love notes."

Reeves picked it up and peered at it. Strands of dessicated pink were strung around the bird's neck. He plucked at them and the dove opened. Water stained Japanese letters marked the bird's spine.

Reeves shook Mikio's shoulder until the grizzled fighter blinked awake. "Can you read this?"

Mikio frowned and took the dove in his good hand. He unfolded it with care, revealing more characters written in pen.

"Aw, you're gonna ruin it," Tara said, eyeing him in the rearview mirror.

"What does it say?"

"Poem," Mikio said. He read on, spreading the paper flat.

"Go on."

"About island. Waves. Friend . . . ship," he said. He stared at the paper a long time, then began folding the paper back into a bird.

"That's all?" Reeves said. He locked eyes.

"Hai," Mikio said, and did not waver.

26.

THE DAY THAT ALL BUT A SKELETON CREW of the rank and file guards shipped out to defend against the inevitable American invasion, Butch waited for the pair of Ass Kissers guarding their hut to circle past, then spidered out the window by starlight.

It felt good to creep again. If Jimmy Prince and O'Neill were here, they could take out the whole camp. He stayed in the shadows and froze when the guards marched into view. They followed a simple perimeter, obedient to a fault. The supply hut was left unguarded. Only the front gate and the prisoner huts were covered.

It seemed too easy. Butch belly crawled along the fence line and tested boards for weakness. Several had rotted, and one popped off its nails at the merest pressure. Butch crept toward the supply hut, its door in shadow beneath a dead electric bulb. He crouched and inserted the nail into the lock.

The makeshift lockpick was hardly ideal, but the lock was worn and he had nothing but time. He eased through the door and closed it behind him. He found a canteen at the back of a shelf, filled it from a sack of rice the rats had chewed open, then catalogued what he could take, one night at a time, if his subterfuge went undiscovered. Blankets. A shaving mirror. Dry food. A tin of black shoe polish. That disappeared into his pocket. No weapons or ammunition. The guards had those. One snapped neck and he would, too.

Butch hid the lockpick in his mouth and filled in the shiny scratch on the lock with shoe polish. His leg began to throb as he moved from one hut to the next, keeping out of the guards' sightline. He could ignore pain, but part of his body no longer worked properly. The nerves were a jumble, as if a stinging jellyfish had made a nest of his hip.

Gantetsu's quarters next. It was as unguarded as the rest. With a knife, he could pry the door jamb and slice a bloody crescent across the maniac's throat.

As Butch neared the corner, he froze. Shadows danced on the dead grass. He inched forward on his belly and peered around.

Men in formation, shrouded in black. Gantetsu at the head, conducting them with the gleaming blade. Butch stared as they struck once, twice, three times, in perfect unison. Kick, chop, finishing blow.

O'Neill had taught the Devil's Brigade this way back in Montana. A Devil was dangerous with only his hands, the equal of a German with a Hitler Youth dagger or a pistol. But this platoon of black-clad men looked like they'd give twice their number of Devil's Brigade commandos a run for the money.

Butch oozed back slower than molasses in January. When he had cover, he took a long breath and warmed his numb hands and sneaked back to his hut. A match flared to Butch's left.

A guard was lighting a cigarette one hut away.

Butch froze, but his leg disobeyed, sending him stumbling against the wall. He caught himself against a rain gutter.

The guard charged with a shout.

Butch tossed the shoe polish under the supply hut and bolted, throwing his traitorous leg ahead of him. Several pairs of feet hit the frozen ground behind him. Butch ran for the men in black. If he was to be caught, might as well get a good look at them in action and see what he was up against. If he escaped, the brass would need to know the kind of insurgency these fanatics could mount.

He rounded the corner and caught one brief glimpse before

his presence became known. Men with swords dueled opponents wielding crazy sickles on chains. They disarmed the swordsmen and held the hooks to their throats, quick as black snakes.

Gantetsu nodded with grave approval. He flicked his eyes toward Butch and his pursuers. The commandos parted like a swarm of cockroaches and disappeared into the shadows.

Butch ran for Gantetsu. If the sonofabitch couldn't kill him, he was gonna get some licks in. Butch feigned a haymaker and snapped one of O'Neill's Chinese boxing punches at Gantetsu's gut.

Gantetsu slapped his jab aside as if Butch was a petulant child. He jabbed Butch's neck with two fingers and sent a jolt of pain down his spine. Butch's cross hand froze a palm's length from the man's face.

"Not bad, *gaijin,*" Gantetsu chuckled, and swept Butch's good leg. Butch hit the ground and rolled into a defensive curl.

The three guards behind him skidded to gape at their commander dressed in black. The Masamune flashed and the first guard fell to his knees, split from shoulder to belt buckle. His rifle dropped in two pieces, the stock severed cleanly from the rest.

The bloodless blade keened like distant funeral bells.

The other two uniforms turned and bolted. Their rifles hit the dirt.

At Gantetsu's nod, black shapes melted from the shadows. A chain looped one runner's throat and yanked him from his feet. The warrior at the other end of the *kusarigama* cradled his victim to the ground silently and buried the sickle in the man's chest.

The last guard ran like mad for the barracks and crossed the building's long shadow.

Gantetsu sheathed the Masamune in one graceful sweep, and whipped his wrist at the fleeing man. Star-shaped blades disappeared into the gloom with a thunk and a cry.

The fugitive guard stumbled into the light. He looked down at the shuriken peppering his chest and collapsed. Black pools of blood spread from his corpse and those of his comrades.

"We are the Black Dragons," Gantetsu said, and put his knee across Butch's throat. His masked men appeared behind him, a silent army of night. "If you are the best the *Ameko* scum have to offer, we welcome your invasion. You will never take Japan."

Butch clawed at Gantetsu until the darkness smothered him.

27.

THE TORONADO WEAVED a few car lengths behind the snowplow on the airport access road. Tara gunned it and fishtailed in the shoulder, sighed and settled back, slapping Reeves' thigh to "Radar Love."

Mikio sat quietly with his brow furrowed, folding the origami bird.

"Can this guy go any slower?" Reeves said.

The plow's brake lights flashed red in answer. Tara pumped the brake and they slid to a stop on the shoulder. The plow driver cut across the road, blocking both lanes. Tara raised her palm to mash the horn.

"The hell?" Tara said.

Black smoke plumed further up the road, drifting down the shoulder like a ghost.

"Hang tight," Reeves said, and hopped out the door. He rounded the back of the truck and saw the source of the smoke. An suv had flipped onto its roof, flaming like a marshmallow left too long in the campfire.

The snowplow driver, decked in a puffy down jacket and a fur-ringed hood, shook his head. "Way they were driving, was bound to happen," the driver said. "Must've been from out of state, you know? Speaking of, you folks are supposed to stay back a hunnert feet. Says so right on the back of the truck."

"Sorry, we're in kind of a hurry." Reeves peered at the truck engulfed in flames. No one could survive that.

"I gotta call this in, and you're gonna have to wait, that's just how it is. Serves ya right for trying to pass a snow removal vehicle."

"Call the cops," Reeves said. Cars didn't burn like this without help. He'd lit up enough of them on checkpoint detail to know.

"Hear me? Call the cops," Reeves shouted, and jogged back toward the car. He'd left the .45 in the glove box.

"Yer darn tootin' I will," the driver hollered. "Gonna tell 'em to write you up for unsafe driving!"

Reeves rapped on Tara's window. She rolled it down.

"Can you get around him? The guy's a real ass—"

The truck's reverse alarm bleeped him out. Reeves dived over the hood as the dump truck roared toward them. Tara threw the car into reverse. Reeves tumbled into a snowbank. The truck roared closer and the dump gate shuddered to stop a foot from his face.

Takehiko waved from the running board, decked out in winter camouflage. The plow driver's coat flapped from the side of the road, the snow stained red where he'd fallen.

Reeves reached for .45 and came up empty. Must've dropped it in the snow. He roared and charged through the hip deep powder.

Takehiko laughed. The truck dumped its payload of rock salt. Reeves ducked and tumbled from the wave of grit spilling over the road into a small mountain. He kicked and scrambled out of the pile as the truck pulled away.

The .45 shone in the snow. Reeves snagged it and fell prone to aim, pushing snow out of the trigger guard. He lined up the sights to fire.

You dumb shit. You want to blow your face off?

Butch, hollering from their blind on Reeves' first deer hunt. Young Reeves had dropped his Savage bolt-action in the snow at the snort of an eight-point buck. Dived for it and made to fire without clearing the barrel first.

Reeves checked the muzzle of the .45 and found it packed with snow.

The snowplow ground through the gears and disappeared down the road. Reeves climbed to his feet and roared at the darkening sky.

28.

BUTCH WOKE WITH HIS ANKLES ON FIRE and his head feeling like a blood-swollen tick fit to burst.

He blinked to clear his vision. The room spun slowly side to side. He reached to rub his eyes and found his wrists lashed together in front of him. He was trussed upside down, hanging like a salami in an Italian delicatessen. The rope creaked as he twisted.

Paper walls. Racks of weapons. He hung inside Gantetsu's private dojo.

The POW camp leader himself stepped around him, a white bottle of *sake* in one hand and a length of bamboo in the other.

"Feels good to stretch," Butch said, turning his head to sneer at his captor.

"You think me murderous," Gantetsu said. "But you forced my hand. Those *yuhei* guards could not live after seeing us. Our secret will die with you soon enough."

"What, you and your boys jumping around in pajamas? It was pretty impressive, but you can't karate chop a five-hundred pound bomb."

In the distance, the buzzing of the B-29s hummed like a swarm of locusts. The drumbeats of falling bombs would come next.

"You will not kill the heart of Japan," Gantetsu said. "This war was foolishness."

"You tweaked the nose of a sleeping giant, one of your generals said."

Gantetsu chuckled. "We should have waited. If Black Dragons

147

ruled, we would have," he said, and sipped his *sake*. "My people have waited centuries to rule again from the shadows. If the Emperor was patient, you would have joined the war in Europe eventually, and become embroiled in battle over the scraps with the Russians and the Germans. You are a flighty people. You cannot endure years and years of war. If we struck when you were weak and weary, your spirit would be crushed and our destiny of ruling all Asia would be within our grasp. Instead, we filled you with dreams of vengeance."

"In a few months you'll be trading that piss-warm wine for a Coca-Cola."

Gantetsu lashed out with the bamboo and struck Butch's bad leg. The abscess inside exploded. Butch writhed in agony like a worm on a hook.

The first of the bombs rumbled off the mountains like thunderheads. He concentrated on the sound. The march of victory.

Gantetsu struck again.

The pain sent shivers through Butch's body. He cried out, and the makeshift lockpick fell from his mouth, jingling on the wooden floor.

Gantetsu plucked the nail between two fingers like a dead insect. He studied it with a deep scowl and snapped at the guards in Japanese.

The guards dragged Kazeta and Zee into the dojo and threw them to the floor.

"The punishment for escape is death," Gantetsu said. "I cannot kill you, Sloane. But I can hurt you."

Gantetsu slid the Masamune from its scabbard. The handle was now decorated simply, differently than before. Gantetsu nodded in admiration and showed it to Butch. The black silk cord gleamed softly, braided intricately over the handle wrap of black rayskin. The iron guard depicted a fox's head with chrysanthemum blossoms for eyes.

"Kazeta has outdone himself," Gantetsu said. "And now he will perish by his own masterpiece."

Kazeta knelt in resignation.

"Choose, Sloane. Both of their lives are worth more than yours. This one was a famous runner. I took it as a challenge to break his spirit. Now he is but a shell of what he once was."

Zee spat. "Go to hell."

"Who dies? Your countryman, or the man who briefly saved your life?"

"Screw you," Butch said.

"Then I behead them both." Gantetsu lifted Zee's chin with the sword's edge. A line of blood formed on Zee's broad jaw.

Kazeta grunted and lowered his head. Gantetsu raised the sword.

Butch squeezed his eyes shut. "Kazeta," he panted.

Gantetsu smiled and stepped behind the kneeling priest. "See, Kazeta-san? Savages. You saved his life, and yet he saves his weak, dying countryman."

"Killing a priest. Damn you straight to hell, you evil sonofabitch!"

"He is no priest, you fool," Gantetsu laughed. "He is samurai! His clan stole this sword from us, and now he will die by it."

A blaze of orange filled the window, and the guards broke away to stare.

Gantetsu frowned and walked over to look. Distant flames lit his horrified face. He barked commands and the guards ran to obey. Gantetsu found his bottle of *sake*, leaned against the wall and took a deep gulp.

Zee raised his hands in surrender and slowly approached the window. Kazeta joined him.

"What is it?" Butch said, twisting to see.

"Tokyo's on fire," Zee said, mouth open. "The whole city, looks like. Never seen anything like it."

The air flushed warm. Tokyo was many miles away. Butch couldn't imagine the kind of fire that could heat you from such a distance.

Kazeta slumped his shoulders and absently raised his stump to rub his brow.

Gantetsu charged forward and severed the rope holding Butch. Butch screamed when his legs hit the floor.

"You will all perish," Gantetsu said, circling. "The Emperor is gone. The Black Dragons will rise and take our rightful place. Kazeta knows. Four hundred years ago, the Shogun slaughtered us. Drove every man, woman and child into the sea. All but one."

Kazeta grunted and sidled toward the weapon racks.

"Cut from his dying mother's belly after Oda Nobunaga himself severed her head. The last of the greatest ninja clan," Gantetsu said. "Tomoyasu Gantetsu, my ancestor!" He dashed to strike.

Kazeta dived into a roll and batted away Gantetsu's sword with a bamboo staff. Ninja and samurai traded a flurry of blows, and stubs of Kazeta's weapon clattered on the floor like champagne corks.

"Untie me dammit," Butch snapped.

Zee jogged to the wall of weapons and returned with a knife. "Sorry, Butch," he panted. "I can't run like I used to." He went to work on the ropes.

"I remember you," Butch said, twisting to offer his wrists. "You stuck it to Hitler."

"That was Jesse Owens, but I did all right." He handed Butch the blade.

The ground shook as the bombers neared. "You gotta take cover," Butch said.

"I'm gonna go warn the men," Zee said and jogged out the door.

Kazeta held his handless arm up like a shield. It was striped with cuts. Gantetsu trembled with fury, his cheeks scraped red and swollen from strikes of the bamboo staff.

Butch hefted the knife and hobbled to his feet. His hip throbbed like a boiler set to blow. He lurched to stab Gantetsu and fell, curling in pain.

"Give me sword!" Kazeta snapped.

Butch pulled himself toward the weapon rack. Gantetsu side-stepped toward Butch, Kazeta intercepted with three quick swipes from his splintered staff.

Butch gripped the rack and pulled himself to sitting. It wobbled and sent sheathed swords, spears, and staves clattering on top of him.

Kazeta stumbled back as Gantetsu's blade cut his stick in half. Butch heaved a sword toward him, then hurled his knife at Gantetsu's back.

Gantetsu struck the flying *tanto* from the air. Kazeta skipped and picked up the sword, scabbard and all. With only one hand, he could not easily unsheathe it. He blocked Gantetsu's swipe and faced off with him, shouting in Japanese.

Butch took a *tanto* knife in each hand and tested their weight.

A guard appeared at the door with a stubby submachine gun. Butch threw a *tanto* into his gut. The guard clutched at the blade, and Butch winged the other knife to his throat. He crawled toward the man's gurgling body while the swordsmen exchanged blows. The Masamune's blade chimed brightly, chipping off chunks of Kazeta's scabbard.

Butch leaned out the door and gaped at the sea of fire roiling down the mountain. Tokyo was the biggest city he'd ever seen, and now half of it swirled to the heavens in tornados of flame. The bombers spread across the clouds like black crosses, payloads whistling down like the merciless judgment of Revelation.

Pappy boosted Zee onto the roof of the prison hut, where he spread out an American flag they had made from scraps of cloth.

They anchored the corners down with combat boots.

The flames of the dying city lit the shadows and betrayed a Black Dragon creeping toward the dojo. Butch perforated him with a tinny burst from the Japanese bullet sprayer. More black-clad ninja swarmed from the shadows. Star-shaped blades spun from their hands and peppered the doorway.

Two on the roof of the supply hut. Butch cut them down with short bursts. One rounded the corner with a rifle and Butch dumped the magazine into him. He whistled to the POWs, and they ran for the fallen enemies and their weapons.

Kazeta and Gantetsu dueled, dancing like two heavyweights in the late rounds. Gantetsu had rage and an infallible blade. Kazeta moved with unpredictable grace despite months of beatings, a mangled arm and a sword stuck in its scabbard. He dodged and deflected killing blows into mere surface cuts, but weakened with every wound.

Butch pushed himself to his feet and staggered with the pain. A knob of bone bulged at his hip like he had an orange in his pocket. The burst abscess had dislocated the hip. He gripped the door jamb and gritted his teeth, then threw his hip into the door frame with enough force to shudder the wall.

Butch screamed at the pain exploding in his side, and yanked a spear from the weapon rack. He staggered toward the duellists, howling and swinging the weapon over his head.

Kazeta flicked his eyes toward him.

Gantetsu took advantage of the distraction and struck overhead. Kazeta ducked beneath and blocked high. The Masamune's blade dug deep into the lacquered scabbard.

Kazeta whisked aside and drew his sword, leaving its sheath attached to Gantetsu's blade. The weight tipped the blade forward and off balance.

Gantetsu's eyes went wide.

Kazeta struck with a shout and severed both of Gantetsu's arms at the elbows.

The Masamune sang as it hit the floor. Gantetsu fell to his knees, staring at his pulsing stumps.

Gantetsu raised his chin and growled, "The Black Dragons will—"

"Shut the hell up," Butch said, and plunged the spear into Gantetsu's mouth, pinning his head to the wall. He staggered and Kazeta caught him.

"Good job, brother," Butch said.

"Domo, nakama," Kazeta said, and steadied Butch on his feet.

"We gotta take cover, Kazeta-san. It's all gone to hell out there."

Kazeta dropped his sword and peeled Gantetsu's fingers from the Masamune. He cleaned the blade on his sleeve calmly as the walls of the dojo shuddered from the bombing. He found the scabbard and tied the sword to his waist.

Kazeta turned back to Gantetsu, who writhed beneath the spearhead, gouging the haft with his teeth as he gurgled out his dying rage. Kazeta narrowed his eyes and gripped the Masamune.

The blade flashed in two blinding strokes.

The severed spear haft hit the floor like a discarded baseball bat, and Gantetsu's body slumped to the floor. Kazeta returned the Masamune to its scabbard and retrieved the length of wood he'd cut.

"Cane," Kazeta said, and handed it to Butch. "We go."

Butch staggered out of the dojo behind him.

The eyes of the head nailed to the wall followed them before slowly going dull. The bonfire of Tokyo painted the mountains a rich copper, and the crags and crevices came alive with flickering shadows like the faces of screaming children.

29.

THEY SLEPT ON THE MOUNTAIN in the freezing cold, buried under pine needles and the wool blanket. Butch woke to the scent of barbecued meat, clutching his commando knife. They had raided the supply hut for kit, and Gantetsu's quarters for their personal belongings before the bombers rocked the camp. Butch found the dagger he'd carried since training camp. Kazeta retrieved his blacksmith stones.

Butch found himself alone and dug out of the grave-like bed. The sun sat pillowed atop the horizon like the yolk of an egg fried over easy. The pack lay next to him, but no Kazeta. Only footprints leading off into the woods.

Probably went for a crap.

He found a packet of crackers and a silver can in their supplies. Lacking a can opener, he peeled it open with the dagger and gagged at the strong fish smell.

It was the first meat Butch had seen in weeks. It stank like the fish soup they served at the camp, but it was solid food. He scooped it out with the crackers and choked it down until his belly complained.

So much for the Montana steaks he'd been dreaming of. He could barely eat a child's portion.

Butch found his cane and followed Kazeta's sign out to the ridge. He found him on a rock that jutted over the edge, staring at the smoking ruins of the great city. Half of Tokyo was knocked flat and painted black, a picture smudged out by a giant thumb.

A thin trail of smoke led from the ruins to the mountaintop. Butch's stomach twisted at the scent. He eased to the ground beside Kazeta.

"I'm sorry, *nakama*."

"We burn China," Kazeta said. "You burn us."

Butch shrugged and offered the remaining fish and crackers. Kazeta tucked the crackers into his pocket, and hurled the can out over the edge. "Stupid!"

The can disappeared into the treetops.

Kazeta pointed past the smoke to the water, where small islands peeked through the rough chop. "We go. Safe. Birds only."

They descended the mountain's zigzag of trails, stopping every few minutes for Butch to rest his hip. It had swollen up like a Ziegfeld girl's thigh.

Butch sat on a stump. "What's the deal with the sword?"

"What Gantetsu say."

"He called it the soul of Japan. Is that why you're warlike?" Butch had never thought much about Japan before the war. He'd learned about Admiral Perry in history class and his school had put on a performance of *The Mikado,* but that was it.

"Japanese soul is not war," Kazeta said, "The *Honjo Masamune* ... great art." He drew the blade and it gleamed in the twilight, the temper line a sinuous river of burnished silver along its length. "Gift to Tokugawa. Shogun. Leader who ... make Japan one."

"So it's a national treasure," Butch said. "Like George Washington's sword. But you risked so much to protect it."

Kazeta shrugged. "Who else will?"

Butch nodded, and looked askance. "You use it pretty well for a blacksmith."

"Grandfather teach," Kazeta replied.

◆ ◆

THEY STAYED ABOVE THE TREE LINE until the sun fell behind the mountains, then began their descent. The moon was fat as a nervous man's thumbnail and it lit on a silvery spring that trickled down the draw.

Butch popped his tin of boot polish and smeared his face black. He offered Kazeta the can.

Kazeta frowned. "Not for face. Go on shoe."

"It's camouflage, smart ass."

Kazeta tilted his head. "Japanese not black," he said, and headed down the trail.

"A comedian," Butch said, leaning heavily on his cane. "You know what a comedian is?"

"Man paint face," Kazeta said. "He comedian."

Small villages terraced the mountains. Kazeta draped the blanket over Butch's shoulders and tied it like an old man's robe. They kept close and silent on the dirt roads, the only sound the trickle of irrigation wastewater from the rice paddies flowing down tiny canals parallel to the roads, orderly and serene. As they neared the foothills, the soft glow of lamplight leaked from the houses and the night was haunted by choked wails and moans.

Silhouettes of women huddled over unmoving forms played on the paper walls. Butch had seen enough in the blasted Italian villages to know the story. The scream of falling artillery still keened in his nightmares.

They picked up a riverbank that led through the city, treading on a white shroud of fallen cherry blossoms beneath the trees. The empty branches clawed the sky. The skeleton of a lone burned-out building stood watch over the gutted ruins, the moonlight beaming through one empty window eye socket. The fallen petals darkened with ashes, and soon their footsteps crunched on charcoal and blackened embers. The delicate air of flowers spoiled and they pulled their collars over their mouths to breathe. As they passed the one remaining edifice, the moonlight gleamed over the water and bared the source of the stench.

A tangle of bloated corpses choked the bend of the river. Eyes bulged and mouths gaped in silent awe. Hands swollen into flippers begged the heavens.

Butch stumbled and Kazeta steadied his shoulder. Neither man spoke. They eased away from the riverbank and froze as the moon lit the road before them. Burned husks littered the ground like cockroaches. One corpse curled protectively around a tinier one. Butch and Kazeta gnawed their fists to remain silent.

They walked acres of human slaughter until they fell into the blackened sands of the beach and covered their faces, ashamed to be human. The shush of the waves was the whisper of a million souls caught in the undertow, folding back into the sea.

A scorched dinghy tilted in the surf. They piled in with Butch at the tiller and leaned toward the islands, the moon behind them an unwavering glare over the cremated remains of Tokyo.

30.

"I'M NOT DRIVING MY BABY OVER THAT," Tara said and jabbed a mittened finger at the mountain of road salt.

Reeves kicked a chunk of rock salt up the road.

Mikio circled the car, windmilling his bad arm, rubbing the shoulder.

Tara popped the trunk and took out a coal shovel, the corners bent from cracking ice. She tossed it to Reeves, who caught it by the haft.

"You wanna catch him, start shoveling."

Reeves lost his jacket and shoveled a path through the snowbank. Tara and Mikio warmed their behinds on the hood of the Olds, teaching each other words in their respective languages.

"Beer," Tara said.

"*Biru,*" Mikio replied.

"That's too easy. How do I order a beer?"

"*Biru ippon kudasai.*"

Reeves worked up a sweat. It felt good to lose himself in the labor, but not as good as a fight would feel. Grandma Jean took to physical labor like religion, and said any time you felt confused, you ought to pick up broom or a shovel. "If you pray while you're working," she said, "you may not get an answer, but at least you got something done."

That hadn't made much sense until Iraq. Stan-land was bad, but simple. There were bad guys who had to get shot. Reeves had been demobilized from Afghanistan before the occupation had time to fester and feed the insurgency. After two weeks R&R in Qatar, the brass sent them to the hotbed of Fallujah, a needle into a boil. The week prior to their arrival, the barbecued corpses of four mercenaries had been dragged through the street.

Fallujah replayed in Reeves' mind often enough that he never sat down and thought about what had happened there. The slack faces of the dead. The wailing of the wounded. White phosphorus fireworks raining down. They were cycled in for a few weeks, then back to the rear so they wouldn't break. Most guys spent the off time playing Xbox or watching bootleg TV shows. Instead, Reeves chose to work.

He helped unload cargo planes. While he cut the metal bands off supply crates with his sawtoothed Ka-Bar, he counted the dead. With each popped crate, he freed the soul of someone he'd killed or allowed to be killed. Their faces wavered through the heat mirages on their way to heaven or hell.

Across the road, the wind whipped up a dust devil of powdery snow. Reeves searched it for ghosts of Butch's face. The snow devil paced back and forth along the tree line, and would not dissipate.

Tara honked the horn and brought him back. "I see cop lights," she hollered. "Get in."

She bashed the Olds through the remaining snow, working both pedals until the car burst through the other side. Tara dropped the hammer and rocketed them down the two-lane road, following the path the snowplow had cleared. The airport appeared as a break in the trees far ahead.

"They're gonna leave before the snow gets bad again," Reeves said.

"Calm your nuts," Tara said. "They won't outrun me."

In the back, Mikio turned the origami dove over in his hands. "I keep."

Reeves turned back. "What? That was my grandfather's."

"I bring you Takehiko," Mikio said, and held up the bird. "I keep."

"I'll think about it," Reeves said. He squinted at the road ahead. "No plow."

"Go around bend," Mikio said, shifting in his seat. "Plane in back."

Tara took the curve hard. Yellow flashers of winter maintenance vehicles strobed beyond the tall chain link fence. The plow's path veered from the road up the embankment. Tara shifted to low gear and followed through a twisted wreck of fence.

"There he is," Reeves said.

The plow scraped a path across the runways. Mikio pointed over the seat toward a big-bellied four-prop aircraft. "There is plane."

"It's a seaplane," Reeves said.

The plow angled away from the seaplane with an airport tug giving chase. The plow bullied the tug aside and sent it careening through a row of single engine aircraft.

"Head to the plane," Reeves said, and popped the magazine of the Springfield.

The plow shuddered to a stop and swung into reverse, heading right for them. Tara yanked the wheel and turned into the spin. "Son of a bitch!" She palmed the wheel in circles and the truck whined past, veering toward the small control tower.

The snowplow hit the air traffic tower with a resounding crash. The structure rocked and tilted, then crashed sideways into the terminal.

"Whoa," Tara said, and skidded to a stop behind the seaplane.

The truck doors opened and two men in white—Takehiko and his henchman—jogged from the wreckage.

"They don't want to be followed," Reeves said. He cleared the chamber of the .45 and blew hard into the ejection port. A fat chalk-stick of snow popped out of the barrel and splattered on the floor.

"Hang back and keep your head down," Reeves said, and tugged the door handle.

"That's your plan, run at them headfirst?" Tara said, revving the engine. "Hell with that. I'll flatten them."

"Bad plan," Mikio said.

"If they're gunned up, they'll wax us easy," Reeves said. "It ain't like the movies. A car is a death trap."

"Not when I'm driving."

"Just stay in the car and back me up," Reeves said, and closed the other handcuff around the steering wheel.

"Oh, that's great!" Tara said. "Are you stupid? How am I supposed to drive?" Reeves mashed a kiss on her cheek. She pushed him away. "Go get killed, stupid!"

Reeves winked and scuttled toward the door.

Mikio looped an arm around Reeves' neck and jabbed the little pigsticker against his throat. Reeves tensed rigid and let the Springfield thunk to the floor mat. "Come with me."

"What the hell you doing, Mickey?" Tara said, kneading the wheel.

"Best way," Mikio said, and tugged him out of the car.

"Easy, man," Reeves said. "You can have the damn paper bird."

"Don't be ass hole," Mikio said. "Go."

The sirens of emergency vehicles wailed as crews responded to the mayhem. Takehiko jogged from the snowplow toward the plane. The Masamune rode in his belt. The seaplane's propellers fired up with a bang.

Mikio dragged Reeves around the nose, away from the blades.

Takehiko snapped his eyes their way and veered toward them. Mikio shifted the blade to Reeves' kidney.

"Fitting, Mick. Stab me in the back," Reeves said.

"Stupid," Mikio said. "Get in plane. Trust me."

"I'd trust you better if you didn't stick a knife in my neck."

Takehiko slowed to a walk and clapped. "Mikio, it seems you have served some useful purpose after all."

Mikio spoke to him in Japanese.

Takehiko tilted his head. *"Hai."* He nodded to a soldier and whispered commands. The man jogged into the seaplane. "Mikio wants a rematch in Tokyo. He thinks beating 'Rage Cage' Reeves will get him back in the game. What do you say, Reeves?"

"You want to see me fight, drop the sword," Reeves growled through gritted teeth.

Five rough men in commando fatigues filed out of the plane.

"I don't fight in competition," Takehiko chuckled. "Only battle. When you're as broken down and scarred as Mikio, maybe I'll let you die."

The soldiers spread out, producing a black hood and zip ties.

Mikio tightened the choke on Reeves' neck. "Don't be pussy," he whispered.

Reeves twisted away, and Mikio pumped a short punch to his kidney. Mikio could hit a lot harder than that. Reeves hunched over and played along. He had little choice. The hood blacked out his vision and someone jerked his arm into a chicken wing. His nerves burned from neck to groin, screaming at him to run. He calmed his breaths the way he did before a fight, ready to be led onto the plane, when a familiar set of tires squealed.

Shouts, a rush of air to his left, then a loud thump. A shove sent Reeves stumbling. He tore the hood off.

Two of Takehiko's men lay sprawled, and Tara hooted from the wheel of the big gold muscle car, windows down. AC/DC's "Whole Lotta Rosie" blared from the stereo. She cut the wheel hard and spun a donut, scattering Takehiko and his men.

Mikio snarled, "Stupid big tit woman!"

A yakuza fired a pistol and the Toronado's rear glass fuzzed and crumbled. Tara spun the wheel and fishtailed, using the plane for cover. Reeves rolled to his feet and shouldered the gunman toward the propeller blades. He tackled with a double leg takedown and planted the yakuza's face to the macadam. The gun skidded away.

Takehiko barked commands and ran up the steps to the plane.

Reeves scrambled after the pistol and was yanked off his feet as the chain of a *kusarigama* whipped around his neck. He hit the ground hard. The commando at the other end of the chain reeled him in, holding the sickle high.

Reeves choked and rolled, clawing at the chain. His cheeks ballooned and the world blurred. He wormed a finger under the chain and eased off the blood choke, feeding his brain a thin stream of oxygen.

Mikio threw a flying knee and folded the commando in half, bringing the pommel of his grandfather's knife down on the man's skull.

Reeves coughed and choked, unlooping the chain from his throat.

Mikio helped him to his feet. "Takehiko in plane," he said, and ran for the steps.

"Wait!" Reeves yelled at his back, and finished untangling himself.

The last ninja dived for the sickle of the *kusarigama* and rolled to a crouch, holding the blade high. He looped the chain around his wrist and tugged Reeves closer.

Tara screamed past in the Toronado. Takehiko's commandos groaned and scuttled out of her way. Reeves twirled the weighted end of the chain over his head and whipped it at her rear wheel. The chain pulled taut and dragged the ninja holding it yelping behind the car.

The commandos staggered for Reeves in a circle, blocking his path to the plane. Reeves snapped a kick to one's thigh and followed with an elbow to a jaw. One opponent grappled and hung like dead weight to keep Reeves planted while his partner chopped for Reeves' throat.

Reeves slipped under the chop and hooked under the man's arm, stuck his other arm in his crotch and heaved him over his shoulder into a fireman's throw at his buddy. The three of them fell in a tangle. Reeves rolled away with a double mule kick and scrambled for the .45.

Tara swung wide and clipped the two men with the Toronado's rear end, sending them tumbling. Reeves skipped over the chain as the sickle wielder rolled past with a scream.

Reeves ducked for the gun and froze when a burst of rifle rounds peppered the asphalt in front of his face.

Takehiko held an M4 assault rifle. Reeves' old pal from Stanland and Iraq. This one had the grenade launcher below the barrel. Behind him, Mikio held his hands high. Three yakuza surrounded Mikio and kicked him to his knees.

The knocked-around yakuza tackled Reeves to the ground and pinned him limb by limb.

"There is no honor in this," Takehiko announced, and raised the rifle to his shoulder. "But the time for games is over." He sighted the Toronado as Tara roared around for another pass.

"No!" Reeves yelled.

The launcher whumped, and the shell exploded beneath the Oldsmobile. The car flipped onto its hood, sheet metal crumpling under the impact, safety glass exploding.

"Tara!"

Takehiko fired a burst into the fuel tank, then swiveled left and fired at an approaching police car. The State Police cruiser jerked and swerved into a luggage carrier, spinning bags across the pavement. A snowball impact in the windshield glass where the driver's head hit.

Reeves groaned as the commandos zip-tied his wrists behind his back.

Takehiko struck Mikio across the face with the butt of the rifle. The grizzled fighter's eyes rolled and he slumped to the ground. Takehiko took one of his men's swords and left it at Mikio's side, then put the rifle in his hands. "Sayonara, Mikio-san."

Takehiko strode up the steps and entered the cockpit.

Reeves fought his captors step by step as they stuffed him into the doorway of the seaplane. Flames spread toward the Toronado's gas tank. The fumes caught with a whoosh, and the rear of the wrecked car rocked with the explosion.

Reeves head-butted the nearest captor and tripped down the folding steps onto his face. They dragged him in by his legs. One cracked an ampule and cupped it to Reeves's face. Reeves wheezed at the sharp chemical tang and fought not to breathe.

The steps folded up and the doors closed on the image of the flaming Toronado as everything went gray and Reeves succumbed to the deepest choke he'd ever felt.

PART THREE

THE SHADOW SHOGUN

31.

BUTCH CREPT THROUGH THE JUNGLE NIGHT with his black stiletto between his teeth, naked as the day he was born. No starlight penetrated the smothering canopy. His bare feet crushed the shells of skittering insects as he followed the distant rhythm of a guttural chant, barely audible above the susurrus of whispering leaves.

A sickly yellow glow peeked through the cover ahead. Butch hid his footsteps in the drumbeats of the chanters circled around the bonfire. Short men in straw hats like upturned bowls struck invisible enemies in unison. Their leader towered over them, clad in black, his face in shadow.

Sweat trickled down Butch's skin like hot rain. The heat of the flames reached across the clearing to lick his flesh. His knees turned to water and he crumpled to the jungle floor. The chanting men quickly surrounded him and held him spreadeagled. Their leader pointed and laughed at Butch's genitalia, and tore the mask off his face.

Gantetsu cackled, the bloody haft of the spear still thrust through his mouth, the point piercing out the back of his neck. He wrenched the weapon out with a crunch and thrust it deep into Butch's side.

BUTCH WOKE WITH A MUFFLED SCREAM on the island's far shore. The cloth wadded in his mouth tasted like dirt from his grave. He hunched and strained against his bonds. The cool sea air like razors against the furnace of his skin.

Kazeta stood above him, the sword at ease in his hand, a grim expression on his face. The surf sizzled away at his feet. A small driftwood fire lit his face, and illuminated his sword, the *Honjo Masamune,* in full polish.

Butch shuddered and his eyes rolled back as the fever wracked down his spine. Kazeta touched the blade to Butch's bare hip. The skin split apart like the eggshell of a poisonous snake. A fat yellow ribbon of pus burst down his thigh.

Butch groaned and slumped into unconsciousness.

Kazeta wiped the blade clean on a leaf, set it out of the surf's reach, and knelt before Butch's wound, with waves lapping his feet. He gripped the waxy flesh with his calloused hands and squeezed out the rest of the ooze, striped red with blood. A black clot slithered through his fingers like a dead jellyfish and was washed away by the surf. He rinsed the wound with seawater while Butch writhed on the sand, eyes bugging. Kazeta swept the cut clean. After Butch collapsed, Kazeta cut his bonds with a *tanto* knife. He took one brand from the fire for a torch and kicked wet sand over the coals, then dragged Butch to their camp in the woods and set him close to the dying campfire.

Kazeta dried the sword, built up the fire, and hung his wet clothes to dry. He hunkered naked before the flames, and scratched the sea-green tattoo on his left upper arm. Resembling a swirling, three-bladed whirlwind, it symbolized the convergence of sky, man and earth and was known as the *mitsudomoe:* the standard of Hachiman, divine protector of Japan since ancient times.

Kazeta fingered the raised lines of ink which scarred his skin. Gantetsu's eyes had flared with murder when he recognized the mark. The only reason he took Kazeta's hand and not his head was to humiliate him before his *oyabun* and bask in the glory of capturing the Black Dragons' greatest enemy.

Kazeta fed a bamboo sliver through one of the prawns he'd

snatched from a tidal pool, and roasted it in the flames until yellow fat bubbled from the scorched shell. He cracked it open and ate greedily, then roasted another for Butch to eat when he woke.

If he woke.

Kazeta was no doctor. He was *bushi*, one who follows the way of the warrior. Not *samurai*, the servants of the shogunate. Not one who lives for battle, like the Satsuma rebels. Kazeta's great-grandsire had been among them, young and brash, when they followed Saigō Takamura to war against the Imperial Army.

Without war or the threat of clan feuds dividing the nation, the samurai were superfluous, their swords mere decoration, heirlooms to be presented to sons as mementos of the greatness the family once held. The yearly stipends of rice paid to the warrior caste were ended, and they faced the dishonorable life of wandering ronin.

The ninja clans weathered the transition to industry better. They merged with the gamblers and became the *yakuza*. But watching the samurai waste away with disuse like a crippled limb was not enough for the Gantetsu clan. While Saigō Takamura pled that the samurai could still serve Japan, his men captured two spies who revealed under torture that they had been sent by the Meiji government to assassinate him.

The samurai were outraged and openly warred with the government over the betrayal. Before the lies of the Gantetsu spies were uncovered, the last of the samurai rebels fell before the repeating rifles and artillery of Japan's new conscript army.

Miyamoto Kubota, Kazeta's great-grandfather, survived. The artillerymen caught his troops in enfilade and cut them down with withering fire. Saigō fell to a bullet, and only a few dozen samurai remained. Beneath his gutted steed, crushed into earth muddied by the blood of his men, Kubota watched as his comrades posed their dead leader as if he had committed *seppuku*, so it would look as though Saigō had died with honor.

Then they charged the Imperial positions and followed him to the peaceful country.

As the final reports echoed across the field of battle, a single dove landed on Kubota's stirrup in defiance of the blistering cannonade.

Doves were the messengers of Hachiman, and though deafened by gunfire, Kazeta's ancestor heard the words of the *kami* spirit:

This is not the way of the warrior.

Then Kubota collapsed.

While the scavengers picked through the dead, he wriggled out of a corpse wagon and shocked the *burakumin* gravediggers as he shucked his armor, retrieved his family sword, and escaped into the rice fields.

Someone would need to protect Japan from the *yakuza* and the shadow clans who slipped into the newly formed government like eels in a bed of seaweed. Hachiman had spoken.

Kubota would recount his dream to young ronin gathered in secret. Telling them Hachiman said that true honor sought no glory. That they could serve Japan while hidden and disguised, and protect the people both from invaders and evil within.

When the shadow clans showed themselves, the Warriors of Hachiman struck in ambush. Creating no witnesses. Leaving no survivors. Fading into their positions as monks, smiths, teachers, soldiers and among the outcasts.

Their enemy, the ninja clans, had centuries of expertise and systems of deception so cunning they had infiltrated every corner of government. They operated openly as The Black Dragon Society, with former samurai families unknowingly in their clutches. Now the war had emboldened them to attempt to wipe out the Warriors of Hachiman once and for all.

Kazeta kneaded the thick pad of scar tissue at the end of his left wrist. It ached deep inside. The bones had not fully knitted.

Few of his brethren remained. He alone could protect the *Honjo Masamune,* the soul of Japan. He would take the blade to the monks in the mountains, and wait for this foolish war to end. When the sword could unite the people to rebuild rather than invade, and its song would not be one of death, but of honor.

Kazeta had avenged his brethrens' death at the hands of the cruel peacock Gantetsu, but felt hollow inside, and without purpose. He knew not to seek vengeance, that the relief it gave was only fleeting, and worse, addictive. The Black Dragons were strong, and Kazeta's allies were scattered and weak, but one man loyal to Hachiman remained.

Kazeta would wage his own shadow war until his dying breath.

Butch moaned and shivered. Kazeta covered him with a dry blanket before joining him in sleep.

32.

SHERIFF JOHANSSON SHOOK HIS HEAD at the mayhem that had befallen Ely airport. Emergency vehicles circled the smoking wreck of Tara's Oldsmobile. The beefy cop sipped a steaming cup of coffee and watched the coroner zip the bag closed on a crispy critter who'd been chained to the rear axle. A fireman had to cut the chain with a bolt cutter.

Two officers injured in a collision with a luggage tug. Two more banged up in an altercation at the diner, their cruiser totaled. A snowplow operator with his throat slit, and two senior citizens and a half-dozen foreign nationals dead at the surplus store. Johansson hadn't seen this many bodies since those snowmobilers drove their truck onto the lake before the ice got thick.

That had been pretty bad, but nothing like this.

He walked to the back of the ambulance where an EMT flashed a penlight in Tara's eyes. Her betrayal had stung, but she was the hottest piece in town, and now he had something on her that would keep her in check for good.

"No concussion?" Johansson said. The EMT shook her head. Johansson loomed until she left him alone with Tara, then offered the coffee. "For the smoke inhalation."

Tara drank it on the ambulance bumper, her other hand cuffed to the blue plastic steering wheel. All that remained of her daddy's Toronado. The horn ring was cracked from where she'd torn the wheel off to escape the explosion.

"You all right, Fireball?"

Tara warmed her hands on the cup. "You don't get to call me that anymore."

"How about Miss Accessory to Murder? Or Terrorist Tara. That has a nice ring to it. Those sound better, ya think?"

Tara sighed and sipped.

"The other survivor, he don't speak English." Johansson jerked a thumb over his shoulder to where Mikio sat in the back of a cruiser. "So that leaves you. And it won't be me asking the questions. The DHS is coming. Department of Homeland Security, kiddo. The TV news is calling it Attack on the Iron Range. Playing up the terrorist angle."

"They're not terrorists," Tara said. "They're ninjas."

"Like some '80s movie?" Johansson laughed. "Come on, Fireball. You gotta do better than that if I'm gonna keep you out of Stillwater prison. You were a hostage, right? The waitress at the diner says you didn't act like a hostage, but I wrote the report. You were kidnapped by Reeves and this Japanese guy."

"No I wasn't." Tara coughed into her sleeve. "We were chasing the guys who blew up the store." She tapped the empty cup against her handcuff. "They wanted some sword Reeves' grandfather had. So they robbed a bank to buy it, and when he refused, they killed him and stole it."

"All this over a sword?" Johansson said, sweeping a glove over the carnage. "It sounds like hooey, Fireball. And when Homeland Security gets here, they're gonna want better. So you were kidnapped. Reeves was in with these guys, and that's why he escaped with them."

"Damn it, Tor! Stop calling me that! Reeves was trying to stop them. He's the one who's kidnapped."

Johansson snatched the empty coffee cup and crushed it. "Why him? It couldn't have been anybody else? He shows up and you fall for him in nothing flat. You had to twist the knife that deep?"

"Because he's over it, and you're not," Tara said.

"What did he lose? Instead of getting his brains scrambled in the ring, he got them screwed up in Iraq. Either way he'd be a bum. I would've gone to State and then the Vikes—"

"All you talk about is how he robbed you of what you coulda-woulda-shoulda been. Maybe when you picked that fight, you robbed yourself. You ever think of that? And if you didn't, you'd have picked a fight with Eli Manning, or Brett Favre or somebody. Get the hell over it."

Johansson dropped the cup and kicked it. He unlocked the cuff from the steering wheel and cinched it on Tara's other wrist. He pushed the wheel into her hands and herded her toward the squad car.

"What the hell are you doing, Tor?"

He pushed her head down and stuck her in back of the cruiser with Mikio. "Get your head on straight and stop protecting him. One of you is gonna burn. It's your choice."

Johannson closed the door and leaned on it, folding his arms.

MIKIO LOOKED SURPRISED TO SEE HER. His hands were cuffed, his pockets turned out. He looked her up and down, then nodded.

"You look shit," he said.

Tara smirked. "You don't look so hot yourself. What kind of crap were you pulling back there? You backstabbing prick."

"Not prick," Mikio said. "Reeves prick. He no follow plan."

"What plan?"

"Go in plane, kick everybody ass. Fly home Tokyo, drink beer with big titty women," Mikio said, as if there were no other possible outcome.

"That was your plan?"

"Good plan." Mikio shrugged. "Reeves fuck up."

"No, *you* fuck up!" Tara hit his shoulder with the steering wheel. Mikio curled away with a stream of Japanese.

"You think maybe you should *tell* the big titty woman your big plan? So she didn't think you turned on us?"

Johansson knocked on the roof. "Settle down in there."

Tara seethed and slammed back into her seat.

"You like cop?" Mikio asked.

"What's it to you?" Tara looked away. Johansson's broad back pressed against the glass. "He can be all right. It's a small town. Not much to choose from."

"He like you. Want release you."

"Only if I snitch you out. And Reeves," Tara said. "That jackass. Almost got me killed."

"Tell cop you snitch," Mikio whispered. "Tell cop . . . me and Reeves, we bad guys."

Tara wrinkled her nose. "Why?"

Mikio's scruffy moustache stretched in a smile. "I have plan."

JOHANSSON MADE TARA KNOCK ON THE WINDOW a good long time before he opened the door.

Tara frowned at the floor. She looked great angry, not so much scared and blubbering. She needed a hot shower back at his place. She was a smart girl and he knew she'd pay him back with interest for this favor.

Their first date was to fix a speeding ticket. And their second. By the third, Gail the dispatcher told him to bring along roses. Tara stopped braking for speed traps, and the back windows of his Trailblazer ss became etched in permanent fog. He joked with the deputies that she'd earned the gold Police Benevolent Association badge he'd stuck in the Toronado's window by getting her card punched ten times, like at Subway.

He took the badge back the night she cussed him out in the diner parking for leaning on the horn when she didn't come out and give him a front seat hummer during her smoke break. She said the gray-hairs all glared at her like they knew. He told her they were jealous she was dating a cop, but she didn't buy it.

Johansson forgot when he'd stopped taking her out on dates to the steakhouse, or why. It just sort of happened. He thought they were past that stuff. She stopped staying over, so he met her at the end of shift, idling outside the diner and blocking her in, no matter how tired she looked. He knew he'd screwed up something good, but she didn't have to be a bitch about it. He forgave her plenty of tickets. She couldn't forgive him a screwup or two?

Thing is, she looked good. Pissed-off redheads always looked good, like they were gonna burst into flames. He'd let her stew while the DHS boys circled the scene in their black Suburban.

"You got your mind right?" Johansson said.

Tara let out a long breath that pushed out her full lower lip. "Yeah."

"Want to go get a steak?"

She shook her hair out, and looked away. "Sure."

Johansson unlocked her cuffs and pushed an evidence bag in her hands. "They're sticking me with the paperwork. Don't open it." He pointed her toward his truck, then turned back to Mikio. "Get out of the car, jerk-off. Time to hand you to the Feds."

MIKIO GRUNTED AS JOHANSSON DRAGGED HIM AWAY by the cuff chain toward two officers flanking a huge blacked-out truck. They sported buzz cuts, watch caps, and aviator sunglasses, and regarded Mikio with matching curt nods.

"Here's your terrorist," Johansson said. "He had a samurai sword and an M16 with a grenade launcher."

"M16, huh? He an antique dealer?" Buzzcut One said, and his partner laughed. "Probably an M4."

Mikio grunted.

Johansson jerked Mikio's arms up behind him. "What you laughing at, tango?"

Mikio grunted and looked away. Americans could always be expected to behave like someone in a television show.

"We'll take it from here, Sheriff," Buzzcut Two said, and eased Mikio's arms down.

Mikio stretched his shoulders while the cops exchanged paperwork. He followed Tara's behind with his eyes to keep his balls from freezing.

"Can he write letters from Gitmo?" Johansson said. "I wanna know if they serve sushi."

The DHS officers rolled their eyes.

Mikio gave Johansson both middle fingers as the Feds put him in the back of their truck. When the door closed, he spat Tara's bobby pin onto the seat and went to work.

TARA WATCHED FROM JOHANSSON'S TRUCK as he strode back to his deputies. She kneaded the steering wheel of her dead Toronado. If Mikio's plan failed, she'd hitch the first ride out of town in the morning after scrubbing herself raw in the shower.

She sighed to herself, watching Johansson gesture and laugh with his cop buddies. Sure, she'd gone on the first date to fix a ticket, but Tor had been sweet back then, and the rest of their dates were honest. The town was slim pickings for decent men, with the Ford plant shuttered. In the beginning it had been all right. He was selfish and farted like a hippo, but he took good care of her at first. She broke it off when she'd become just another stop on his patrol, a coffee break with a side of steamy windows. And he'd made her pay for it.

Her lip twitched as Tor laughed it up with his men. They all knew. The cops had given her a glove box full of tickets, some deserved and most not. All burned up in the wreck of her Daddy's Toronado.

Her own plan would be to wait until she and Tor were alone and brain him with the steering wheel. The slimy sonofabitch. But she knew that wasn't in her. Easier to give him what he wanted, then skip town.

THE BACK DOOR POPPED OPEN and Mikio crawled in. She looked back at the black truck's tinted windows. "What did you do?"

"Plan," Mikio said. He held his forearm across his throat and mimicked rolling his eyes and passing out. "Choke cops, drive away."

"What about those other dozen cops, idiot!"

Mikio waved his hand. "Make dumb cop drive away. He like you," he said, and cupped his palms with fingers spread wide, like he was lugging two sugar melons.

Tara swatted his shoulder. "They're not that big, jerk. If we get out of this, we need to discuss what 'plan' means. Get your ass down." She reached over him and pulled the blanket from the back, the one she made Tor keep for their old 'dates.' She spread it over Mikio and the rear seats, pushing his head down. "He's coming. Wait for my, uh, signal."

Johansson strutted over and climbed in, flashing a smug grin that brought out his dimples. They'd been cute once, but now Tara saw him as a baby-faced bully, daring you to glance at his harelip scar.

"Saved your sweet ass again, Fireball. You're in the clear." Johansson revved the throaty V8 and warmed his fingers against the heat vents. Tara curled against the passenger door and let her breath fog the window.

"You could be grateful," he said. "You really goofed up this time."

"I am grateful, Tor. Just tired."

"How about a hot shower back at my house? You look like you need it."

"Thanks."

"You need to stop being so high and mighty. You were too good for me, back when you first came to town. When you needed something, then you came sniffing around. Then I started looking pretty good."

"How many parking lot blow jobs is it gonna be, officer?"

"There's no need for that kind of talk," Johansson said. "But that's a good start. This ain't no speeding ticket. It's a hell of a lot worse. You got a smart mouth, you know? You want to share a cell at Gitmo with that oriental fella, we can go talk with the Feds."

"Drive home, Tor. I'm just worn out. I'm sorry."

"Maybe I want it right here," Johansson said, curling his scarred lip. "Let the boys see just one head in the window. Yeah, I'd like that." He unzipped his trousers slow, letting her hear it. "The guys all thought it was funny, you hooking up with Reeves. You owe me good this time."

Tara drew a big round smiley face in the fog with her finger. She etched dimples on it, then squeaked her thumb across the glass and wiped the smile off its face.

"Well? What are you waiting for, Valentine's Day?"

Tara reached over and touched his knee. In the back seat, she saw Mikio peel back the quilt and reach for Tor's throat. She gave him a quick shake of the head.

"Can we do it on the road? I know you like it better."

"Okay." Johansson shifted into gear and pulled away. "That's more like it."

He drove past a news van with a satellite dish on the way out of the airport. "I took you for granted, I admit. And I'm sorry. You hear that? I said it. *I'm sorry.* It's not easy for me to say it, because you sorta took me for granted, too. And you kinda cheated on me with Reeves back there."

"We broke up three months ago, Tor."

"There you go with the smart mouth again. You broke up. I didn't break up. I knew you just needed to cool off."

"So banging Heidi Knutson behind the Perkins is okay?"

"You were throwing your tits around like you were hot shit! I got needs!" He flipped on the lights and passed a salt truck, the pellets rattling off the paint. "Let me tell you how it's gonna be. You're gonna start appreciating me. And you can start right now."

Tara rolled her eyes and hissed a resigned sigh that Johansson found all too familiar. He held the stare until she relented and bent down. He eased the seat back, set the cruise control, and gave an insistent push on the nape of her neck.

"What's the hold up? You're a waitress, you ought to want a big tip."

Tara bit down hard.

Johansson shrieked and the truck swerved side to side, and but she held on like a trophy muskie on a trolling lure.

Mikio threw his arm around Johansson's throat and cut him off in mid-scream. Tara sat up with a smear of blood on her lip and fought to keep the wheel steady as Johansson pinned the accelerator and the Corvette-powered truck roared down the highway.

"You better put him out!" Tara said.

Mikio clamped down tighter. "Arm weak! Reeves ass hole!"

Tara blinked at a curve approaching fast. She threw a leg over Johansson's lap and stomped on the brakes, sending the truck lurching as the two pedals fought for supremacy. She popped the ignition off, and Johansson jerked his sidearm from the holster and aimed wildly.

"Mickey!"

The steering wheel locked in place and the truck wound down and coasted. The anti-lock brakes shuddered in the snow and the truck spun into a snowdrift, burying the windows in white. Tara tumbled under the seat and Mikio groaned and tightened the choke.

The radio spouted, "Sheriff, please respond. DHS states the prisoner has overwhelmed them and escaped."

Johansson twitched and fired the Glock into the radio, just before his eyelids fluttered closed and he slumped forward with a string of drool dangling from his lip.

"Holy shit." Tara wiggled a finger into her ear. "I think I'm deaf."

"See? Good plan," Mikio said, and untangled his arm from Johansson's neck. He rubbed his elbow, then nudged her with it. "I like your signal."

"Shut up."

They stripped and cuffed Johansson, and gagged him with one of his red-striped tube socks. Tara pushed him out the door with both feet. Johansson snapped awake when he hit the snow. He groaned in pain and attempted to blink away the predicament he found himself in.

"Does it hurt? Good," Tara said. "I should've bit it off. Think on that while your nuts get frostbite."

The sheriff squirmed and hopped toward the road like a walrus in tighty whities.

Mikio frowned. "Can't leave here," he told Tara. "He die."

"Let him."

Mikio helped Johansson to his feet and prodded him into the trunk with a pinch to his floating ribs. He patted him on the cheek and slammed the trunk shut.

AT THE FIRST GAS STATION, they left Johansson cuffed to a toilet and dumped his cell phone in the bowl. They swapped license plates with a beater parked behind the convenience shop, then loaded up on coffee and jerky and trail mix. Mikio grabbed a maroon sweatshirt with "Go Gophers!" emblazoned across the chest.

Tara pointed the truck west and put the Chevy small block through its paces. "What's the plan now, Kato?"

"Drive San Francisco," Mikio said. "Meet friend." He peeled off his undershirt, revealing a chiseled abdomen so thin his broad shoulders and chest resembled a triangle balanced on his waist.

Tara reached over and squeezed his deltoid, admiring the swirling three-bladed symbol tattooed there in green and black. "Nice ink. What's it mean?"

"Domo, Akane-chan." Mikio pulled the baggy Gophers sweatshirt over his head. "Means 'Warrior,'" Mikio said, and slapped his shoulder. "Like grandfather."

He removed the flattened origami dove from the evidence bag and unfolded its wings. He set the bird on the dashboard, beak aimed toward the open road.

33.

REEVES WOKE FROM A DRUGGED SLEEP to the drone of propellers and the pillowy yaw of the seaplane. The sun bobbed like a new penny over the clouds. Reeves peeled his face from the window and rubbed the painful red ligatures the now-severed zip ties had left on his wrists.

He was groggy but unbound, belted into a seat in the middle of the plane. Black-haired heads nodded and rocked in the seats in front of him. Six he could see. No guards in the aisle, front or back. Reeves stretched to banish the pins and needles, then ducked out of his seat toward the rear of the plane.

He took two steps before pain seared down the side of his neck. He reached for his throat and his assailant twisted his finger back into an arm lock. Years of grappling made Reeves acutely aware of what his joints could take, and his attacker seemed equally knowledgable. The guard whirled Reeves off balance with his wrist poised to snap, depositing him back into his seat.

Reeves gripped the guard's arm by the wrist and another bolt of pain shot down his neck. He sneered up into a pair of cold almond eyes, framed by locks of black.

"The captain has not removed the safety belt sign," the woman said, and ground her fingertips into the nerve cluster below Reeves' earlobe. "You will remain seated."

She smiled at Reeves' surprise, and how he fought hard to ignore the pain.

Reeves raised his hand from the seat rest, and she responded with an uppercut deep into his groin.

Mixed martial arts had also made Reeves well-acquainted with strikes to the testicles. Grazing blows that caught up with you three seconds later. Solid shots that felt like your nuts were pinballs bouncing off your internal organs. And the worst kind, which set a disco ball of lights spinning in your head while your spirit left your body, as if embarrassed to be seen with you.

She hit Reeves with that kind.

Reeves' spirit admired her from a distance while his body hunched in half. She was beautiful in the way most young Japanese women seem to Americans, her features smooth like the air-brushed faces of the models in fashion magazines. She wore a checked blazer over a black tank that stuck to her trim abdomen.

She released Reeves from the nerve strike and sank into her seat. "If you want to know who just kicked your ass, my name's Oki," she said, folding long mantis legs sheathed in denim.

A short old man with a face like a shriveled apricot passed them on his way back from the lavatory. He grinned at Reeves and wagged a wizened finger.

Reeves pushed his nuts out of his throat with a series of powerful exhales. He glared at the old man's back. He looked like an ancient judoka. If ninja existed, Reeves bet the old guy knew some *dim mak* five finger death touch moves. Probably the most dangerous man on the plane. The woman took an e-reader from her black-webbed handbag and tapped the screen.

"Belt up," she snapped, her accent rising to the surface. "We're landing soon."

The winds buffeted the seaplane's belly and lifted Reeves from his seat. He found the belt and strapped in. He'd been bounced around in a C-130 and had no desire to do it again. He leaned toward the window and looked over the wing as they emerged from a cloud bank. Only open ocean below.

Reeves craned to look out Oki's window on other side. She ignored him, unfazed that they appeared to be landing in the middle of the Pacific. Reeves watched out the window for an atoll or some small island. Hawaii, maybe. The Japanese practically owned that, he heard. No island appeared during their steady descent.

The woman braced and Reeves followed suit. The plane's belly skidded across the waves, and a looming black shape filled Reeves' window. He pressed his face to the glass.

An enormous cargo ship sat low in the water, stacked with a multi-colored array of shipping containers. Tall letters in white painted along the side. *Kokuryukai Maru.* The long red boom of a crane swiveled out from the deck like the arm of a toy grabber machine at an arcade. The plane rocked gently with the waves, then jolted as it was lifted out of the water. Stevedores on the ship waved them in.

Oki gripped the back of her seat with one hand. Reeves quietly unbuckled his seatbelt, planted a foot, and watched the deck approach.

The plane thumped on its landing gear and shook the passengers side to side. Reeves launched himself down the aisle toward the cockpit, spinning as the plane lurched and bounced him off a Black Dragon's shoulder.

Oki shouted and her commandos unbuckled and jumped into action. Reeves hit the first with a flying knee to the sternum and ducked a snap kick from the next, shouldering under the man's leg and heaving him down the aisle into his comrades. They cursed and tumbled, and Reeves gripped two seat backs and leapfrogged over them as they untangled themselves. Oki shouted angrily in Japanese and pushed men out of her way.

Takehiko popped his head out of the cockpit. He wore a captain's hat.

Reeves didn't need a cage to unleash the rage that gave him his fighting name. He roared and leaped into an elbow strike.

Takehiko held his hat and somersaulted out the exit door with the grace of a gymnast. Reeves plowed into the back of the copilot's seat, knocking the man face first into the controls. Reeves cursed and clambered out of the cockpit.

The old man blocked the door. His face stone. Hands held up calmly.

Death touch or no death touch, Reeves was going through him. He snapped a probing jab and knocked the old man's head back into the seats.

Reeves stared at his blood-flecked fist, and the old man crumpled into the tangle of Black Dragons blocking Oki.

"Now you've pissed me off!" Oki snarled, climbing over the seat rests like a spider.

Reeves shrugged and dived after Takehiko onto the ship deck.

The stevedores locking down the plane shouted and stumbled out of his way. The plane sat in a small cubbyhole between shipping containers on the edge of the deck. Takehiko danced behind the crew like a flyweight, hands at his sides, a smirk on his face.

A stevedore ran screaming at Reeves with a set of wheel chocks over his head. Reeves slipped left and hit him with a liver punch. A burly sailor threw a haymaker and Reeves dropped him with a combo. Another swung a knotted rope like a lasso. Reeves let the rope bounce off his back and ran for Takehiko. "Fight me, you sonofabitch!"

Takehiko dodged his wild strikes like a ghost. He prodded Reeves in the knee to trip him, then slipped behind the stevedores.

Takehiko's soldiers boiled out of the plane in their identical white collared shirts, black ties and slacks. Most of them battered and bruised. He wouldn't mind kicking their asses. If they wanted him dead, they could have tossed him out of the plane over the Rockies, much less the Pacific. No, they wanted him alive.

Then they would pay for it dearly.

Oki pushed through the men, then circled Reeves with careful bare steps. Her feet looked somehow both dainty and too large for her body. The office ninjas formed a jeering mosh pit around her and Reeves while the Old Man smiled and watched, holding a silk handkerchief to his nose.

"I don't hit women," Reeves said, and dropped his hands.

"Your balls didn't *feel* small," Oki said. "Did I bruise them? I bet they look like two pickled plums." The men laughed.

"I want your boss, not you."

"Then you go through me," Oki said, and beckoned with her palm.

"He killed my grandfather and two innocent people," Reeves said, snapping his scarred knuckles up into guard. "I don't want to hurt you."

"Well, I want to hurt you!" Oki laughed and swept a high kick over Reeves' head, chain punching jabs to his rib tips with her knobby little fists.

Reeves skipped aside and bit back the pain. She was good. But he'd never hit a woman. Couldn't. He had pushed a girl in the mud as a tyke when she'd called his grandma a hillbilly. Grandma Jean made him apologize and scrub the girl's dress on the washboard.

Reeves gripped one of the ninjas by the belt and hurled him at Oki. She chopped the man's shoulder and sent him barrel-rolling with a judo throw. Reeves pushed three more into her path and Oki dispatched them with sweeps and surgical jabs that left them curling in agony.

Reeves cashed in the few seconds he gained to charge Takehiko. The Old Man stood watching, his wispy beard twitching in the wind. Takehiko handed the Old Man his captain's hat and shot his cuffs. Reeves opened with his best, the Rage Cage Combo. Jab, jab, front kick. The jabs rattled brains and the kick launched opponents into the cage.

Takehiko slapped away the jabs and dodged the kick, cracking Reeves across the temple. Reeves stumbled. The ship seemed to tilt.

"I've watched all your fights, Reeves." Takehiko laughed. "Haven't you learned anything new?"

"I'm gonna strangle you with your own guts," Reeves slurred.

Oki jabbed her fingertips between his ribs. Reeves should have felt agony, but his anger dulled it to a distant ache. She leaped on his back and ground the point of her elbow into a nerve between his shoulders. Reeves' arms went numb.

Reeves willed his arms to move, but they floated to his sides, full of needles.

"Oki's father was a masseur," Takehiko said. "He was blind, like all the masters. A cartographer of the human body. Every nerve, muscle and blood vessel. Oki puts his knowledge to better use, don't you think?"

Oki whispered in Reeves' ear. "Be a good boy, or I'll teach you entire continents of pain." She squeezed above his hips with iron thighs, and ran a knuckle down his spine.

Reeves's legs buckled and he fell to his knees.

"If you had behaved, you could ride with the crew," Takehiko said. He snapped orders in Japanese to the stevedores.

Oki padded to Takehiko's side. She stood as tall barefoot as Takehiko did in loafers. She licked a finger and neatened his hair. He hooked his arm around her waist, and they left Reeves struggling to pump feeling back into his limbs.

A long shadow fell over the deck and the stevedores shouted warnings. The crane lowered a large red container, blotting out the sun. Two ninjas dragged Reeves toward the open doors as the crane picked up another load and finished bricking them in.

34.

BUTCH WOKE TO BRIGHT LIGHT. Jean Marie smiled beneath a nurse cap, and bent to kiss his cheek.

"Wasn't sure you were gonna make it, big fella."

Butch smiled and stroked her hair. "I said I'd be back for you."

"Let's see that wound," she said, and unbuttoned his uniform. "Not so bad. You'll be home quicker than crap through a goose."

Her lustrous curls haloed her face and tickled his chest as she leaned in for another kiss. "It's the swelling that's got me concerned. Let's take a look at that."

She unbuckled his belt and reached in his pants. Butch closed his eyes.

"You will drown in shit like your traitor friends," Gantetsu whispered in his ear. His snarling rictus exhaled fetid death into Butch's nostrils. He plunged his arm elbow-deep into Butch's wound.

Butch writhed in agony as Gantetsu tore out a chunk of flesh and held it up like a trophy. "You took my head, I take your balls!"

Butch woke panting beside the extinguished campfire. He tried to sit up then fell back exhausted. His arms were wrapped tightly in a wool blanket, like a spider's meal. Sea birds cried overhead, beyond the canopy of green.

Kazeta knelt shirtless beside him, frowning at Butch's wound. "Smell bad," Kazeta said. "Not good." He washed it out with spring water from a container made from a palm leaf, then dressed and bandaged it with a clean strip of cloth.

He helped Butch sit up against a palm tree, then walked off into the woods. He returned with more water and a stringer of round butterfish, shiny as silver dollars. He gave Butch the water, and set to cleaning the fish.

"My fever broke," Butch said. "That's something."

Kazeta grunted and deposited the fish heads in an empty helmet. He cut slivers from the rich peach-colored meat, and popped one in his mouth. He balanced another on the edge of the knife and held it out to Butch.

Butch wrinkled his nose. "Can't we make a fire?"

"No fire, day time. Smoke. Soldier see." Kazeta tapped the knife impatiently. "Eat, make strong."

Butch choked it down. He'd never been a fan of battered wall-eye back home. Slimy raw fish straight from the ocean stuck in his throat like undercooked egg whites.

"How long was I out?"

"Three day," Kazeta said, then held up three fingers.

"You said it right." A squadron of planes buzzed in the distance. Butch squinted through the trees at the water. Morning fog shrouded the coast, leaving only the white shoulders of Mount Fuji bare. "After what we saw, it's gotta be over soon. I know you guys fight to the death, but what'll be left to fight for?"

Kazeta nodded and ate another chunk of butterfish. "People fight long after lose battle."

BUTCH REGAINED HIS STRENGTH on broth and whole fish baked in the coals. He carved a notch in their camp's big palm tree each day. Kazeta carved spears and hardened the points in the fire. Butch fished with a cane pole, and hobbled along the shore to dig clams with his toes. They camped on the island's windward side, away from the coast, and lit fires only at night, deep in the hat-shaped isle's peaked cap of trees.

Tokyo smoldered for a week before the ants began to rebuild. A destroyer cruised the bay, a lone shark protecting its territory.

Butch read the letters from Jean and dreamt of her riding across the ranch in her boots and lady Stetson and not much else. One morning he woke as the horizon swelled purple with the sun's ascent, and watched Kazeta wield the *Masamune* blade against an invisible foe. The battle raged until the morning sky lit with soft flame. The first ray of sunlight cut across the ocean and lit up the blade like a lightning-stroke, cloaking Kazeta in electric white.

Butch rubbed his eyes as if he'd stared into the sun. When he could see again, Kazeta cut through a six-inch thick bamboo trunk as if it were air. He sheathed the blade and bowed deep, his broad back glistening with sweat. He held his bow in silent prayer, then picked up the cylinder of bamboo he'd severed and began hollowing it out with a knife to make a container.

Butch peeled a couple of satsumas for breakfast. He spit the seeds for distance to have something to do. Kazeta ate baby bamboo shoots and some seaweed, and sharpened a knife on his rust-colored stone.

"Kazeta, tell me something," Butch said. "Do you really believe the Emperor is a living god?"

Kazeta chuckled. "Never met Emperor. Don't know."

"Is it true you can't even look at his photograph?"

Kazeta scratched his chin. "Children, in school. They pray to Emperor."

"Huh," Butch said. "Who do you pray to?"

"Hachiman," Kazeta said. "God of warriors. Protector . . . of Japan."

"You could use him now," Butch said.

"We failed him," Kazeta said. "That is why he . . . scorns us. We will learn, not to take war . . . lightly."

Butch nodded. "Tell me about the sword."

Kazeta sat leaning against a palm tree, and picked at his teeth with a sliver of bamboo. "Sword very old."

"That's all? Tell me all about it. Practice your English."

"Say please," Kazeta said, concentrating on the L sound.

Butch furrowed his brow. *"Onegai . . . she . . . shimasu."*

"Yoku dekimashita," Kazeta said, and scratched his tanned back against the palm. "Very good." He looked across the water, and his eyes went far away.

THE SWORD HAD BEEN FORGED BY MASAMUNE, the greatest of all Japanese swordmakers. A priest whose identity was lost to legend and time, his blades were the finest of cutters. He took no wife, and committed himself to the craft of the sword, taking on students in his later years. The most gifted was a slender young boy named Muramasa, whose father left him at Masamune's forge one morning with nothing but a stack of gold *ryo*.

The boy spoke little but obeyed without question, and soon became Masamune's favorite apprentice. When he became a journeyman and hammered his own blades, his edges quickly surpassed even the master's in sharpness.

A Masamune blade would slice a falling leaf in two after splitting ten tatami mats rolled to mimic the resistance of a human torso. Muramasa would dab his blades with nectar, to demonstrate how a butterfly lighting upon the edge was cut in twain. Soon the garden sparkled with their iridescent corpses.

"I prefer their wings in the trees," Masamune said.

The young students who cleaved to Muramasa told him the old master was jealous of his talent. When ambitious samurai came looking for swords, Muramasa thrust his blade into the nearby stream, where it glimmered like minnow scales. The water roiled, and two halves of a snakehead pike swirled to the surface, riding a slick of blood.

"There is more to a blade than cutting," Masamune said, but many young samurai disagreed. Muramasa swords became famous, and he left to create his own smithy. When the *daimyo* in charge of the prefecture rode into battle against an aggressive neighbor, he did so with a Muramasa blade.

His horse returned riderless. The sword had broken on the helmet of his enemy.

The sons of the *daimyo* razed Muramasa's forge to the ground and dragged him to the square to be boiled alive. Masamune pleaded for mercy, that his student be granted the honorable death of suicide by *seppuku*. The sons scoffed. *Seppuku* was only for samurai. Masamune argued that one who had dedicated his life to the sword should die by it. Would it not be fitting?

The sons convened. "You will be his second," the eldest said. "And his head will rot on a spear outside our castle."

Masamune bowed deeply in thanks. "Allow me one week to make a sword for the purpose."

In one week's time, Muramasa would kneel before them and open his belly with a sharp blade. As second, Masamune's duty was to sever his head. However headstrong and misguided Muramasa had become, Masamune had raised the young man like his own. He had failed to give the boy peace. He would grant him a swift and peaceful death.

He prayed to Hachiman, the god of warriors, and set to work on his greatest blade. He smelted the ore from iron-sand and clamshells. He forged the blade long into the night. Hammering into it his sadness for failing his adoptive son, loathing for having been blinded by pride, and the raw pain of duty and honor tearing his heart in two. He polished the blade a dull silver and fitted it to a simple iron guard and cord-wrapped handle without decoration. For the sake of his adopted son's neck, he sharpened the edge until it would cut a falling hair.

The night before the execution he visited Muramasa's cell, flanked by many guards. The sword hung at his side in its deep black scabbard. When they reached the dungeon, they found it littered with bodies and the iron stench of blood. Muramasa had escaped, and the guards lay slaughtered at their posts.

"Did Masamune hunt him down?" Butch asked.

"No," Kazeta said. "Masamune commit *seppuku*. Suicide, with own sword." He held up the blade. It seemed to soak up the sun. "Seishin Chokudo, youngest son of the *daimyo,* take sword. Become shogun. Never lose battle. Very . . . honorable. Muramasa never seen again. Make sword for *shinobi.*"

"What's that mean?"

"Shadow warrior," Kazeta said. "Spy. Never see. Ghost, in darkness. Black Dragon."

"Why do they want the sword?" Butch asked. "It sounds like a jinx. Bad luck."

"Muramasa's escape was . . . greatest treachery . . . committed by Gantetsu clan. Clan Gantetsu become . . . *Kokuryukai.* Black Dragon."

"That's some *ii desu* English, *nakama.* We get off this island, I promise I won't let those shitbirds get the sword."

"What mean . . . shit bird?"

Butch chuckled. "A shitbird's . . . well, a shitbird. They can't do shit right. They're uh, as good as bird shit. On your head."

Kazeta nodded and laughed. "Black Dragons, they are shit of big bird."

35.

TARA AND MIKIO DROVE STRAIGHT THROUGH to Wyoming before they swung into a truck stop to scrub off the road stink. Tara bought a sack of foil-wrapped cheeseburgers and a six-pack of Cokes from a roadstand, and they took turns at the wheel: four hours driving, four hours sleeping under the quilt in back, four hours shooting the shit and searching the radio for rock 'n' roll. They had chased a fuzzy station blaring honky tonk all the way through Nevada when Mikio swerved into the black desert down an off-ramp labeled 'Gerlach.'

"We low on gas?" Tara said, yawning.

"No," Mikio said.

"Then why're we pulling off the interstate?"

"Hot spring," Mikio said. "Good for you."

"Pfft. You just want to see me in a wet t-shirt. What would your wife say?"

"Wife want see them, too." Mikio laughed. "Take picture."

Tara walloped his shoulder. "Pull over. I'll hitchhike."

"Joke, joke." He followed a curve around dead black mountains, toward a cluster of businesses. "San Francisco . . . dangerous, maybe. Need rest first."

They bought overpriced swimsuits at a convenience store up the road from the steam-kettle pond. A silver dollar of shining water in the dull gray wasteland. They sank to their necks in the natural cauldron and let the heat seep through their bones to melt the aches away.

"I hope Reeves isn't getting killed while we're boiling our butts,"

Tara said.

"They want kill Reeves, they shoot. He is good fighter. Takehiko want him alive." Mikio windmilled his left arm until the shoulder popped.

"Your English is getting better," Tara said. She stretched under the steaming water, white as a freckled ghost.

"Learn in school," Mikio said. "No use, it get . . . rusty."

"Who are we meeting in Frisco?"

"Akashi Uchida. Old fighter, run school in Little Osaka. He get us passport, fly Japan. There, many friend. Find sword."

"And Reeves," Tara said. "Right?"

Mikio nodded.

"Then let's go," she said, and climbed out of the water. A stylized heart with a racing slick burning rubber in the center marked the pale field of her gas-pedal thigh. The words "Heart Like a Wheel" scrolled beneath.

"Nice ink," Mikio said.

"You betcha."

Mikio shadow-boxed while Tara dried off. His punches snapped the water droplets from his ropey forearms.

Tara took the wheel and kept the speedometer pinned on the straightaways until they left the desert and crossed the Golden Gate into the city. Mikio called out directions from a gas station map as they navigated San Francisco's labyrinth. They parked next to a ringed concrete tower with a corkscrew on top. A sign named it Peace Plaza.

"Wait here," Mikio said, and slipped out the door before she could kill the engine. He jogged up the street.

"Dammit," Tara said. She took Johansson's magnum from the glove box, checked the cylinder, and tucked its nickel barrel under her AC/DC t-shirt. She padded after Mikio as he disappeared into a dojo with a sign in Japanese out front.

The building crouched in a strip mall between a yakitori joint peddling fried meat on skewers and a tax preparer's office. The sign read Iron Dove Fighting in small letters beneath the brushed ink symbols. Tara leaned on a palm tree out front. Inside, men sparred in white karate uniforms on red mats. A bald man with thick legs, who looked as rough and scarred as Mikio or Reeves, casually walked between students and corrected them with quick taps of his thick hands.

Mikio kicked his shoes off in the lobby and half-bowed at the edge of the mats. He stepped around students punching square burlap pillows nailed to the walls, slapped his chest and gestured at the teacher in the universal language of challenge.

The teacher responded in kind. The two fighters circled. The students slowly drifted closer, staring in disbelief. A tall blond surfer boy jabbed a finger at Mikio.

Mikio side-stepped and planted a palm in the surfer's chest that sent him sprawling on his back. The teacher snapped a kick to Mikio's thigh and their hands blurred in a flurry of strikes. The students made a circle around them. Mikio held his position, and the teacher kept moving, looking for weakness.

Mikio shot for a leg and took a knee to the ribs and an elbow to the shoulder before they plowed through the white-robed students like bowling pins. Mikio landed with his knee on the teacher's belly, and students crowded around as the two masters traded blows. Mikio's hand whipped like a snake, hitting one student in the crotch and another under the arm, leaving the men gasping.

A student ran for the weapons rack and took a wooden sword off the wall. The teacher rolled to his feet. Two students grabbed Mikio's arms and got elbows in their bellies, but not before Mikio took the teacher's kick in the gut. He grunted and trapped the leg, chopping the back of the knee, sweeping a forearm into the teacher's chest and taking him back to the ground. Mikio raised his fist and a blast cracked through the room.

A burlap *makiwara* punching bag exploded, showering the brawlers with unhulled rice. Students gaped and rubbed their ears. Tara swept the room with the magnum's barrel.

"Get your karate chopping asses face-down on the floor."

The students complied.

"We friends, *Akane-chan*." Mikio raised his hands. "We just fool around." He helped the teacher to his feet.

"In other words, chill," the teacher said with a grimace, and wiggled a pinky finger into his ear.

"Uchida-san, this Tara," Mikio said.

"You fighters are crazy," Tara said, and tucked the revolver away. "Every one of you."

Uchida bowed, a grin beneath his sparse moustache. His face was streamlined, vaguely serpentine. "Lucky that's a brick wall," he said, and shook his head. "We're crazy?"

The students stood up warily. Uchida waved them off. "We're closing for the day. Let's keep this quiet, okay?"

The blond student bowed to Uchida and whispered, "How would I defend against this, sensei?"

"Which one?" Uchida said. "The fighter several time zones out of your league, or the gun?"

"Uh . . . both?"

Uchida smirked. "Sometimes you run."

36.

UCHIDA LIVED ON THE THIRD FLOOR of a condo in Telegraph Hill with a postage stamp–sized garden terrace and a view of the bay. The stainless steel kitchen was split from the spartan living room by a butcher block island with copper pans dangling above. Tara and Mikio followed Uchida into an office with boxes of paperwork stacked to the walls, surrounding a desk with a compact computer workstation, photo printer, leather sewing needle, pens and ink.

"Two non-biometric passports," Uchida said, and picked up a large Nikon camera from atop a box. "Forgery is still an art, but now it is mostly done with computers."

They each posed in turn, and Uchida printed out their tiny photographs onto pages cut from existing passports. "Your new name is Jin Watanabe," he said, examining the page with a jeweler's loupe.

Mikio grunted.

"And you'll be Kyra Bloustein," Uchida said, picking a passport from a stack.

"That looks completely fake," Tara said, frowning at the photo printed over the original.

Uchida smiled. "It won't when I'm done with it."

Tara and Mikio drank bottles of Anchor Steam on the terrace while Uchida painted a false luster onto their photographs, and restored the golden eagle hologram with meticulous strokes.

Uchida sewed the pages back into the passports over another beer. Then he sandwiched the pages between sheets of crumpled tin foil, wrapped them in a towel and set an iron atop them on low.

"They have to dry for an hour," Uchida said, and carried a six-pack onto the terrace. "Let's relax. Some jerk bruised my ribs."

They sipped crisp ale in the cool breeze and watched the green parrots flutter from one perch to another. Uchida offered Tara his Santa Cruz Banana Slugs hoodie. "It gets colder than people think."

"I'm from Minnesota," she said, and took a sip of beer. "This is a heat wave."

Uchida reached out and squeezed Mikio's stub of a pinky finger. "You really went deep cover."

Mikio shrugged.

"So Takehiko finally made a move," Uchida said. "You know why?"

"Talk to angry old men." He switched to Japanese, and Uchida nodded.

Tara said. "Hey. What's Zainichi? Are you talking about me?"

Uchida chuckled. "No, just things difficult to explain with Mikio's limited English." He gestured at Mikio with the bottle. "*Paizuri tatsujin* was more interested in our English teacher's breasts than her lessons."

Mikio shrugged, and took a slug of beer.

"We're talking about . . . nationalists," Uchida said. "Japan has many old enmities with Korea. Some fools want war."

"With North Korea? That Kim guy's crazy."

"Both Koreas. Like I said, old feuds long past making sense. The Zainichi are Koreans living in Japan. They get treated the same way anti-immigrant Americans treat Mexicans: illegal until proven innocent, lazy, and probably up to no good. And many yakuza gangsters are Zainichi, so that doesn't help. After the War, some embraced the future, others dream of a mythical past. Some want the Emperor to return to power and challenge China for the rule of Asia."

"Good luck," Tara said. "I think you're outnumbered."

"Plus they have the bomb," Uchida said. "And plenty of justifiable hatred for what Japan did in the war. But you can't argue with fanatics. They think a return to the Shogunate would make Japan invincible."

"The Masamune," Mikio said. "Takehiko found the *Honjo Masamune*."

Uchida nodded. "That makes sense. It was lost in the War, and symbolizes all the glory we had before it. The greatest treasure from the Kamamura era. With it, we defeated the Mongol horde. Takehiko wants it to get the nationalists behind him. But why? He's never been interested in anything but money and fighting. He made his father rich, running brothels and underground fight clubs." Uchida rubbed his chin. "Could the Black Dragons profit from war with Korea? The North fired another missile over Hokkaido. Tensions are pretty high."

"Black Dragons always . . . profit from chaos," Mikio said. "Takehiko grandfather, Matsuhiro Gantetsu, rose from shadow during the War. Maybe Takehiko want same."

"This shit's too complicated," Tara said, and drained her beer. "I should quit while I'm ahead. If I had somewhere else to go, I'd ditch your ass."

"Mikio doesn't have an ass." Uchida chuckled. "It's flat as a board. Look at it."

Mikio frowned. "No talk about my ass."

Uchida grinned. "I make my friend uncomfortable."

"He not *gay,*" Mikio said, and turned to Tara with a sneer. "I see Uchida with many, many women." He tipped back his bottle.

Uchida shrugged. "I got better."

Inside, Uchida pored over the passports one more time. "This will get you into Japan. I'm not guaranteeing them for a return trip. These weren't stolen, but the original owners might find their way into the Federal prison system. So they could generate a hit with customs on the way home."

"Great," Tara said.

"You like Japan," Mikio said. "Good food, fast cars."

"And the sexiest men in the world," Uchida said. "You have tickets?"

Mikio waved a hand at the computer impatiently. "Put on my bill."

Uchida sat and space-barred the screen to life. "It's a pretty big bill, *Paizuri*."

"Very big," Mikio grunted. "And thick." He peered at an ornate wakizashi shortsword on a shelf.

Uchida rolled his eyes, and tapped his way to a travel website.

"*Paizuri* means warrior, right?" Tara asked.

"Hardly." Uchida sniggered. "It's something teenage boys call each other."

"What about *Oppai desu Akane*?"

Uchida went red-faced and sniggered. "That means Big Tits Red."

Tara kicked Mikio in his non-existent ass.

UCHIDA BOOKED THEM ON A DIRECT RED-EYE to Narita airport. Tara suggested they ditch the car in long term parking and wait in the lounge, but Uchida insisted on cooking dinner. They ate seared yellowtail over wilted greens and watched the sun fizzle into the bay like a scoop of vanilla in an orange soda.

"Come inside and I'll put on some coffee," Uchida said.

He tweaked a gleaming espresso maker and produced three bitter cups.

Mikio frowned at the handle of the magnum sticking from Tara's pocket. "Can't take that on plane."

"I'll hang onto it for you," Uchida said.

She handed it to him. "Thanks."

Uchida's smile faded as his fingers closed around the checkered grip.

Mikio's ears twitched. He turned and saw dark shapes flip over the rail onto the balcony.

"Relax, old friend," Uchida said, snaking an arm around Tara's throat, jamming the pistol into her ribs.

"You piece of shit," Tara choked.

"I had no choice," Uchida said. "They have the Shadow Shogun."

Three black-clad ninja padded through the sliding doors in split-toed *tabi*. They wore no masks. Hard-faced Japanese all. One produced zip ties, another held a gleaming syringe. The third hefted a cattle prod.

"We are sons of Hachiman," Mikio growled. "We fight!"

"Make this easy, Mikio," Uchida said. "It's you for him."

The trio closed in. One ninja gripped Mikio's wrist, and the other held the prod inches from his face. Current sizzled between the prod's electrodes.

When the man looked down to cinch the restraints, Mikio slammed his forehead into the ninja's cheekbone and slapped the cattle prod into his neck. The ninja screamed, and all four fighters— Mikio included—jerked back with the electric jolt.

Mikio spun drew the wakizashi from the wall. He parried the cattle prod, then dived behind the kitchen island and rolled to his feet.

"The Shogun is too important!" Uchida shouted. "Remember your duty!"

The ninja with the syringe stabbed it into the sofa and snapped open a telescoping steel baton. He nodded to his comrade and they rushed the island from either side.

Tara ground her chin into Uchida's forearm to bite, but he tightened his grip and cut off her air. She clawed for his groin and he laughed. "You think this is Hollywood, big-tit bitch?"

Mikio snagged a cleaver from the knife block with his off hand and hurled it into the cattle prodder's shoulder. The man skidded to his ass on the tiles, clutching the wound. Mikio hopped over the fallen ninja, took a club strike to the ribs, and turned to trade blows with the baton wielder, their weapons clanging off the hanging pots and pans.

Uchida aimed the revolver and shouted angrily in Japanese.

Tara fell with all her weight and pulled Uchida off balance. The shot pierced three copper pans, which clattered to the tile floor.

"You made me pull the trigger, you stupid bitch!" Uchida growled, and wrestled Tara to her feet.

Mikio ducked behind the island while his opponent took the moment to snap out a second steel baton. He charged, twirling his weapons in a whirlwind of fury.

The head-butted ninja wobbled to his feet, his hair spiking in all directions from the electric shock.

Mikio rolled over the butcher block and sprang toward the office, pushing the woozy ninja into his pursuer's path. The baton-wielding ninja swatted his comrade aside.

Uchida let Tara thud to the floor. She gripped his arm and wrapped her legs around his ankle.

"They want Mikio alive, not you," Uchida snapped, and jabbed the revolver into Tara's chest. "Settle your tits before I blast them off."

She released him, her face twisted with rage. "Why didn't you just poison us!"

"Mikio can do more damage as a captive," Uchida hissed under his breath. "If you haven't noticed he's a walking shitstorm."

Mikio yanked the matching katana off the wall and whipped his wrist, sailing its scabbard into Uchida's head. He traded blows with the ninja. Blades and batons rang as he drove his opponent back.

Uchida rubbed his temple, and opened his eyes to Tara's snarling face. She roared and tackled him into the office, plowing into the stacks of banker boxes. The sagging wall of cardboard collapsed and buried them in an avalanche of paperwork.

Mikio crossed his blades to parry an overhead double baton strike, then scissored them closed and thrust both swords through the ninja's chest. The man choked out a silent curse from his two pierced lungs, and collapsed to his knees.

Mikio kicked the groaning man off his blades. He stepped for the office and the first ninja wrenched the cleaver from his shoulder with a yelp. Mikio cut him down in passing and tossed the katana to the floor on his dash after Tara.

Uchida struggled to his feet with a seething Tara hammering his side. He raised a backhand to strike her, and Mikio kicked him in the kidney and sent him to his knees. Mikio struck the nerve cluster under Uchida's arm and kneed him in the ribs with a crunch.

Uchida curled in defense, quivering in pain. "You don't know what you're doing," he wheezed.

"*Baka iunayo!*" Mikio shouted at Uchida, and helped Tara to her feet. "Get passports!"

Tara ran into the living room.

Uchida groaned and clutched his side. "You'll get Mitsuru killed."

"Sons of Hachiman *fight*," Mikio said. "If he dies, he dies with honor." He raised the blade to strike.

Uchida did not flinch or waver.

Mikio snarled and punched the door jamb. The wood shivered under his fist.

"I'm sorry, brother," Uchida said. "You have a father. I have Mitsuru."

Mikio grunted.

"There are more coming," Uchida said. "You should run. I'll take care of them."

"Don't do favor!" Mikio shouted back.

"Got my passport," Tara said, stuffing them into her jeans. "Can't find yours. Do you think they'll even work?"

"I wouldn't betray my art," Uchida said, probing his ribs with a thumb.

"No, only people," Tara said, and slammed the office door behind her.

As they approached the front door, feet stomped up the stairs in the condo hallway.

Mikio dropped the sword. "Out back," he said, and led Tara by the wrist.

The last shocked and battered ninja sat up with a groan. Mikio yanked a baton from a corpse's hand and cold-cocked him on the way to the terrace.

MIKIO SLID DOWN THE NINJA'S NYLON ROPE with Tara on his back and the baton clenched between his teeth. As they fled into the alley, a square head popped over the balcony rail. Lead ricocheted off the stucco walls and shell casings rained onto the garbage cans.

They ran for the Trailblazer. A jacketed Japanese man leaned against it, smoking. He dug under his coat and Mikio clubbed his arm with the baton. The bone snapped and Tara gagged. The man winced and stumbled to his knees. Mikio pushed him aside and climbed in.

An explosion shook the block and Mikio ducked behind the passenger door. Uchida's windows belched smoke, and shattered glass peppered the sidewalk. The square-headed man from the balcony stepped out of the lobby. Pock-marked cheeks and a flat-top as well-trimmed as a putting green. He reached beneath his sleeveless fatigue jacket.

"Drive fast!" Mikio said, and hung onto the oh-shit handle. The truck was sandwiched in by Mini Coopers. Tara floored the pedal and bullied the truck forward with a crunch of safety glass. They squealed away while a rattle of suppressed gunfire echoed off the buildings and rounds slapped the tailgate.

"Which way to the airport?" Tara shouted, swerving around a double-parked delivery van.

"How fuck I know?"

They approached a red light and Tara stomped on the brakes. The oncoming lane was crammed with traffic. "Get the damn map."

Mikio clawed at the glove compartment. From behind them came the whine of a turbocharger and a burbling exhaust note. A purple Toyota Supra shrieked to a stop two cars back. The brick-like Japanese man popped from the passenger window and casually aimed a machine pistol fitted with a fat silencer as long as his tattooed forearm.

"Go sidewalk!" Mikio shouted, and cupped Tara's neck, pulling her head down and shielding her with his body.

Tara screamed in protest, flooring the pedal and one-arming the wheel. The truck's windows exploded and the yellow padding burst from her seat's headrest.

The truck plowed between parked cars and the wagon in front of them, shedding the passenger mirror and resculpting the sheet metal. She roared through the intersection and tires screamed. Tara peeked and saw traffic at a dead stop ahead of them. She leaned on the horn and jumped the curb. Pedestrians belly flopped onto parked cars and flattened against buildings as they passed. She took out a wrought iron fence and swerved onto a cross street, dragging their front bumper.

Tara leaned to peer through an uncracked section of windshield and passed a line of traffic in the oncoming lane. Mikio leaned out the window with the baton cocked to throw until they hit the highway for the airport.

"What the hell," Tara said. "I thought he was your friend."

"Can't trust anyone," Mikio said, rolling up the window. "We fight alone."

Tara kneaded the wheel and passed on the right. "This is too much," she said. "I just want to hide somewhere safe."

"Nowhere safe," Mikio said. "Black Dragons find you."

"They don't seem so tough for you."

Mikio chuckled. "I am bad ass," he said, and thumped his chest. "My people are last samurai. Kick ninja ass one hand, drink beer other!"

"Then why are we running?"

"Samurai know when retreat," Mikio said.

37.

THE RHYTHM OF THE MASSIVE DIESEL ENGINE thrummed in the belly of the ship like the heartbeat of the earth. The Black Dragons had locked him in with a case of bottled water, emergency rations from one of the lifeboats, and a plastic bucket for his waste. Reeves trained in the dark of the empty cargo container.

He measured his days by the brief sliver of sunlight that lasered across his rectangular cell. It only lasted the duration of a round or two. He quit his workout, grabbed the stack of Butch's letters, and picked up where he'd left off.

The invasion of his dead grandparents' privacy twisted like a worm in his gut. They had been private people. Reeves remembered sneaking home past curfew, some years after his parents died in the wreck, to see the silhouette of Butch and Grandma Jean in the front window. Butch wobbled on one leg and held Jean in his arms, swaying to Hank Williams crooning "Setting the Woods on Fire."

They kissed. And more. Reeves curled up to sleep on the porch rather than disturb them. An hour or so later, Grandma Jean opened the door. She wore her nightgown and a broad grin. She told him to get inside before he caught cold. Reeves ran inside with his heart thumping and cheeks red, for spying on their private romance.

Reading their letters felt the same.

He only gave in when he went loopy in the dark, unable to tell if he was asleep or awake. He opened his eyes to a grim face lit by the cherry of a Lucky Strike. Young Butch, with both legs and a full

212

head of hair slick with Vitalis.

"You really tripped over your dick this time," Butch said. "You got plenty of heart, but you have mule shit for brains. I told you charging like a mad bull and swinging like a freight train would only get you so far."

Reeves fought to respond. His mouth was gluey, his throat parched.

"Don't say anything. What's there to say? You did it again. And this time you got a girl killed." Butch faded to a small floating ember as he gestured with his cigarette in the black. "You need to get your shit together. What the hell you moping for? You got a few hundred square feet of training space. Chickie's basement was smaller. And we jerry-rigged our equipment. Use your body weight. Do it until you can do a one arm handstand, and do push-ups on it like the strongman at the State Fair."

Butch's face glowed orange, older now. "Read my letters. They'll keep you sane." He stood and began walking into the darkness. "And don't expect me to pop in your head and give advice like Yoda. I don't even know who he is."

Reeves crawled after him, croaking wordless sounds.

"Besides—" Butch flashed a wicked grin. "—I'm dead. You may be crazy as a shit-house rat, but you're alive. Protect the sword. Avenge me. And stop feeling sorry for yourself. You got both legs, you sonofabitch. It's more than I had."

The cigarette grew enormous and Reeves flinched from its heat.

He woke in a slice of sunlight and tore open a bottle of water to quench his thirst. He drank it dry and threw the empty in the corner. Then he sat and opened a letter and read.

When he couldn't read, he trained. Pounding the corrugated walls until his knuckles grew flat with callus. Running the box's perimeter. Forty-four and a half feet long, seven foot eight inches wide, almost nine feet high. He lost count of the exercises. Hand-stand and one-arm pushups. Warrior lunges. Back bridges, pistol squats. Pull-ups and hanging leg raises from the edge of the ceiling beam.

He worked out until he collapsed, paying penance for his failures. He shredded until he was hard as marble.

When the diesel engine stopped, the silence hit Reeves like a mortar shell hitting camp in the middle of the night. The door clanked open and four shadows appeared in the blinding light. The sun stabbed his eyes and he fell with his palms mashed into his eye sockets. Reeves scrambled for his chamber pot bucket and heaved it at their silhouettes with a roar.

The Black Dragons looped the noose of a catch pole over Reeves' head and dragged him out of the container. He lashed at every sound. His captors choked and prodded him off the ship and into a cage in back of an unmarked van.

Reeves rubbed his eyes. The inside of the cargo van stank of cig-arettes. Horns and traffic outside sounded like a symphony after the monotony of the ship's engine. After a time the van stopped and the doors opened on a grimy, claustrophobic alley. A forklift whirred close and slipped its forks under the cage, unloading Reeves like a pallet of goods. The lift backed up the ramp of a warehouse loading bay.

Four hard men in suits followed him into stale cold air and dim fluorescent light. The forklift deposited his cage against the wall of a musty underground storage area. Other cages were spaced along the walls, and in the center loomed the largest cage of all.

A dome of chain link, spikes and iron rebar, Reeves recognized it immediately. It looked nothing like the octagon of the Ultimate Fighting Championship, or the makeshift cages he'd fought in at arenas and fight gyms and rich men's backyards. The scent of old blood, long-ago crusted into flaked black paint, told him what it was.

The biggest fight cage he'd ever seen.

38.

FROM THE RUINS OF A BUDDHIST SHRINE atop the island's small mountain, Kazeta watched ships flying the American flag thrust their prows through the harbor. Ten days ago a distant rumble shuddered through the island at noon.

Nothing since. Kazeta wondered if the war was truly over. If the Emperor would seek peace before millions threw themselves against the American guns in a great divine wind.

They had behaved like slaughterers, not warriors. So they had failed.

The divine wind did not blow.

Kamikaze no fuki sokone.

No matter who had won the war, the sword would need protection. And the best protection was secrecy. The American had been trustworthy, but might turn Kazeta in to his superiors to satisfy his sense of duty and to quench the shame of being captured. His wound made the point a moot one. Butch would likely take these secrets to his grave.

His leg had gone black with gangrene, though neither man spoke of it. The wound was too high on the leg to cut and cauterize. Butch would bleed out within seconds.

Kazeta meditated on what a Son of Hachiman should do.

He left fish skeletons where hungry sea birds could not find them.

Kazeta made his rounds of the black sand beaches, collecting seaweed and shellfish from a tidal pool. Spearing a plump cormorant for their dinner, collecting dew into leaf containers to drink, burying one manure pit and digging another. He also collected a handful of fat white maggots from the picked-clean bones of the baitfish he had piled in the shade several days earlier.

Kazeta's great-grandfather Kubota had lived in the mountains with his disgraced samurai brethren after the gunners crushed the Satsuma rebellion. There they learned to survive from the Ainu tribes who made the mountains their home. At first the aboriginal people had fled. They were considered lower even than the *buraku-min*, the lowest caste of workers, the gravediggers and butchers and dung sweepers.

But Kubota preached peace with them. He married an Ainu wife, who taught the Sons of Hachiman to disappear into the wilderness and live there undetected. To hide in plain sight like the *shinobi*, disguising his features, voice and gait.

Another such skill was healing on the move. Infected wounds meant death. Maggots would eat the diseased flesh and leave fresh pink muscle beneath.

Kazeta delicately sprinkled the slick white grubs into Butch's wound. He washed his hands in sea water and began making a small breakfast of seaweed and wild radish topped with fat chunks of buttery raw scallop. He ate with a pair of handmade chopsticks. Butch stirred awake.

Butch sat and rubbed the sleep dust from his eyes. "Good morning."

"Ohayo," Kazeta said, and handed him a folded leaf of water.

"Kentucky," Butch muttered, and sipped. He scratched his leg and glanced down at his wound. He threw the cup and made to claw out the maggots writhing in his flesh.

Kazeta snatched his wrist with a grip like iron.

"What the hell?" Butch said.

"Good for heal," Kazeta said. He released Butch's hand, and went back to his meal. He popped a quivering slice of white scallop into his mouth.

Butch gagged. "Are you crazy? Get these filthy things off me."

"Trust," Kazeta said.

Butch staggered to his feet, walking stiffly. "I have trusted you," he yelled to the trees. "I'm stuck on a damn island with a rotten leg and I'd be better off back with the crazy shitbird beating the hell out of me every night! At least the prison camp had that drunk-off-his-ass doctor!"

Butch punched the palm tree until his knuckles were bloody. He leaned against it and slid down the trunk, staring at his hands.

Kazeta offered Butch a folded leaf with his half of the meal.

"Thank you, *nakama*," Butch said, panting. "I'm sorry. I can't eat that slimy stuff first thing in the morning."

Kazeta tossed him two satsuma oranges.

"Can I at least cover up the wound? It's making me queasy," Butch said, peeling an orange.

Kazeta ate the food off the leaf, then set it over the wound.

Americans, Kazeta had learned, complained about everything. He could see why the Imperial officers loathed them so. A Japanese soldier would never debase himself as Butch had. The shame was too great. Schoolteachers said keeping face made you stronger, but Kazeta's Ainu grandmother laughed at Japanese ways. He had seen her kill a bear with a knife and cook its liver, so he knew strength came from things other than face.

"Today you gather seashells," Kazeta announced.

"Why?" Butch asked around a mouthful of orange.

"Keep mind off leg," Kazeta said, and drew the *Honjo Masamune*. He strode to a sheltered clearing and felled the few remaining stalks of bamboo within it. Then he began gathering large stones and piling them in the grass.

Butch ate his second orange. He had begun writing letters to Jean on the back of her pages. She might never receive them, but he liked to imagine her reading them even if his bones were bleached white in the Pacific sun by the time they got to her.

"Get shells," Kazeta said.

"I don't need your damn busy work. Ignoring this leg ain't gonna heal it."

Kazeta sighed. "Favor. Bring sea shell. Many."

Butch shook his head and hobbled toward their shell pile.

Kazeta gathered more stones. The island was a small mountaintop of crumbling basalt. Its beaches were black with magnetic sand. The rich soil was thick with trees and green. Kazeta lugged every brick-shaped stone to the clearing until he had enough to build a wall, one that would make good neighbors. He built a small beehive of the stones while Butch amused himself with the pile of shells.

"Here's a pretty one," Butch said, holding up a purple moon scallop, which resembled a small lady's fan. "Can I make a necklace?"

Kazeta ignored him and began cutting down a large tree with the *tanto* knife. He wished they'd brought a hatchet, but soon it would not matter. He stacked his logs inside the beehive, then soaked branches in palm oil and stacked a teepee of kindling atop the logs. He lit it with a waterproof match, coaxed the fire to life, and removed one of the bricks to make a chimney.

"You making a fireplace? I thought they'd see the smoke."

Kazeta hefted a bamboo bucket of iron sand and poured it into a crucible of cracked basalt. He threw in a double handful of shells and smashed them to shards with a bamboo pestle.

Butch squinted at the fire, tapping the purple shell against his palm. "Mind telling me what this is all about? You gonna bake us a cake?"

Kazeta snatched the scallop shell from Butch's hand and crushed it into the mess of black sand.

"Hey!"

Kazeta set the stone bowl into the forge. He picked up two long bamboo tubes and thrust one into Butch's hands.

"Blow."

Kazeta aimed the bamboo pipe under blazing logs and puffed hard into the other end. The flames flared white-hot.

"Not make cake," Kazeta said. He ran his fingers through the black sand. "This . . . *satetsu*. Make iron."

"If I had something better to do," Butch said, "I'd tell you to go pound this sand into a rat hole."

He filled his lungs and bellowed the blaze white hot.

39.

TARA DUMPED THE TRUCK in long term parking and tossed the keys down a storm drain. Inside the terminal, she tugged Mikio's elbow and veered toward baggage claim. "Hustle, amigo. Our flight leaves in forty minutes, and we need luggage."

"Why?" Mikio said.

"We'll stand out with no bags. Probably get cavity searched," Tara said. She wriggled her fingers. "Elbow deep up the ying-yang."

Mikio sneered. "Okay."

Tara scanned the conveyors, ticking off bags that made the circle a few times without being taken. She snagged two plain black rolling pullmans and a Louis Vuitton valise.

Mikio grunted and stuck his grandfather's knife into one of the bags. "Need passport."

Tara marched him toward international arrivals. "Can you pick pockets?"

"No."

Tara chewed her lip, and walked faster. "Maybe I can."

From the crowd of chauffeurs holding hand-printed signs, they waited as a group of Japanese businessmen herded down the escalators. A slim young Asian man trailed behind, thumbing his phone. Tara pushed the valise into Mikio's hands. "Stay put," she said, and tied off the corner of her t-shirt, snugging the fabric taut over her chest.

Tara intercepted the young man broadsides with her prow and his eyes went wide. Mikio chuckled to himself. Then his hackles rose.

He took cover behind a concrete pillar and swept the crowd in his peripherals. He caught the hard cheekbones and balanced gait of a fighter, then lost him. The man Tara was vamping shouted and hurried away.

"Just leave me alone, lady!"

Two security officers converged on her. Both bald. One Latino, one black.

As Mikio stepped to intervene, his hackles flared. He sidestepped to avoid a squat Filipino lunging with a butterfly knife. The blade gouged the concrete support.

Mikio smashed his elbow into the man's knife arm and wrenched back his wrist, driving the attacker behind the pillar. The man snapped a knee at Mikio's groin, and Mikio checked it with his own, pinning the knifer's thigh against his own belly, driving him to the floor.

The man's elbow crunched like a dog gnawing soup bones. Mikio cut off his scream with a knee under the jaw. He eased to the floor with his shin across the man's throat, and peeled his fingers off the knife. Mikio swung the blade closed and rifled through his attacker's pockets. The man's eyes fluttered shut.

The man had no passport. His driver's license said his name was Arnel Weng, and the young photo barely resembled the face beneath Mikio's knee. Mikio left the knife and license on the man's chest and stuffed the valise under his head like a pillow.

"Ma'am," the black officer repeated. "We're gonna need to see some identification."

Tara handed the officer her passport. "I'm looking for my friend, that's all."

Mikio jogged over with a big smile and their luggage in tow. *"Konbanwa!"*

"Sir, please stand back," the Latino officer said, and extended a palm while his partner scrutinized Tara's passport.

"Kore wa watashi no yujin wa oppai akagedesu," Mikio said, and hugged Tara tight. *"Kanojo wa, Gorden Gaeto bur-idge, o mite watashi o totte iru!"*

"This is him," Tara said, forcing a laugh as she pushed Mikio's face out of her cleavage. "We met online. See the resemblance?"

"Not really," the officer said, and handed Tara her passport. "Next time, take no for an answer."

Mikio nattered in Japanese, and lifted Tara off her feet. "I miss so much!"

They exited hand in hand, weaving through the crowd, feeling the officers' stares. The tattooed yakuza tracked them with a suppressed MAC-10 from the Supra parked in the passenger pickup area. He slung the weapon under his coat, pulling the fabric to cover the stick magazine.

"We got company," Tara said. She shielded herself behind Mikio as they ducked into ticketing.

"I know," Mikio said. "Get on plane."

"What about you?"

"They kill Uchida," Mikio said. "They die."

"He betrayed us," Tara said. "What do you care?"

"Still Son of Hachiman," Mikio said, and slipped into the crowd.

"If you shoot up the place they'll lock the place down and ground all flights." Tara wheeled their bags toward the security line.

Mikio caught the yakuza's eye and jerked his head in challenge. The gunman regarded him through blacked-out glasses, then nodded. Mikio entered the men's room, and the yakuza peeled off to follow.

A big man in shorts and sandals stood at a urinal. Only the large handicapped toilet stall door was closed. Mikio quickly pulled the other stall doors shut, then stood next to the bearded man at the urinal and pointed at his penis.

"You very big," Mikio said and unzipped. "Mine bigger."

"Fucking weirdo," the man said, stumbling backward and urinating on the floor. He zipped up and hurried out, his luggage bouncing behind him. He stopped at the exit to shout, "You give this town a bad name!"

Mikio sank at the knees, getting his legs springy.

"Your boyfriend's waiting," the big man bellowed in the hallway.

Mikio hit the hand dryer buttons on his way to the entrance. When the yakuza skidded around the corner against the wall, Mikio had already launched into a sprint. He hit the fat silencer with his knee and mashed the barrel against the yakuza's chest. The gunman flattened to the wall, his arms tied up in the weapon's strap and trigger guard. A burst of rounds turned ceiling tiles to confetti and pelted Mikio's face with hot brass casings before he jammed his thumb behind the trigger guard.

The yakuza head-butted him. Mikio grunted and struggled for the gun. The man reared back to butt him again. Mikio thumbed the magazine release and yanked the 30-round stick free, clubbing the yakuza across the temple. The man rolled with it and kicked out Mikio's leg.

Mikio fell to his knees and blocked two blows of the gun barrel. The yakuza spun behind him and choked him with the submachine gun under his chin. The yakuza's forearms bulged with effort. Mikio's jaw crunched. He fought against the gun. Pieces of shredded ceiling tile fell around them like snowflakes.

It was only an air choke. Something Mikio had trained to fight through while other Japanese children traded baseball cards and jabbed each other's behinds in games of *kancho*.

Mikio reached up and jerked the trigger.

The MAC-10 fired the round in its chamber and hot gas seared the yakuza's hand through the ejection port. The bolt slammed closed on the stump of the yakuza's ritually shortened little finger. Mikio blasted up to his feet and slammed the yakuza in the chin with the back of his head.

Mikio spun and kicked him through the doors of the handi-capped stall. The yakuza landed ass-first on the toilet. Mikio leapt and straddled his lap, punched his nose flat with two fast jabs, then stabbed the steel magazine into his eye socket. The man's head lolled forward, blood oozing from the mouth.

In the dead man's pocket, Mikio found a roll of twenty dollar bills clipped to a rumpled Japanese passport. He took both and slammed the stall door shut behind him.

Mikio trudged toward the door. A spike-haired Japanese man burst into the hallway, drawing a small pistol. Mikio forearmed him across the throat and snapped his neck before he hit the tile floor.

Mikio tossed the handgun into the trash can on his way out. The hand dryers whined to a stop.

40.

REEVES SPENT HIS DAYS keeping fit in the cage and eating chunky bowls of *chankonabe,* chicken on the bone swimming in broth and noodles. Soon he was performing one arm pull-ups and push-ups, pistol squats and hanging leg raises with ease. Exercises he once used to show off in the Corps he now performed in countless repetitions.

His neighbors were an enormous sumo wrestler, a beefy yakuza tattooed from head to toe, and a dozen fighters of every weight class. They were given fight shorts and fed three bowls a day. They woke to a guard hitting the cage bars with a shock baton for their first meal. Then they were led out in threes to a gym, guarded by two bored chain-smoking yakuza with spiked hair and machine pistols slung from their shoulders.

The weight room was state of the art, crammed with top of the line equipment. A shell-shocked pretty-boy trainer sat on a stool and gave direction in lightly accented English.

"You fight in two weeks," the trainer said. "To the death."

Reeves had carved himself to scarred marble on the boat ride over. He nodded, then hit the weight pile to pack on more muscle.

He had built a wall in his mind when he joined the Corps. There was fighting, and there was killing.

First day of MCMAP training—Marine Corps Martial Arts Program—the gunny taunted the biggest and baddest to step up and be made an example. The recruits had all seen that movie before, the one where the drill instructor flings the big gorilla around like a ragdoll to show just how bad-ass they'll all be if they were declared Marines.

Reeves stepped up and threw a wild haymaker to make the instructor commit to a sweep, then shot for his leg for a takedown, passed to mount and scissored his forearms over the big black man's throat.

D.I. Dunlap kept his stony expression throughout the choke, and tapped out gracefully. When Reeves relented, the D.I. told him to wipe the shit-eating grin off his face. Then he made Reeves his assistant martial arts instructor.

Reeves had wanted a week in the brig, not a promotion. Butch's disappointed face still stung in his mind, and he didn't see himself as a soldier. More of a professional fuck-up. But D.I. Dunlap refused to allow Reeves that escape route. He drove Reeves to challenge himself at every turn, to drag the other recruits along with him, and to teach the most useless shitbird how to throw an opponent and take command of their weapon. Reeves breezed through basic and plowed through Advanced Infantry training like a rhino with a lightning bolt suppository.

After graduation a grizzled Brigadier General and old friend of Butch offered Reeves a spot with the Embassy Guard Battalion.

"Thank you, sir," Reeves said. "But no thank you. I didn't train this hard to babysit spooks and diplomats."

The BG smirked. "Your grandfather fought under my old man," the axe-nosed man said. "He was some soldier. I understand you wanting to follow his footsteps, but I think you underestimate the situation in Libya. It wouldn't be a picnic. And you'd make good contacts, for when you come home."

"I appreciate it, but I wouldn't be able to live with myself, sir."

"Okay then. You want combat, you can babysit Army convoys instead. They need us devil dogs to keep the insurgents running scared. Consider your wish granted."

◆ ◆

CLEARING HOUSES IN FALLUJAH, Reeves learned that even a shorty M4 rifle was a liability in enclosed spaces. Inside were two insurgents with one AK. His training kicked in and he plugged the armed man with a three round burst. The second tackled him, and pinned the M4 against Reeves' throat like a crowbar.

Reeves locked the man's legs in guard and torqued his hips, ramming the tango's head into the stone wall. He yanked the man's arm around his own throat and sank in a cobra choke.

He heard the roar of a crowd that wasn't there. His comrades shouted over the din in his head. *Snap his neck, Reeves! Snap it!*

PFC Jenkins drilled a hole in the insurgent's forehead and chunked the wall with his brains. Reeves untangled his arms and kicked the twitching corpse away.

"What, you waiting for him to tap?" Jenkins laughed, eyes glinting behind his combat goggles.

Reeves blushed and retrieved his rifle, just in time for another shooter to pop Jenkins through the neck.

Killing with guns was easy. But people, they were supposed to tap. Or get beat until their corner threw the towel. That was what Rage Cage Reeves did. Hammer or choke you until it was done. The leash, however invisible, had always been on.

Now he was loose with the mad dogs, and had to teach himself to kill.

In his head there was the cage, and there was combat.

Now they would be one and the same.

A BLIND MASSEUR KNEADED REEVES' SHOULDERS after his workout. The trainer took his payment in illegal steroids and was escorted away. That left two guards, watching Reeves as if he were a tiger at their watering hole. He could heave a dumbbell through one gunner's skull, but the other one would cut him in half.

There was only one way to Takehiko.

Through the deathmatch.

Reeves thanked the masseur and left the gym. He snapped a roundhouse kick at the heavy bag as he passed. The bag bent in half, barely wobbling with the blow.

Just like Butch and Chickie had taught him. Put all the force into the target.

"When you throw a good punch, it feels like hitting marshmallows," Butch said, echoing O'Neill's words from fifty years earlier. "That's how you know all the power hit the other guy."

Back in his cage, Reeves listened to his future victims breathe.

The yakuza dragged in a new friend with their mid-day meal. A hooded fighter whose legs looked like they'd been grafted on from a much stronger man. Covered in bruises old and new, and a crest of three swirling blades tattooed on his shoulder.

The guard glared at Reeves with his unswollen eye and shoved a food bowl through the bars quick.

"Keep your thumb out of my slop, shitbird," Reeves said, and snagged the soup.

The cage door clanged shut. The fighters slurped until their spoons scraped empty bowls.

"Tomorrow you fight to the death," the guard said and laughed. "I will feed your body to the dogs."

"We'll see who gets fed to who," Reeves said.

He felt nothing. Inside and out.

41.

THE SHADOW SHOGUN POURED TEA while Takehiko held the *Honjo Masamune* in the rays of the morning sun. The house was constructed in the old style atop cliffs overlooking the Pacific, north of Tokyo. The crash of the surf and the mournful cry of seabirds were the only sounds.

"The blade won't shimmer for me," Takehiko said, admiring the sword's temper line. "I tarnished my soul to retrieve this artifact. I hope you're satisfied."

"A small price for your grandfather's soul to rest peacefully in Yasukuni shrine, is it not?" The older man pushed a stone cup to the opposite side of the table. "Drink."

The Shadow Shogun wore a traditional kimono marked with the hollyhock crest of the Tokugawa shogunate and knelt on sandaled feet as he gracefully labored through the meticulous rite. He was unnaturally lean, with a white beard and eyebrows that flowed like the crests of waves in a Hokusai woodcut. A dull red welt scored the bridge of his nose where Reeves' fist had landed. His name was Takashi Mitsuru, and he had risen through the ranks of *kempeitai* secret police to join Japanese intelligence prior to the Greater East Asian War. As a field operative, he sparred with agents of the Shanghai Municipal Police while gathering intel prior to the Japanese invasion. Then on to Burma, where he fought to deflect the damage done by Merrill's Marauders.

His greatest act of espionage occurred thousands of miles from his presence and was never uncovered as such: the deadly sabotage of the Port Chicago munitions facility on the California coast. Civilians, but a military target. Unlike the barbaric Americans, who burned entire cities as a matter of business.

Mitsuru claimed allegiance to only Japan itself, yet after the war his knowledge of Japanese military and political figures and their motives became instrumental in MacArthur's restructuring of the post-war government. Some considered it treason to work with the Occupier. Mitsuru did not. The Americans had won the war; the divine wind had failed. You could either help Japan rise from the ashes, or let your pride keep it in ruins.

His wealth proved the wisdom of his decision.

Every election, the rumors flew that he would run for prime minister. Mitsuru remained a quiet kingmaker and intelligence merchant in the gentlemen's clubs of the Ginza district, easily spotted by his traditional dress. His fellow agents and officers would attest that despite his advanced age, Mitsuru's broad consideration of possible threats made him as dangerous as a cobra, still able to inflict a deadly bite long after its head was severed.

Takehiko sheathed the blade and sat to drink. "You are certain this is the blade?"

Mitsuru ignored him and continued the tea ritual. He drank and set down his cup. "The temper line is said to be a dirge for Masamune's failed son," he said, removing a flute from the sleeve of his robe. "Shall I play it?"

Takehiko drew the silent blade, turning it until the wavy *hamon* gleamed.

Mitsuru brought the flute to his lips and played. The surf beat a slow rhythm beneath the flute's tale of sorrow. A tiny speckled seabird lighted on the railing and cocked its head.

"It is the one," Takehiko said and smiled. "Soon the last of the Sons of Hachiman will be dead. Who shall I test it upon?"

"Don't be foolish," Mitsuru said. "Carrying on the knowledge of the *shinobi* is honorable, but once you are allied with the *Uyoku dantai*, you must become a true shadow warrior." He reached into the sleeve of his robe and scattered a few grains of rice on the rail. The bird shied away with a flutter, then hopped back to peck.

Takehiko nodded. Even though the *Uyoku dantai* nationalist groups raised money through the yakuza—gangsters who had evolved from low-caste gamblers and peddlers in the Edo period—they idolized the samurai and felt that restoring the warrior caste's former glory would revive their once-great military power and bring them out of decades of economic stagnation.

"Your grandfather sought to ally the Gantetsu clan with the Emperor," Mitsuru continued. "But you will be the new, young samurai who sees that the shogunate lies not in the palace, but within the glass towers of the Kobutocho district. Wealth has always been tied to power. A good shogun provided his samurai with many *koku* of rice. Those who did not found themselves facing insurrection."

Takehiko nodded. Old men liked to repeat themselves, and see young lions nod at the supposedly new morsel of knowledge they have imparted. Takehiko considered the nationalists to be rich old fools with tons of hidden war gold, and Mitsuru a doddering patriarch. Albeit one about to cash in seven decades of secrets and owed favors for the ability to name one last king from the shadows.

Takehiko would gladly wear the crown. Not longer after he'd learned to walk, he had trained to climb walls, strike from the shadows, and snap his own neck if captured. He excelled at all of these—the last practiced on his father's enemies, of course—but the shadow warrior's greatest skill, and the one Takehiko practiced most keenly, was the ability to hide in plain sight.

"I will present the sword at the *Kumite*," Takehiko said. "The leaders are all invited. The grandson of the American who slew my grandfather is my captive, and will die in the tournament. At one warrior's hands, or if he should last until the end, I will kill him myself."

"I will give you my blessing," Mitsuru said, "and I will spread word of it in the clubs of the Ginza strip, and my admiration for your honor. Upon your election to the Diet, the Masamune will be returned, and the people may not realize it, but they will yearn for the old ways upon seeing this glimmer of our former glory. And then we can strike the *kankoku* of the North and eliminate that cultish rogue state once and for all."

Takehiko bowed. A decade ago, the Shadow Shogun's only daughter led a sabotage operation against North Korea's nuclear program along the Chinese border. Her team had been vaporized in the resulting explosion. Since then, several Black Dragons had allowed themselves to be captured by North Korean operatives. Once Takehiko was in power, the Dragons would escape and fire all of North Korea's missiles at Japan and the South.

Given their reliability, most would miss Japan. Seoul would not fare so well. Nor would the 50,000 American soldiers guarding the DMZ. With casualties of that magnitude, Japan and the United States would have no choice but to retaliate. China's financial deathgrip on the West would be released, freeing Japan to rule all of Asia once more.

"China's only strength has always been in numbers," Mitsuru said. "Their hearts follow only money. They will let the North fall, if the price is great enough."

The bird tilted its head, and Mitsuru held a grain of rice between its fingers. The bird hopped closer, then back. He set the rice close to him on the rail. The bird stared at it, unmoving.

Takehiko smiled outwardly in agreement, and inwardly at the old man's outdated opinion of the Chinese. How the old clung foolishly to the land beneath their feet. The Black Dragons had been shackled to the land of the rising sun for far too long. Takehiko's grandfather had thought bigger than all those before him, and as scion, Takehiko thought bigger still.

"What of the Sons of Hachiman?" asked the Shadow Shogun, as he poured more tea. "My sources say they have so far eluded you."

Takehiko's face turned grim. "A handful of obsolete fanatics," he said, looking out to the sea. "You overestimate them, Mitsuru-san. The Gantetsu have tracked their every move. Their greatest warrior landed in Tokyo yesterday. We have followed him ever since."

The old man watched the bird take tentative steps. "Yet he hid beneath your nose until I revealed him."

"He will die soon enough."

The old man smiled. "Does your father know that Miyamoto Mikio lives?"

Takehiko flared his nostrils. "He knows what he needs to know!"

The bird ran for the last piece of rice. Takehiko's sword flashed, and the bird fell headless onto the railing. A thin stream of crimson pooled around the single grain.

The Shadow Shogun sipped his tea. "You are far too enamored of the physical arts of *shinobi*. Someday you will learn."

Someday you will as well, old man, Takehiko thought as he cleaned the blade with his silk handkerchief.

42.

TARA SLEPT THROUGH THE MEAL SERVICE and woke ravenous and exhausted. Mikio studied the dead yakuza's passport. His own sat among a stack of Uchida's fakes at the Hachiman shrine in Akita, deep in the forest. The monks trained in secret, passing on the old ways. Protecting the Warriors of Hachiman and their families.

The back of the airline seat had a telephone in it. Mikio wished he could call his wife Yumi and hear his son's voice. But there were no phones at the temple. No electricity. Only a small village of samurai who posed as priests and farmers, who walked down the mountain to sell vegetables at the market, and on occasion, take the *shinkansen* off the island to snap a man's neck or sever it with a *katana,* when he planned to bring evil upon the world.

Tara snored quietly, her head on Mikio's shoulder. He admired her spirit, her loyalty. She reminded him of Yumi in those ways. Though his wife was much more beautiful, in his mind. A woman of iron, whose fiery heart soothed and purified him like a boiling hot bath after battle.

Their son, he promised, would be peaceful. Mikio's father served Hachiman without spilling blood. Their son would follow that path. *Our boy will grow so old he will drag his balls behind him like the tanuki,* he'd told Yumi, the night before he left for the mission. He would be gone many months. Playing the washed-up fighter, to infiltrate the *Kumite.* When Takehiko told him he would go to America to fight "Rage Cage" Reeves, Mikio continued the mission. Gathering intel for the Shadow Shogun.

Now according to Uchida, the spy master had been captured. Old Man Mitsuru had always been off limits. He was the closest they had to a national hero everyone could respect. During the war he served bravely. Yet when confronted with the atrocity of the Rape of Nanking, he informed his superiors of the disgrace it brought upon them without flinching. And it had cost him dearly.

Tojo himself had Mitsuru committed to Unit 731, the infamous bioweapons and medical experimentation program performed on Chinese and Allied prisoners of war, who the doctors called "human logs." There he was injected with tuberculosis, and caged to watch men die of bubonic plague, gangrene, and syphilis, as well as mundane forms of execution such as grenade tests and vivisection. When the war was lost, the doctor in charge of the facility, one General Ishii, destroyed the grounds and left the prisoners for dead. Mitsuru walked out of the camp a gaunt skeleton with scarred lungs that gave a faint whistle to his every breath.

Mitsuru saved what evidence he could and passed it to American agents prosecuting war crimes. He was not surprised when nothing came of it. The knowledge gained by the evil doctors was too valuable. He bided his time and regained his strength, working as an information broker with the Allied occupiers and the criminal underground. And when General Ishii's housekeeper became unlucky at Pachinko, she chose to pour thorium in her employer's tea rather than work off her debt in the brothels of the *akasen* district.

Ishii died of throat cancer not long after.

MIKIO TOYED WITH THE ORIGAMI DOVE and its necklace of dried abalone. The traditional gift of a samurai to his comrade, when neither may return from battle. He studied several of the cryptic haiku written inside by the grandfather he'd never known.

Vigilant on a sea of steel
The warrior's true heart
Stands bending but unbroken

Mikio folded it gently. He would bring it to his father at the shrine. He would know what to do.

THEY ABANDONED THEIR BAGS after customs and took the *shinkan-sen* bullet train north through the mountains. Mikio traded the dead yakuza's dollars for yen and purchased tickets for a sleeper cabin to Akita prefecture. He studied the haiku once more while Tara thumped against the thin walls of the tiny shower stall, her towel blocking the bathroom door's porthole window.

His grandfather died protecting the *Honjo Masamune*. The greatest sword ever forged, it hid waiting for a true warrior to retrieve it. The nationalists said an American soldier had stolen it as war booty, and the Japanese government offered a no-questions-asked amnesty for the return of any historically important swords and trophy skulls of the war dead. On occasion, a disgusted heir or a police department would return a skull, but only rarely would a blade be returned by collectors.

The lure of history and the hum of power resonating through the steel like an unrung bell was too much. The treasures of Japan's master smiths hid in climate controlled vaults and gun safes packed with desiccant, removed only to show the most worthy of syco-phants who would never reveal the owner's secret; in steamer trunks in Grandpa's attic, his knees too shot to risk climbing the retractable stairs; or underneath the floorboards with stacks of silver certifi-cates and Krugerrands, to be found by a house-flipper with a prybar after the old soldier's mummified corpse was found merged with his La-Z-Boy.

Mikio had his own blade, of younger vintage than the Masamune. His great-grandfather's *dotanuki* blade, from the final battle of the Satsuma rebellion. A battle blade, thick-cored with a simple iron guard and furniture. In dull polish, for cleaving meat and bone. Mikio could scrape stubble off his cheek with the edge, but it would never slice leaves or silk like a Masamune.

For separating heads from torsos, it worked fine.

Mikio didn't spot any Black Dragons tailing them at the airport. This disturbed him. Takehiko had sacrificed his green recruits for the overseas mission, but if the *shinobi* following them were this good, Mikio wondered how formidable their inner guard would be.

He and Tara looped and doubled back as if they were tailed. She purchased new underwear and a t-shirt that read "Peace Fish" across the chest from a vending machine. They boarded a Japan Rail East car and disembarked at the last moment. No one followed as they ran for the Akita train.

The new *shinkansen* reached 360 kilometers per hour once they left the Tokyo metro area. It would be safer to rent a car, but Tara's nerves needed a rest. She was strong for a soft American, but there were only so many bullets one could take.

She emerged from the shower with her hair towel-turbaned and a white kimono tied around her waist. "Your turn," she said, and collapsed on the bench seat, her chest reverberating with the impact. Mikio looked out the window to avoid staring at the triangle of flesh below her throat, pale as the belly of a speckled trout.

"Shower," Tara said. "You smell like New Jersey."

Mikio shrugged and tore the plastic off his new boxers and plain black t-shirt. "No peek," he said, and closed the door behind him.

Tara rolled her eyes. She liked when men had a bit of boy in them, but not when it manifested as constant dick jokes. Reeves had treated her with respect, which had been rare in the dying town she'd found herself trapped in. The boy in Reeves was wounded, but still cracked a smile now and then. They hadn't much time together, and he'd gotten her in more trouble than she'd managed in her entire life, but he *got* her. And Tara thought she got him.

As an EMT, she'd once crawled into a Bronco that flipped on the highway, spewing gasoline. Her partner couldn't squeeze in. She cut the seat belt and they tugged the driver out by his Redwing boots, a goose egg where his left eye should be. The engine sparked when the firemen hit it with foam, and the *whump* of displaced air followed her for weeks. One more minute, and she would have been a crispy critter.

The adrenaline became a drug. And when there wasn't action, Wild Turkey did the trick. Her shift boss smelled whiskey on her breath and gave her leave, saying she could come back when she had a 90-day keychain from the friends of Bill W.

Tara put the bottle down, but couldn't drag herself back to ask for her old job. The shame was too much. She waited tables instead. Then her Ma died and left her the Toronado, and every time she had enough scratch to get out of town, she got another ticket or the Olds needed repair.

Now she was in a foreign country with a fake passport, no wheels, and a wad of fives and singles that smelled like wet leaves. And she was cool with it. With what little she'd seen of Tokyo's neon steel sprawl, and the bonsai forests and ice cream mountains flying past the train, she could give Japan a shot. She'd seen *Lost in Translation* and *Tokyo Drift*. They liked cars and booze and so did she. They'd spring Reeves, and he and Mikio would beat the hell out of the bad guy, who owed her a car. Mob guys always had money and fast cars. They'd steal one and get away. An Evo, maybe. Those were sweet.

Tara drifted off to the hum of the shower and the high-revving turbo whine of a hot engine.

Mikio stepped out shirtless in his new heart-spangled boxers. His chest was check-patterned with slice scars, his shins leopard-spotted with bruises. Tara snored, half-spilled out of her kimono. Mikio frowned and tied her belt, then carefully lifted her onto the small bunk, folding her legs at the knee so she fit.

The winter sun reflected off Tara's legs like snow sculptures. Mikio eased the blinds shut. He held the sole of his foot beside hers and shook his head. Western women were gigantic.

Mikio pulled on pants and slipped into the hallway, quietly closing the door behind him. He checked each cabin window. Two opposite each other had their shades closed. The rest were empty. The ticket seller had given a broad wink when Mikio asked for the pricey sleeper car in the middle of the day.

Mikio wanted privacy, but not for sexual athletics. He knelt by the first shaded cabin door and listened. Then he palmed his grandfather's knife and tested the lock. It turned. He slid the door open a notch and bent at the knee, ready to attack.

Empty.

The door at the southbound end of the car opened and a uniformed conductor appeared holding a small scanner. "Tickets please," he said.

"I left it in my jacket," Mikio said, pocketing the knife. "Just stretching my legs."

"I'll need to see it," the conductor said, peering into the empty cabin windows. "And please don a shirt and footwear when you leave your cabin."

Mikio shuffled down the hallway.

The whisper of silk before the noose cinched over Mikio's throat was enough to snap his hands to guard. The conductor yanked him into an empty cabin, spun so Mikio's back slammed into his, then hunched over to lift him off his feet.

Mikio dangled from the garroting conductor's broad shoulders, legs flailing for purchase. Mikio twisted the garrote away from his jugular, fingers turning purple beneath the silk cord.

Above him, a ninja in black suspended himself with his hands and feet pressed to opposite sides of the walls. Mikio grabbed for his knife and the ninja dropped and landed an elbow to his stomach.

Mikio's face ballooned.

Only seconds before the lack of blood shut down his brain. Mikio snatched the knife from his pocket and plunged it into the conductor's kidney, then curled in half and ran across the ceiling to flip himself over his strangler's head. Joined by rope, they collided against the wall. The conductor clawed for the blade in his side. Mikio gouged two fingers into his eye to the last knuckle and charged out of the room. The conductor screamed and fell, and the garrote yanked Mikio down with him. Mikio flipped onto his back in the hallway and tugged the silk rope from his throat.

The ceiling ninja drew a short sword and gave chase. Mikio rolled and kicked off the walls like a crab on his back. The ninja raised his sword high and Mikio scissor-kicked the swordsman's knees out. The ninja tumbled nose first into Mikio's palm strike.

Mikio gave him three more, then gripped his chin and the back of his skull and snapped the man's head backwards. He kicked his way from under the corpse and picked up the straight-bladed *ninja-to* sword.

The garroter stumbled out of the car with Mikio's knife in his bloody hand. He flicked the knife at Mikio's throat. Mikio blocked it with the sword and sliced him from jaw to sternum.

The assassin's conductor hat rolled down the hallway as he crumpled at Mikio's feet. Mikio breathed a heavy sigh, and knelt to retrieve his grandfather's knife at the far end of the car.

The six cabin doors opened. From each, a black-clad swordsman emerged silently.

"Fuck!" Mikio hurled the knife. The first ninja batted it aside. The six huddled and approached warily.

"Come die, assholes," Mikio said, his blade held low.

There were no comers.

The door opened behind them. A conductor stepped through, and his jaw fell.

The ninja at the rear thrust his blade through the real conductor's throat. He held it there while the man gurgled his life away, his mouth working like a dying fish's.

Mikio cursed and charged with a shout of *"Kiai!"*

The first ninja met his charge, but could not match his rage. Mikio struck his blade aside and side-stepped, drawing his own edge across the ninja's throat.

The bloodspray painted Mikio's cheek. He faced his next opponent before the first hit the floor.

The second, tall ninja drew a second blade and crossed his swords to deflect Mikio's strike. They locked blades and Mikio's arms bulged. Blood dripped from his face. The ninja behind his opponent raised his blade for a thrust, looking for an opening.

Mikio turned his knees to water and sank to a crouch. He rolled through his opponent's legs, blade over his shoulder. The ninja squealed as Mikio cut through his groin, gripped his leg for purchase, then lopped the next ninja's leg off at the knee.

The amputee hit the wall and fell, splattering Mikio's chest with blood. The third ninja reversed his grip for a downward thrust. Mikio sprang up and skewered him under the chin. The ninja's swordpoint sliced across his trapezius.

Mikio's blade snapped in the dying man's skull. The ninja stiffened on tiptoes and toppled backward, eyes flowing blood.

The one-legged ninja took a wild swipe. Mikio caught it on his half-sword and stomped the man's jaw. He pried the ninja's sword from his fingers while the three remaining opponents dodged their falling comrade's corpse.

Mikio snarled, blood-soaked, his face a seething *shikami* demon mask of righteous anger. He held the new blade low in two hands, padding on bare feet.

The rearmost ninja sheathed his blade for a *kusarigama* sickle and chain. The frontman nervously hurled a trio of *shuriken*. Mikio flattened to the wall. One flying blade nicked his shoulder before thunking further down the hallway.

"Japan is ours, *samurai*," the lead ninja spat.

At the temple in Akita, the Sons of Hachiman trained from morning until night. With weapons and without. Finding their center. Balancing their war-worship with honor toward nature and servitude under the weak and needy. They chopped wood and carried water until they took on the tree's fortitude and the stream's fluidity.

The ninja trained only to win, at any cost. To live in pure deception. Between and beyond rules and expectations. To combat their enemy's shapeless soul, the Warriors of Hachiman were trained to have no expectations of attack. Opponents struck without warning, at any time, until the young samurai reacted like water. Adapting, enveloping, overflowing, however their opponents attempted to contain them.

"You know it is true!" The ninja shouted.

"Keep talking." Mikio laughed. "Little dicks in funny pajamas."

Behind him, Tara opened the cabin door and gasped at the walls painted in blood. The ninja followed their training and used this moment to strike in unison.

The first struck Mikio's blade while the second leapt over his head, scraping the ceiling and diving for the floor behind him.

Mikio cut the first ninja down. The ninja with the *kusarigama* whipped the chain around Mikio's weapon's hilt. The ninja behind him rolled to his feet and swiped with his blade.

Mikio launched forward to dodge the strike and caught the sickle on his sword, spinning his opponent with his momentum. "Tara! Get sword!"

Mikio's voice held such command that shock-struck Tara bent and picked up a fallen blade. Her heart pounded, the adrenaline flushing her skin red. She saw a leg with no body attached. Her stomach lurched.

"Throw!" Mikio shouted.

Tara took two steps and froze. This wasn't road racing. This was scary shit.

"You look like black sperm," Mikio snarled, and slammed his opponent into a wall, kneeing his ribs with *muay thai* strikes. The chain man absorbed them without complaint, his eyes flicking behind Mikio.

"Throw now!"

Tara hurled the blade down the hall like a spear. The ninja swordsman dodged its clatter, and Mikio released his own blade to the chain-wielder's grip. With his opponent off balance, Mikio backflipped over the swordsman's strike, the bladepoint cutting a red line across his shoulder. He landed in a roll, snatched the sword Tara had thrown, and thrust it through the swordsman's belly.

Mikio ran him through, spun him sideways and jerked the blade clean to face the ninja with chain and sickle.

He hooked Mikio's blade with a fierce chop that sunk his sickle into the wall and trapped both weapons, then whipped the chain around Mikio's neck.

Mikio stared into the ninja's eyes as the chain pulled taut. He kneed the ninja in the liver and gripped him by the throat. He leaned in to whisper, crushing the man's larynx against his spine with his thumbs. "I hung for an hour from the thousand-year old *yakusugi* tree outside our temple, *shinobi*. And the monks call me 'weak-neck.'"

Mikio lifted the kicking ninja up against the wall to die. The ninja tugged other end of the chain, twisting the sickle until the blade snapped and its haft flew into his hand. He squeezed the wooden haft and a small blade sprung from the end.

Mikio smashed his forehead between the ninja's eyes, dropped him, and forced the hideaway blade deep into the ninja's collarbone. Blood spritzed across his eyes. Mikio held the ninja close until his pounding heart faded.

"*Tansyo,*" Mikio spat, and dropped the corpse to the floor.

Tara stared while he dragged bodies into an empty cabin, tossed weapons in another, and chose one sword to keep. He patted her shoulder and left a bloody handprint on her kimono.

"Very good, *Akane-chan,*" Mikio said. "You are bad ass."

Mikio turned on the shower and stepped inside.

43.

THE FIRST METAL TO EMERGE from Kazeta's forge became a hammer head.

Their lungs burned with effort before the white coals turned the iron sand red and molten. The flux of shells burned away and left a spongy mass of iron, a black brain giving off a dim red glow.

Kazeta pounded the iron to a rough square with heavy, one-handed blows with chunks of stone. Butch kept the coals hot while Kazeta shattered stone after stone.

Long after the sun set, they left the iron to cool and collapsed on their straw beds.

In the morning after a breakfast of raw scallops, Kazeta attached the crude hammer head to a haft of bamboo and admired their work.

"Want me to go find a coconut?" Butch said, and peeled the shell off a prawn. "When we get off this island, I'm never eating fish again."

Kazeta grunted, and hammered the flat rock he'd used as an anvil. The dull iron rang high and bright. Kazeta nodded in approval. "Light fire," he said. "More work."

"Shouldn't I be resting?" Butch peered at the new pink skin on his leg wound. The maggots had crawled away in the night, to digest their meal of gangrenous flesh and join the island's ranks of bluebottle flies. He wiped a hand on his shirt and gave his wound a gentle prod. It looked and felt pink and greasy as an Easter ham, right before it went in the oven.

Butch limped to the haystack of bamboo and maple staves Kazeta had chopped, and lugged an armful to the forge. He bellowed the smoldering coals until they flared into a bed of marigolds, and laid the wood like cigarettes in a case. Once they caught, he stacked on more.

Kazeta jogged back with six bamboo buckets of iron sand yoked on his shoulders. Then he double-timed back for more.

They spent the day making a crude anvil. Kazeta worked long into the night hammering it flat and true. Butch served as his left hand, adjusting the flame. Bringing him water, which Kazeta drank greedily, and grilled filets of a skipjack he'd speared, which Kazeta refused.

The moon was high when Kazeta nodded at the anvil's blood-red glow and collapsed against his palm tree. Butch handed him a container of water.

Kazeta sipped and frowned. "No beer?"

Butch laughed and they shared a cold meal of grilled fish.

THE NEXT DAY KAZETA SLEPT. Butch speared fish and gathered water from the spring that trickled down their tiny mountain. He scratched his beard and squinted at a distant ship, crouching behind cover. The craft's flag was too small to see.

That evening, Kazeta shaped a leftover ingot into a dull hook. Butch whittled a disc of bamboo and fitted it to the end, then sliced the top off a boot, and laced it to Kazeta's stump. He pulled the laces snug.

Kazeta studied his new left hand in the sparks of their fire.

"If you shave off that little moustache, you can be Captain Blood," Butch said.

Kazeta taught Butch to hammer wrought iron from crude ore. The ringing blows squeezed impurities from the metal. The charcoal in the forge baked carbon into it and it became steel. Butch's arms became thick and chiseled, with horseshoes of muscle above his ashy elbows. Butch had lived in Minnesota's Iron Range all his life, and the blacksmith work brought him back. He had left his father's farm and fallen in love with a sassy cowgirl a thousand miles from home. Seen the glory of Rome, the lush French countryside, the serene mountains over Tokyo.

But he had also seen brutality beyond measure. Shell-holes and skeletons pocking the landscape. Families scrabbling to survive as merciless, dead-eyed soldiers crushed them beneath their boots. His own hand slicing soft young throats of mere boys, who like him, had chosen to march under their country's flag rather than break rocks on a chain gang of deserters. Acidic sweat ran off his shoulders as he pounded the iron into mild steel, purifying himself along with the metal. From the pigs of ore they made chisels. Tongs. Files. Hatchets for cutting down fuel for the greedy flames.

They dug thick clay from the foot of their mountain and fired bowls and drinking cups in the forge. Then a large cooking pot, which Kazeta used to boil water and pour it over green camellia leaves.

"*Matcha*," Kazeta said, and gave a deep groan as he sipped the steaming brew. He offered Butch a cup. "Tea."

"No thank you, *nakama*," Butch said. The black Chinese stuff he had in San Fran was all right, but he didn't like the piss-yellow Japanese 'green' tea. "Don't suppose there's a coffee bush on this rock?"

Kazeta shrugged and finished his cup.

Butch carved another chop into his palm trunk. They'd been on the island two months.

They spent the next evening firing a huge clay pot which barely stood under its own weight. After they blasted it in their kiln, Butch hefted a new steel-tipped spear. "I'm gonna nail one of those black ducks and make you some soup you'll never forget."

Kazeta waved his hand. "Not for food."

"Then what the hell's it for? Taking a bath?"

Kazeta shook his head. He could use a hot soak in an *onsen*, but had more important plans. He took their hatchet and sank it into the trunk of a black pine sapling. "Chop all tree like this, bring wood here. Many." He held the blade of his hand chest height, suggesting a woodpile worthy of the bitterest Minnesota winter.

"Are we building a raft? Please say we're building a raft."

Kazeta heaved his yoke of buckets to his shoulder and marched toward the black side of the island.

When the sun fell, they began the fire. The soft pine burned low, and Kazeta studied the coals, inserting new wood at measured intervals. Sometime after midnight, he began pouring from their chest-high pile of sand and leftover charcoal. The smoke had a tang, like blood in the back of the throat, as iron was born.

Butch fell asleep in the middle of the night, and in the morning woke to find Kazeta adding more iron sand and charcoal.

"Did you sleep?" he croaked.

"No," Kazeta said. "Make tea, please. Need bad."

"What about the smoke?"

"Take risk," Kazeta said.

Butch started a fire, and picked a few satsumas. He gagged as he passed a rack of fish Kazeta had left drying in the sun. He found two crabs dueling in the sand, pulled their claws off and brought them back for breakfast. He poured tea, and then dropped the struggling crabs into the boil.

"Domo," Kazeta said, and sipped his tea. He sprinkled another bucket of black sand into the crucible.

"We're gonna get found out, we keep forging and hammering, *nakama.*"

Kazeta nodded, studying the fire. "Work hard. Soon, we leave island."

KAZETA STAYED AWAKE THREE DAYS tending the fire, waving away Butch's offers to stand watch. On the third night, the iron in the crucible bloomed like lava flowers. They dumped the clay *tatara* out of the flames and it cracked like an egg, spilling bright orange yolk. The ground began to smolder, and Kazeta stumbled for the buckets. Butch poured sea water around the molten iron while Kazeta muttered directions.

The molten iron resembled a bright orange coral, quickly fading to ashy gray. Kazeta knelt close and studied the bubbled metal. *"Tamahagane,"* he said. He held up a thumb and collapsed in the dirt.

Butch carried him to his straw bed, then roasted his dinner over the meteorite they'd forged. The stars hid behind a pebble-bed of clouds, the red brain of hot ore the only light.

Kazeta slept through the day.

When he woke, he took tea and chipped off pieces of iron and started the forge. When the pieces glowed hot, he hammered them flat, and then held them with tongs while Butch pounded them into one large ingot. Butch swung until his bad leg throbbed. Kazeta heaved the sledgehammer over his shoulder, guiding it with his hook, and folded steel over steel countless times.

After a week of labor, the ingot became long and slender, the needle tooth of a sea creature hauled from the abyss. Kazeta painted it with wet clay in a delicate pattern, thick by the back and thin on the edge.

Butch fired the forge into a dull orange, and Kazeta thrust the blade into the coals. When the metal glowed with the fury of the rising sun, he quenched the blade in a trench of spring water. The blade hissed as its fire was banished within, curving into a thin iron fang of a sky dragon huffing flame.

Once it cooled, Kazeta held the sword in the moonlight, comparing their unfinished blade with the majesty of the *Honjo Masamune*.

"You're not really a country blacksmith, are you?" Butch said.

"I am Miyamoto Kazeta," he said, and crossed the blades before him. "Warlord and Armorer of Hachiman Samurai Brotherhood."

44.

TARA CLENCHED HER JAW to keep it from trembling as she stitched Mikio's shoulder with the complimentary sewing kit. She had seen blood as an EMT. People with parts missing, kicked down the highway. Just never so much, and not all at once.

"How . . . how could you kill all those people?"

"They would kill us. They are *shinobi*." Mikio said.

"Yeah, but . . . why do they fight to the death? It's crazy," she said.

Scars cross-hatched the wings of Mikio's muscled back. He hummed to himself while the needle pierced his skin. The tang of blood filled Tara's nostrils and she looked away.

"They choose *gokudo*," Mikio said. "Means, 'ultimate path.' No going back. Cannot quit."

"I just don't understand. It's not a war. Is it?" She hissed as the needle struck deep. "Sorry."

Mikio waved her on. "Yes, is war. Not born samurai, Tara-kun. Trained, very young, yes. When old enough, I choose. Choose to be samurai. Fight for Hachiman. Win or die. *Shinobi,* yakuza . . . they choose also."

"But how could you know, when you're that young?"

Mikio grunted. "Every day, wake up. I choose. They same, they choose. Choose enough, no more choice. Only one way. They choose be *tansyo*." Mikio chuckled.

Tara chewed her lip, pinched his wound closed and sewed quick.

"What's that mean?" she said.

"Mean they have very little dick."

Tara smirked. "No offense, but isn't that kinda the norm here?"

Mikio chuckled. "Not me."

"Okay, Godzilla." Tara laughed.

"Ask wife," Mikio said, puffing his chest. "She tell."

"Uh huh." She tied off the suture with a triple knot. "Can't wait."

Mikio stood up to stretch and test her work. A dark gem of blood appeared on the wound. He smeared it away with a finger. "Reeves big?"

"Oh yeah," Tara said, and held her hands two feet apart. "Like a damn crankshaft. I needed surgery."

"Oh . . . ." Mikio nodded in awe.

Tara rolled her eyes. "I thought samurai had to grow up."

"I special," Mikio said, and pulled on his shirt.

Tara mussed his hair. "You're very special. You have your own bus."

They wrapped the sword in a clean kimono and moved to empty seats near the front of the train. At Akita station they quickly switched to a boxy shuttle bus that climbed into the mountains. Tara wiggled a finger in her ears until they popped.

They hopped off in a small tree-crowded village full of short, friendly buildings and streets festooned with signs in Japanese, English and colorful pictograms. Mikio bought skewers of fried dumplings called *takoyaki,* and Tara crunched three down while they marched toward a peninsula of shops with wide roads on either side.

"That guy should open a shop at the Minnesota State Fair," Tara said, watching storm water run down the tiny canal below the curb. "He does fried stuff on a stick pretty good. What is this?"

"Tako," Mikio said, mouth full. He wiggled four fingers. "Octopus."

Tara wrinkled her nose. Then looked at the lone dumpling left on her skewer, shrugged, and ate it. "Guess I can cross that off the list."

Mikio left her behind a motorcycle shop, its back lot crammed with yellow scooters and small road bikes. Boxed in by 250cc Honda dirt bikes, a Russian heavy-duty Ural motorcycle sat mated to a sidecar built of thick gauge steel. Tara straddled an older Yamaha VMAX muscle bike with a bent fork, kicking her tennis shoes against the pegs and watching scooters and hatchbacks drive on the wrong side of the road, breaking her view of the white-capped crags in the distance.

Mikio stepped out the back, followed by a skinny, shoe-gazing mechanic in a grease-smeared yellow motorcycle jacket he couldn't possible zip closed over his potbelly. The mechanic held two helmets.

Mikio held up a key, and stuck it in a Honda CR-500 with hybrid off-road tires. He climbed on the bike and revved it to life.

Tara hopped off the Yamaha and nodded to the grease monkey. "Nice VMAX."

"*Oppai ii desu,*" he mumbled with a grin.

"*Domo,*" Tara said, looking him up and down. "*Tansyo.*" She yanked the helmets from his hands.

"Oh," the mechanic flinched. "*Baka ona.*"

Mikio laughed.

Tara slapped a helmet into Mikio's stomach. "I never ride bitch." She swung a leg over the gas tank and pushed Mikio to the second seat. She pulled on her helmet and took off up the mountain road.

The road disappeared into the trees and the bike hugged the outside lane up the mountain. Tara hadn't ridden in years, not since the EMT job. Too many helmetless riders had grated themselves to ground chuck on her shift.

The engine buzzed and Mikio tilted like a veteran rider, pointing over her shoulder toward turns without signs, leading them onto a logging road with two tire ruts and flattened weeds in the middle.

Tara eased to a stop and steadied the bike with one leg.

She peered up the steep grade and told Mikio he'd better take over.

They switched seats, and Mikio gave her wrists a little tug to suggest she hang on. Then he hunkered down and dug in the combo tires, jouncing them up the switchback trail. Tara gripped around his waist and hooted as the rear tire kicked dirt on the turns, only a hump of weeds and scrub separating them from the cliff's edge.

Mikio paused at a ridge with a clear view of the coast. He tapped helmets, then slapped his heart and with his fist gestured at the vista of lush foothills speckled with villages, gridded with rice paddies, rolling down and into the sea.

Tara nodded and squeezed his chest. It was beautiful. The country seemed chiseled from malachite and rich brown stone, everything short and sturdy, dotted with homes that blended into the landscape. Mikio goosed them up the trail with a curl of the wrist, and soon their helmets scraped low pine branches, forcing them to hunker down and coast to a stop.

Mikio killed the engine and they pushed the bike along the wagon trail. A few minutes later Mikio stopped, backtracked a few steps, and parted the weeds to reveal a lean-to constructed of fallen boughs. Within it he found a camouflage tarp. They covered the bike and helmets with it, and hiked on.

The trail thinned to a deer track, and the pines grew thick and squat, like fat old men with shoulders thrust back to bare proud bellies. The canopy swallowed the sunlight as their feet trod the rotting bark floor. Wind shook the treetops, and snow monkeys chattered warning.

A five-story pagoda appeared among the fat thousand-year-old pines, and Mikio walked past it as if it was as natural as a tree stump. Tara stared at the structure's ornate beauty and Mikio waved her on. A half mile later the trail opened into a clearing ringed by the ancient pines. Mikio patted her on the shoulder before kneeling in the grass.

She followed suit. "We praying?"

"Shh."

An arrow thunked into the dirt by Mikio's knee. He pulled it from the grass, stood, and marched across the clearing. Tara got up and jogged after him.

A slender young woman stepped from the trees, holding a bow as tall as she was. She bowed deeply to Mikio and chattered in bright tones. He nodded and returned her arrow.

The archer bounced through the forest carrying her slender weapon, and they followed.

"This is beautiful and all," Tara said, "But what's the plan, Mickey?"

Mikio scratched his chin. "Talk with father. Eat big bowl soba noodle. Then give wife boom-boom, and go stick sword up Take-hiko ass."

Tara rolled her eyes.

The trees parted a second time, revealing a small village of traditional Japanese homes straddling a brook. In the field, twenty white-robed students performed katas in formation, learning karate. Across it, six archers lobbed missiles at distant haystacks. Villagers in modern garb tended their small farm, and upstream a waterwheel spun a mill to grind buckwheat flour.

"I hope you have one of those guys selling octopus on a stick," Tara said. "I'm starving."

The young archer laughed. "Sorry, no *takoyaki*."

Mikio barked in Japanese. The girl stiffened and bowed, then marched back to her post.

Tara frowned. "Don't be a dick."

"Not dick," Mikio said. "She must guard."

They crossed the brook at a footbridge and approached the archers. A small woman led the instruction, correcting one's stance or another's grip. She wore a white kimono marked in red with the swirling symbol from Mikio's shoulder, and a black lacquer breast-plate strapped to her chest. She took the longbow from a student and nocked a white-fletched arrow. The bow nearly touched the grass as she aimed at the farthest hay bale, a hundred meters away.

Mikio paused and touched Tara's shoulder. "Beautiful, yes?"

The archer brought the feather to her cheek, the talon of four calloused fingers gripping the bowstring. She loosed the arrow with a thrum and nodded, lips in a hawk's grin.

The archery teacher's eyes went soft when they fell on Mikio. The students cheered as the arrow struck its target. Yumi wrapped her arms around her husband, bow in hand, and dismissed her charges.

Mikio lifted her off her feet, face buried in her neck.

The students jogged away, leaving Tara with the amorous couple. Japanese were supposed to be private about this stuff. After a minute, she cleared her throat.

"My wife, Yumi," Mikio said with a proud nod.

"Pleased to meet you, Tara." Yumi smiled, and offered her hand. "Welcome to Hachiman Temple."

THEY STOPPED AT A SCHOOLHOUSE ON THE PATH, and a small round-faced boy ran from the playground to leap into Mikio's arms. Mikio swung him around, and set him on his feet to introduce him to Tara.

The boy gawped.

"Please forgive Shiro," Yumi said. "He hasn't seen many Western-ers."

Tara crouched and made claws of her hands. "Ra," she said.

Shiro stepped back in a fighting pose.

Tara laughed. "Just like your Pop."

Mikio patted him on the head. "Tara-san *nakama,* Shiro."

The children followed them in line to the temple, a graceful wooden structure beamed in dark pine, decorated only with an enormous bell and two red banners emblazoned with the swirling three-bladed symbol of Hachiman.

Teachers and villagers converged carrying their tools, and robed men—and women—with *katana* in their belts emerged from homes and guard posts in the woods. A young man in orange robes ducked into the temple, and returned with a bald, older man wearing red raiments stitched with white doves.

The crowd quieted under the elder's blank expression as he descended the steps. His sun-scoured skin fit tight to the bones of his face, making him resemble a watchful lizard.

"This is our elder, Miyamoto Kenshin," Yumi whispered to Tara. "Mikio's father."

Mikio bowed deeply.

The old man spoke sharply in Japanese. Mikio stammered his reply. His father glared at Tara.

"Bow," Yumi whispered. "Bow low."

Tara curtseyed, then quickly turned it into a bow.

The old man nodded to Tara in return, then led Mikio away. The crowd murmured and dispersed, the children filing back into their school.

"You are the first Westerner to enter the Temple grounds," Yumi said. "My husband says you saved his life at least twice. Come, we have much to talk about."

THEY SOAKED IN THE HOT SPRING nestled in the crags atop the mountain, surrounded by ghosts of steam. Tara had kicked off her tennis shoes outside the Miyamoto's modest home, where Yumi gave her a kimono and sandals. They followed the brook to its source, and Tara told her of her adventure, as the heat melted the aches from their bones.

"You are very brave," Yumi said.

"I'm just doing what anyone would do," Tara said. "I guess. I don't know what people do when ninjas kidnap their friend. I used to drive an ambulance, maybe I just miss rescuing people. It felt good."

Yumi rolled her shoulders. Her right bulged larger from years of pulling the bowstring. "You have the heart for it. Warriors win the glory, but there is great honor in what you do."

"I never thought about it," Tara said. "I mean, I was always the one who made my Dad pull over when we saw a dog or a cat hit on the road. Wrap them in a blanket and take them to the animal hospital. They'd smile and take them, tell me they'd do everything they could. Then I volunteered and saw how many they gassed. Even the healthy ones.

"I wanted to be a veterinarian, but after that I couldn't do it. Too much like quitting, you know? To not even try. At least with people, they pretend to do their best. Triage, they call it. You need to decide what battles you're gonna fight. Sometimes well, you can see it in the doc's eyes. Someone's not gonna get their A game. Maybe the patient's a drunk, or elderly and frail. They don't have much fight in them, or let's face it, sometimes they brought it on themselves. That's one reason I quit, I couldn't deal with that. I feel like no matter what, they deserved everything I got, you know?"

Yumi nodded, staring off the mountain to the sea.

"Well, that's what I think," Tara said. "Guess I'm—"

"You fight your own battle," Yumi said, and held up a finger. "Even when your comrades are weak in spirit. Your bravery will inspire them. Do not quit simply because they are not as strong as you."

Tara bit her tongue. Nobody called her a quitter. She moved to speak, then flushed.

Yumi was right. She *had* quit. From what she loved.

Tara closed her eyes and sank to the bottom. The rocks jabbed her behind and elbows as the undercurrent spun and caressed her with fiery hands. She saw only red behind her eyelids, as if she could see into the mountain's fierce volcanic heart.

She had punished herself enough at Johansson's hands. She would not quit again.

Tara pushed off the rocks and burst from the water, the early spring air an ice-bucket splash of gooseflesh and needles.

"Careful," Yumi said. "You can slip away down there."

"Yeah," Tara said, and stood up in the cold. Skin tight with gooseflesh, her breath pluming. Voices rippled around the stones. She folded her arms and sank back to neck deep.

Mikio and Shiro shucked their kimonos without a care and joined them in the water, Shiro in his father's lap.

Yumi examined Mikio's shoulder. "You stitched him very well."

"Thanks," Tara said.

Shiro whispered and Mikio laughed.

"I think I'm gonna go take a nap, okay?" Tara said, exiting the water behind the rocks.

"There are towels in the closet," Yumi called.

"Why is the big woman leaving?" Shiro asked.

"Foreigners have different ways," Mikio said. "They bathe alone."

"Why?"

"They're afraid they'll fart in the water," Mikio said, and ruffled Shiro's hair.

MIKIO'S FATHER JOINED THEM FOR DINNER. Yumi served big bowls of fried noodles, *yakisoba,* with a pot of green tea. They sat at a low table, the room lit by paper lamps.

"Tara-kun," Kenshin said. "Mikio tells me you killed two Black Dragons." He spoke careful and clear.

Tara shrugged. "I hit a couple with my Toronado. Helped here and there."

"You are very brave. And I thank you. My son is quite reckless," Kenshin said, and wagged a finger. "But let us eat."

Mikio slurped down three bowls while Tara fumbled with the chopsticks. Shiro squeezed to her side and showed her how to hold them properly.

"Thanks, little guy."

"You have a big nose," Shiro said. "Mama says you are not a *tengu*. But you look like one."

"What's a *tengu*?"

"A red demon with a big nose!"

"Ha, very funny," Tara said, and tweaked Shiro's nose. She stuck her thumb between her fingers. "Now I got *your* nose."

Shiro gasped. "Give it back!"

"Nope, not until you say I'm not a demon."

"You're a nose-stealing demon!"

"Shiro, be polite," Yumi said.

"But she has my nose!"

Tara poked Shiro's nose with her thumb. "There," she said. "Protect it better next time."

Shiro squeezed his nose and warily hunkered over his noodles.

"It is very disturbing to lose Uchida," Kenshin said, speaking to Yumi and Mikio in Japanese. "He was one of our best. The Shadow Shogun cannot be trusted. After the war, our causes were briefly aligned. He is old, and the world is not to his liking. His daughter's death at *Kita-Chosin* hands has weighed heavily on him."

"Uchida said they *had* him, father," Mikio said. "Like it was against his will."

"What do they have to use against him?" Yumi asked, pouring tea. "His children are dead. His bloodline is finished. But he can't work with them openly without betraying us."

"Poor Uchida was deceived," Kenshin said, and stared into his tea cup. "If the Mitsuru has allied with the Black Dragons, it will be to avenge his daughter and strike North Korea."

"Then why ally with *kigyoshatei* like Takehiko?" Mikio said. "The corporate yakuza brothers are full of Koreans."

"The snake knows best the ways of the serpent," Kenshin said, and raised his cup. "That has always been the reason for our alliance with Mitsuru. His spying against the Koreans during the war would make it impossible for him to recruit Korean spies directly. Yakuza care only for money. That is why he beds with them. For operatives."

Mikio slurped down a mouthful of noodles. "Takehiko can get into Korea. He has a container ship he uses for a base of operations," he said. "Perfect for a *shinobi*. Looks like shit outside, but within, very luxurious. He has a seaplane he hides on it. Get close, fly below radar."

"My old sources at the *Yomiuri-Shinbun* political desk are whispering about Takehiko running for office," Yumi said. "They've been pressured to write glowing articles. We can't let him get that powerful."

"When he heads back to Seoul," Kenshin said, "You mine the ship. End of problem."

"We can't wait that long, father," Mikio said.

"Why not, my reckless only son?" Kenshin said. "You never were good at waiting."

Mikio told him about Reeves. "Why keep him alive? I think Takehiko wants him for the *Kumite*. To rouse the nationalists. They would love to see one of our fighters defeat an American."

"So?"

"Reeves fought well. I do not want to see him sacrificed," Mikio said. "He would make a strong ally."

"What is your plan?"

Mikio shrugged. "Go to Tokyo, find the *wants rem*. Bring the police," he said, and nodded to Yumi. "You still have a contact at the Shinjuku precinct, that greasy loser?"

Yumi smirked. "Yes, Takagi still works there."

"We strike during the raid and break him out," Mikio said. "We'll need all the fighters we can get."

Kenshin frowned. "This may conceal our motives, but it is too dangerous. We can't risk you on a mission of such little consequence."

Mikio looked in his empty bowl.

Tara cleared her throat. "These are very good noodles, Yumi," she said. The defeat on Mikio's face, so soon after Reeves' name was mentioned, made the question and answer clear. "Thank you. I don't understand Japanese and all, but I recognize names. Reeves stood up for Mikio in a fight, when he didn't have to. Because it was right."

Kenshin ignored her. "Yumi, perhaps you two should clean the table."

Yumi nodded, and began clearing the bowls.

"Hey," Tara said. "I saved your son's ass, that doesn't count for much, huh? Reeves may not be one of you, but he's one of me."

Mikio sighed and scratched at the stub of his little finger with his thumbnail. "Father, forgive her rudeness, but she is right. We traveled together, ate together. I owe them a debt."

Kenshin reached across the table and pinched Mikio's hand. "What have you done to your finger?"

Yumi ducked to examine Mikio's pinky finger. "Why?"

"To get close to Takehiko!" Mikio said. "My body is covered with scars from fighting for our cause. What is one fingertip? All you do is talk. I was his bodyguard. I learned more than Uchida did with years of snooping."

"Is your body vandalized with tattoos as well?" Kenshin snapped.

"Only with this, father," Mikio said, and bared the symbol of Hachiman on his shoulder. "Grandfather would rescue an ally."

"You have his foolishness," Kenshin said. "Mother should never have told you of my father's tattoo. Or the stories of the sword. You would've been a priest, and known peace. Instead you let the blade fall into the hands of our enemy, and now our best chance is to send it to the bottom of the ocean. They will never let it go!"

"And we should?"

"If you have to die to get it, yes! You are talking like a *chinpira* yakuza punk, not like a samurai! I should have never allowed this mission," Kenshin said. "The sword is a symbol, nothing more. It cost me my father, and I will not sacrifice my son to possess it!" He stood and straightened his robe.

"Father, wait."

"Thank you for the meal, Yumi. Please talk some sense into my son, as I have failed to teach him respect." Kenshin patted Shiro on the head on his way out.

AFTER THEY PUT SHIRO TO BED, Yumi poured *sake*.

"We're not going after Reeves, are we?" Tara said, shivering at the cold ether taste.

"His father is right," Yumi said. "It is dangerous."

"More dangerous, sit here on top of mountain playing with our balls." Mikio sighed. "Black Dragons very strong, because we sit, do nothing."

Yumi nodded. "That is all the more reason for us to strike with care."

"Give me a bike, a gun and a phrase book," Tara said. "I'll do it."

Mikio patted Tara on the shoulder. "Sleep first, plan later. Yumi make him see eye to eye." He tapped beneath his eyes with two fingers. "She very good, talk to father."

45.

BUTCH PICKED DELICATELY at the pink skin on his leg with a hand-shaped scratcher he'd carved from bamboo. The wound had healed over, but still felt wrong. He walked around the island to get back muscle he'd lost, powering through the ache in his hip. He spied the shore of the mainland, which had begun to buzz with activity. They heard no bombing for weeks, nothing since the far-off rumbles.

American ships cut between them and the harbor, but the only vessels close enough to signal were Japanese fishing boats trawling the bay. Butch considered waving one in. What if they'd merely called a ceasefire? After what he saw of Tokyo, he feared what civilians would do to him.

Cut him up and use him as bait, most likely.

Kazeta had sent him to fill a bucket with the seeds of the camellia bushes that covered the island. Their white flowers blanketed the paths, and lime-green seed pods rolled in the snowfall of their petals. Each pod held four brown seeds the size of a brazil nut. Butch cracked the pods over his bucket like eggs, and the seeds thumped in.

He had carved thirty marks on the palm tree since the last bomb's thunder rumbled across the waves. Covered every inch of paper with letters to Jean. He gave Kazeta his word, but was tired of eating fish and oranges and sleeping outdoors. His gut told him that the central thrust of the war had changed. Another strike on Hirohito had succeeded, maybe. Something big like that.

He couldn't escape without Kazeta. And if an American ship

caught them, Kazeta would need Butch to explain that this sword-wielding one-armed Jap was one of the good guys, and had helped him break out of a POW camp.

Butch rolled a pair of seed pods in his hands before crushing them. Until Kazeta was done with the sword, Butch was stuck on the island playing with his nuts.

BACK IN CAMP Kazeta showed him how to press the camellia seeds between slats of bamboo and release their sweet oil, catching it in a hollowed bamboo pole three inches wide and three feet long. Each seed leaked but a tiny squirt.

"Fill," Kazeta said, tapping the bamboo rod.

Butch had forearms worthy of Popeye before the job was done.

Kazeta bent the sword true against a tall bamboo tree, then laid out his seven stones atop the anvil. He soaked the pale red *arato* stone in spring water and powdered clamshell, then put a bevel on the blade by rubbing the sword against the quick-cutting grit one section at a time.

Kazeta worked his way up the stones, using his hook to steady the blade and his hand to finesse it. Part of him ached as he rushed the work, considering only the sword's beauty. His own blade—hidden away at Hachiman temple—was no Masamune, but it would cleave thick torsos and not fail.

This blade would look the part and cut well enough, but would not be trustworthy in battle. More Muramasa than Masamune.

Their beards grew long while Kazeta gave the sword his best polish. The dull gray *kaisei* stone gave the blade its first edge; the soft brown *koma-nagura* keened it; the swirled black *uchigumori* refined it, so it could shave hair; then the final edge with the speckled white *karasu* stone and a mirror polish with the ivory *honyama awasi* stone, veined with brown like a great stag's antler.

Kazeta held up the blade by the thick tang, turning its gleam in the mid-day light. He brought the edge to his throat. Butch looked up from his chore and caught the hollowed tube full of oil before it spilled six days of his labor.

The bristly hairs on Kazeta's throat popped off like porcupine quills before the sword's edge.

"Huh," Butch said and scratched his beard. "I'm gonna hold out for a Gillette."

Kazeta grunted, and shaved his face clean with careful strokes. When done, he set the two swords across the anvil for Butch's inspection. Butch leaned over the swords and nodded.

"It's a ringer," Butch said. "Now let's get off this rock."

Kazeta dipped a finger into the camellia oil, coated his palms and rubbed it into his freshly shaved face. The scent was cool and bright, like green tea. "Tomorrow," he said, and began unwrapping the Masamune's corded silk grip to transfer it to the new sword.

Kazeta placed the Masamune blade in the bamboo tube filled with camellia oil and sealed the ends with pine tar. Butch followed him up the mountain, stopping to rest his aching leg. He found Kazeta at the top, kneeling before the ruins of an abandoned shrine. The small hut lay crushed beneath a fallen pine, its stone markers crooked and spotted with lichen.

Butch caught his breath and let his friend meditate in peace.

Kazeta pried away the floorboards and they took turns digging a deep, narrow grave with the hatchet. Kazeta placed the bamboo capsule in the hole and covered it, then replaced the boards and brushed his palms clean.

THAT EVENING THEY CELEBRATED with a meal of grilled prawns and abalone. Kazeta dived and brought up three fat mirror-blue shells, knifed them open and hammered the flesh tender on the anvil as though he was working steel.

He cut thin slices of abalone and skewered them between sat-suma wedges and cooked them over the fire. They drank tea and watched the sun drown in the ocean, the horizon aglow with the same pastel luster of the abalone's mother-of-pearl.

As darkness fell, cruisers patrolled the bay like sharks, their horns echoing across the water. The men sat silent, listening to the ships and the surf.

"My leg don't feel so great," Butch said, rubbing his hip. "Feels green inside. I don't make it, promise me you'll get my letters to Jean."

Kazeta nodded.

"Jean Marie Dundee, in Helena Montana. The address is on the envelopes. Beautiful woman," Butch said, slapping the sheaf of let-ters against his palm. "Beautiful country, too. Her land is at the foot of the mountain. Like Fuji, only bigger. And serene. You say there are spirits in everything, well those mountains will make anybody believe it. They're like gods, watching you. Goading you to make something of yourself.

"And Jean's that kind of woman. Before the war, I worked alone out in the woods. I was a park ranger. I don't know if you got those. My job boiled down to chasing men who weren't trying to do nothing more than put food on the table, and I was a mean sonofa-bitch about it. All I gave a damn about was following the law."

Butch looked out at the waves, phosphorescent in the half-moon's light. "They made me angry, for not following the rules. That was when I thought rules were something real. As a kid, I got whupped if I didn't follow the rules. Rules were always there, even if you couldn't see them, like barbed wire in the dark.

"I was a kid, what the hell did I know? I remember taking a poached deer from a man with hungry kids at home, and I'm ashamed of what Jean would think," Butch said, and paused to scratch hard at his beard. "So if my leg rots off, I need you to get these to her. You promise?"

"I promise," Kazeta said, staring at their dying fire.

"What about you, *nakama*?" Butch said. "I can bring the sword to someone. Or deliver a message."

Kazeta's wife and son were hidden with the monks, deep in the woods atop Mount Hachimantai. An ordinary *gaijin* could never find it. This one showed spirit. One leg or two, he would find a way. But if he could, so could the Black Dragons.

"Wife and son," Kazeta said. "Far away. Safe."

"You never talked about 'em much."

Americans loved to talk of personal matters. Kazeta did not understand it. Every evening while Butch yammered, Kazeta watched the fire and visited his wife Reiko, and played with his son Kenshin in his mind.

"I die," Kazeta said, "Bury me in forest." He took a sheet of paper inscribed in Japanese from his pocket. He folded it in tight creases with his blackened, calloused fingers until he held a white dove, the symbol of Hachiman. "When samurai go to battle, he give friend *haiku*. Poem."

Kazeta took a dried ribbon of abalone and twirled the ends into a necklace for the paper bird, then placed it in Butch's palm.

Butch held the bird carefully. "Thank you, *nakama*. What about your kid? He should have something to know you by."

Kazeta nodded. Little Kenshin's spirit was not born for combat, but even at his young age he settled playground conflicts with ease. He would serve Japan in other ways, without bloodshed.

"Protect sword," Kazeta said. "Black Dragon come, you kill."

"What about the real sword?"

Kazeta grunted. "Better lost, than in hand of *shinobi*."

Butch frowned. "You said it was your country's treasure. Something like that shouldn't disappear—"

"Promise!" Kazeta said, jabbing Butch's chest with a finger.

"Okay," Butch said. "I promise."

IN THE MORNING, Butch woke alone to a dead fire. The sword was gone.

Butch's heart pounded. He snatched his dagger and limped to the black sands where they had pulled the dinghy ashore. The pit of Butch's stomach steeled to anger at the abandonment. His leg ached as he hobbled along the rocky shore.

Kazeta didn't trust him. He wouldn't even give him a message to bring his family if he died. After all Butch had confided in him. It hurt, but he should have known. There was a gulf between the two countries as wide as the Pacific, and Butch cursed himself for forgetting it.

Butch had a knife, and that was all a commando needed. He would build a raft and get out of this crazy damn country. If he had told Lt. Frederick to go screw, he would have been rolling in the literal hay with Jean Marie by now. Learning to fall off horses and shovel cow shit. Better off than being stuck on this turd in the Pacific, stranded with a crazy swordsman.

In the bay, a gray cruiser skirted the fishing boats. Ants stood on deck, and Old Glory flapped at the bow. Butch shouted across the water and waved both his arms. He held his commando dagger in the sun, flashing the blade like a signal mirror where the bluing had worn off.

Butch kneaded his hip and followed the island's bay side as the ship scudded past. He kicked at the undergrowth, then clutched his foot in pain.

He spread the sea grass, and pulled up an oar. He chopped the brush with it, swinging in broad strokes like a mad knight. Parting the green until he revealed the dinghy he and Kazeta had ridden to the island.

Shit. Kazeta hadn't ditched him.

Butch used the oar as a crutch and limped back to camp.

He found Kazeta practicing swordsmanship on the slick rocks. Kazeta hopped from stone to stone like a mountain goat, his sword held low. "You find boat?"

"Yeah." Butch heaved the oar over his shoulder like a rifle as he approached. "I thought you skipped town."

Kazeta peered his way, and strode into the water, fighting an invisible opponent.

Butch watched his friend's effortless grace and berated his own lack of faith. He had more faith in a country girl he hadn't seen in years than in the man who had saved his life. All because of where he was born. No one could help that, but it was the one thing you could be sure to have held against you.

Born to money? You're a rich prick. Born poor, go starve somewhere else, we don't want you here. Born black, drink from that fountain over there. Born white, you're a nasty whip-cracker. Born on a reservation and you can't drink. Born in Asia, you were a sneaky rat. Born Irish, you need not apply. Italian, you're a ditch-digging guinea. Born in the city, your shit don't stink. Born in the country and you cuddled cousins and the occasional livestock.

If you were born a bohunk like Butch's father, you got swindled out of your best land for not knowing English, and you were stuck plucking chickens the rest of your life.

Butch swung the oar at the rocks, cursing to himself. He should have known better.

A distant shout echoed across the beach. Butch looked up.

He remembered Kazeta jerking with the impact of the rounds,

but could never recall hearing gunshots. Kazeta sank into the waves, sword held high. Butch pulled his limp body from the water, the iron sands stained a deep red.

Four GIs with Garands walked from the forest. "Looks like we saved your bacon, Robinson Crusoe," one laughed.

"Dibs on the sword," a swarthy bent-nosed soldier said. "It was my damn bullet."

Butch tackled him and tore the rifle from his hands. The GIs clubbed Butch with the butts of their rifles until he saw only black.

The agony in Butch's leg woke him as the soldiers tossed him in a stretcher. He struggled to get up, and ate two big fists.

"Want us to leave you here?" The Roman-nosed sergeant said, and tucked the sword into his belt. The soldiers carried Butch like pallbearers toward a Higgins boat beached on the rocks. Butch craned to look back at the shore.

The cratered body of Kazeta made angels in the sand as the surf slowly dragged him out to sea.

46.

TARA LAY ON THE HARD FUTON of the guest room, *sake* gone sour in her belly. The urgent sounds of Yumi and Mikio's muted lovemaking rippled through the paper walls.

Tara pulled on her jeans and tiptoed outside. The half moon lit the mountain with a mocking smile. Mikio's love song joined that of the crickets. Tara squeezed into her sneakers and followed the path down to the village, a beautiful tomb for a way of life that would never again flourish.

If the guards thought she was a big-nosed demon and sank an arrow in her ass, so be it. Enough of sitting still. She'd sat still in that podunk town, and look what happened. She would head to Tokyo on the motorbike and find Reeves.

Tara cut around the schoolhouse and froze as shadows flitted through the trees.

She crouched behind a stump. Four shapes passed quick, padding on pine needles as they fanned out among the houses.

Ninjas. *Shinobi.*

More shadows rippled from the woods, converging on the dimly lit homes. Cutting off her retreat to Mikio's house. Tara ran past the temple to the forest gates where the archer girl had held post. As she rounded the path, a young samurai reached for his blade and called out. *"Tomare! Stop!"*

"Shinobi!" Tara shouted back, skidding to her butt on the packed dirt. "They're everywhere."

The guard wore his hair in a ponytail resembling the classic top-knot. He knelt to help her up. "It's okay, Tara-san," he said "Give me your hand."

Tara gripped his hand and he pulled her to feet. His hand tightened and ground her knuckles together. "Hey!"

Blood gurgled from his lips and a bright blade sprouted from his chest.

Tara jerked her hand away. The samurai stumbled as a black-wrapped assassin yanked the blade free. Tara pushed the dying samurai into his attacker with a grimace and bolted into the woods.

Boughs lashed her face. Cold air burned her lungs. The masked slayer's fingers inches from her neck. A root snaked around her ankle and sent her tumbling into the brush, pinecones clawing into her shoulder. She sat up with a dead branch for a weapon, gasping.

The murderer had not pursued her.

She was no threat. She was not samurai.

Tara climbed to her feet and dashed for the temple.

Three shadows floated out of one darkened home and into the next. The lamps inside blinked out one by one.

Tara's throat choked closed. Ahead, the shrine's great iron bell hung like a death cap. Pain shot up her shins as she pounded the path. One of the killer shadows peeled away to intercept her. She pushed harder.

The shadow was tall and thin and drew a sword from over his shoulder. Tara leapt up the stairs and clubbed the bell with her broken branch. The branch snapped in two, and the bell tolled a muted keen.

Tara jumped and pounded the bell with her fists. It swayed, mocking her with its silence.

The ninja took the steps slowly, laughing when Tara collapsed panting against the wall.

"Bakaryo gaijin," he spat. "That means 'stupid foreign bitch.' We

all learn your idiot language." He raised his blade. "Only good for watching movies."

Tara raised a shielding hand.

An orange blur struck the ninja and sent him tumbling down the steps. The sword clattered to the stones. A bald young monk pulled Tara to her feet and shoved her toward the wooden clapper swinging on the bell's other side. Then he leapt down the steps and planted his knee in the back of the fallen ninja with a sickening crack.

Tara heaved the counterweighted beam toward the bell. The tone rippled through her like warm water. Three more monks burst from the shrine with fighting sticks in both hands, and chased after shadows.

Tara rang the bell twice more. Kenshin stepped outside and blocked her way with a long wooden staff. "Go inside," he said. "They only want warriors."

MIKIO CURSED LOUDLY and threw on a dark kimono. The bell rang three times. Yumi's bell had rung twice.

Everyone's bell got to ring but his.

He took his great-grandfather's *daisho* from the display rack. The heavy-bladed battle *katana* and its shorter, keener partner, the *wakizashi*. Yumi emerged glowing with sweat, pulled a kimono over her lithe form, and lifted her bow and quiver from the wall.

They traded grim nods. The night they dreaded had finally come.

Shiro ran into the parlor. Mikio crouched and pressed his cheek to his crying son's face. "Stay with mother, brave son," he said. "We will play in the morning."

Yumi nocked her bow at the door as Mikio dashed into the night with both swords drawn.

Mikio circled the village on a deer track. The ugly song of death shouts and steel on steel echoed through the forest. A young samurai slumped at his post, nailed to a tree with a black arrow. An archer lay sprawled as if sleeping, a jagged smile slashed across her throat. Three shinobi stepped from the home of Takashi Harada, their best spearman. Mikio crept upon them as they flicked the blood from their swords.

Grandfather's blades sliced two from shoulder to waist with ease. The third ninja's arm fell to the porch before his sword was drawn. Mikio speared him with a backthrust and crouched to listen at the door.

The home was silent. Harada's wife and child did not wail for him. The Black Dragons had taken no prisoners.

Mikio jogged for the temple.

THE MONKS' STICKS WERE NO MATCH FOR NINJA BLADES. Two remained, facing seven. Kenshin handed Tara a broad *tanto* knife in a decorated scabbard. "My father made this. He was no legend. Not a Masamune. But he was a master. If they come for you . . . slice your own throat."

Tara stared.

"The Black Dragons have no honor," Kenshin said. "This is a slaughter. My son was right. They have merged with the new yakuza. Their money from drugs and enslavement of women. If they don't kill you, if they take you to Roppongi and Kabuchiko as a sex slave, you will regret not spilling your blood a thousand times before they dump your wasted body into the sea."

Tara checked the blade and stuffed it into her jeans pocket.

Kenshin descended the steps and swept his long staff in a wide circle, scattering the ninja skirmish.

Three Black Dragons charged. He speared one with the shaft and cracked another twice, shifted grip and parried the sword of the third only inches from his face. Moving with speed belying his age, he stepped crosswise to their movements, as if they existed in only two dimensions and he alone inhabited the third axis. His weapon cracked in metronomic sweeps, tumbling them to the dirt.

Kenshin's two acolytes shielded themselves in range of his strikes, clubbing ninja limbs until they cracked and the joints bent unnaturally. As the houses of Hachiman samurai fell, Black Dragons converged on the temple and took the place of the fallen.

MIKIO RAN PAST SLAUGHTERED SAMURAI who had risen to the bell's warning only to be cut down in the village streets. An arrow snapped past his cheek and sent him behind the blacksmith shop for cover. His grandfather's anvil sat inside. The man he'd never met, the one who had recovered the *Honjo Masamune* and died for it on a nameless island after escaping a POW camp run by Gantetsu, leader of the Black Dragons.

Mikio wanted so badly to bring that sword to his father. To let his grandfather's spirit rest, and not wander the earth knowing his task was undone. His father had given up and lost himself in worship of the past.

Shouts from the blacksmith's house where his cousin Jin lived. Mikio burst inside and found Jin guarding his family, holding two ninja at bay with a long-bladed *naginata* pole-arm. Jin bled from a slash down his chest.

The ninja held their swords in reverse grip in tight quarters, the blades held against their wrists. One spun and deflected Mikio's katana. Mikio skewered him under the breastbone with the wakizashi.

Jin used the opening to hack the second ninja's thigh to the bone. Mikio nodded to Jin and left him stabbing the fallen assassin again and again, crying out with the shock of those freshly blooded in battle.

Mikio cursed himself for not having rebelled against his father more strongly. They could not hide away as an example of a dead age. After the war they'd become complacent, content to allow the Black Dragons to merge with the yakuza and rule from below.

They had escaped to high ground, and now they were being cut off at the knees.

YUMI CURSED AT THE EMPTY GUEST ROOM. Tara had run. Her husband had been foolish to drag her into the Akita mountains, where the only ghost-white foreigners were German hikers and Americans who wanted to venture to places where tourists didn't normally go.

Shiro hugged her leg. She gave him a squeeze and led him through the house as she snuffed out the lamps. She upended the thick dining table and sat him behind it, then perched by the secret arrow slit in the northeast corner, covering the mountain path.

Yumi had practiced the bow as a hobby before she'd met Mikio. The yakuza had funded Japan's largest political party from its inception. The corruption was an open secret. The players changed, but the stories did not. When she dared report on it, she was demoted to a backwater post in Niigata. An orphan since her twenties, when her parents were ruined by a yakuza real estate scam and committed suicide on the bullet train tracks, she was delighted to find a funny, handsome fighter teaching at a dojo outside Niigata city.

She had never met anyone like him. Intense, chivalrous and old-fashioned. Mikio cared little for money and viewed the country like a child, as if the skyscrapers were anthills that could crumble without consequence and reveal the Japan of the past.

When Mikio pledged marriage, he told her his secret. He trusted her never to speak of the Sons of Hachiman, should she be unable to accept his proposal.

She took his hand and walked into legend.

They spent years trying to convince his father that living in a mountain village unchanged since the Satsuma rebellion was no way to fight yakuza who hid tattoos beneath Saville row suits, and had no compunctions against slaughtering entire families of those who stood between them and greater wealth and power.

They had failed.

Yumi had hoped the Black Dragons would simply allow them to fade into irrelevance, but they had come to settle the blood debt.

Mikio would fight to the death. And so would she.

THREE SHINOBI MARCHED INTO THE MOUNTAIN VILLAGE with purpose, one taller than the rest. The alarm having sounded, their comrades fought samurai openly. Blades rang loud in the night. The fallen screamed and flailed, their hot blood steaming the air.

These three kept silent. Blades sheathed on their shoulders. Faces blacked beneath their mask wraps.

Short-barreled M4 assault rifles slung from two of their shoulders. Tipped with suppressor cans. Loaded with thick, hi-cap magazines jungle-rigged with hundred-mile-an-hour tape. The tallest carried a chunky black pistol fitted with a fat black silencer.

As they came upon skirmishes, they took turns shooting samurai down. Flat slaps of suppressed fire crackled through the trees, no louder than the sweet spot of a monk's staff connecting with skull. Single shots. Conserving ammunition. Making every bullet count.

MIKIO SLICED HIS WAY THROUGH THE BATTLE outside Hachiman temple with his *dotanuki* blade. It meant *cuts thick torsos*, and the sword lived up to its name. He cleaved one Black Dragon from ear to breastbone, and another across the waist. The dying ninja tore handfuls of grass, dragging his chest away from his severed legs, innards trailing between.

Kenshin whirred his staff overhead and clubbed a ninja aside. Two Black Dragons with *kusarigama* sickles on chains lassoed samurai and yanked them off balance for their swordsmen to cut down.

Mikio fought his way toward them. There were too many. They had lost their spearmen, their archers. They had no time to don armor. This was street fighting, not war. Mikio was one of few who had fought real battles. His father had approved fewer and fewer missions, weary of sending men to their deaths. The best had died in their sleep.

TARA HOPPED OFF THE STEPS and hugged the wall. She dashed to a fallen monk and dragged him from the fray. Legs slashed, his right arm cut to the bone. Tara ripped the hem of his robe and tied off the arm. He thanked her, with eyes glazed and face pale. The arm was probably lost, but she left the knot loose and told him to count off each minute and release the pressure.

She ran to the next. There were so many. Moaning, gurgling, dying. More blood than she'd ever seen on the drunken snow-strewn highways of the Iron Range. The air stank with it. Every breath a mouthful of tinfoil.

And they battled on.

YUMI FOUGHT THE TREMBLING IN HER LEGS that told her to run. She felled the first shadow with an arrow to the throat. The second sent his own arrow through her cross-shaped window and nicked her cheek. The moon betrayed his cover, and she put an arrow in his gut. The third belly-crawled through the rocks, and three of her missiles shattered on stone. Now he hid at an angle that forced her to step outside to hit him. And she doubted he was alone.

Yumi scooped Shiro from where he lay behind the table and slipped out the back. The ninja pressed himself against the wall and shimmied toward the arrow slit, his sword drawn.

"Ma!" Shiro cried.

Yumi dropped Shiro on his butt in the grass and drew her bow. The ninja dived into the garden. She followed him with her arrow and released. A grunt came from the darkness. She nocked another arrow and clutched Shiro to her chest, hurrying toward the deer track. A shuriken flashed through the branches and thunked into her shoulder blade. The pain squeezed the air from her lungs, but she kept running for the temple, hot blood running down her spine.

"KEEP FIGHTING, MY SON!" Kenshin shouted over the battle, levering his staff to crack two opponents on either side. "Retreat to the temple!"

The bloodied monks fell back up the steps, their sticks gouged and split. Tara bandaged a samurai with scraps of his own kimono, staunching the blood from a gaping wound.

Mikio crossed his blades to parry a Black Dragon's sword, then sidestepped and attacked the blade, snapping it at the hilt. He switched the wakizashi to reverse grip and slashed the ninja's neck as he passed.

Mikio's muscles screamed and his lungs blazed. The Black Dragons outnumbered him, but his mad-wolf eyes and blood-slick blades held them at bay. He joined his father on the steps of the temple, guarding the retreat of beaten-down monks and wounded samurai.

"I see why you crave battle," Kenshin shouted, fending off two swordsmen with a quick sweep and reverse.

Arrows whistled into the Black Dragon ranks from afar. Yumi and three of her students fired volley after volley from the woods. The ninjas began to rout. Mikio stepped forward, driving them back with exaggerated strikes. Kenshin followed suit, and tired samurai joined them.

"Scurry back to your gambling dens," Kenshin shouted. "The Sons of Hachiman will never surrender!"

Mikio smiled and cut down another. Father and son drove the Black Dragons down the temple steps as Yumi's archers peppered their backs.

Three warriors stopped on the temple path and raised their weapons. Sharp staccato bursts crackled the air. Monks and samurai fell. Archers tripped, their bows shattered. Kenshin stared into infinity and his staff clattered down the stairs.

Yumi ran for the woods with Shiro in tow. Tara flattened against the back wall of the temple, hand on the *tanto's* grip.

Kenshin tumbled down the steps.

"Father!" Mikio dropped his wakizashi and knelt at his father's side, guarding him with his katana.

Kenshin gripped his son's kimono, baring a bloody-toothed grimace. "No . . . ." he groaned. "You will not die for me! I do not permit it."

The gunmen surrounded father and son.

Kenshin coughed blood and Mikio cradled his father's head. "Then I will kill for you."

"Drop your sword, samurai."

"Fight me, Takehiko!" Mikio snarled. "Coward!"

"The Sons of Hachiman are finished," Oki said, and peeled back her mask. "Takehiko has more important business to attend to." She nodded to the riflemen. "Take Mikio. Execute the rest."

A rifleman fired on the monks inside the temple. The other trained his weapon on Kenshin, and Mikio lunged and pressed his chest to the barrel.

"Fuck you!"

An arrow punched through the rifle's trigger guard and severed the gunman's finger, pinning the weapon to his chest.

Mikio seized the rifle and Oki clubbed the back of his skull with her pistol's suppressor. He stumbled to his knees, and the Black Dragons fell on him with feet and fists.

Oki aimed into the woods and fired her magazine empty.

"Tie him up," Oki said.

She stood over Kenshin, leering down at the old man's face as he coughed blood. "Japan no longer wants samurai," Oki said. "War is a video game. But the world will always need assassins."

Oki holstered her pistol and cupped her phone to her ear. "It's done."

TARA CROUCHED BEHIND THE TEMPLE as five Black Dragons hogtied Mikio. The rest wandered the battlefield, skewering the wounded. She held the *tanto* against her chest. She could kill the tall bitch. But then what? They'd cut her to pieces.

Tara stuck the knife in its sheath. The old plan would still work. Get the bike. Go to Tokyo. Find them. Free them. She took a deep breath and bolted for the woods where she'd last seen Yumi firing arrows.

"BOSS," THE LAST RIFLEMAN SAID, and jerked his head toward the ghost-white gaijin running from the temple.

Oki took his M4 and followed the woman through the red-dot sight. The crazy bitch with the car at the airport had chased them six thousand miles.

She had spirit.

The temperature was already near freezing. Oki made a bet with herself. If she saw the redhead again, she would buy her a drink.

And then kill her.

Oki dumped the rifle with the other firearms and stripped down to a motorcycle jacket covered in black and red patches. She piled her discarded kit on the rifles, then tucked a thermite grenade at the bottom and primed the pin.

"Clear out," she said. "Back to base by oh-five-hundred."

She followed the men lugging Mikio down the mountain, and hurled a second thermite grenade into the temple.

The ordnance burst into molten orange fireworks. The temple blazed through the trees as the Black Dragons descended, the mountain erupting in flames that shot high in the black night.

47.

TAKEHIKO POCKETED THE PHONE and smiled. He found his glasses and robe and walked the plush carpets of the Ginza penthouse to his father's room. He rapped three times on the solid oak.

A bark from his father beckoned him to enter.

The thick old man lay on the bed with a glazed-eye blonde Roppongi whore under each tattooed arm. One had her hand beneath the sheets, keeping the Black Dragon *oyabun* aroused.

"Yes?" Gantetsu Abe barked.

Takehiko bowed deeply. "The Sons of Hachiman are no more."

"About time," he said. "You may go. Unless you wish to join us? They are quite talented. And clean."

"Thank you, father," Takehiko said. "But there is still much work to do. The *Kumite,* and the deal with the nationalists . . . they are paying in gold. I have a connection to launder it, but it will take time."

Abe sneered. "You test my patience. It took you ten years to slaughter a bunch of idiots dressed as samurai on the mountain. Do not make me wait ten more for my rightful due." He pushed the unoccupied blonde's head beneath the sheets.

Takehiko looked out the wall-length window. "Yes, father." Tokyo's lights gleamed like a treasure room floor. Treasure he had long been denied.

Abe hiked the sheet and revealed the girl's behind. "Come, enjoy yourself. Oki is beautiful, but not a ripe peach like these."

"Pleasing my father is its own reward," Takehiko said, turning away.

"Extinguishing the Miyamoto line makes all your failures bearable," Abe grunted, his flabby chest shaking.

Takehiko closed the door behind him. He wished Oki were here. She was a boring fanatic, but athletic and fierce. His father had arranged their marriage to wed the Gantetsu to her ninja lineage, which stretched back to the Tokugawa Shogunate.

It was a pity to use her, but what else were true believers good for?

His father would be furious when he saw Mikio in the battle cage, but would not be able to deny the visual impact of their followers seeing Takehiko behead him with the *Honjo Masamune*.

Takehiko would escape his father's wrath by joining the war gold on its journey to the States, where doomsday-obsessed militiamen would pay handsomely for it not only in cash, but with military weapons. When Takehiko returned, he would not be the richest yakuza by many billions. But he would be the best armed and the most cunning.

With the blessing of the Shadow Shogun, and Oki and her shadow warriors on his side, Takehiko would geyser to the top in an eruption of blood. Promising citizens he would wipe the corrupt stain of the yakuza from the streets once and for all, while the war with North Korea kept them willfully distracted.

Takehiko pressed himself to the window pane with his robe open, naked before the jeweled sprawl of the metropolis his bloodline would rule again.

A true shadow shogunate. One that would endure for centuries.

48.

REEVES WOKE TO HIS FISTS and feet pounding the floor and his heart playing hummingbird. The black-eyed guard held a stun gun to his leg.

Reeves leapt to strike and slammed into an enormous, tattooed fist. The huge baby-faced bruiser at the other end of it dragged Reeves out by his foot and threw him to the floor.

Baby-face was checkered with Polynesian inkwork on his knees, chest and shoulders. He bulged with muscle and a Buddha belly of hard fat, wearing only a spiked collar and red fighting shorts. A tan, tattooed Hulk.

The guards noosed Reeves with a catch-pole and dragged him to the gym.

Another fighter howled as he got the shock treatment next.

Men packed the gym, some suited, others in jeans and work shirts. Takehiko sat on a folding chair, the *Honjo Masamune* across his sharkskin lap. Reeves lunged to the end of his leash. The Hawaiian Hulk slapped him across the face with a walrus flipper of a hand.

"Sorry, Reeves." Takehiko chuckled. "I'm afraid I am a mere observer." He turned and spoke in Japanese to two frog-faced older gentlemen in pinstripes beside him.

The pinstriped men nodded at Reeves warily.

The Hulk shoved Reeves into the chain-link hexagon of the sparring cage, its mat a Jackson Pollock of bloodstains. Razor wire ringed the top of the fence. Reeves rattled the supports with a kick.

"Fight me, Takehiko," Reeves said. "Do your cronies know what a coward you are? How do you say coward in Japanese?"

"American." Takehiko laughed. "You will sate your bloodlust today, but not on me."

The guards pushed in a hooded fighter at the end of a catch-pole. The New Guy. He walked calmly before them, his body cow-spotted with fading bruises and burns, chest striped with old scars. A green and black tattoo of three whirling blades wax-sealed his upper arm.

Takehiko drew his blade and addressed the crowd in Japanese, conducting with razor sharp steel. Reeves couldn't understand the words, but recognized the cadence.

Announcing the fight.

Reeves held up his fists when Takehiko shouted his name. The crowd clapped politely.

His opponent did not follow suit. Hulk yanked off the man's hood, revealing a bald Japanese bullet head, cheeks rouged with abrasions.

"Akashi Uchida!" Takehiko shouted to the crowd's boos.

The trainer weaved handwraps between Uchida's fingers, then approached Reeves with the roll of tape.

Reeves stuck his fists through the cage and spread his fingers. The bones of the human hand were weak; Reeves learned that on Johansson's jaw. The wraps turned fists into bricks of meat, bone and athletic tape.

The Hulk strapped on a pair of Roman cestus, sheathing his fists and forearms in spiked leather. Studded shin guards covered his thick calves. He pushed Uchida into the cage ahead of him. The guards slammed the gate shut and padlocked it.

Hulkboy lifted a spiked fist. "Fight to death," he said, pushing the fighters together. "Tap fist!"

Reeves glared at Uchida and bumped fists.

"That is some crazy *Conan the Barbarian* shit," Uchida said, jerking his head at the Ref.

Reeves ignored him. Better not to get friendly with the guy he had to kill. He remembered what Mikio said his name meant in Japanese. He pounded his chest and shouted, *"Paizuri Tatsujin!"*

The crowd burst into laughter. Hulkboy raised his fist.

Uchida snorted. "Don't know what that means, do you?"

Takehiko shouted, *"Tatakau!"* and the Hulk dropped his fist.

Reeves fell into a rhythm and snapped an exploratory jab.

"You gotta be Reeves," Uchida said, parrying with ease. Reeves gave chase, pounding his forearms.

Reeves slipped a fist past his guard and opened his cheek.

"They're gonna kill us anyway," Uchida shouted. "Let's take this fuckhead out, and see what they do then. Maybe we'll have a chance."

The Ref shouted "No talk! *Tatakau!*" and thumped Uchida on the back. The spikes gashed his flesh.

Uchida groaned and pounded the Hulk in the belly, then skipped sideways to hook Reeves in the ribs. "Mikio said you were a knucklehead!"

Reeves countered with a kick to the thigh. "Shut up and fight!"

The Ref circled, goading and prodding them with spiked fists, keeping them from waiting the other out.

Uchida threw high, raked his knuckles over Reeves' eye and drew blood. Reeves hammered Uchida's bruised body, driving him into the cage.

Reeves squinted through the blood. No bells, no cut man, no one in his corner. The only towel thrown would be the sheet over his face.

"Don't make me kill you," Uchida panted, clubbing Reeves down with his forearm as he threw a knee to his face. Reeves slipped it and heaved Uchida's legs with a double takedown, hammering at his face when they hit the mats.

Let's see how you ninja pricks like ground and pound.

Uchida head-butted Reeves in the chin and swept him. Reeves pulled guard, snapping his legs around Uchida's abdomen.

"Tara's looking for you," Uchida snarled in his ear, and thumped his ribs with a fist.

"Fuck you say?" Reeves heel-kicked Uchida's back and locked down his arm.

"The redhead with the tits," Uchida panted.

Reeves saw PFC Jenkins laughing, blood gushing from his throat. *You waiting for him to tap?*

Survival mode. Freight train heart thundering down the line. No rules, no taps, no surrender. In combat the worst ally is the guy who isn't afraid to die. Reeves had nothing left. No future, no family, no friends.

He was only afraid to die before Takehiko's face came apart beneath his fists.

"I'm sick of you fuckers and your tricks!" Reeves broke his guard and kicked Uchida away, then scrambled to his feet.

Reeves leapt with a flying knee. Uchida dodged and socked Reeves in the ribs. Reeves chain-stepped knees until Uchida dodged into his overhand right. Uchida bounced off the cage, dazed.

"Why should I trust you?" Reeves kept him flattened to the cage, shouldering him in the face to keep the Ref at bay.

"I could've killed you three times already," Uchida said, slamming the knife of his hand into Reeves' throat. "Quit being a dickhole!" Reeves gagged.

The Ref spiked Reeves between the shoulder blades. The pain turned to red mist behind Reeves' eyes.

Reeves charged for the kill. The Rage Cage Combo. Uchida ate the jabs and took a front kick to the gut hard. The crowd jumped from their seats and roared, folding chairs clattering to the floor.

The handwraps shredded Uchida's cheeks and his eyes rolled white.

Reeves pounded him into the mat as adrenaline danced through his veins. For the first time in his life the Ref wasn't there to pull him off. The fruitless fury at Butch's death, Tara's car up in flames. The judge nodding to the Johansson family after the gavel fell. Jenkins shivering in his arms. Reeves' father ignoring him when he popped up in the back seat to tell him there was a truck on the bridge.

Takehiko held the sword high and voiced a bombastic oath that sent the crowd into a thundering chant. The pinstriped men stood and clapped.

"Kokuryukai! Kokuryukai!"

Reeves pounded until the Hulk finally pushed him aside. Even Takehiko the butcher stared at what Reeves had done.

When Reeves saw what remained of Uchida, he shouldered into the beefy Ref and drove him through the cage door. They slammed into the floor and Reeves rattled Hulkboy's jaw with the whip of an elbow.

The crowd scattered back as Reeves launched for Takehiko.

Takehiko raised the blade, his face blank with fear. "Guards!"

Reeves flopped to his face. His spine bowed and he bit a chunk off the inside of his cheek. Two thin wires ran from barbs in his back to the black-eyed guard's Taser.

The Taser barbs burned in his lats as Reeves struggled to his feet, the electrodes rattling like a viper's tail. He hissed through his teeth as he staggered across the gym toward Takehiko, jerking with the current.

Butch's face burned into his retinas.

The crowd chanted, *"Ganbarre!"*

Keep fighting.

Reeves staggered until the barbs ripped from his back, freeing him from the current. He lunged for Takehiko's throat.

The Hawaiian tackled Reeves from behind, looping a Hulk-thick arm around his throat and driving him to the floor.

Reeves groaned in impotent fury as the choke cut the blood to his brain, drowning him in the claustrophobic dark with nothing but his own heartbeat hammering him to sleep.

49.

TARA HUDDLED IN THE FOREST, shivering beneath a pine bough with Kenshin's *tanto* clutched to her chest, watching the last of the Black Dragons limp away from the slaughter. The temple blazed, a fiery dust-devil on the windswept mountain, and tree branches rattled like chattering teeth. Tara warmed her palms with steamy breaths and pressed them to her cheeks to thaw. She'd fared much colder nights in Minnesota, but not alone in the woods with nothing but jeans and a t-shirt.

She crept low and hurried toward the bonfire, looking away as she passed the slit throats of the samurai she had bandaged. So much death. She moved like a puppet, watching herself from far away.

The warmth chased the numbness from her bones. The framework of the temple glowed orange in the flames. The thick beams cracked and spat sparks. The structure creaked and shifted. Tara ran around to the other side in case it collapsed.

Four bodies sprawled on the steps. Three monks, their orange robes stained red, and Mikio's father, staring dead-eyed at the stars. Tara knelt and brushed his eyes closed with her fingertips.

Kenshin gripped her wrist. "Tara-san," he gasped.

"Jesus!"

"Tell my son I am sorry," Kenshin said through gritted teeth.

"They took him," Tara said.

"Then we have truly lost," Kenshin said, jaw trembling.

Tara held him while his ragged breaths faded. She squeezed his dry, papery hand and they watched the temple collapse in on itself.

A beam clattered down the steps, scattering embers. One of the dead monks began to smolder.

Two figures in white walked out of the darkness to warm at the fire. Yumi leading her stunned boy by the hand. Her kimono was torn and streaked with blood.

Yumi raised her chin toward Kenshin. Tara shook her head.

"Mama, is Ojiisan asleep also?" Shiro asked, and hugged his mother's leg.

"No, my son," she said. "Ojiisan has joined the spirits."

Shiro nodded. The fire played off his black eyes. "Sayonara, Ojiisan," he whispered.

Yumi scanned the steps. Mikio's blades were among the discarded weapons. "Your father dropped his swords, Shiro. Please collect them carefully and place them in their scabbards."

While Shiro performed his chore, Yumi lifted Kenshin's body by the legs. Tara looked up at her.

"Please," Yumi said. "We do not bury our dead. We must put them on the pyre."

The horizon glowed pink before they were done, their faces dark with soot, the air acrid with scorched flesh. They washed in the spring. Yumi pulled on a pair of jeans and dressed her son in modern clothing. Tara squeezed into one of Yumi's shirts. Her jeans reeked of smoke.

TARA LED THEM TO THE MOTORBIKE. She peeled back the tarp and gripped the handlebars of the Honda. Yumi clamped a hand on her shoulder.

"What?"

Yumi pointed with a thin, calloused finger. "You see?"

Tara squinted. The thinnest of wires led from the bike's fork to the base of a tree. Yumi brushed away the leaves, revealing a fragmentation grenade.

"They left us alive because they feel we are no threat," Yumi said. "But they know we're coming." She untwined the wire and checked the grenade pin.

"They don't know who they're fucking with," Tara said.

Yumi nodded, and pocketed the grenade.

Tara couldn't get the bike started. At first she thought it was just cold, then found the snapped fuel hose. The Black Dragons took no chances.

They took turns carrying Shiro down the mountain. The monkeys did not chatter, and the birds did not sing. The creatures hid away in the silent trees, as if the mountain itself mourned the night's slaughter.

The town had not yet stirred. No one awake but a hunched old woman sweeping the sidewalk.

The motorcycle garage bay was open. Several bikes in various stages of autopsy, parts spread out on dingy sheets. The mechanic squatted on an upturned bucket, puffing a strong Russian cigarette. Belly pooched out, his navel puckered as if waiting for a drag of his smoke. He perked his eyebrows as Tara short-stepped around the corner.

"*Ohayo, ushipai,*" the man chuckled.

Tara's feet burned from the hike. She ignored him and flipped through her phrasebook. "I want to buy a . . . bike," she said. Switched to English. "The Ural with the sidecar." Then back. Flip, flip. "How much?"

He scratched at a scab on his scruffy chin, "*Demio kazamesa teka,*" he said, leering.

Yumi marched from around the corner, Mikio's swords crossed at her belt. She yanked the *tanto* from Tara's back pocket and thrust it at the mechanic's crotch, piercing the bucket and sinking it to the hilt.

He yelped and dropped his cigarette, squirming back into a shelf overflowing with parts.

Yumi jammed her thumb into his Adam's apple and spat angry rapid-fire Japanese. "You want some head? Maybe I cut yours off, the little and the big, you pervert piece of shit!"

The mechanic held up two grease-lined palms.

Yumi traded Tara the *tanto* for a wad of yen. She feathered off five ten-thousand notes and let them flutter to the floor.

"Tansyo," she sneered.

Yumi tucked Shiro into the sidecar and Tara topped off the Ural's black tank from a battered red gas can. She kicked it to life while the mechanic glared and picked at the slit in his jeans.

"Be happy I didn't take your balls," Yumi said in Japanese, and straddled the seat behind Tara. "Mikio won't be so kind." She flipped down her helmet's visor, and Tara eased them onto the street.

She took a wide curve around an old man staring up at the plume of white smoke rising to the sky.

Shiro pointed to the sunburst hidden by the plume. "Mama, look. Buddha's rays."

The beams shot toward a Tokyo shrouded in mist, with only the death cap of Mount Fuji standing above the smog.

50.

"DINGLEBERRY, DINGLEBERRY, DINGLEBERRY," a voice sang. "Hee hee hee hee!"

"Shut the hell up, Wooster," a man wheezed in reply.

Butch woke to the smell of cigarettes, iodine and human waste on top of the low tang of sour sheets. A fat cargo plane buzzed overhead, and a hefty oscillating fan cooled the sweat on his greasy brow. He felt weak, like he'd been painted to the bed.

In the bed to his left, a man with a bandaged head stirred the contents of a white enamel bedpan with his fingertip. Wooster laughed and broke into song. "Jimmy cracked corn and I don't care!"

"I'll shove that chamberpot down your throat," gurgled the bedmate to Butch's right. "You're a phony! The war's over, quit acting like a damn loony bird!" Hook-nosed and wasted away, his chest sagged like a pair of ungartered stockings. He wheezed and spat into a yellow-stained rag.

Restraints creaked as Butch tried to sit up. His left arm was shackled to the bed frame. He leaned over and unbuckled it.

"I wouldn't try to get up," Wooster said, wagging a brown-smeared finger.

"Hell if I'm staying in this nuthouse," Butch said, and swung his leg over the edge. He stood up, gripping the bed for balance. The room spun and he tumbled to the floor. Pain jolted up his spine.

"Told ya!" Wooster cackled.

Only one leg hit the floor. Butch slapped the bare spot on the green tiles. He patted his hospital gown, as if a pickpocket had made off with his right leg.

The bandage leaked fresh blood where his leg had been. Butch screamed and pounded the floor. A thick Filipino nurse ran in with two orderlies and heaved him to the bed, holding him down.

"Easy big fella," the nurse said, and jabbed a hypo into his one remaining ass cheek.

"You stole my leg," Butch gasped. The meds washed over him like lukewarm bath water. He clutched the nurse and cried against her breasts. "Jean, Jean, don't leave me," he said.

The nurse patted his head. "Sleep, big fella. Don't cry. You got more left to you than a lot of guys got."

The bright light above the bed became the sun, blanking his vision in a white shroud.

BUTCH RESTED AS MUCH AS HE COULD. He rolled shreds of newspaper into balls and plugged his ears to shield himself from Wooster and the lunger screaming at each other. The lunger's name was Luce, and he played a good game of chess. The nurse did as well, and she could belt a tune like a Filipino Ethel Merman.

The nurse's name was Emlyn. Butch asked her if the soldiers who brought him in left any of his things, and she said she'd look. When she came back to dole out pills, she held a bundle of sun-bleached fatigues pinned between her breast and elbow. She set them on Butch's lap.

He thanked her, and unfolded the package.

"Your pigsticker's in the locker," Emlyn said. "Can't have that in here."

Butch found the rusted, beat-up Tetley tea box wrapped in his shredded pants. The scraps and letters were dry inside. Butch smiled. "Thanks, hon. Could I bother you for some paper and a sharp pencil? I promise I won't stick it in Wooster's ear, no matter how loud he gets."

Butch wrote five letters to Jean and tore them up. It was better that she think he was dead. He was worse than half a man. There were no one-legged cowboys.

And the sword, let that prick keep it. When those Black Dragons showed up looking for it, he'd shit his pants.

Butch killed time reading the letters he had received from Jean and his folks, and the scraps he'd written in the POW camp. To tell the world how they'd been starved, beaten, tortured. And in Johnny Nagaki's case, murdered. Would Johnny's family want to know? Better if they didn't. Let them think he died a Hollywood death.

The war was over. Millions had suffered worse than they had. Countless had died. Butch stared at the empty side of his chair where his leg had been. What made him so special? The hospital was full of busted and broken men. At least he wasn't Wooster, fishing for corn in his bedpan and giggling like he found gold nuggets.

Butch collected the scraps and stuffed them in the tea can. The origami dove floated to the floor.

Butch picked it up, and thumped his forehead with his knuckle three times.

Kazeta, dying in the surf. Unburied.

"An unburied soul wanders the earth forever," Kazeta had told him. "Promise you will bury me."

When the sun glowed red over the surf, it brought Butch back to Montana. Kazeta had called it *setsunai,* a deep sadness you can't shake. The sunset gave him *setsunai.* He felt it again now, turning the dove over in his hands.

He couldn't appease Kazeta's spirit, if it wanted his bones buried. The crabs that scuttled between the rocks had surely picked them clean. But he could complete Kazeta's mission, to fool the Black Dragons into chasing him for the ringer sword.

Butch knew who'd taken the blade. If the son of a bitch hadn't traded it for a Nambu pistol or a bag full of gold teeth, Butch would get it back.

And when the Black Dragons came calling, he'd fight for it like it was the real one.

Butch set the paper dove atop the tea can, and gripped the rickety table by the edges. He stood on an equally rickety leg, snatching his wooden crutch for balance.

He held the crutch out like a bird with a bum wing, bent at the knee, and hopped.

Wooster looked up from his bed pan and laughed. "Pogo stick! Pogo stick!"

Butch hopped closer, and swiped the crutch at Wooster's head. Wooster ducked and flung the bedpan high into the air.

The bedpan hit the ceiling and dumped its contents with a splatter. Luce dived under his sheets and Butch hopped away, catching himself with his crutch. Wooster looked up with a Stan Laurel expression of dread and surprise, poking at the wet lumps of shit leopard-spotting his tow-headed noggin.

"Oh Christ!" Wooster hollered, and ran for the head.

Luce slapped his pillow. "I knew it," he wheezed, and spat a brown oyster into his rag. "I knew he was a phony."

51.

YUMI AND TARA PARKED THE BIKE OUTSIDE a Lawson's convenience store to stretch their legs. They ate triangles of rice stuffed with tuna that resembled white bread sandwiches, and took cheese biscuits and pickled plums for the road. The Tokyo metro area seemed a country into itself, buildings spreading from the bay halfway across the isle of Japan.

They followed a tentacle of highway into the city. Yumi lifted her visor and shouted directions. The streets converged on the skyscrapers and crowded out the buildings themselves, doubling up on top and below each other with ramps, overpasses and twisty concrete capillaries.

"People get lost here even with GPS," Yumi said, pointing over Tara's shoulder. "Left at the light. Watch that bus. They have the right of way."

The bike buzzed through traffic, circling around an enormous park where costumed teenagers posed in flowing dresses, peacock hair and ghostly makeup, like extras from a punk rock sci-fi film set in Victorian England. They dodged through salarymen hustling toward bars and clots of bubbly minivans and stately black taxis pumping through clogged rush-hour arteries.

Tara nosed the bike into a narrow parking lot crammed with police cars, black on the bottom, white on top. A sign on the concrete fortress read "Shinjuku Precinct No. 7" in steel text beneath the Japanese symbols.

Inside the institutional beige lobby, a chirpy clerk worked the queue of unhappy citizens. Tara stood to give her ass a rest from the bike's harsh ride. Cops did cop things, dressed like cops. Blue shirts, black pants. Haircuts at least a decade out of touch.

A round-faced man in a blue suit pushed through the gate.

Yumi waved. "Takagi!"

The cop smiled. "Yumi-san."

His smile sagged as Yumi rushed up with Shiro in tow.

TAKAGI LIT A CIGARETTE and sat on the desk of his cramped basement office while Yumi caught him up on the past seven years of her life.

"You've been legally declared dead," he said in Japanese. Thick in the middle and hair slicked back, he resembled the yakuza he investigated. "When you just disappeared . . . ." He looked at Shiro, napping on a chair, and exhaled. "I assumed the worst. I never imagined you could be living in the mountains with a samurai cult. I knew the reporting got to you, but if you were gonna go crazy, you should've just become a cop."

Yumi grinned. "I've put more yakuza in jail than you, so what does that say?"

Takagi sighed. "That I'll live to have grandchildren, and you won't."

Yumi rubbed his shoulders. "I should have told you. I'm sorry."

"You trust me now," Takagi said. "When you have nowhere else to go."

Yumi rolled her eyes. "We can hit the Gantetsu family hard, if you still care."

Takagi waved his cigarette at the windowless office. "This is where caring got me." He pointed at Tara. "Is she another foreigner who thought she'd be a classy hostess, who got tricked into working in a suck-off parlor? The courts don't give a damn about them.

I've tried to get them out of the life. And you know what? I took a transfer to homicide, instead. This way I can't get any more of them killed," he said, and took a deep drag. "Because when I deal with them, they're dead already."

Yumi bit her lip. "You weren't a quitter when I knew you."

"What about you? Going off into the mountains."

Tara flipped through her phrasebook. *"Sumimasen,"* she said. "I'm done, okay, Yumi? I don't know what you two are saying."

"Apologies, Tara-san. We'll speak English," Yumi said.

"Thanks," Tara said. "Now I'd really just like to go to the American Embassy. I just want to go home."

Yumi clenched her jaw. "Takagi, tell her what'll happen if she tries to leave the country."

Takagi furrowed his brow. "The first girl I bought a ticket home didn't make it to the plane. Disappeared. So I escorted the next one. She made it all the way back to Estonia." He puffed, and exhaled. "But not home. They mailed me photos of the pieces. If the Black Dragons want you, they'll find you. And no one else will."

"What the fuck," Tara said, and bit her knuckle. "I just wanted to get the hell out of a bad place. I helped your damn husband, and now I have a death sentence."

"What about your boy Reeves?" Yumi said. "You were hot to trot just a day ago. Now you're quitting again."

All that blood. "I . . . I didn't know what those ninja guys could do."

Yumi exhaled through her nostrils. "When my son gets out of shock, I'm going to have to tell him that everyone he grew up with is dead. Children. Babies. You're alive," Yumi said. "Start acting like it."

Tara stared down at her blood-flecked tennis shoes. "Damn it. Just, damn it. What can I do? I can't kill someone. I just can't, okay?"

"You can drive, can't you? Or was my husband making that up because he likes your big tits?"

Tara pinched her eyebrows together. "I can drive, bitch."

"Good," Yumi said. She unbuttoned her blouse and checked her bandage. "And you can field dress a wound, and suture it closed. And you stayed alive when twenty of the best Black Dragon commandos massacred a whole village.

"You can die running, or you can die fighting. What's it gonna be, rock 'n' roller girl?"

Tara thought of what Reeves had said. *I fight to know I'm alive.* Tom Petty on her stereo, after they'd made love. Reeves held her and laughed. *This guy is kind of mellow for me, but I like what he's saying. About being up against the gates of hell, and not backing down. That's what fighting's about.*

"Let's fuck these fucking fuckers," Tara said, and punched her palm.

"Mikio said you had spirit." Yumi smiled. "Takagi, the Dragons captured two fighters. My husband and this Reeves guy. What does that tell you?"

"Time for a *Kumite*." Takagi huffed, and took a final drag on his butt. "You said they had guns, right?"

"Big guns," Tara said.

"Military weapons," Yumi said. "American."

"From Okinawa?"

"Takehiko has controlling interest in a Korean shipping line," Yumi said. "Mikio said he uses a container ship like his secret yacht. They met with militiamen in the States—American *uyoku dantai*— and bought crates of weapons. Is that enough to light a fire under the chief's ass?"

Takagi grunted. "With hearsay evidence from a foreigner with a forged passport and a pain in the ass reporter who's been declared legally dead and is in possession of two unregistered swords and a stolen motorbike? Chief Ishikawa's gonna love that."

"He's chief now? Ho, ho. He'll go for it. You know why?" Yumi bent to whisper in Takagi's ear.

Takagi blanched.

"Tell him that will be in tomorrow's *Yomiuri Shimbun* unless he gives you full cooperation."

Takagi lit another cigarette and moseyed to the door. "Yumi-chan, if I ever make you angry," he said. "Just kill me."

Yumi smiled. "Not my style."

Takagi returned twenty minutes later, patting his neck with a handkerchief. "We'll have vice squad, and a rapid response team, and I'll be provisional lieutenant for the operation," he said, and straightened his tie. "But you'd better go back to your mountain when we're done."

Yumi said, "I'd like nothing better."

Takagi folded his handkerchief and nodded to Tara. "Can you dress up and pretend to be impressed by dumb-ass tough guys? I know Yumi can."

Yumi blushed and clucked her tongue.

"Only been doing it my whole life." Tara laughed.

Takagi ground out his cigarette in an ashtray glazed with the scorched logo of the Tokyo Metro Police. "Then let's go shopping, ladies. We're crashing the *Kumite*."

52.

"**PUT A DOUBLE CREW ON THE VAN DETAIL,**" Takehiko panted into Oki's neck. He sprawled in his leather office chair with her straddling him, dress hiked up at the legs and down at the neckline.

"I know how to run security, *wakagashira*." Oki smirked, flipping a salute before she eased from his lap. "The shipment will be protected, and so will the *Kumite*." She tugged her dress back into place, heels clicking as she hurried to his private washroom.

Takehiko smiled to himself, inhaling her lingering scent. He wondered if ambition soured with age. If someday he'd become a frightened old lion eyeing the young contenders eager for his throne. That was his curse, always thinking forward. The rest embraced the old ways, the cozy corruption tolerated by the authorities. Tonight that would change.

He lifted the *Honjo Masamune* and admired its gleam. He'd gripped the handle while Oki pounced him and sated herself. She was always hungry after battle.

Takehiko had withheld. If a man could not control that impulse, what could he control?

He would celebrate with her afterward, atop the forecastle of the *Kokuryukai Maru* on the open sea, as they sailed toward victory.

A knock at the door. "Master, it is time," a Black Dragon called.

"Come in."

The commando looked away as Takehiko tucked himself back in his pants.

"That is your commander's scent," Takehiko said. "She is a fierce one."

"We would die for Oki-san."

"Tonight you may have the opportunity," Takehiko said. "We have gathered the most brutal fighters in the world. If one should escape, you must take him down alive. They must die in the cage."

The man bowed. "Seven died luring the samurai home, Lord Takehiko. Without complaint."

Takehiko nodded. "Bring me to him."

MIKIO KNELT CHAINED AND HOODED on the concrete floor of the training gym.

He perked at the sound of footsteps.

Takehiko kept his distance as the commando yanked off Mikio's hood.

Mikio lunged and snapped his teeth on the inside of the soldier's thigh. The man grunted and gripped Mikio's head.

"Alive! Alive, I said!"

The commando ground his thumbs behind Mikio's earlobes until he fell limp and rolled to his back. Mikio rattled the chain leashing him to the squat rack.

"Nearly cut my femoral artery," the commando said.

Takehiko stared at the soldier until he left the room.

Mikio grinned with bloody teeth.

"You made a fool of me," Takehiko said. "My trusted bodyguard. Relish it. Your people are slaughtered, and tonight I cut off your head and toss it into the ocean."

Mikio's expression faded to blank.

Takehiko drew the Masamune, and admired his reflection in the blade. "What do you say to that?"

"I can smell your pussy," Mikio said. "Give me a sword. Fight me, and I'll cut off your little dick, and your father's. Unless his rotted off in a diseased pig's asshole."

Takehiko breathed deeply. "This is not your Japan, *samurai.*" He spat the last. "Your war destroyed it. We are its new soul. The Black Dragons. The most ruthless of the yakuza, and the last of the ninja, banded together."

"You have always been with us," Mikio said. "You did what you needed to survive beneath the shogun's heel. When the rebels of Satsuma fell, we stepped aside. The People of the Sun had spoken. We retreated to the mountains. We left you to your gambling and whores, your drugs and pachinko parlors. But for the Gantetsu, that was not enough. You always craved power."

"Power belongs to those who take it," Takehiko said. "Rather like this sword. Or your father's head."

Mikio sneered. "He died a warrior. Unlike you. You'll die stinking of shit."

Takehiko held the blade to Mikio's throat.

"Kill me now, coward." Mikio glared.

The edge drew blood.

"But you won't." Mikio chuckled. "You geisha in an Italian suit. You want a kabuki show for your father."

Takehiko smirked and walked away.

"Your father won't change," Mikio called.

Takehiko turned and rushed with the sword gripped to strike. He froze ten steps from Mikio, who tensed with one foot planted, ready to launch his teeth at Takehiko's throat.

Mikio smiled. "He will still call you a weaselly little shit."

Takehiko sheathed the blade and straightened his tie. "I'll take your head soon enough," he said, and marched from the room.

Mikio listened for a long time. When he was sure he was alone, he sat on the floor and allowed himself to cry for his family.

53.

ALONE IN HIS CAGE, Reeves rattled the letters in the Tetley tin, hoping they could summon Butch's ghost. Uchida's wrecked face glared at him from the shadows. In the neighboring cages, spoons clicked in empty bowls and fighters muttered in languages Reeves didn't understand. He pushed them out like the voices of doubt before a fight.

"Pop," Reeves whispered, "I done bad."

Reeves closed his eyes and hit the metal tin against his temple.

"You were right," Reeves said. "My temper finally got someone killed." He squeezed the metal tin until it buckled. "You said I never listened to you, but I did. I worried so much about killing someone in a fight that it got my buddy Jenkins killed. I been carrying that a long while. I was ashamed to tell you. And today I got so mad I beat a guy to death, a dumb bastard stuck here like me. For nothing. He did nothing to me. He was trying to help me."

Reeves deflated, the adrenaline gone from his muscles, leaving them weak and empty.

"I told you about war, didn't I, kid?" Butch said. His face flickered in the dark, lit by the black and white TV they used to watch Ultimate Fighting Championships on. "You do what you can. You'll never feel like a hero unless you're full of shit."

Reeves picked at the dried blood crusted between his fingers.

"The heroes never made it home," Butch said. "We get medals so we can forget for a while, about how much it hurts that we couldn't save them."

Butch's image shrank into a vanishing white dot.

IN THE MORNING, workers installed new lights above the cage. Reeves flipped through the scraps of paper in the Tetley can. Butch wrote in tiny chicken scratch, using every bit of space. Reeves hadn't read handwriting in ages. The neatly written letters, with long looping script, had been easy. Reading the scraps felt like deciphering hieroglyphics.

He picked one at random.

> *Hung from ankles three hours today.*
> *Told Shitbird it made me taller.*

> *Kazeta stood, hands at sides while beaten with sticks.*
> *Toughest S.O.B. I ever saw.*

Reeves flinched at the calm recollection of torture. Worse was when Butch talked about how good his leg was healing. Reeves ached, knowing the outcome.

> *Fowler wants to smother Kazeta in his sleep. Bopped him one.*
> *Leg better. I may limp like Wallace Beery but I ain't a pegleg yet.*

> *Kazeta taught me how to say "Fireworks" in Jap. Hana-Bi.*
> *Good nickname for Jean. Her hair in the sun.*

Reeves squinted at the page. He thought Kazeta was a Polish name. Butch never talked about the war, and Reeves assumed he hated the Japanese.

He read on.

> *Tokyo burned. Bad. Never want to see that again.*
> *Island beautiful. Black sands. Kazeta calls it Toshima.*
> *Please don't let me die here.*

Kazeta can die for a damn sword. I won't.

The sword. Reeves picked through, looking for mentions of it. Several scraps were smeared and illegible. Others had dried out, and crackled into yellow shards in his fingers.

Sword is called Han Joe Massa Muni. Amazing thing.
Shines like the sun.
Kazeta says it is better lost than put in the wrong hands.
He spent a month making a ringer.
But hidden treasure should get found, someday.
We buried the real one under a shrine on top of the island.
Whoever reads this, dig it up and get it to
the Monks of Hachiman Temple.

Reeves laughed so loud his cellmates jumped in their cages.

"Screw you, Takehiko," he shouted, his voice echoing off the walls. "The joke's on you, but I'm still gonna shove that sword right up your ass!"

54.

"AT LAST, AFTER SIXTY YEARS OF LANGUISHING in the filthy hands of barbarian invaders, the *Honjo Masamune* has been returned to Nippon," Takehiko said, and unsheathed the blade.

A hush of drawn breaths fell over the table in the Shadow Shogun's private room at Club Tachi-aoi on the Ginza strip. Five magnates in bespoke suits stared at the blade's glimmer, as did the stunning hostesses at their sides. Some in traditional geisha dress, others in designer sheaths.

Mitsuru took the head of the table, the club's elegant *mama-san* at his arm. "It has been verified by the curator of the Society for the Preservation of Japanese Art Swords," Mitsuru said. "And by myself. It is the same sword my agents hid away from the occupiers, until they were lost in the firestorm."

The men bowed their heads.

Takehiko's father had insisted on this revision of history. He had remolded the Gantetsu into a yakuza clan, while a distant cousin had kept the *shinobi* tradition alive by training assassins and commandos for hire. The Sons of Hachiman were soon to be wiped from existence, and their hidden history was best not repeated.

Mitsuru nodded to the *mama-san*. "Dearest Lady Shurayuki, the next we discuss in private," he said. "Please, ladies. Let it be known that the sword has been recovered, and will soon be returned to its rightful place in the Imperial Palace."

The hostesses bid the men goodbye and filed from the room. Once the paper door closed, Takehiko sheathed the blade and passed it to the iron-haired statesman to his right. Each man slid the sword partly from its scabbard, marveled appropriately at the ghostly polish of its temper line, and passed it on. The Shadow Shogun received it last, and held it across his lap.

"Gentlemen, it is time to bring forth the treasure myself and your fathers did not lose," Mitsuru said, stroking wizened fingers over the Masamune's lacquered scabbard. "That of the *Awa Maru*. Takehiko has contacts in the States who will pay top price for gold and platinum, in cash. And with cargo ships under his control, he has the clandestine means of transporting it." He lifted his hand to quell their questions.

"Tell them, young prince," Mitsuru said. "They must learn to hear it from my inevitable successor."

Takehiko bowed deeply, and stood. "The Americans printed and shipped billions in hundred-dollar bills to fund the rebuilding of Iraq in their latest misadventure," he said. "Twelve billion went unaccounted for, written off as soft money payments to warlords and militant groups. Five billion was believed destroyed when a munitions dump in Samawah was ignited by a suicide bomber who murdered seventeen Japanese members of our Self-Defense Forces Iraq Reconstruction Group, martyrs to our continued enslavement to the Occupier."

The men nodded solemnly.

"Black Dragons were among the dead," Takehiko continued, "and the survivors. They could not retrieve the currency, but placed tracking devices. A C-47 cargo plane returning war dead brought five pallets, one billion dollars each, back to the States, where they were transferred to two trucks in the Norfolk Naval Shipyard. One truck disappeared by Mount Weather, the American 'shadow government' facility, and the other went to a militia group operating near the Canadian border, the Fist of Liberty, led by former servicemen.

"They are isolationists, and while we disagree on much—" Takehiko laughed, "—particularly which race is superior, we have one common belief, that American military bases have no place on Japanese soil."

The men muttered agreement.

"They also correctly believe that the American dollar's value only exists due to the strength of the government they actively undermine, so they wish to hoard precious metals without alerting the authorities.

"Gentlemen, that is a service we are in a unique position to provide."

The men conferred quietly while the Shadow Shogun tapped his manicured fingernails on the Masamune's scabbard.

The gray-haired statesman nodded. "Forty metric tons of gold, and fifteen of platinum have lain barren in our vaults since the Shadow Shogun and our fathers smuggled it from the hold of the *Awa Maru* before its final voyage. It has weighed heavy on our hearts, this betrayal of the Emperor," he lamented. "But the betrayal of the Emperor himself cut us more deeply. Under your leadership, Japan will be vassal to the Americans no longer. We will release one half of the treasure for these purposes."

Takehiko bowed, and the men returned it as equals.

"We will keep the police distracted with the *Kumite,*" Takehiko said. "Use your black vans, and deliver the treasure to Shinagawa container terminal. We will load it on our ship."

The black vans were the perfect cover because no one noticed them as they cruised Tokyo, blaring their message of nationalist nonsense.

Now they would carry three billion in gold and platinum instead, to a ship that would be tragically lost at sea, when the Black

Dragons executed the crew and detonated the scuttle charges. But not before the most valuable container was loaded onto another, smaller ship.

When Takehiko returned, flush with cash and weapons, his father would be as surprised as the rest of the yakuza.

And the first to die.

55.

BUTCH SAT CARVING A CEDAR BRANCH with his combat knife while two Irish Marines pounded each other in the makeshift boxing ring on their base in Nakano ward. Both fighters had heart, but only one had brains. Any brains the other guy had were about to get beaten in, if he didn't stay down.

A small crowd of Japanese servants had gathered to watch. The GIS were grizzled by battle and eager to ship home. They cursed the points system that kept them here for clean-up, and bet on anything to pass the time.

Sometimes they beat the hell out of Japs, and sometimes they beat the hell out of each other.

A green kid named Malone took the beating this time.

Butch admired his whittling and put his new crutch into the crook of his arm. He walked to the ring for a closer look. The technical bruiser was a tow-headed Boston bigmouth named Halloran. He had good reach, but not much else.

It took Butch one round to figure out Malone's weakness. He hated being in the pocket, where ape-armed Halloran would be vulnerable. Halloran capitalized on it, keeping the kid at the end of his reach.

Butch didn't give a damn. Some people needed their head knocked in, to learn better. Then he saw Guiffrida, the big Italian who'd taken his sword, waving a handful of bills, cheering for Halloran to finish the job.

Time to have a little fun.

"Malone," Butch shouted. "Get inside and uppercut him, you dumb prick!"

Malone popped his head up and ate a hook. Butch groaned, and the crowd cheered.

Malone wobbled into a clinch. Butch caught his eye. "You hear me, stupid? Get in the pocket! He don't like you in there!"

Malone nodded and pushed away. Halloran was cocky. He'd made a mess of Malone's face and felt invulnerable. He tried to finish him with an overhand right, and Malone slipped inside to hammer the body. Halloran buckled, and Malone cracked his jaw with an uppercut driven from his heels.

Halloran hit the ropes.

"Finish him!" Butch hollered. "What are you waiting for, Christmas?"

Malone fired a combo and Halloran's knees turned to water.

The crowd booed.

Halloran's friends splashed water in his face and an old Japanese man mopped the ring. Malone hopped the ropes and slapped Butch on the back. "Thanks, Sloane. You should oughtta be a cut man or somethin'." When he collected his winnings, he tucked a fin into Butch's pocket.

"Anytime," Butch said, leaning against the ring.

Guiffrida jabbed Butch with a finger. "You just cost me a double sawbuck, gimp."

"You wanna take it?" Butch said. He wore a fatigue shirt with the sleeves off. His Devil's Brigade ink—fresh from the tattooers in Shitamachi ward—glared from his biceps. A black devil brandishing a red spear in his claws and a dagger in his teeth.

"I don't fight cripples," Guiffrida sneered.

"And I don't fight cowards," Butch replied.

The crowd oohed.

"You'd think I'd get thanks for saving your sorry-ass life," Guiffrida said. "I didn't make ya a gimp. You lost a leg. That's the hand life dealt ya." He laughed. His buddies chuckled along.

"You took my samurai sword," Butch said. "You're a thieving big-nosed prick."

Guiffrida bared a mouthful of snaggle. "Your life ain't worth that? I guess it ain't." He turned his back.

Butch gripped his shoulder. "Give me one round in there. You can beat a one-legged gimp, can't you? You win, you keep the sword."

Guiffrida rolled his eyes. "I ain't beating on no cripple. Go find a sideshow to be in."

Butch let his crutch drop, and hopped to the ring. He grabbed the ropes and swung over with ease. He took a moment to balance himself.

"Knock me down three times, you big guinea thief," Butch shouted. The words felt sour, but he needed to piss the guy off enough to fight. "Then you can keep the sword you stole from me while I was out cold."

The Japanese ring man tied Butch's gloves on for him.

Guiffrida's friends pushed him toward the ring. He shook his head and unbuttoned his shirt, baring shrapnel-pocked muscle. He pulled on a pair of mildewed leather gloves.

The bell rang and the crowd laughed as Butch hopped around like a kangaroo with a hotfoot. Guiffrida waved his arms and grinned.

Butch hopped in with an overhand right and rattled his opponent's jaw. He caught his balance in the clinch, and hopped away.

Guiffrida rubbed his chin and charged like a linebacker, knocking Butch on his ass. Guiffrida offered a hand, and the crowd laughed.

Butch got his leg under his ass and popped up like a daisy, pounding Guiffrida in the ribs. Big guys hated that. Most had heads like concrete, but bodies like the Princess and the Pea.

Guiffrida gulped air and covered up. He had no rhythm, just bravado and muscle. Butch bounced from side to side, and Guiffrida whiffed haymakers and ate sharp jabs in return.

Butch popped him good in the nose. Guiffrida kicked Butch's leg out with a snarl.

The crowd booed. "Come on, Frito! Don't cheat!"

"That counts," Guiffrida panted, rubbing blood from his lip.

Butch pulled himself up the ropes and said nothing. He hadn't picked up much Italian in Rome, but he knew one goodie from the street kids.

Butch flexed one biceps and put the opposite glove in the crook of his elbow. *"Va fa' in culo!"*

Guiffrida blinked and charged, fist high. Butch hopped right and cracked him below the ear with everything he had. Guiffrida hit the mat and skidded on his face, out of the ring into the dirt.

Guiffrida woke with a grapefruit for a jaw as his friends splashed him with another bucket of water.

"You want more?" Butch said, hovering over him.

Guiffrida tried to speak, then just shook his head.

Butch limped to the barracks and came back with Kazeta's sword tucked in his belt.

BUTCH CRUMPLED YET ANOTHER ABORTED LETTER TO JEAN as two uniforms entered the hospital lobby. Emlyn the nurse pointed them his way. A moustached officer with scrambled eggs on his cap and a Japanese lackey sniffing his ass, one step behind. The lackey looked almost skeletal.

"Sgt. Sloane," the officer said. "I'm Colonel Faraday."

Butch stood to salute, and the colonel waved a dismissive hand.

"I have a message from Lt. Frederick," he said. "First, he'd like to congratulate your extreme bravery in the mission in which you were captured, which you will never mention again. The war's over, son. Hirohito says he's not a god any more, and we need to keep the Japs in line. So no mention of how we almost got him. Are we clear?"

Butch nodded. "Aye, sir."

"Secondly," Faraday said, and turned to his aide. "Mitsuru."

His gaunt Japanese aide handed Butch an envelope.

"You are exempted from the points system, and the duration plus six requirements. You're shipping out. It's no medal, but it's all you're gonna get for your actions in the Pacific, soldier. So pack up, the boat leaves tomorrow."

"Thank you, sir."

The colonel shook Butch's hand. Butch gripped it, and the man's moustache squirmed like a wounded caterpillar.

"One favor, sir, before I go," Butch said. "I promised a Japanese—a good fella, I wouldn't be here, if it wasn't for him—that I'd tell his family how he died. But all I got is his name, and the unit he was in."

"Well, soldier, you'll be on that ship tomorrow," Faraday said. "Unless you want to stay here and whittle chopsticks. You can dictate a letter to Mitsuru. He will transcribe it into Jap, and we'll do our best to get it to the man's family." He pulled his hand away. "Mitsuru, five minutes. I'll be in the Jeep."

Mitsuru produced a pad and pen, and sat at Butch's table while the colonel walked away, patting Emlyn on her ample behind as he passed.

"That guy's something else," Butch said.

Mitsuru nodded. "Yes, he is," he said, in barely accented English. "What was your friend's name?"

"Kazeta," Butch said. "Kazeta Miyamoto."

Mitsuru penned in Japanese. "Did you know his village?"

"Hachiman," Butch said. "Said he came from Hachiman."

Mitsuru paused, then wrote some more. "I know it," he said, "Great blacksmiths come from that village. Was he a knife-maker?"

"Just a grunt," Butch said.

"So, what do you want to tell his family?"

Butch rubbed his brow. "Some GIs saw us and thought I was his prisoner. They shot before I could say a damn thing. They left him on the beach. He said your spirits can't rest if you're left for dead like that. Eats me up, you know?"

Mitsuru nodded.

"He was a good man," Butch said. "Put that in there, will you?"

"I will tell them he died honorably," Mitsuru said, and scratched away. "Miyamoto is a very common name. May I ask his profession, sir? It will make it easier to find his people."

"He was just a priest," Butch said.

Mitsuru locked black-marble eyes with him. "I see."

56.

"MY INFORMANT SAYS HE CAN GET US IN," Takagi said, practicing faces in the mirror of his bachelor pad. He wore the black suit from his vice days, and had spent thirty minutes slicking back his hair. "Most yakuza die of liver cancer," he said, while Tara and Yumi tapped their feet. "Goro says it's because of the tattoos. Hepatitis, and no sweat glands. But I think it's from trying to look mean all the time. I feel like a monkey trying to shit a coconut."

"You still have a way with words," Yumi said. "Maybe you should retire and be a reporter."

"I may be a professional ass-kisser, keeping the brass and politicians happy. But I have more self-respect than that."

THEY DROPPED SHIRO OFF WITH TAKAGI'S MOTHER, who brightened to see her son with Yumi again, then wilted to learn she'd be babysitting another man's child. Takagi shrugged. "Cop's life, Ma."

Takagi checked out a yakuza's confiscated silver Mercedes G63 street tank from the impound lot, and picked up Goro at Shinjuku station. A beefy bruiser with an ill-fitting suit, scarred cheeks and shots of gray in his hair, Goro owed Takagi for warning him of a hit that took out his boss and three soldiers. Goro quit the life, and now did bodyguard and muscle work piecemeal. He leaned over the seat and eyed Tara and Yumi like cuts of steak.

Goro gave an appreciative nod. "Sweet pair of peaches, but we're still gonna max out your credit cards."

He directed Takagi to the Ginza strip, and escorted the women into one designer shop after another while Takagi chain-smoked and coordinated the teams on his cell phone.

Tara and Yumi exited the shop sparkling in Gucci. Yumi wore black, sheathed from heart to thighs, heeled in stilettos, with a cape cinched at her throat. Tara was draped in sea-green, crossing her chest and slit up the thigh. She pulled the dress closed and pinched her reddened lips together. "I'm not used to this shit," she whispered to Yumi.

Takagi's cigarette dipped as he gazed at them over his shades.

"Want to buy us a drink, bad boys?"

They filed the edge off their nerves with slugs of 12-year-old Yamazaki whiskey while the black Benz sharked through traffic toward the leering neon of the Kabuchiko brothel district. The fight would be held in a squat warehouse with dark windows. Pock-faced men in black suits guarded the doors. The *Kumite* was as open a secret as a pro wrestling script.

Yumi tied a silk obi around her waist and wore the swords crossed.

Tara rubbed her feet and slipped into her heels. Takagi perfected his glower in the rear view mirror.

"Perfect," Takagi said, "Takehiko loves only swords, and his old man loves beautiful women. If this goes south, I'll trade you both for my life."

Yumi smirked. "If this goes bad, you'll make sure my son doesn't become a cop or a reporter. Promise?"

"Promise," Takagi said, then spoke into his phone. "The teams are in place. Let's do this."

He puffed up his chest and offered Yumi his arm, nodding as if she belonged there. Yumi broke into a vapid smile and hung from his side.

Tara did her best to look as bored and beautiful as a supermodel, and slinked her arm around Goro's meat hook.

"Never had a date with a woman like you," Goro said. "You were beautiful before you got dolled up. You know that, right?"

Tara blushed and gave his arm a squeeze. "Thanks, big guy."

"I'll get you out of there," Goro said. "No matter how bad it gets."

"Even if I'm spoken for?"

Goro looked wounded. "Whoever it is, he's a lucky guy."

They approached the huddle of pinstriped men smoking outside the doors. Takagi barked and the group parted, ogling the women openly until Goro met their stares.

Two of Goro's uglier brothers guarded the doors. One planted a palm on Takagi's chest and pointed at Yumi's swords. "Why the blades? Is she fighting?"

Takagi grunted and slid the katana a foot out of its scabbard. "Dotanuki battle blades," he said. "Gifts for Takehiko."

The guard nodded. "Keep them sheathed," he said. "Our guards are packing heat. They'll ventilate you and feed you to the dogs."

The doors opened and they walked into the roar inside.

57.

REEVES KNEW HE COULD KILL when he heard the roar of the crowd. That morning, the guards threw black sheets over the cages. When their evening meal didn't show, Reeves knew the score. He hunkered in his shrouded cage like a hooded warbird eager to strike.

Not long after, a muted hush of voices and the flat slap of men's dress shoes, the clack of women's heels. Reeves warmed up, stretching his limbs and neck.

Game time.

An announcer worked the crowd in bombastic Japanese. The room thrummed with drumbeats. The polite applause rose to thunder as seats filled and the bloodlust grew.

Their excitement flushed hot in Reeves' veins. Knowing that crowd was there to see you fight, whether to cheer your victory or defeat, tingled down deep.

The emcee's voice crescendoed and the barrel-gut trainer tore away the curtain separating Reeves from his audience.

"Rage-u Cage-u Reeves!"

A yakuza shocked the bars with a stun gun. Reeves gripped the bars tight, bared his teeth and howled. "I'm gonna shove that thing so far up your ass you'll piss lightning!"

The crowd shouted back, applauding his spirit. Japanese men in dark suits, hair cut high and tight, chanted and stomped. Trophy women clapped at their sides. Young and old, some waving the Japanese battle flag, a broad-rayed red sun on a white field. The one Butch used to call "the meatball."

Reeves scanned the audience for Takehiko's smarmy weasel face. Guards with short M4 rifles patrolled the aisles. Oki cheered ringside, sleek in a black dress slit to the thighs.

No Takehiko.

The guards unlocked the cage of the next fighter and noosed him with a catch pole, a sumo wrestler with a lazy eye and man-tits as big as Reeves' head. The guards herded the fighters toward the huge hemispherical cage.

Just like the Thunderdome from the Mad Max movie. *Two men enter, one man leaves.* The guards led one pair at a time, taking the muay thai kid and a blue-eyed karateka next. Then a pair of chiseled Burmese boxers, two tall Japanese shooto fighters, two European kickboxers, and a Chinese fighter with knuckles calloused to stone.

They noosed Reeves last. He jogged ahead of his captors, flexing his throat and chomping at the bit. The crowd pumped their fists in approval. The fighters spread around the ring like the numbers on a crowded clock face.

A shirtless yakuza with blue demons tattooed across his chiseled back twirled a pair of fighting sticks and beat out a thunderous rhythm on a *taiko* drum the size of a steamroller wheel.

The crowd cheered louder. Takehiko marched out, the Masamune at his belt. The Hawaiian Hulk lumbered behind him in full gladiator regalia, leading a hooded fighter in chains, a ropey statue of scarred bronze.

Takehiko took the microphone and worked the crowd.

Reeves felt his temples begin to boil.

"THERE ARE MORE GUNS HERE TONIGHT than we've captured in a year," Takagi whispered.

Yumi eyed the crowd from their ringside seats, noting the guards armed openly and concealed. "There is Gantetsu Abe," she told

Takagi, nodding toward the frog-faced clan leader. "I don't see his son." She gasped softly. "Takashi Mitsuru is by his side."

"The Shadow Shogun," Takagi said. "Why would he dirty his hands here?"

"This isn't like any *Kumite* I've been to," Goro said. "Usually it's one on one."

Tara squeezed Goro's hand as Takehiko pushed the hooded fighter toward the cage.

"And our last combatant, you knew as . . . 'Psycho Monkey' Kimitake!" Takehiko tore the hood off, revealing Mikio's unbowed glare. "We caught him informing on us, so if he survives, I will fight him to the death!" Takehiko howled into the mike, holding the sword high.

Mikio gave the crowd twin middle fingers.

Yumi bit her lip. "Can't we call in the squad? There are guns everywhere," she whispered to Takagi.

"Not until we have something on Takehiko. That was the only deal the chief would take."

Yumi gripped Takagi's knee. "If Mikio dies, I'll spread your guts all over this floor."

"I'd expect nothing less, little tiger."

TAKEHIKO SHOVED MIKIO TOWARD THE CAGE. "See your friend in there?"

Reeves beamed hate at them across the thunderdome.

"He killed Uchida." Takehiko laughed. "Your queer samurai. Stomped his face like *mochi*. If he doesn't kill you, I will."

Hulkboy hurled Mikio in the cage by his chains. Takehiko kicked the door shut and tossed the cuff key to the dirt.

Reeves stomped his way across the circle.

Mikio picked the key up with his toes and transferred it to his hands, then leaned against the cage to work the lock.

Hulkboy snickered. "Your friend died hard," he said in Japanese.

"With his dick in your ass," Mikio shouted, and whipped the chain at the Hulk's face. The brute caught it on his spiked cestus and yanked Mikio off his feet. He warded off Reeves with his other mailed fist. "Not yet, American."

"When the bell rings, I'm coming for both of you," Reeves said. Mikio unlocked his chains and threw them to the ground. He hopped to his feet, nose to nose with Reeves. "You kill Uchida," he said, and slapped his Hachiman tattoo. "You die last."

"I beat your ass once," Reeves said, not giving an inch. "I don't wanna kill you, but to get to Takehiko, I will."

"Good," Mikio sneered. "Maybe I let you live that long."

Hulkboy spooled the chain around his arm, leaving the shackles dangling like a morningstar. He whirled them over his head, and jabbed his other fist toward the other end of the ring. "Take place!"

Reeves jogged back to his place.

THE VEINS IN TAKEHIKO'S FOREHEAD THROBBED as he drove the crowd to a frenzy. The Masamune in one hand, the mike in the other. Buxom ring girls waved Japanese battle flags and play-boxed with each other. The drumbeats quickened to a machine-gun patter.

The fighters strained on invisible leashes, their faces twisted into rictuses of bloodlust and fear. Reeves stretched his neck and avoided the ghosts of the dead mingling with the crowd. Bearded men with blood pouring from ears and eye sockets. Women with cell phone detonators, bodies burst apart like rotten fruit. Boys barely able to lift AKs, cratered with exit wounds.

Sacrifices to the War God, the green-eyed iron beast always ravenous for more flesh.

The drummer pounded the final tattoo. The crowd's bloodthirsty roar hit the cage like a tsunami.

The fighters charged.

Reeves bent at the knees and brought up his fists. Bodies collided in the center, the sumo trampling the shooto fighters and smothering one with his bulk. The Burmese boxers spun and weaved through the mosh pit in a whirl of knees and elbows.

Hulkboy whirled his chain, swiping at any fighters who hovered at the edges.

Reeves ducked the shackles and caught a knee to the ribs from the scrappy muay thai fighter. The man gripped Reeves behind the head to pull his face down for the coup de grace.

The pain ignited behind Reeves' eyes and misted everything red.

Reeves fired an uppercut and popped his opponent's head back, then dropped his elbow on the collarbone. The bone cracked and the fighter's arm went limp. Reeves chopped him in half with a body kick, then caught the gladiator's chain across his back.

Mikio caught a rangy kickboxer with a flying knee to the chest and snapped his neck before he hit the floor. He threw himself into a roll and came up by Reeves, and pulled him to his feet.

"Only save you so I kill you later, ass hole," Mikio snarled and pushed him away.

"Keep talking shit, you'll die with a mouth full of it!" Reeves said, jabbing Mikio's shoulder as he circled away from his opponent's incoming assault.

"Life or death, *Tatsujin!*" Mikio shouted, before a Chinese boxer drove him away, pedaling chain punches.

A towering kickboxer intercepted Reeves with a high kick. Reeves pummeled his ribs with a jab-cross-hook. They traded blows until Reeves hooked the leg and head-butted the kickboxer's jaw. The bone cracked like a gunshot. Reeves clocked him with an overhand right and dropped him like timber.

The crowd screamed and pumped fistfuls of yen. "*Rage-u Cage-u Reeves!*"

Reeves leapt onto the cage and shook the bars. "I am *Paizuri Tatsujin!*" he shouted.

The crowd burst into laughter. "*Paizuri Tatsujin! Paizuri Tatsujin!*"

"WHY IS EVERYONE LAUGHING?" Tara asked Goro.

Goro frowned. "Your friend calls himself, um . . . 'king titty fucker.'" He peered at Tara's bust, hoisted into zero gee by her dress. "I don't like this guy. He's no good for you."

Tara rolled her eyes. "Someone told him it meant bad-ass warrior," she said. "How do you say that?"

Goro pointed at the Polynesian gladiator with a sausage finger. "Whatever that guy's name is," he said, and winced as the hulk tore open a crippled fighter's throat with his spiked cestus.

WHILE MIKIO TRADED FLURRIES OF BLOWS with the Chinese wushu fighter, two Burmese boxers charged for Reeves, their raised fists bloody. The small hard-eyed men struck in tandem, one kicking at his knees while the other used the opening to rake knuckles across Reeves' brow and open a cut above his eyes.

Reeves countered with a liver kick that should have cut one in half. The little wedge-headed man bounced back up like a spring toy, and his partner chopped Reeves hard on the thigh. He staggered under the blow. Reeves had toughened his shins on sandbags, but the Burmese kicks felt like concrete rebar.

"Get him, Reeves!" Tara shouted.

Mikio took a snap kick to the gut and trapped the Chinese boxer's leg. The boxer gripped Mikio's shirt and swung his free leg at his face.

Yumi winced, and gripped Takagi's hand.

Mikio took the blow on the forearm and trapped the man's second leg, then spun to keep his opponent off the ground. Circled once, twice. On the third revolution Mikio clanged the boxer's skull off the thick bars of the cage in a spray of blood.

The crowd howled in approval.

REEVES BRACED FOR A SUICIDE CHARGE from one of the Burmese twins. Reeves broke his guard open with a one-two, then elbowed him on the ear and sent him face first into the cage.

The Hawaiian Hulk hefted the body of a fallen fighter and hurled it at Mikio, who dodged and smacked back to back with Reeves. "Kill you later," Mikio shouted. "Fight together, now!"

"For now," Reeves replied, trading jabs with the remaining Burmese fighter. "Wouldn't be here if you hadn't stabbed me in the back!"

"No stab back! Plan to trick Takehiko. You too stupid to play along!" Mikio kicked the stunned Burmese fighter in the spine and bounced his face off the cage. The man fell with a groan.

Reeves smashed his knuckles into his little opponent's nose with little effect. "Don't these little guys stay down?" The little man shook it off with a glazed-eye smile, and his fallen twin again crawled to his feet. Reeves rolled his eyes. "They're like zombies!"

"Don't whine! Fight!" Mikio snapped, and dodged a tackle from a huge black heavyweight. "How big pussy like you kill Uchida? Take Tyson!" He shoved Reeves toward the big bruiser and checked the Burmese boxer's counter kick.

'Tyson' smiled through bloody teeth and drove in with hooks and elbows. His skin hung loose on his beefy frame like a mastiff, but he moved like a greyhound, slipping past Reeves' guard to flatten his nose.

Blood exploded in the back of Reeves's throat. He hung in the clinch and thumped the bruiser's barrel belly with high knees while

Mikio spun one fighter in a headlock and traded kicks with the other.

Take him to your hurting place, Butch's voice echoed.

Reeves stomped the boxer's foot and swept it for a takedown. As the man toppled, Reeves slipped in blood and hit the dirt beneath three hundred pounds of furious muscle.

Tara and Goro jumped, and the crowd gasped.

The big man cut Reeves' cheek with a hammer fist, then planted a hand on his chest, rearing up for a finishing blow.

Get the arm, kid!

Reeves sprang like a snake. He hooked his leg over the bruiser's beefy neck and clamped him into a deep armbar. The big man body-slammed him into the dirt, and Reeves cranked both legs against his one huge arm.

The man's eyes went wide.

The joint gave way with a crunch like a dog gnawing chicken bones, and the big man flailed in agony. Reeves silenced him with a trio of up-kicks to the face.

The bruiser slumped to the dirt.

"FUCK YEAH!" Tara shouted.

Goro clapped. "He fights good, but I still don't like him."

Tara slapped Goro on the back. "Chill, big guy. We should've smuggled in beers."

"This is taking too long." Yumi cracked her knuckles around the handle of Mikio's blades. "I'll kill Takehiko right now."

"They're stationed right outside," Takagi said, "I'll call as soon as Takehiko steps into the ring. Attempted murder."

THE SHOOTO FIGHTER BROKE HIS SHIN on the sumo wrestler's battered skull, and screamed as the *sumotori* flopped over him like an elephant seal and twisted the mangled limb. The shrieks were silenced with a spiked fist to the throat.

"You are done!" The Polynesian Pit Fighter looped his chain around the crippled sumo fighter's neck and choked him purple.

Reeves eyed the Hawaiian's open back. *Climb up the mountain and choke him out.* Then he saw Mikio fending off the two Burmese boxers, his face gashed and bloody.

Reeves spun and swept a boxer's ankle. He leapt and flattened the wiry man face down in the dirt, and hooked an arm around his neck. The little boxer squeezed out of the choke and chomped down on Reeves' forearm.

"About time!" Mikio slammed his knee into the other Burmese boxer's face until he slumped at his feet. Mikio staggered against the cage and spat tooth chips.

Reeves hammered the base of the boxer's skull with his elbow until the man fell limp. He pried the man's teeth from his arm. "Thanks would be nice!"

Mikio panted and grinned. *"Anata no manko ga nurete imasu ka?"*

"What's that mean?"

"Is your pussy wet?"

"You are one sick little shitbird." Reeves laughed. "So what does *Paizuri Tatsujin* really mean?"

"King of Tit Fuckers," Mikio said with a grin of jagged teeth.

Reeves held out shredded knuckles. "Still wanna kill me?"

Mikio bumped bloody fists. "You dumb ass," he said. "You get yourself killed soon enough."

Reeves shrugged and wiped blood from his eyes. "Can't deny that."

The crowd booed and shouted *"Ganbarre! Ganbarre!"*

Hulkboy twirled the shackles overhead and approached them warily. "You will fight!"

Mikio and Reeves exchanged weary glances.

"Let's kill this crazy bastard," Reeves said.

THE SPECIAL ASSAULT TEAM OFFICER at the wheel of the Tsukiji Fish Market panel truck pretended to flip through papers on his clipboard while he watched a yakuza chase his drunk girlfriend down the block. The girl wobbled on her heels, and stopped to tug off her shoe.

The driver stifled a laugh as she jabbed the spike heel at her boyfriend and shouted something about tattoos making him impotent. She stomped past the van in a huff. Her boyfriend waved his arms incredulously and ran after her like an obedient puppy.

The officer leaned over his seat to repeat what he heard to the dozen armed police hunkered in the back of the van when something thunked against the side. Light poured through a small hole in the sheet metal. The team jumped and charged their weapons.

Just as quickly as it appeared the hole was plugged up, with a hiss of gas.

The driver drew a pistol from beneath the dash and tugged the door handle. His face met a slapjack as he cracked open the door. A slender hand with painted nails pushed his slumping form back inside and pressed the door shut.

The police rammed shoulders against the rear doors as they succumbed to the fumes.

Oki patted the padlocked rear door handles as she passed, then took the arm of her 'date.' "Two more to go."

MIKIO AND REEVES CIRCLED the bloody-spiked gladiator, and the crowd stood roaring.

"Make them fight!" Takehiko spat into the microphone.

"They are making fools of you," Abe sneered at his son. "The crowd loves them!" He folded his arms. "Can you do nothing without shaming me?"

Takehiko drew his blade high. "The *Honjo Masamune* will take two heads tonight!"

The crowd stomped the floor as Takehiko stepped into the cage.

"FIGHT FAIR!" Yumi shouted. "Give them swords!"

Takagi tapped his Bluetooth headset as she squeezed past him down the aisle. "Pick up, team one! Pick up, damn you!"

Yumi rushed the cage, blades high. The crowd applauded and repeated her words. "Sword fight! Sword fight!"

MIKIO HEARD HIS WIFE CALL HIS NAME. He blinked and caught a kick to the chest.

"Go, go!" Reeves shouted, pulling the pit fighter's chain to keep him off Mikio. Hulkboy sneered and threw his weight into the tug of war.

Reeves flew into a belly flop in the dirt. Hulkboy stomped Reeves on the shoulder and mashed his face into the droplets of blood dancing atop the dusty pit floor like quicksilver.

Takehiko charged across the battlefield, sword held high.

Mikio scrambled to his feet and ran for the cage. Yumi held out the swords, shouting herself hoarse. Mikio thrust his arms through the bars and pulled Yumi close, kissing her cheek with a smear of sweat, dirt, and blood. "You are alive!"

"Our son, too," Yumi cried. "Take your sword!"

A guard pushed Yumi away. Mikio gripped the sword handle and drew his great-grandfather's blade. He turned to meet Takehiko's attack.

Their blades rang bright, and the crowd rushed and climbed the cage to watch them battle.

◆ ◆

TAKAGI TAPPED HIS EARPIECE. "Something's wrong."

Tara ripped the keys from Takagi's pocket and pushed Goro ahead of her, into the crush.

"Make yourself useful, big guy!"

Goro shouldered his way through the crowd toward the doors.

HULKBOY SCOOPED REEVES UP with both arms and flung him over his head like a kid in a swimming pool. The impact knocked the air from Reeves' lungs. The pit fighter's kick made him gasp it back in.

The baby-faced monster laughed and looped the chains around Reeves' chest. Reeves choked as the big man dragged him in circles, showboating for the cheering crowd.

Mikio dodged and deflected Takehiko's blade with care. The *Honjo Masamune's* reputation of slicing men from shoulder to groin and snapping *dotanuki* battle blades like dead branches kept him reined-in and wary.

"This sword will taste Miyamoto blood once more," Takehiko said, lashing with wide strokes. "Your name dies with you!"

Mikio stepped back, sword held low. Edge forward, seeking an opening. He sidestepped and cut open the left shoulder of Takehiko's suit.

The crowd gasped.

Mikio shouted, "What is the *Honjo Masamune* in the hands of a weasel?"

"You shall see," Takehiko spat, feinted, and sliced Mikio across the chest.

Reeves pulled himself up the chain, spun and kicked. Hulkboy fell to one knee, spikes gouging the dirt pit.

"Mikio!" Reeves shouted. The two swordsmen circled, eyes locked on each other's form.

Reeves ran to the end of his tether.

"Mikio, he doesn't have the real—"

Hulkboy yanked him off his feet and cut off the rest.

YUMI ARGUED WITH THE BLACK DRAGON GUARD and stepped backward, thumbing the wakizashi from its scabbard. The commando beckoned her to give up the blade, patting the sand-camo assault rifle slung around his neck.

Takagi gripped the commando's shoulder. "Police," he said.

The Black Dragon turned and laughed. "Who are you kidding?"

Yumi jerked the rifle under the commando's arm and flipped it, pulling the strap taut to his neck and judo throwing him over her shoulder. He landed in a tangle of folding chairs, and she rushed to sink her heel in his throat.

Takagi blinked.

Yumi nodded. "Get the rifle and take out the guards," she said. "I'm going for Abe." She prowled through the crowd, the short sword at her back.

Takagi frowned at the guard's dead eyes and knelt to untangle the rifle strap from his throat.

His phone rang, and he crouched behind a chair to take the call. "Where the hell are you guys? You're missing a great fight."

A woman's voice laughed. "Your men are all dead."

Then the line was dead, too.

ACROSS THE CROWD, Oki smashed the dead cop's phone beneath her heel and snapped commands to her men. "Remember, the bitch is mine."

Her Black Dragons filtered through the crowd as Takehiko

dueled with the samurai. Oki reached into her purse and flipped off the safety on the compact Warthog .45 within.

Takehiko was a great swordsman. And today, he wielded the greatest sword their country's masters had ever produced. But she had men seen lose battles with greater advantage.

Takehiko's weakness was the rage within for his whoremaster of a father. Oki had hitched her destiny to his and would not allow him to fail. She flicked on the pistol's laser sight and slinked through the aisles, seeking a better vantage point.

REEVES DUCKED A BEAR SLAP and hammered the pit fighter's body with hooks. It felt like punching a tan tiger shark. The man slammed the anvil of his forehead into Reeves' own, and sent him stumbling out of the clinch.

Reeves blinked. Just when he thought it couldn't get worse, now there were two of the big S.O.B.S.

Use your head, shitbird! That chain is connected to both of you.

"I tried that," Reeves said. "He's too heavy!"

Then tangle his big ass up in it. He's the only ass bigger and dumber than you. Look at him. He looks like he can't count his balls and get the same number twice.

"Hey," Reeves said. "How many balls do you have?"

The pit fighter tilted his head in confusion, then snarled and threw a spiked haymaker.

Punch-drunk, Reeves laughed and slipped the blow, thumping Hulkboy on the kidney and circling him with the chain.

The pit fighter roared and swiped at Reeves with the spikes. Reeves leaped and put all his weight into the chain, jerking the man's foot out and sending him to the dirt. Reeves cracked him across the face with his shin and sent teeth downrange. With the monster stunned, Reeves made his move.

Mikio and Takehiko circled with blood-flecked blades. Mikio's chest striped with surface cuts, Takehiko's Saville Row suit razored in shreds. Takehiko parried and cut Mikio above the knee. The samurai stumbled, blood trickling to his feet.

"Mikio!" Reeves shouted. "That's not the real sword! It's a fake!"

The pit fighter clubbed him with a spiked fist and he went down with a gash across his shoulders.

Mikio narrowed his eyes, touching blades with Takehiko.

"He lies," Takehiko said. "The Shadow Shogun gave me his word!"

Mikio spread a tight grin. "The snake knows best the ways of the serpent."

Takehiko trembled with rage. The crowd pressed their faces to the bars. He back-stepped, sword held defensively.

"Kill him, Weasel!" Takehiko's father shouted.

The crowd broke into laughter.

Takehiko seethed and charged. Mikio roared and met him with his sword held high.

Steel rang and the crowd gasped. Takehiko staggered, holding only half a blade. The other half clattered to the dirt.

"Butch pulled a fast one on you, shitbird!" Reeves laughed through bloody teeth.

Takehiko touched the gash in his cheek with trembling fingers.

Mikio held his blade overhead and shouted, "One last Son of Hachiman still lives!"

A dark murmur rumbled through the crowd.

Oki knelt and braced her elbow. The laser's red death pointer crossed the dirt and flickered on Mikio's chest.

Yumi shoved through the huddle. Abe laughed, aisles away. Takagi struggled with the rifle straps while five Black Dragons converged on him, hands under their suit jackets.

The pit fighter pressed his foot to Reeves' chest. He spat blood in Reeves' face and raised a spiked fist.

"Kill them all!" Takehiko shouted to his men. "Every one of them!"

The crowd went silent.

The building shook with an enormous impact. Asbestos snowed from the ceiling beams and the lights flickered. Women screamed. The doors crashed open with the thunderous roar of a V8 engine as the silver Benz luxo-tank plowed in with a yakuza gunman's body plastered to the grille.

Oki fired and starred the truck's rear windows.

The truck rammed the cage and tore through the gates. Tara howled behind the wheel, leaning on the horn. She chased down the Polynesian gladiator as Reeves kicked himself away.

The pit fighter scampered until he ran out of chain and disappeared beneath the truck with a whump. The truck rocked to a stop with a wheel parked on his chest. The pit fighter clutched at the metal, gurgling blood as his spiked fists gouged steel.

Tara opened the door. "Get your ass in here, Reeves!"

Takehiko dropped his broken sword as Mikio slowly approached. "Time to die," Mikio said.

Takehiko disappeared with a bang and flash of smoke. Mikio charged the clouds, sword held rudder-low.

Takehiko flipped over the truck and dived through the smashed gates. Black Dragons fired to give him cover. Their bullets sparked off the bars of the cage and peppered the dirt.

Takagi fell prone and fired the M4 to scatter them. Oki returned fire and punched a hole through the seat beside Takagi's head.

Reeves wriggled out of his chains and hopped on the truck's running board. He threw a bloody arm around Tara and buried his face in her hair. "Never thought I'd see you again."

"Told you I wasn't a quitter," Tara said. She backed the truck off the fallen hulk.

The dying gladiator reared up to spike the front tire and explode it with a hiss.

As Mikio ran past, he severed the Hawaiian's head with blinding swipe and yelled, "Bad ass, *Akane-chan!*"

TAKEHIKO SLAMMED THROUGH the panicked crowd toward the gym. Beyond lay his office and the alley exit. Just a short ride to the docks and his gold.

"Takehiko!" Mikio shouted, stalking with his sword held low. "Come die with honor!"

Takehiko drew a slim gold automatic and fired two shots. Mikio took one in the shoulder and slumped against the bricks, clutching his wound.

"No!" Yumi shouted. She cut down Gantetsu Abe's bodyguard with slash to the throat, spraying his suit and the Shadow Shogun's white kimono with blood.

Abe fell off his chair in terror.

Yumi crouched behind him, holding her blade beneath his chin wattle.

Takehiko paused.

Abe squeaked and trembled. "Kill her, you worthless coward!"

Takehiko screamed and fired his magazine dry. Yumi dived aside as the crowd shrieked and stampeded in full panic.

Abe stared agape as his shirt blossomed red. A mouthful of blood engulfed his last cry of disbelief.

Mikio leaned into a wobbly charge at Takehiko. Two Black Dragons intercepted him with short blades. Takehiko spat on his father's gaping face and stomped toward the exit.

The Shadow Shogun had not flinched throughout. He stood

carefully, wiped the blood spray from his beard with a silk handker-chief, and followed.

TARA PLOWED THE CRIPPLED TRUCK through the folding chairs in reverse. Black Dragons peppered the vehicle with rifle fire, popping the tires one by one. Reeves grabbed her and piled out the passenger side, taking cover behind the engine block as rounds punched through the sheet metal.

"We're gonna die," Tara said, and gripped his shoulder.

"Not yet," Reeves said. He grabbed a mangled chair. "Keep your head down."

Reeves ducked beneath the truck's frame to get the shooters' positions. When they split to come around the vehicle, he heaved the chair over the hood, and sprinted when he heard the gunner grunt with the impact.

Bullets snapped past Reeves's face like a passing freight train. He hit the shooter in a running tackle and plowed him into a pile of tumbled chairs.

TAKAGI SHOUTED INTO HIS PHONE, huddled behind chairs, trading potshots with his snubnose. A red dot blinded him, and he shielded his eyes. Oki's bullet clipped his shoulder. Takagi dropped and clutched his wound, phone skittering across the floor.

Oki slapped in a fresh magazine and stalked toward the truck.

REEVES SPUN TO SIDE MOUNT and drove his knee into the man's head. The M4 leaped into his hands like a loyal pup. He feathered the trigger and put a single round through the other shooter's skull. He jogged toward Tara with the rifle held port arms before the body flopped to the ground.

Reeves slung the rifle and hooked Tara with one arm. A panicked jam of bodies crushed at the demolished front doors.

"Takehiko went this way," Tara said, and led him.

As they rounded the truck, a laser bead flashed on Tara's forehead.

"Drop the weapon or she dies," Oki said.

Reeves shrugged off the rifle strap.

Oki moved the laser to Reeves' chest and waved at Tara. "Come with me."

Bullets rang off the truck. Goro ran down the aisle firing two Berettas, cursing loudly in Japanese.

Oki double-tapped Goro in the chest and he tumbled into a rolling heap.

"No!" Tara shouted.

Reeves yanked up his rifle and fired. Oki gazelle-leaped over the hood of the truck. He rolled to his feet and traced her in his sights. She crashed into the crowd. His finger depressed the trigger, but she squirmed away like a snake.

Tara knelt over Goro, counting out chest compressions. Goro's eyes were flat as wet river stones.

Reeves squeezed her shoulder. "He's gone," he said.

Tara brushed Goro's eyes closed with her fingertips, and they ran for the exit.

MIKIO AND YUMI CIRCLED BACK TO BACK, surrounded by three Black Dragon swordsmen. Mikio's left arm hung useless at his side. He slowly angled his blood-slick blade. Yumi held the wakizashi two handed, wavering the point between her target's throats.

Yumi reached behind her and squeezed Mikio's cold hand. They raised their blades in silence. Three short bursts of rifle fire and the swordsmen jerked and crumpled. Reeves marched to a fallen ninja and put a round through his skull.

Tara ran up and pressed her palm to Mikio's bullet wound.

"Takehiko escapes," Mikio panted. "No time."

"You're gonna bleed out and go into shock," Tara said. She took Yumi's cape and began binding Mikio's shoulder in a makeshift sling.

"I got this, Mick," Reeves said.

"Wait," Yumi said. She took the grenade from her purse and slapped it in Reeves' palm.

Reeves grinned and jogged after Takehiko.

58.

REEVES KICKED OPEN THE GYM DOOR and ran for the cover of the weight tree as rounds peppered the cinderblock wall.

Wounded businessmen groaned on the floor and clutched their wounds. The black-eyed yakuza guard peek-a-booed from behind the heavy bag, firing a machine pistol. Rounds sparked off the iron plates as Reeves dived prone on the mats, and cut the yakuza's legs out at the knees with a quick burst.

The rifle clicked dry. Reeves scooped up the fallen MP7 machine pistol on his way out. Takehiko's office sat empty. A door slammed down the dimly lit hallway, and Reeves bolted for it.

The rear door opened on an alleyway. A silver Bentley Continental GT squealed away as Reeves burst through the door. He aimed to fire and a slender arm fired a pistol out the passenger window and sent him dodging behind a trash can.

Reeves stood and cursed, then flattened to the wall to let a black Toyota Century limousine roar past. "Fuck!"

The exit door banged open and Reeves drew on it.

"Jesus!" Tara held up her hands.

"We lost him," Reeves said. An engine whined and a horn blared behind him. He spun and fired two rounds into the cobblestones, and a sleek white Nissan GTR coupe squealed to a stop. Before the bug-eyed driver could reverse, Reeves smashed the man's nose through the window glass with the MP7. He heaved the driver into the trash cans.

Tara gaped.

"Drive!" Reeves rolled over the hood and took the passenger seat.

The GTR screamed out the alley into the street.

Reeves leaned out the window and pointed Tara toward the silver coupe racing away from the limousine. Tara spun them in a four-wheel drift through the chaos of the streets. Police vans and yakuza saloons bumped noses as troops of armed police swarmed toward the warehouse.

Reeves aimed at the Bentley and Tara fishtailed through the gears, drifting in a plume of white smoke and clipping a police sedan's rear bumper. Reeves planted his feet against the windshield to keep from flying out onto the asphalt.

"Woo!" Tara shouted. "Hang on tight, ya sissy!"

The Bentley left a mess of traffic in its wake. Tara swerved and dodged the limo as it got caught in the snarl, then stomped the brakes for a trio of cars that crunched together and blocked the street.

"We're losing them," Reeves said.

"No we're not," Tara said.

She jumped onto the broad sidewalk, horn pinned. Tourists and café girls handing out flyers scattered. Tara popped the clutch, the supercharger whine echoing off the steel and glass canyons.

The silver Bentley skipped down a side street, and the supercar followed.

"Hang back," Reeves said. "They don't know we're onto them, let's keep it that way."

Tara hugged the curb until the Bentley zipped right on red and a taxi plowed into a light pole to avoid it.

She tailed the Bentley to the docks, where the streets spread out into a concrete wasteland. Takehiko roared toward a quay with his container ship in dock. Two cranes tended the enormous vessel, which looked beached, as if it had rammed into the city. A deep horn blasted and Tara swerved to avoid a forklift the size of a dump truck, which hustled a shipping container toward the towering container stacks.

She killed the headlights and rolled behind a wall of pallets.

The Bentley parked by a crowd of black vans with megaphones sprouting from their roofs. A trio of corrugated shipping containers sat behind. The crane operator sat in a plastic cage two hundred feet up, and plucked a container into the sky.

"Six armed men I can count," Reeves said. "You stay here."

"Reeves," Tara said. "Don't die stupid, okay? I hauled ass a long way to get you."

"I'll kill smart," Reeves said. "Promise." He squeezed her hand and jogged toward the endless multicolored stacks.

Tara eyed a row of parked forklifts and unbuckled her seatbelt.

Reeves took a running jump with the MP7 slung over his shoulder and slammed into a container, fingers over the lip of the top. He pulled himself up and over, crawled to the edge, and spied the Bentley.

Takehiko and Oki jabbed fingers and shouted commands over the roar of gargantuan machinery. Reeves closed one eye and sighted on Takehiko's shredded suit.

Fifty yards in darkness, half-lit by mercury lamps a hundred feet high. Eight shooters with hard cover. Half a mag of shit pistol rounds. Not the best circumstances.

Reeves unhooked the grenade from his waistband. He primed the pin and hurled it overhand, then flattened to his belly.

A van's windows exploded and the two shooters fell. The rest scattered, shadows disappearing behind the vehicles. Muzzle flashes sparked in the darkness and rounds thunked into Reeves' shipping container, then stopped.

They waited for Reeves to fire and reveal himself.

The crane hoisted the second box and set it on the ship's loading deck. Men in hardhats locked it in place.

Reeves slipped down behind the container and ran in the crane's shadow toward the edge of the pier. Rounds ricocheted off the asphalt, and he hunched behind an iron pylon by the ship.

Bastards must have night vision.

He fired at the vans and their return fire lit up like a starfield, bullets sparking around him.

"Reeves," Takehiko called. "That's you, isn't it? Stick your head out so we can shoot you. Or swim away like garbage on the waves." He laughed.

"How did holding that broken sword feel?" Reeves shouted back. "Everybody saw you with your dick in your hands."

"Your grandfather may have tricked me with the sword," Takehiko said. "But not before he died by it."

The red mist fogged Reeves' brain. He pressed his forehead against the cold steel.

Don't die stupid, Reeves. You read my letters. I did everything I could to come home to Jean.

Reeves checked the magazine. Five rounds. As long as Takehiko died first. That's all that mattered. Die trying.

You keep charging like a bull and you're gonna die by the matador.

The red mist shrieked in Reeves' brain like an incoming missile, then faded away.

Bullets ricocheted and a crash echoed down the concrete. The forklift plowed through the vans like they were toys. Steamrolled gunmen screamed and scattered. Panic fire sparkled in the dark and the mangled Bentley spun into the ocean.

Tara waved to Reeves from the forklift's cage and looped back to flatten two vans over the gunmen cowering behind them.

See? Patience, kid.

Takehiko and Oki clambered onto the final container. The crane locked on and lifted it away.

Reeves stepped out and sighted on the crane operator's bubble. He took a deep breath, released it, and squeezed the trigger between heartbeats, firing until empty.

The crane's window fuzzed to opaque and shattered.

The boom swept wide.

Takehiko rode the box like a veteran surfer. The container wrecking-balled into the ship's cargo stacks, and Oki cartwheeled off into the darkness. Takehiko tumbled like an acrobat. He gripped the container's edge, hung for a moment, then hit the deck hard.

The containers toppled like children's blocks, bursting open around him, spilling their piñata guts. Takehiko looked up. The ripped-open container rained gold and platinum bars onto the ship deck.

The ingots rang out their anvil chorus and mashed Takehiko to paste.

REEVES TOSSED THE GUN INTO THE WATER. A platinum brick clattered to the pier, and he hefted it beneath his arm. Tara climbed down from the forklift to meet him, barefoot in her green designer sari. They held hands and walked through the smoking wrecks of the nationalists' vans, away from the yard.

A black limousine eased to a stop between them and the white GTR.

The driver and passenger exited, two bulky Japanese men with chauffeur caps and bulges beneath their left armpits. One held up his palm. The other opened the rear door.

Mitsuru smoothed his kimono and slowly exited the discreetly luxurious interior, waving off assistance.

Tara bowed. She elbowed Reeves when he did not follow suit.

Reeves ignored her and met the Shadow Shogun's marble-black eyes.

Mitsuru gave Reeves the merest of nods, and Reeves returned it.

"Takehiko is dead, I presume," Mitsuru said.

"Affirmative."

"Oki?"

"She took a dive into the water," Tara said.

Mitsuru nodded. "If I were you, I would not linger in my country unless her body is found."

"If she comes for us, her body *will* be found," Reeves said.

"You have my property," Mitsuru said. "Platinum. Five hundred ounces. At today's price, approximately seventy-five million yen, or three quarters of a million of your American dollars."

Reeves held out the ingot in his palm.

"Keep it," Mitsuru said. "And return to your country."

"Done," Reeves said.

"Or," the old man said and raised a finger, "Take as many as you wish, and tell me what your grandfather and Kazeta did with the true *Honjo Masamune*."

"I would if I knew," Reeves said. "I just knew we had the fake one. He told me the guy who ran their POW camp forced Kazeta to make the ringer. They killed him with it during a bombing raid, and Kazeta gave the fake to Butch as a gift. They never saw each other again."

"A pity such a treasure was lost. But the world lost so much with that foolish war," Mitsuru said. "Ah, you do not want to hear the prattling of an old man. You fought bravely. Enjoy the spoils."

Tara released Reeves' hand and fired up the GTR.

"I plan on it," Reeves said. He stepped toward the car.

Mitsuru placed a hand on the platinum brick. "I trust if you learn anything more of the sword's whereabouts, you will be sure to tell me?"

Mitsuru's smile resembled a deep-sea creature never meant to see the light.

"Sure thing," Reeves said, and climbed into the passenger seat.

"And tell Mikio to reach out to me if he wishes to enter politics."

They answered him with a blast of exhaust note.

59.

BUTCH HOPPED OFF THE TRAIN nimble as a jackrabbit, with a smile for the porter who handed him his crutch. The train stop was a long walk from town. He kept the mountains on his right and headed for the cluster of shops that had sprung up after the war. On the long ride from San Francisco, Butch had felt new life across the land, fresh shoots bursting from blood-soaked soil.

Almost a year after VJ day, the country was still flushed and joyful to be done with the war. As Butch reached the edge of town, men doffed their Stetsons with solemn nods. He tipped his black beret in return, cracking half a smile and hefting his pack with the trophy sword lashed to his back.

An old rancher with a broom moustache offered him a lift, and Butch threw his gear in the pickup bed of the Model A Ford.

"Where you goin', son?"

"If you can drop me by the Dundee Ranch, I'd be, uh, mighty obliged," Butch said.

The man narrowed his poached-egg eyes. "Sorry, fella. That's Stallings land now."

"Oh," Butch said.

"You looking for Miss Jean, I reckon?"

"Yeah." Butch squinted at the sun behind the clouds.

"She's the foreman," the man said, with a bright little laugh. "Fore woman, I guess. Let's head on up there."

The truck wobbled up the mountain road like a weary ox. The rancher told him how after Jean's father had passed, she ran into a patch of bad luck and lost quite a few head. With most of the men gone to war, she couldn't get good help, so she sold the land to the only family not trying to skinflint her out of her birthright, the Stallings clan.

"She talks a good line about leaving town, but she's stuck with us for two seasons now," the man said. "The Stallings fella—Big Jake—he's asked her to marry twice now."

The old man cleared his throat.

"Drop me at the gate," Butch said. He thanked the old man and shook his hand, then crutched his way toward the ranch house. It looked the same except for a third gravestone beneath the hemlock.

A big red-faced man leaned on the fence and smoked a cheroot. As his eyes fell on Butch, the ember drooped past his chin.

"I know what you're gonna say, big fella," Butch said. "I can't dance, and I can't ride a horse. But I made it here. And not 'cause I got nowhere else to go. You know why."

The man nodded slow and made to speak.

"Hold on a minute. I'm sorry to wreck your plans, but the damned war wrecked everyone's plans. I didn't ask to meet a Montana girl like Jean Marie, but I sure as hell won't give her up, either. So how about we let Miss Dundee decide. And if she tells me to take a hike, I promise I'll hoof it back the way I came without a fuss."

Butch raised a finger. "But if you don't think I won't fight for her, I'll pole vault off this crutch like Earle Meadows and kick you right in the ass. So, now what you got to say?"

Big Jake furrowed his brow and pinched the end of his cheroot to save it for later. "I was gonna say 'good morning.'"

Butch laughed and shook Jake's bear paw of a hand. A rider galloped across the green, astride a glossy palomino. The hoofbeats echoed from far away. Butch felt them in his boot, and gripped the fence as his knee turned weak.

"She don't say much about you," Jake said. "But her eyes do. I got a busted shoulder myself. Bronc threw me when I was a kid. That's why I didn't serve."

"You didn't miss a thing," Butch said.

Jake nodded. "Reckon I will, though. You make Miss Jean happy, now."

"I swear I will," Butch said, and returned Jake's crush of a hand-shake.

Jean slowed her horse to a trot and pulled along the fence. The sun behind her Stetson set her curls afire. "You came back," she said.

Butch swung his leg over the fence and sat on the rail. "Some of me," he said.

Jean smiled. "I'll take what I can get."

60.

THE FIVE OF THEM TOOK THE FERRY to Toshima island in the morning. Mikio's left arm in a sling, Shiro hanging from the other. Yumi held her son's other hand. Tara and Reeves leaned over the rail and watched Mount Fuji poke through the misty clouds. They shared the ride with two marine biologists, a handful of birdwatchers and a fisherman's daughter.

Shiro poked at his father's pinky finger. Doctors had replaced the severed digit with Mikio's little toe. He couldn't bend it, but it looked normal at first glance.

After they disembarked in the village, they found an outdoor cafe and ate hash and bacon pancakes called *okonomiyaki*. Then they walked barefoot on the black sand beaches ringing the island until they found the well-marked path to the mountaintop.

Shiro led the way with his father jogging alongside, pretending to race.

Reeves squeezed Tara's hand. "I knew you were crazy," he said. "Didn't think you'd chase me halfway to Timbuktu for skipping out on you like that."

Tara rolled her eyes. "You still owe me a set of wheels," she said. "It killed me to give up that GTR."

"I owe you an Oldsmobile," Reeves said. "Besides, we're using the cash to start a dojo. How about a Honda, you like Hondas? Like *Fast and the Furious*?"

"Don't cheap out on me," Tara said. "I saved your ass. Means I own it." She grabbed what she owned.

Reeves pulled her close. "Anything you want. As long as you don't leave me in the dust."

"You get sappy on me, I'll take the first plane out of here."

Yumi rolled her eyes at young love. She had cajoled her way into her old job at the *Yomiuri Shimbun* crime desk and wrote the story of the *Kumite* being a cover-up for a failed power grab by the now-shattered Gantetsu crime family. The government scolded her paper for spreading conspiracy theories, but it had outsold their competitors three to one for the week of her story. Her boss censured her publicly and demoted her to the Niigata desk, just like she asked.

They climbed to the top of the hill and found a humble shrine to Inari, the goddess of the rice harvest.

Mikio, Yumi and Shiro knelt at the shrine and prayed for the spirits of the dead. Tara and Reeves nodded their heads politely.

A priest in red stepped out of the bamboo hut, bowed and smiled. "You are not of the island," he said. "It is good to meet you. I am Hiraoke."

"Is this the only shrine on the island?" Mikio asked. "I thought there was an older one, dedicated to Hachiman."

"Oh, I was told there was one here from before the war," the priest said. "From the Edo period, when the island was a prison colony. My predecessor built this on its ruins, I'm afraid."

"Did anything remain?" Mikio said. "I recently learned that my grandfather died here during the war. We were hoping to find his grave."

The priest wrinkled his brow. "I'm sorry, but there are no grave markers on the island. When one of the fishermen dies, they are taken by the ferry for cremation in Yokohama. But you are welcome to come inside. Some of the original shrine was reused in the construction."

Reeves let go of Tara's hand and took a slow walk around the perimeter of the shrine. The Tetley tea tin rattled in his jacket pocket. When he was out of sight, he removed an entrenching tool from his pack and unfolded it. Butch had written that they buried the sword, but there was no way to dig beneath the shrine without a steam shovel.

Reeves leaned on the wall and squeezed the tea tin, popping it like a bottle cap.

Tara walked up and kissed his chin. "Whatcha doin'?"

"Thinking."

"About what?"

"Where Butch buried the sword."

"Beneath a big W. Remember that old movie?" Tara said. She squinted over his head. "Huh."

"What?"

"That piece of bamboo looks different than the rest."

Reeves looked up. The outer walls were built of wide bamboo columns yellowed with stain. One stood out. It was darker, cracked. Older.

"Mickey!"

A commotion inside the shrine. A crash. The older bamboo pole tipped out, then disappeared inside.

Mikio popped his head out of the hole he made in the wall. "One step ahead you, ass hole."

They gathered around Mikio as he split the bamboo stave with his grandfather's knife. Reeves pried it open with the e-tool. Oil poured from the wood. Mikio carefully reached inside, and wiped down the contents with his sleeve.

The priest stood with his hands on his hips, frowning from the doorway. He gasped and stepped back.

The last Son of Hachiman stood and raised a brilliant blade.

A sunbeam broke through the autumn clouds and struck metal, spinning in a hypnotic scintillation as it enveloped the warrior in blinding armor.

Reeves shielded his eyes. For a moment, down in the gleaming waves, he swore he saw two soldiers in a skiff laughing as they rowed away into the rising sun.

JAPANESE TOUGH GUY DICTIONARY

Akane — Red.

Ameko — American, with bad connotations.

Baka iunayo! — Stop saying stupid things!

Baka ona — Stupid bitch.

Benjo mushi — Toilet insect, dung beetle. Insult.

Biru ippon kudasai — One beer, please.

Bukkoroshite yaru zo — I'm going to kill you.

Chinpira — Showy young yakuza with no honor or class.

Demio kazamesa teka — Give me some head.

Dewa, mata chikai uchini — See you again soon.

Domo or arigato or domo arigato — Thank you, in increasing levels of formality.

Gaijin — Foreigner, outsider.

Ganbarre — Keep going, keep fighting. A cheer of encouragement.

Gokudo — 'The Ultimate Path.' For old-school yakuza, 'the life.'

Hai — Yes.

Hiretsukan — Bastard, son of a bitch. Literally: "despicable person."

Issunbosi — One inch dick.

Itashimashite — You're welcome.

Kampai — Cheers.

Kempeitai — Japanese secret police, the Gestapo of Japan in World War II.

Kigyoshatei — Yakuza businessman. Corporate, or a runner of front companies.

Kocha koi! — Come get your ass kicked.

Kokuryukai — Black Dragon.

Kono yaru — Coward.

Kuso Tori — Shit Bird.

Kutabare — Fuck you.

Manko — Pussy.

Mou osoi node watashi wa kaeri masu — It's getting late, I must be going now.

Mukou ike — Fuck off.

Ohayo — Good morning.

Ojiisan — Grandfather.

Omae no manko wa kusai —Your vagina smells (directed at a man).

Oppai ii desu —Very large breasts.

Oyabun — Boss of a yakuza family.

Paizuri Tatsujin — Rage Cage Reeves.★

Sayonara — Goodbye.

Shatei — Lowest-ranking yakuza. "Little brothers."

Shinobi — Shadow warrior. Also known as ninja.

Tansyo — Little-dick.

Tatakau! — Fight!

Urusai — Shut up.

Ushipai —Tits like cow udders.

Wakagashira — Highest-ranking yakuza lieutenant below the oyabun.

Yasukuni de aou! —We will meet in the peaceful country. "See you in heaven!"

Yowayowashii — Chickenshit.

Yuhei — Useless soldiers.

Zainichi — Foreigner living in Japan, used as a slang term for Koreans living in Japan.

★**Not really.**

ABOUT THE AUTHOR

THOMAS PLUCK writes unflinching fiction with heart. He also lifts heavy things and wrassles. He works with computers now, but has worked on the docks, in construction sites, flipping burgers, washing dishes, and even cleaned the crappers at the Guggenheim. His work has appeared in *The Utne Reader, Needle: A Magazine of Noir, Burnt Bridge,* PANK *Magazine, McSweeney's, The Morning News, Beat to a Pulp,* and numerous anthologies.

He is also the editor of *Protectors: Stories to Benefit* PROTECT which collected 41 authors to fight child abuse, all proceeds going to PROTECT: The National Association to Protect Children.

Thomas also writes *The Big Eat* for *Devil Gourmet,* interviews writers for *The Big Thrill,* and blogs for *Criminal Element* and *The Good Men Project.*

You can find him on his website, thomaspluck.com, and on Twitter as @tommysalami

ABOUT
THE TYPE

BEMBO was designed in 1496 by Francesco Griffo da Bologna, a punchcutter working in Venice for Aldus Manutius in Venice. It is a calligraphic Old Style Humanist typeface, showcasing a beautiful diagonal tail on the R. It was first used in in the setting of a book entitled *Petri Bembi de Aetna Angelum Chabrielem liber,* by the Italian humanist poet Pietro Bembo. Six years later, Griffo was responsible for the first italic types, cut for Aldus.

MUNICH was designed in 1992 for FontBureau by Richard Lipton, an American type designer. Inspired by Ludwig Hohlwein's original 1922 letterforms for the Bremen typeface, Munich is a small-cap typeface that is very angular in form.

Printed in Great Britain
by Amazon.co.uk, Ltd.,
Marston Gate.

4307268R00205